D0545206

Praise for Anna Jacobs

'[Anna Jacobs' books have an]
impressive grasp of human emotions'
The Sunday Times

'A powerful and absorbing saga – a fine example of
family strife and struggle set in a bygone age'
Hartlepool Mail

'Anna Jacobs' books are deservedly popular. She is one
of the best writers of Lancashire sagas around'
Historical Novels Review

'A compelling read'
Sun

'This is a rare thing, a pacy page-turner with a ripping
plot and characters you care about . . . [Anna Jacobs is]
especially big on resourceful, admirable women.
Great stuff!'
Daily Mail

'Catherine Cookson fans will cheer!'
Peterborough Evening Telegraph

ANNA
JACOBS

Silver Wishes

Jubilee Lake Saga Book One

HODDER

First published in Great Britain in 2022 by Hodder & Stoughton
An Hachette UK company

This paperback edition published in 2023

1

A CIP catalogue record for this title is available from the British Library

Paperback ISBN 978 1 529 35134 7
eBook ISBN 978 1 529 35132 3

Typeset in Plantin Light

Printed and bound in Great Britain by Clays Ltd, Elcograf S.p.A.

Hodder & Stoughton policy is to use papers that are natural, renewable
and recyclable products and made from wood grown in sustainable forests.
The logging and manufacturing processes are expected to conform to the
environmental regulations of the country of origin.

Hodder & Stoughton Ltd
Carmelite House
50 Victoria Embankment
London EC4Y 0DZ

www.hodder.co.uk

Silver Wishes

I

1895 – Lancashire

Reginald Stafford died of an apoplexy while shouting at the gardener's lad for some imagined carelessness.

Typically, he still had a look of anger on his face even after the last breath had left his body. The gardener tried to smooth the snarling features before sending for his master's step-daughter, because the poor lass had had enough to put up with, but he couldn't get rid of that look.

When the gardener's lad came running to tell her what had happened, Elinor was so surprised it took her a moment or two to summon up her usual calm expression before she walked slowly outside to the area where her stepfather smoked his cigars. It was a trick, it must be; another of his stupid hurtful pranks.

When she saw the body lying on the ground, one arm out-stretched as if beckoning to her, she paused again. But there was no sign of movement of any sort. The first trickle of hope slipped into her. Could she really be free of him at last?

She bent down and steeled herself to check the body care-fully, half-expecting him to grab her and roar with laughter at making her jump in shock. She let out a heartfelt sigh of relief when she found no pulse and looked across at the gardener. He gave her a little nod as if to say she wasn't mistaken. It was true! Her stepfather really was dead.

She stood up. She was free at last. When she turned, she saw his manservant standing behind her and vowed to be free of him as well, and soon.

'Is the master—?'

'Dead? Yes. Could you and the gardener please carry him up to his bedroom, Denby?'

She followed closely behind the men. Once they had laid the body down on the bed, she moved to stand near it, asking them to leave her alone with him for a few moments and to send someone for the doctor.

Denby hesitated, looking at her doubtfully, then as she gestured towards the door, he walked slowly out of the room.

She whispered to the gardener as he passed her, 'Keep your eye on the master's study, would you, please, Barker?'

He nodded, his eyes going to the manservant. He knew perfectly well why she had said this. That fellow would steal the butter off a piece of bread!

She'd have asked Maude to come and help her, but the maid, who was as close as a sister to her, was out at the shops. She'd have to manage on her own.

Elinor locked the bedroom door and steeled herself to search her stepfather's pockets for money. She knew he always carried some on him and if she didn't find it, Denby would take it, she was sure. She searched very carefully, letting out a huge sigh of relief as she found it.

But something made her continue searching and when she found some folded banknotes in an inner pocket as well as what was in his wallet, she stared down at the two bundles of notes in fury. Household bills left unpaid, skimping on food for her and the servants, her clothes mended and so old-fashioned she looked like a maid herself. And all the time *he* had been walking round with this much money in his pocket, ready to waste it on gambling and any loose woman who caught his fancy.

She tidied his clothes, not wanting her search to show, then tucked the banknotes down as far as she could push them into her bodice. What a good thing she didn't wear the fashionable corsets that pulled in a woman's waist and upper body so tightly you could hardly breathe. Well, she was so thin she had no need to 'improve' her figure.

She didn't wear the popular leg of mutton sleeves either, because she not only did not care about keeping up with the changing fashions, she couldn't afford the extra material it took to make sleeves like that. On the rare occasions she managed to scrape the money together to buy a dress length for a new outfit she looked only for the cheapest and most hard-wearing material she could find.

Someone knocked on the door and called, 'Are you all right, miss?' Reginald's manservant had returned and was trying to poke his nose in as usual.

'I'm fine. I'll call if I need you, Denby.' He could stay out there till kingdom come! She wasn't opening that door to anyone except Maude till she'd checked everything in the room.

She continued to search till she found her stepfather's desk key with two other small keys in a bowl on the windowsill. After she'd hidden them in her clothing as well and investigated every one of his pockets a second time, she went quickly through the drawers. No money there, but she did find her mother's wedding ring and didn't scruple to take that.

Only when she'd searched everywhere did she unlock the door and call for Denby. He came almost immediately and must have been waiting near the stairs.

'The gardener's lad has gone for the doctor, miss.' He stared past her as if trying to see signs of what she'd been doing in the room.

'Good. I've finished praying over your master now. You can stay with his body until the doctor arrives. Better not touch him, though.'

He looked from her to the body suspiciously but she didn't care. He could no longer tell his master if she did something her stepfather would disapprove of. In fact, the sooner she got Denby out of the house, the happier she would be.

Downstairs she nodded dismissal to the gardener, who was still standing guard, and went into the room her stepfather had called his study. It contained very few books and was actually where he sometimes boozed or played cards with one or two seedy cronies. Once again, she locked the door before searching the desk.

She knew which was the desk key and found by trying them that the two smaller keys opened the locked bottom drawer and the box it contained. In it she found some more money and the few pieces of her mother's jewellery that were still unsold. She took all its contents and stowed them in her underclothing, then locked the box again and put it back.

There had been no sign of a will in any of the untidy drawers, though her stepfather had made a big thing of going to see the family lawyer last year, telling her he was updating his will and promising her that she'd be taken care of. Presumably Mr Calwell had a copy.

When she opened the door again, she found Maude standing there as if on guard.

'Barker told me about your step father as I came in. Are you all right, love?'

'I shall be a lot better now.' She didn't have to pretend with Maude.

'Denby had crept down and was trying to listen to what you were doing, so I stayed here. I'm sorry I was out when it happened.'

Maude had officially been their maid for nearly twenty years but was more like a member of the family than a servant. Elinor glanced over her shoulder then gave her friend a quick hug before she said in a low voice, 'We'll both be better off now, I'm sure. And we can show our friendship openly.'

She couldn't voice a single word of regret for his death because she had hated her stepfather ever since she'd been old enough to know what hatred was – and cruelty. She'd feared as well as hated him after her mother died suddenly a few years ago following a fall down the stairs, because she suspected him of deliberately pushing his wife down them. But she could prove nothing, so had been helpless.

And you couldn't leave home when you had nowhere to go and no money of your own, so she'd had to stay here, relieved when he'd mostly ignored her presence. She knew perfectly well that he only kept her here because respectable people spoke to him because of her and he knew they'd never speak to him again if he threw her out.

'I need to send for the lawyer, Maude.'

'The gardener's lad can go when he gets back from fetching the doctor.'

'Wait with me and I'll write a quick note to Mr Calwell.'

When the doctor arrived, he made a cursory examination of the body then sought her out. 'Your stepfather died of a seizure, Miss Pendleton, and I'm not surprised. Only last week I warned him that he was drinking far too much and that was damaging his health, but he told me to mind my own business.'

'He hasn't looked well for a while.'

'I'll write you out a death certificate. You'll need it for the formalities. You can send for the undertaker straight away.'

Good. The sooner the body was taken away, the happier she'd be, she thought. She wondered whether anyone would miss Reginald Stafford or even attend his funeral.

After the doctor had left, the house fell silent as they waited for the undertaker. It was wonderful not to have her stepfather shouting and upsetting people, not to be waiting for him to burst into the house, half drunk usually.

The only person he visited socially was his equally horrible nephew. She hoped she'd never see Jason Stafford again after the funeral.

Elinor's relief at being free was short-lived, however. As soon as the lawyer arrived she knew something was wrong from his pitying expression.

'Please come into the sitting room, Mr Calwell.'

She asked Maude to stay in the hall and make sure no one eavesdropped on them.

The lawyer gestured to a chair, looking at her sadly. 'You'd better sit down before I start, Miss Pendleton. I'm afraid I have some bad news for you.'

She did as he asked with a sinking feeling, wondering whether her stepfather had driven them to bankruptcy.

After clearing his throat and fiddling with some papers from his briefcase, Mr Calwell said, 'I'm afraid the will leaves everything your stepfather owned to his nephew, Jason Stafford.'

She could only stare at him, shocked beyond words.

'And even if he hadn't done that, you'd not have got much. I fear the house will have to be sold to pay off his debts. It's not a large dwelling, though it has a nice big garden so should easily find a buyer.'

He took a deep breath and added, 'He had just asked me to sell another piece of your mother's jewellery.' He fumbled in his pocket and held a lumpy envelope out to her. 'I feel this should come to you, at least, because she left you all her jewellery when she died even though *he* took it from you. Please put it away quickly and don't tell anyone.'

She took it and shoved it into her pocket. 'But the money and house came to him mostly from my mother! Surely something has been left for me? He *promised* I'd be taken care of.'

He hesitated, looking even more reluctant to speak.

'Please go on. It can't get much worse.'

But it did.

'You'll only be taken care of financially if you marry his nephew. In that case, there is a small annuity that will be paid to you, so you'll be able to manage should Jason Stafford predecease you. I had to fight hard to get even that provided and safeguarded.'

She felt physically sick at the idea of marrying *him*. Last time Jason Stafford had visited his uncle, he'd tried to grab her several times. When she'd complained to her stepfather, he'd merely laughed and said the Staffords were a lusty bunch and she should be grateful for any man being interested in a frump like her.

Thank goodness for Maude and her rolling pin. They had shared a bedroom the whole time he was visiting.

'I could never marry that man. Never, ever, Mr Calwell.'

'I don't blame you. He is . . . despicable, has a dreadful reputation. I wouldn't even introduce him to my wife or daughter.'

He waited a moment then continued, 'Last month your stepfather came to see me about a minor matter and I tried once again to persuade him to change his mind about you marrying his nephew, but you know what Mr Stafford was like once he set his mind on doing something. I am so very sorry I couldn't do more.'

He glanced towards the door and lowered his voice. 'If you have relatives you can seek refuge with, Miss Pendleton, I will arrange to take you to them after the funeral at my own expense.'

She didn't even have to think about her answer. 'There is no relative close enough to ask for that sort of help. My real father was the last of the Pendletons and my mother was an only child. I don't even know where most of her more distant relatives are living now.'

'Oh, dear.'

'I need to think, to work out some kind of plan to get away.' She started to stand up and he reached out to stop her.

'Well, um, look. If you wish to leave, you can come to stay with my wife and me for a while after the funeral. We'll keep you safe from him, I promise. And I'm certain we can find you a respectable job as a governess or companion to an elderly lady. Do you have any money at all?'

She shook her head. She didn't intend to tell anyone what she had found.

He fumbled in his pocket and pulled out a five-pound note. When he offered this to her, she decided that she couldn't afford to be proud about anything and took it.

'Keep this in case there are any problems and your need to leave becomes urgent. You can use it to pay for a taxi cab to bring you and your possessions to my house in the next village. This is our home address.' He handed her a card. 'My wife knows about this shameful occurrence and will take you in if I'm not at home.'

'Thank you. You're very kind. I'll pack my things and leave with you immediately after the funeral, if that's all right? And may I bring my maid? She's been a tower of strength since my mother died and she too may need help escaping from Jason Stafford.'

'Ah. Well, yes, I suppose so. We can provide her with suitable references for getting another position because she's been a faithful servant to your family. And she can help out in the house while we're looking for a job for her. There's always someone searching for a good maid.'

Elinor dug her fingernails into the palms of her hands to prevent the protest she wanted to utter and say that was a poor reward for the years of faithful service. 'She's the best maid you could ever find.'

'I'm glad to hear that.'

She wanted to tell him that Maude was far more than a maid to her, more like a cousin or sister even, but this would do no good. He was at least willing to help them both in a limited way.

But she'd only go to him if she were desperate. She'd had enough of being told what to do. And she wanted, no, she *intended*, to stay with Maude. They had already decided that.

*

Unfortunately, two hours later Jason Stafford arrived, almost erupting into the house and looking extremely cheerful for a man who'd just lost a close relative. His arrival proved that someone must have sent word to him, probably Denby.

Jason stared at her with a gloating smile. 'I know what was in the will. My uncle and I laughed about it together. So tonight you had better not deny me my marital rights.'

She looked at him in shock. 'But we're not married.'

'We shall be, so why wait? You're from a good enough family to produce a legal heir and then a couple of other children for me. And marrying you will help prove to people that I've turned respectable.'

That man would have a long way to go to be considered even vaguely respectable, whatever he did. There was something particularly sly and nasty about him.

He continued to eye her possessively. 'It'll be a good bargain for you because unlike my uncle I don't waste my money. You'll be guaranteed a roof over your head, good food to eat and better clothes than those shabby rags you usually wear. I shall wish you to do me credit when you are my wife.'

He flicked a contemptuous finger at her clothes and added, 'In fact, I'm going to take them off now and enjoy myself.' He followed that by moving towards her, hands outstretched.

Utterly horrified, she fled from him and ran up the stairs, locking herself in her bedroom. She'd made sure years ago that there were bolts on the inside of its door as well as the old-fashioned key lock.

He banged on the door, shook it a few times then called, 'I'm warning you: I'll break it down tonight if I have to. And you had better do as you're told then. I won't put up with being defied by a woman.'

2

Once she'd heard Jason go back downstairs, Elinor began to pack her things, hastily thrusting clothes into her pillowcases for lack of a suitcase or even a shopping bag. She sacrificed some space for her paintings. Thank goodness she'd only ever done small ones that she could hide easily. She'd have hated her stepfather to get his hands on them.

She'd have to leave immediately, though she wasn't sure yet how she was going to get out of the house without him stopping her.

But she was quite sure she was going to try.

To her surprise, as she was stuffing a few final garments into the second pillowcase, there was the patter of small stones against the outside of the window. She looked out to see Maude standing below her, dressed in outdoor clothing and the neat little felt hat trimmed by a feather that she wore to church. It was much newer and smarter than Elinor's own.

Maude always stood out among the congregation anyway, being nearly six foot tall and strong with it. Even Reginald Stafford at his drunkest hadn't dared try to fumble with her.

Her friend glanced round then came a little closer and called up, 'He's just sacked me and told me to leave immediately. He's in the study now going through the drawers. Good thing that's at the front of the house. Barker is bringing a ladder. Throw what you can into a pillowcase and climb down quickly. This will probably be our only chance of getting you away safely.'

'I've packed already. Here.' Elinor opened the window as wide as she could and dropped her two pillowcases down from the window one after the other just as Barker and the boy rushed round the corner carrying the old ladder.

She didn't hesitate but squirmed out of the window on to it, not caring how much of her legs and underwear she showed to the world. As she began to clamber down the ladder, one of the rungs gave a loud cracking sound when she put her weight on it and she moved on quickly, heart pounding.

By the time she got to the bottom, Maude had picked up one of the pillowcases as well as two full shopping bags of her own.

'Barker will take the ladder back while we get away as fast as we can. Come on!'

When she set off at a run, Elinor followed, terror lending her the extra speed needed to keep up with Maude.

'Where are we going?' she panted.

'To Barker's mother's house till it's dark, then he'll take us to the nearest railway station in his neighbour's gig.'

'How kind of him.'

'He's going to find himself another job, says he won't work for Jason.'

They had to pause at the main road, crouching behind some bushes to avoid being seen by pedestrians, cyclists or carriages until it was clear to cross the road.

'Where can we go from there, though, Maude love? I don't know anyone who'll take us in.'

'We'll go wherever our feet take us to start off with. I've got some savings, not much but it all helps. And you've still got that money you took from your stepfather, haven't you? Unless that Jason took it off you?'

'No, he didn't.'

'Good. It'll last us months if we're careful.'

'Most of it's safe in my bodice, but I put some in my purse. The lawyer said he would help us, so I suppose we could go to him if we were desperate.'

'I was eavesdropping. He'd help you find a ladylike job as slave to someone who pays only spending money and your keep, and he'd help me get another maid's position, and who knows where that might be? We might never see one another again.'

'Look out. The road's going to be clear in a minute. Oh bother! There's another cyclist coming. Keep your head down. I couldn't bear us to be separated, Maude. Only, where can we go?'

'Blackpool.'

'What? We don't know anyone there.'

'That's part of the reason. There are lots of people coming and going even now, before the summer holiday season has started, so strangers won't stand out. We can start off by booking into a lodging house while we have a look round. And there would be jobs available as maids if we got desperate.'

'I'd never have thought of that. I'd like to go there anyway. I've never even seen the sea.'

'There you are, then. That'll be a good start for our new life.'

'Quick! There's no one in sight. Let's get across this road.'

Later, as they tried to rest in Barker's mother's front room, because she insisted on giving them the best the small house could offer, Elinor pulled the money out and they counted it. After that she showed her friend the remaining pieces of her mother's jewellery, including the brooch Mr Calwell had passed on to her, one of the prettiest of them all, and her mother's wedding ring.

Maude studied them all. 'I think you should keep quiet about the jewellery, love. If people ask, look sad and tell them your stepfather took it from you a while ago to sell. And say you have a little money but not much. You should sew most of these banknotes into your petticoat and only keep a little money in your purse.' Maude gave a wry smile. 'You're a far more capable needlewoman than I am.'

'You should take some of it as well. I'll sew some into your clothing too, if you don't mind. We'll be safer spreading the risk of it getting stolen.'

'All right. You know you can trust me.'

'I know.' They smiled at one another.

'Now, how about you stop being my maid and call yourself my sister? You certainly feel like one. You're the person who cared for me when I was younger and my mother fell ill. You *feel* like a sister.'

Maude shook her head. 'No one will believe that because we don't look at all alike. Not only am I much taller, but my hair's dark and yours is a light chestnut brown.'

'Well, you've been more like a relative than a servant for as long as I can remember so I'll say you're my cousin, then. No one expects cousins to look alike.' Elinor reached out to grasp Maude's hand briefly. 'Agreed?'

'I'd like that. We'll be cousins and we'll stay together. I'm sure we'll manage somehow.'

'Thank you for rescuing me today.'

'It's a husband you need really to keep you safe if that horrible man comes after you.'

'I never got the chance to meet anyone.'

'Neither of us did. I'd like to have got married and had children too. If you were able to dress better and ate properly, you'd be pretty enough to attract a husband still. At nearly forty, I'm well past hoping.'

'I'm nearly thirty and scrawny.' Elinor scowled down at herself. 'I look more like a scarecrow than a woman. Who'd want me?'

'A widower might. And you're not thirty. Stop saying that. You've only just turned twenty-eight and you'd make a wonderful mother, the way you love children. And you're only scrawny because of him spoiling meals with shouting and nasty remarks, so that you could never eat in peace when he was around. That man made your whole life a misery.'

Elinor shuddered. 'I have no desire to marry after I've seen how *he* treated my mother, no desire whatsoever. How does a woman ever know what a man will be like after the wedding? I was only ten but I remember how happy Mother was when she thought she'd found someone to look after us. Her happiness soon faded after she married *him*, didn't it?'

'Men aren't all like that pig of a fellow was.'

'But you can't know for certain beforehand, can you? And by the time you're married, it's too late to do anything about it. No, I'm never going to risk that.'

'You'll change when you meet some happily married people.'

Elinor hugged her suddenly. 'Never mind that. I just want to thank you for staying with me all these years. I was always surprised he let you stay.'

'He wasn't stupid. He knew he'd have difficulty finding another maid who'd stay on or work as hard.'

'You acted as housekeeper, really, but he only paid you a maid's wage.'

'I stayed to be with you. That made it worthwhile.'

They both fell silent, thinking about their predicament.

A few minutes later Maude's eyes closed and she began snoring softly. Elinor smiled fondly across at her. Her dear friend's hair was tightly drawn back into its usual knobbly bun, emphasising her gaunt appearance. You'd never call her pretty, but she had the kindest nature and a smile that lit up her whole face.

Elinor wished she had the ability to fall asleep so easily. But she couldn't stop her mind from going over and over what had just happened and wondering how this would all turn out.

She couldn't shake off the worries about what she could do to earn a living when the money ran out. She hadn't trained as a lady typewriter or done any of the other jobs in an office, hadn't worked in a shop, hadn't been able to go to college and become a teacher because she'd been caring for her mother, as well as doing some of the housework.

Her only experience had been in sewing and she was an expert at making one penny do the work of two. She was quite good at sketching and painting, but that was just a hobby.

She dozed off and woke with a start when Barker brought the neighbour's pony and trap round and his mother came in to fetch her. He gave her some sacks to put their clothes in, apologising that he couldn't provide proper bags or suitcases. The sacks looked better than the pillowcases, but only just.

As they set off, Elinor stared down at the lumpy bundles pushed against her feet, suddenly realising that they contained all her worldly goods now, every single thing she owned.

Anger at what *he* had done, what she had lost, seared through her yet again – as well as utter determination to stay out of Jason Stafford's clutches.

After Barker had left them, apologising for needing to take the pony straight back, the two women had to pass the rest of the night sitting on a hard bench at a small local station, pressed closely together for warmth as they waited for the first train of the day. He said this would be the train taking the farmers' milk to be bottled and it usually stopped here about five in the morning.

They didn't chat much; they were too exhausted by now.

An elderly railway employee arrived to open up before the milk train and seemed surprised to see them. He sold them tickets that would take them all the way to Blackpool, chatting cheerfully and giving them instructions about where to change trains.

When Maude took the opportunity to ask about how they might get to a place called Ollerthwaite from Blackpool, he knew that too, because he'd worked on most of the railway lines in the north of England. Now that he was older he'd chosen to settle near his family and earn less money by running this small station, which he said was a 'halt' more than a station.

He seemed to enjoy having company and hardly stopped talking for a minute, raising his voice when he had to do something at the far end of the platform. And although she knew Maude was encouraging him to chat in order to get as much information as possible, Elinor wished her friend wouldn't tell him so much about their plans.

When they got on the train, she asked Maude why she had been asking about this Ollerthwaite place.

'I have distant relatives there. I'm not sure whether to ask them for help or not. I'm just asking in case he comes after us and we have to run away again.'

It was after midday when they arrived in Blackpool and the first thing they did was find a little café where they could buy something to eat and a pot of tea. The milk train hadn't stopped for long at any station, and when they'd had to change trains, there hadn't been time to eat, so by now they were ravenous.

They chose the cheapest and most filling meal on the menu, eating it quickly and not lingering in the café.

Maude asked the friendly waitress where they could buy proper travelling bags, and when she looked at them curiously, she explained that they'd had to leave in a hurry after the death of the relative they'd been lodging with, and his cousin had tried to get at them.

The waitress was instantly sympathetic. 'Some men are awful, aren't they?' After studying their clothes she suggested trying a local pawnshop.

The idea of going to such a place startled Elinor, but Maude beamed. 'That's a really good idea. Thank you so much.'

When she tried to tip the waitress, the woman shook her head and looked at Elinor's clothes pityingly. 'I reckon you two need the money more than I do, love.'

'Bless you. We do need to be a bit careful at the moment.'

'Are we really going to a pawnshop?' Elinor asked as they walked along the street in the direction the waitress had told them.

'We certainly are. And while we're at it, we'll see if we can find you a better coat and hat as well. You need to look a bit smarter than that, love, to show you're respectable. Don't look so disapproving. They sell some good things that haven't been redeemed at pawnshops as well as lending money on items. I've several times bought clothes in such places.'

Before they got there, however, they had their first view of the Blackpool Tower, which had only been finished the previous year. It was gigantic, towering over the buildings around it and they both stopped to gape at it.

'Would you like to go up it?' Maude asked.

'No, never. I'd hate it.'

'Me too. But some people love it. I'm glad to have seen it, though.'

They found a smart hat and coat, as well as a skirt and blouse, and two scuffed Gladstone bags at the pawnshop, all much cheaper than Elinor would ever have expected.

'I'm learning new ways of doing things already,' she said. 'I think you'd better take charge of where we go and how we travel. You know far more than I do about how best to do things. I feel as if I've been shut away from the world ever since my mother remarried.'

'I've not really seen much. I've only ever travelled round Lancashire.'

'Well, at least you used to get away on your annual holidays when you visited your aunt. I've never been this far away from home before, never even seen the sea.'

'She was a lovely person. I was sorry when she died last year and I had to pay her neighbour for a room, just to get away from *him*. My aunt would have taken us in and helped us settle somewhere if she'd still been alive and known how desperate we were. Anyway, come on. We need to find some respectable lodgings.'

All the streets near the station seemed to be displaying little signs in their windows saying things like 'Respectable rooms' or 'Vacancies' or occasionally 'No vacancies'.

'There will be a lot more signs saying "No vacancies" when the summer holiday season really gets going,' Maude said. 'At this time of year, we can take our time and choose a place we like the looks of.'

'Surely Jason won't try to follow us?'

'He might. He's nasty enough to want to get back at us for running away. But he won't know where we've gone. And how will he find that out? I think we'll be safe now.'

'I'm not sure about that. He's always been very cunning and I think he'll come after my mother's jewellery as well as wanting to get me back there, for some strange reason.'

'He's desperate to find a respectable wife and if you refuse him again, Elinor love, he'll try to find a way to punish you. He's a spiteful brute.'

'We'll have to pray that he doesn't find out where we are, then.'

'If he does, we can run away again. Now, let's look for some decent lodgings then spend a few days here and see whether we'd like to live in Blackpool.'

It wasn't hard to find lodgings, there were so many on offer. They walked round a few streets and decided on a smaller house within walking distance of the sea in the north part of the town, which seemed quieter than the south.

The landlady said they were welcome to leave their luggage and they could trust her to take care of it, but she didn't allow lodgers to stay in the house from ten in the morning to four in the afternoon. 'There are over two miles of promenade and it's a fine day. I'm sure you'll enjoy a walk.'

They decided to stroll along the promenade so that Elinor could see the sea for the first time. Both were feeling exhausted after their nearly sleepless night and they simply ambled along the 'front' as people called it.

The tide was out and after a while Elinor frowned at the smooth sand and calm water. "The sea doesn't do much, does it?'

'It's famous for being calm enough here for children to paddle in. There will be a lot more going on later in the season. Donkey rides and Punch and Judy shows. Things like that.'

But to her surprise, Elinor felt a bit disappointed. The pictures she'd seen showed pretty little bays or waves crashing on rocks. This was . . . rather tame.

After walking a little way, they sat down on a bench to watch the holidaymakers, who seemed very loud and cheerful. Even this early in the season there were family groups, young women in twos and threes, walking along with arms linked, and young men also in groups eyeing the lasses.

Maude was right about one thing: nobody gave them a second glance.

When they returned to the lodging house, their landlady recommended a nearby fish and chip café for tea, because she only provided breakfasts. The food was excellent but all they wanted to do now was lie down and sleep so they went back to their room.

'There isn't much greenery at the seaside, is there?' Elinor said as they lay in bed chatting.

Maude gave one of her soft chuckles. 'No. People come to look at the water or build sandcastles on the beach not walk through woods. I hope it'll be fine tomorrow then maybe we can have a paddle.'

'I don't think I'll bother to paddle. I might get my clothes wet and I don't have many spare clothes. Let's just walk round a bit. How about we go on one of the piers? The landlady said there were three of them now.'

'Good idea.'

They had to leave their lodgings again after breakfast the following day, so began to walk along the promenade, pausing at the entrance to North Pier, then pausing again to look at Central Pier and when they reached the South Pier they stopped to buy a pot of tea and a couple of sandwiches in one of the many cafés.

'This is the newest pier, only recently completed,' Maude said. 'I read about it in a brochure at the lodgings. Do you want to walk along it or would you prefer one of the others?'

'I feel more like strolling along the promenade again. I feel sort of suspended. I don't think I shall feel right in myself until we have more idea what to do with our lives and have found somewhere to settle. Being without anywhere to live makes me feel vulnerable.'

'I'm a bit the same. Anyway, more than anything else we need to find a way to earn a living. We're not here to have a holiday. We could run a boarding house, I suppose. We have some money to set up with if we're careful.'

Elinor frowned and paused for a few moments, one hand on the rail at the sea edge of the promenade, trying to work out what that would entail.

'That'd only bring in an income for half the year,' she said eventually, 'and we'd have to sell my mother's jewellery to get enough money to rent a suitable house and set it up with furniture for boarders. If we didn't do well, we'd be in big trouble and lose most of our money.'

They both shivered involuntarily at that thought.

'Anyway, it'd mean running round after people we don't know, some of whom might not be pleasant to deal with,' Maude said.

'Hmm. I don't actually fancy living my life with one set of strangers after another. Do you?'

'No. We have to be very careful what we do. The money won't last for ever.'

They went on the North Pier to end the afternoon, just on principle because they might never come here again. They found a sheltered spot to sit and watch the sea, but were mostly silent, then Elinor said quietly, 'I don't think either of us would feel comfortable living in Blackpool. It's a lovely place to visit, and the people are friendly, but I'm missing the greenery already. I like trees and gardens more than bare sand.'

'And there seem to be plenty of small shops in the town already,' Maude added. 'So that's not a good business to get into, either.'

'It's not hard to decide that you don't want to do something, but it's going to be far harder to find something we do want to do with our lives. I can't even think where to go next. I've been racking my brain.'

'Well, it's early days yet, but that's why I was asking about getting to Ollerthwaite. I may have an idea. Let me think about it and we'll discuss it tomorrow. Come on. I'm hungry even if you aren't.'

Maude linked her arm in Elinor's and they left the seafront to explore an area where there seemed to be shops and even a theatre.

But they ended up having tea at the same fish and chip shop near their lodgings, because at least they knew the food was good, and they were tired as well as worried. They went to bed early again.

3

In the small village near Oldham, Jason Stafford decided to postpone looking for Elinor until he'd sorted out his uncle's house. He told the lawyer he'd like to move in and might be able to scrape some money together to pay his uncle's debts if people would give him a little more time to sell his present house.

He ended up asking, 'You haven't heard from those two bitches, I suppose? Heaven knows why they ran away like that. You have to wonder about their morals.'

Mr Calwell sucked in his breath in shock. 'I haven't heard a word. And I shan't agree to see you again, let alone answer your questions if you insult the ladies like that.'

'Well, they stole the rest of my aunt's jewellery. You can't deny that.'

'Yes, I can. They didn't steal it; it was left to Miss Pendleton by her mother years ago so it belonged to her quite legally. It was your uncle who took it from her and sold a couple of pieces unlawfully. I have a copy of that lady's will to prove Miss Pendleton's ownership – as I shall inform the police if I hear you or anyone else saying she stole it.'

That made Jason even angrier with Elinor, but he held his tongue. He wanted to move into his uncle's house, and Mr Calwell had admitted that he might manage to do something to prevent it being sold if Mr Stafford could pay some money off the debts on account.

When he got back from the lawyer's, Jason told Denby he could stay at the house for a while as long as he made himself useful. 'After working for my uncle for so long, you may remember something to give us a clue about where those two have gone. I intend to bring them back because they'd both be useful to me. Elinor is the best I can hope for in a respectable marriage because people are so narrow-minded. They'll gradually forgive me my so-called sins,' he rolled his eyes, 'if they see her married to me. I gather she was well liked in the village, too. Well, she must have been for people to help her escape.'

'I'll do my best to remember something useful and in the meantime I could ask at the pub and find out whether anyone saw them leaving.'

'Good idea. People there are more likely to talk to you than to me.'

'You'd have to pay for my drinks. I need to be careful with my money till I've found a new job. I have a sick aunt to support, remember.' He'd been saying that for years to get out of spending any of his own money.

Jason stared at him thoughtfully. 'You can work for me for a while, if you like. We can see how we go and I'll pay you the same as my uncle did.'

'Doing what exactly, sir?'

'Whatever's needed.' He repeated emphatically, '*Whatever* is needed.'

Denby nodded and winked at him. 'As I did for your uncle.'

'Exactly. And your first job will be to ask around the village and see what you can find out about those two. Someone must have seen them leaving.' He fumbled in his pocket for a coin or two and gave them to his companion.

Denby went out for a drink at the poorer of the two local pubs but no one admitted to knowing anything about where the two women had gone. He was about to leave and try the other pub when he saw a man wearing the uniform of the local railway come in.

He managed to get chatting to him and when he offered to buy the next round, the man accepted. And he could certainly talk the hind leg off a donkey.

Most of what he said was just general gossip but Denby fixed a smile on his face and let him run on for a while before asking casually, 'You don't happen to have seen two women catching a train in the middle of the night or in the very early morning recently, do you?'

'There aren't any trains in the middle of the night round here. But there were two women as got on the early milk train a couple of days ago. Why?'

Denby stiffened. 'My master's looking for his poor cousin, who hasn't got all her senses.' He tapped his forehead. 'She ran off when her stepfather died. Frightened of her own shadow, she is. There's a maid looks after her who vanished too.'

'Well, it could be them because the older woman did most of the talking.'

'Was she very tall?'

'Yes, she was. Far too tall for a woman. Well, fancy that. They must be the ones you're looking for, and just because we got talking you've found out where they've gone.'

'Chance is an amazing thing, isn't it? You, um, don't have any idea where they were going, do you?'

'Oh yes. I sold them tickets right through to Blackpool. And then the older one asked about a place called Ollerthwaite as well. Not many people have heard of it, let alone could have told her how to get there, but I've worked on the railways all my life, mostly in Lancashire, and I know every minor line as well as the major ones, so I was able to help her.'

'I'm amazed at how much you know. You're a marvel. I've never even heard of this place, either. Where exactly is it?'

'Up near the Forest of Bowland, nestled in the Pennines. All right for them as likes to live in a valley near the moors. Wouldn't suit me. Nothing much to do round there except go hiking on the moors, and I get enough walking in my job, thank you very much.'

As the man continued to talk, Denby nodded and smiled some more, then asked, 'Why did she want to go there? Did she say?'

'To visit a relative.'

'You've been very helpful. Let me buy you another drink.'

'Thank you, sir. Much obliged.'

'Did she say what her relative was called? We'd like to make sure the poor thing is all right.'

'No, sorry.'

Denby had memorised how to get to Ollerthwaite, but the man he'd been talking to couldn't help him guess where to look for the two women in Blackpool.

'It's too big these days, sir, full of people coming and going from all over the north for holidays by the sea now the weather's getting warmer. And usually it's only for a week, so there are different people there all the time.'

Denby finished his beer. 'I've enjoyed chatting to you but I'm sorry to say I have to go now.'

The man looked at him hopefully, as if expecting another drink, but Denby was keeping the rest of the money Stafford had given him, so just nodded goodbye and walked briskly out.

When Denby got back, Jason listened intently to what he'd been told. 'We'll find them.'

'Not if they stay in Blackpool.'

'It's my bet they won't stay there. They're neither of them used to towns, let alone big places like that, and it'll be expensive to stay in lodgings. I'd bet a hundred quid they move on to that Maude's relative. What's her surname again?'

'Vernon.'

'I'll remember that. It's not a common name. We'll give them time to look round Blackpool then move on before we go after them. I've got enough on my plate at the moment sorting out my house and moving. I have to get it ready to sell and there will be plenty of jobs for you to do there.'

He was pleased with Denby's first efforts at looking for *her*, very pleased indeed. Smart man, that one. After thinking it over, he said, 'When we've given them a little time and it's convenient for me, you can go after them.'

As Denby went back to work, he heard Stafford mutter, 'No woman messes around with me. I'll teach that Elinor what's what.'

He sniggered. The escape would be that Maude's doing, not Elinor's. She was the clever one of the two. He wouldn't bother to go after them at all, if it was him, just for a bit of jewellery. She'd probably have sold it by now. Or was Stafford so determined to marry her he'd go to any lengths? He was fooling himself if he thought respectable people would deal with him socially, whatever he did.

It'd cost his new master dearly to send him to find them, though he doubted Jason Stafford would be as careless about money as his uncle had been. But Denby would wait to see if they found the two women before he found another job. There was money to be made in pursuing them.

In the morning Maude woke early and couldn't bear to wait any longer to share her thoughts about what to do next with Elinor.

'This distant relative of mine lives further north in Lancashire in a small Pennine valley and that porter told me how to get there. I remember my mother talking about her cousin Walter, saying he had a farm and other business interests as well, and was a very kind man. She said he wasn't rich but he wasn't short of money, either.'

'Go on.'

'Well, I woke in the night and couldn't get back to sleep so I lay thinking about what we could do next. I decided you and I don't know enough about the world to make this big decision about our futures on our own. We're lucky that we have some money, but we don't want to waste it, so I think we need advice or help from someone wiser. How about we go there and throw ourselves on Cousin Walter's mercy, ask for his advice?'

Elinor gaped at her. 'Not even ask him if he'll be willing for us to visit him, just turn up at his farm?'

'That's right.'

'I can see that he might be willing to help you but why should he help me?'

'If he's as kind as my mother said, I don't think he'll turn you away. It's worth a try, don't you think? I know I'm not a Crossley by name, but my mother was and families usually look after their own.'

She took Elinor's hand in hers. 'I won't leave you, love, whatever this cousin Walter says or does, but I feel lost, not sure where to turn and I can tell that you're feeling a bit that way. Besides, what if Jason Stafford comes after us? He could claim we stole that money from him and tell all sorts of lies about us. And some people might believe him.'

Silence hung heavily between them, then Elinor said slowly, 'Let's give it a try.'

Maude gave her a big hug. 'The man at the little railway halt where we started from told me how to get to Ollerthwaite but he didn't know what time the trains were these days. We can go to the railway station today and check that I remember correctly then buy tickets and leave as early as we can tomorrow morning. I think we'll have to go via Preston and then some little railway no one's heard of: Cross End Line, I think it's called.'

'Well, if you're sure.'

'I'm not sure of anything, Elinor love, that's the trouble.'

'Neither am I. So we'll go and see if your relative will help. He can only say no, after all.'

4

Walter Crossley went outside to stare across his land. He always thought better when he could see the moors up above his farm and feel the fresh air on his face. He couldn't bear to think that the property might pass into the hands of strangers if he couldn't find a suitable heir.

The only thing he could think of was to write to his younger son. James had run away to travel the world at the age of eighteen and had never returned, while his older son had stayed at home in Ollerthwaite.

It was years before James got in touch to say that he'd settled in America, was doing well there and now owned a small farm. Who'd have thought such a wild lad would settle down like that?

From then onwards a letter each Christmas had brought the latest news and Walter had reciprocated in kind. In his second year's letter, James revealed he'd fathered an illegitimate son but hadn't wanted to marry a poor woman so was looking for a wife who brought him a decent dowry. That upset Walter, it sounded so heartless.

Since then James had indeed married well and now owned a larger farm. In further annual letters he said he'd become the proud father of three sons and a daughter. He'd never mentioned the bastard son again, so neither did Walter.

When the wife of his older son Frank died in childbirth at the age of forty, after an unexpected late pregnancy, Walter had wondered if his son might remarry. But Frank made no effort to do that, declaring that no one could replace his Vicky. Well, Walter had been fond of the wife he'd lost to pneumonia so he knew how hard that loss of a spouse could hit you.

Then fate struck a cruel blow and it had taken Walter a few months to recover from it. At sixty-five, he'd had occasional bad patches in life, as most people did, but this was the worst thing he could ever have imagined: he lost both his elder son and grandson in one dreadful accident when a pantechnicon suddenly rolled over on an icy road, colliding with his son's pony trap and killing them both.

His son and grandson had been the light of his life and not only had he loved them dearly, but he'd felt happy to think that Frank would be a good man to take over Cross End Farm one day, and they even had a backup heir in Frank's son Timothy, though at barely nineteen, his grandson hadn't even got to the stage of considering marriage.

And so, suddenly, Walter's whole family had gone, either dying or going overseas.

The loss of the two people he loved most in the world had left him struggling even to get out of bed in the mornings. If the animals hadn't needed feeding, he might not have bothered.

Eventually there came a morning when the sunlight seemed brighter than it had for a while and when Walter looked out of the window, he saw a blue sky that seemed to be beckoning him outside. It wasn't quite spring yet, but the weather was beautiful today. Not only were the plants and animals responding to nature's caress, but the snowdrops had bloomed vigorously.

For some reason he was starting to recover. He didn't let himself feel guilty because he'd lived long enough to know that you had to learn to live with the bad things that happened to you, painful as that was.

He got dressed quickly then went outside to lean on the fence and look across what he'd once called the home field.

Groups of cows used to munch the grass there. After the accident he'd given them to his former stockman, Henry, and told him to take them home and care for them.

He'd given his flock of sheep to a neighbour, keeping only his hens.

Walter had already been moving away from the time-consuming daily tasks of farming even before the accident and he knew now that he wouldn't go back to the same way of making a living as before. He'd continue to buy and sell things, look after the various small houses he had acquired over the years and live off the rents.

Was it his imagination or did the hens seem livelier than usual today, looking up at him with their heads held slightly to one side and taking sudden runs at one another, as if they had too much energy to spare?

What should he do today? He felt restless, needing to do something worthwhile to prove he was starting to recover, and suddenly he knew what he'd start with. He'd been putting it off for months but now was the time.

He went back inside, found Flora from the village there and remembered that it was her day to mop the floors and take away the dirty washing from the laundry basket – if he'd remembered to put his things in it. He hadn't always done that lately.

He really ought to hire a proper housekeeper and bring the family home up to scratch again, but he'd just kept asking Flora to do an extra day here and there, and he'd lived mainly on bought bread and cheese or eggs, as well as apples and tinned fruit.

There had been enough eggs to see him through winter and give Flora a few, but now the hens were starting to lay better and there were eggs left over to sell in the village. He'd neglected things and should be ashamed of himself. It was a wonder the poor birds had survived the winter.

'Sorry, Flora. I forgot to sort out my dirty clothes. The sun tempted me outside. I'll go up and grab them.'

'I'm glad to hear it. And it doesn't look as if you've had breakfast yet, either. Shall I fry you a couple of eggs?'

To his further surprise he was hungry for the first time in ages. 'Yes, please. And I'll have some strawberry jam on a piece of toast as well if there's any left.' He'd have to buy some more jars of jam from the village shop. It was one thing they never ran out of, because it was very popular.

She nodded and studied him as if noticing that he'd perked up a bit, so he said it for her. 'I'm feeling a bit better today.'

'I'm glad to hear that as well, Mr Crossley.'

While she was cooking, he went into the sitting room, got out the writing materials and sat down at the little roll-top desk to write to his younger son. Of course the fancy fountain pen Frank had once bought him for Christmas was lacking ink, and even the ink in the bottle had dried up. But there was a new, unopened bottle in the drawer, so he rinsed out the fountain pen and filled it, checking that the nib was all right. Nibs seemed to last longer these days than they had in his youth.

By that time his meal was ready and Flora had called him twice, so he left the letter till later.

After breakfast he turned to his task. He needed to write and tell James about his brother's death, should have done that months ago, and ask for his help in finding an heir. Three sons, James had had. No, four, but one had been fathered out of marriage and didn't live with James and family. He'd never spoken of that one again so perhaps the mother had moved away and they'd lost touch.

Surely James could spare one of his sons to move to England and take over Cross End Farm and the other business activities after Walter died?

Not that Walter was in ill-health, but at sixty-five he wasn't exactly young and it would only be prudent to work out what to do with the farm and his other business interests. He'd once hoped to build a hotel by the side of the lake, and had bought rights to some of the land along its edge when they became available. That was another dream that had been lost. Now, the best he could hope for was to have enough years left to train a new heir and help him to understand how to look after the land round here. He'd need to do what he could for the valley and its inhabitants, too.

It had upset Walter for years to see how lack of work locally had seen people move away to nearby towns, or even across the sea to Australia or America. He had become determined to find a way to bring his valley back to life again. People needed little businesses and jobs to keep them here and bring others too.

He went over in his mind what he needed to say in the letter as he went back into his farm office across the yard and tried it out in pencil, altering a few details. Once he was satisfied that this was the best he could do, he wrote the letter in his very best handwriting, then knuckled away a tear or two.

Later that morning he harnessed his pony and drove the short distance down the valley into Ollerthwaite in his trap. It was the only town round here, not big as towns went but considerably larger than the tiny village of Upperfold near his farm. Ollerthwaite had, among other services, a large general store, a post office, three pubs, a barber's shop, a haberdasher's, an ironmonger's which also sold farm supplies, and a small timber merchant that sold the sort of wood often needed for minor repairs on a house or shed, as well as the nails and hardware to go with it.

As he drove home again after posting the letter to his son, Walter faced the fact that all he could do now was wait for a reply – and pray that it'd be the response he desperately needed.

But a couple more tears escaped him as this again brought memories of his older son and grandson. It was so hard still to remember that he'd lost them and had no close family nearby now. He still turned round sometimes to say something to one of them.

5

New York

When a letter from England arrived in upstate New York and was delivered to James Crossley's farm together with a bundle of business letters and bills, he placed everything on his desk to look at later. Correspondence with his father was his duty but not his pleasure, and they only normally wrote at Christmas. There wasn't usually anything urgent about it.

Nonetheless, he hesitated, staring down at it. Was there a problem? Should he open his father's letter straight away?

No. At the moment he had other matters on his mind that were far more important. He was having serious problems with his youngest son, who had never been a hard worker but had now fallen in with a group of troublemakers and become increasingly involved in gambling, which occasionally led to fights.

In the past month Caleb had gambled away his three months' allowance within a week of receiving it, got into two fights with other ne'er-do-wells like himself, and avoided work on the family farm as much as he possibly could, vanishing for two or three days at a time.

James was at his wits' end as to how to deal with this because all his sanctions so far had failed, and though he'd begged her not to, he knew his wife was secretly slipping Caleb money.

Lately his son didn't seem to care about anything he said or did and no threats worked to bring him in line. Caleb had disappeared several times now and refused to say where he'd been. And he was too big and strong to beat a bit of sense into him. He was a real Crossley physically, though not like the rest of the family in character. Most people grew out of their foolish ways. Caleb hadn't.

Even his older half-brother Cameron, James's illegitimate son from before his marriage, couldn't get much information out of Caleb this time, and he was the only member of the family who might have managed it.

Not that Cameron was exactly part of the family. James's wife wouldn't have stood for that. James had mentioned his existence to his father, or at least he thought he had. He couldn't remember exactly what he'd said in his first letter after their years apart, and hadn't had the sense then to keep a copy.

Cameron was a son he'd have been proud of in any other circumstances. When his birth mother had married and moved away while he was still a boy, James had found a family to foster the lad, because his mother's new husband didn't want him to live with them.

James had continued to keep an eye on him over the years and had made sure Cameron was properly housed and fed as he grew up. He hadn't needed to do anything to make that son try hard in school because Cameron had soaked up learning like a sponge. Now, he was a man grown, tall and strong like most Crossleys, and with a far sharper brain than his half-brothers.

At just turned thirty, he had been living independently for several years in a small one-room house he'd built for himself on a plot of land he'd bought with his own money. He worked for James on and off, as needed, and was a good worker too.

James had steadfastly refused to send him away, which infuriated his wife because Cameron resembled his father so closely. In fact, he was a thoroughly decent, hard-working young chap. Pity he had never married.

James forced himself to stop thinking about Cameron and turn his mind back to his youngest legitimate son. He was wondering whether he should disown Caleb completely and throw him out of the family home, but that wasn't a solution that appealed to him. Family should stick together through thick and thin.

Besides, it would devastate his wife, who doted on her youngest in spite of everything.

That evening he went to read his letters and realised he hadn't yet opened the one from his father. He read it quickly, gasped then re-read it slowly and carefully, feeling desperately sad.

His elder brother and nephew had both been killed in an accident. Both of them! As a result of this dreadful loss his father was offering to make one of James's sons his heir if the young man would move to England, learn to manage Walter's farm and business interests, and marry a woman of whom his grandfather approved.

James let the idea sink in, nodding a couple of times. It might be the ideal solution for Caleb if only he could persuade his troublesome son to do this.

The family farm in England was in a poor area but James's father had other strings to his bow these days, not necessarily connected with farming. Surely even his youngest might consider this inheritance a prize worth having?

And it'd get his son away from here without needing to cast him out of the family. Caleb living a long way away would please everyone except for James's fool of a wife.

He'd get Cameron to help him persuade Caleb to do it, yes, and send the older brother with him to make sure he got to England all right. Cameron was eight years older than Caleb and had more sense in his left hand than Caleb had in his whole body.

When he first mentioned the offer, Caleb merely laughed. 'No way am I going to move to a farm in England, father. When will you accept that I hate farming? It's filthy, back-breaking work and it bores me to tears.'

'But it's not just farming. There are other businesses and keeping accounts isn't dirty work.'

'I'm not fond of fiddling around with figures either. It's tedious.'

'You'd inherit a fortune when your grandfather died! Surely that's worth being bored for?'

'I'd still have to work on a farm and marry some woman I've never met, probably an ugly one, to get such an inheritance. Life's too short. I won't do it.'

'I'll accept your refusal when you find some other worthwhile way to earn a living. In the meantime I'm not reinstating your allowance until you learn to pull your weight round here. Everyone has to pay their way in the world, you included.'

'Well, I'm *not* going to England and I'm *not* becoming a farmer, here or there.'

'Caleb, please give this some serious thought. It's a wonderful opportunity. You'd be rich eventually.'

'Couldn't I just go over there and sell the farm when the time comes and the old man dies?'

'Of course not. Your grandfather is only sixty-five and we Crossleys usually live to a ripe old age.'

'Then that sort of inheritance is of no use to me.' His son scowled at him and nothing anyone in the family said or did would make Caleb consider the offer seriously, let alone change his mind.

But only a few weeks later, Caleb had to change. His gambling had left him in debt to the most dangerous man in the state, and he'd come running to his father for financial help to flee from the law and get right away from here.

James scowled at his son. 'I'm not helping you unless you take up your grandfather's offer and move to England.'

'Even if I wanted to, I don't have the money to get there.'

'I'll supply that.'

'But I don't *want* to become a farmer. I loathe it. I've told you that time after time. Why will you not believe me?'

'Because you have lost all your money, which shows you're no good at gambling. And you're now in trouble with the law for nearly killing a man as well. It's more than time you grew up and started acting sensibly.'

'That man won the game by cheating. He deserved a good thumping. It's just a pity he has an uncle who's a judge.'

'You gave him more than a thumping by the sounds of it; you nearly killed him.' James banged his fist down on the table. 'That's my only offer. If you don't take it, they can put you in jail with my blessing.'

He saw the moment when Caleb realised he meant it and accepted the offer with a black scowl.

Since he was concerned that his son would still try to get out of it, James added, 'And I'm sending your half-brother with you to England to make sure you get there. Cameron will manage the money and keep an eye on you during the journey.'

'He won't want to go to England either.'

'Doesn't matter. Unlike you, he'll do his duty by the family. He may not be a Crossley by name, but he's one by nature. Besides, his job will only be to get you there, then he can come home again because *he* isn't wanted by the law. If I give him that outlying piece of land he's renting from me as a reward for undertaking this unpleasant task, he'll jump at the chance. He plans for the future, your brother does, and he's good at everything he's done so far. I'm proud of him. You, on the other hand, need to sort your life out and I'm ashamed of you.'

It took another half an hour to make Caleb see sense and agree to go to his grandfather in England and give things a try. James quickly got down to planning it all.

'How did you get here from the station? Who knows you're here?'

'No one. I had no money left so I had to walk.'

'Good.'

When they heard the sounds of horses approaching the farm, James stiffened. 'No one normally comes out to the farm at this hour of the night, so you must have been seen. Go and hide in the inner cellar till we see who it is. I'll fetch you once they've gone and we'll see if we can get you away without them noticing.'

He slammed his flat hand down on the family Bible. 'And I swear this will be the last time I'll ever help you.'

This won him another scowl and not the slightest sign of gratitude.

Before he went to speak to the law officers, James sent his foreman to fetch Cameron. 'Tell him I have a proposition to make to him which will bring him good money and say he should bring clothes for a long journey to earn it.'

The man looked at him in surprise and he knew why. He didn't often invite his illegitimate son into the house. They usually met somewhere on the farm.

Although Cameron was perfectly polite, James suspected that his son had always thought him wrong not to have married his mother when Alice found out she was expecting. From then onwards people had looked down on her for bearing a child out of wedlock, just as they looked down on the child itself. No wonder she'd married someone who took her away from here.

James too sometimes thought he should have married Alice, especially when he saw what a fine young man his illegitimate son was, with the same kind nature as his grandfather in England. But Alice would have brought nothing to the marriage, so he'd set her up in a small house and married Rose Wilson instead.

Rose had brought him another farm as big as his own, and had given him two fine sons and a daughter before she bore Caleb. It was a pity she was such a whiner, always complaining. It was hard not to yell at her sometimes.

He spent an hour persuading the officers of the law that he hadn't seen Caleb for a couple of days. He had to let them search the house and stables before they'd believe him.

Once they'd left, James told his wife what he intended to do.

Rose let out a little mew of anguish. 'You're sending my Caleb away? No! No, you can't! Pay the fine, whatever it costs.'

'It's not a fine; it's either get him away or let them put him in jail for several years. Which do you prefer?'

She burst into tears and it took him a few minutes to persuade her that Caleb really didn't have any choice.

Afterwards she said stiffly, 'Well, I don't want to see that Cameron of yours. Keep him out of my way. You know I don't like him coming to the house.'

'He's a good person. It's not his fault he's illegitimate; it's mine.'

'You always say that. You're probably sorry you married me instead of *her*.'

'You know that's not true. She got married to someone else years ago and I haven't seen her since well before then.'

He kept reminding her of that but it didn't stop his wife throwing his ex-mistress's name in his face regularly. 'You've given me children and we've made a beautiful home together. Please, Rose, accept this situation. The only choices for our youngest son are going to jail or fleeing the country.'

She went up to bed in tears and left him to put the proposition to Cameron who was waiting for him in the small room he called his office, but which was just as much a refuge from his wife.

After James had explained what he was offering for escorting Caleb to England, his son stared at him, face expressionless.

He was taller than James now and stronger too. He had a full head of the dark, wavy Crossley hair and bore a distinct resemblance to the family in features as well, more so than any of his half-brothers, strangely enough.

When his son turned to stare out of the window at the darkness outside, James waited, forcing himself to be patient. He knew this man liked to think things through and could rarely be pushed into rushing heedlessly into anything. It was a good trait, so he waited.

At last his son turned round again. 'Very well, father. I'll do it.'

'Thank you.'

'Caleb and I should set off tonight and travel to New York as quickly as we can. If we catch an overnight train, he can stay out of sight in the sleeping compartment. Can you send a telegram to book passages on the next ship going to England for us? The sooner he's out of the country the better.'

'I agree. I'm going to give the money to pay for the journey to you. Don't give him any of the money at all. All he does is gamble it away.'

'I know what he's like. But he's right about one thing: he really isn't suited to farming.'

'I don't know what he *is* suited to and farming is what our family does, so it's the only thing on offer from me or his grandfather, that and helping in some little business or other that my father runs. And Caleb is physically lazy as well.'

'He gets breathless if he works hard.'

'That's because he lacks practice at it. You have to build your muscles. They don't happen by chance.'

Cameron shrugged, knowing he'd never persuade his father that Caleb wasn't cut out for physical labour and wasn't strong physically, however healthy he looked. 'Well, that's water under the bridge now. He should pack his things then he and I had better go back to my place and use my horses to get to a railway station further away than your local one. I'll need to pack some things for myself too, of course.'

Another pause, then, 'If I arrange to send the horses back from the station, will you pay the man who brings them and keep an eye on them and my crops while I'm away?'

'Of course I will. And when you return from delivering Caleb to his grandfather, I'll gift that top field to you. I swear. Do you want me to put that in writing?'

'No. Your word is good enough for me. Hmm. Just one other thing: if anything happens to me, if I get killed doing this, I want that land given to my cousin Tom from my mother's side. He's got the makings of a good farmer and I'll pay him to look after it for me while I'm away. All you'll have to do is go there occasionally to check it.'

James rolled his eyes. 'What the hell's likely to happen to you? People travel to England by steamship every day of the week. This is 1895, not the Dark Ages.'

'I agree that probably nothing will happen. I just like to plan for every contingency. It's a long journey and Caleb can be a loose cannon, as we both know.'

'He wouldn't *kill* you. In fact, he's as fond of you as he is of anyone.'

'He'd not kill me on purpose, I know, but he might get me into trouble with the wrong type of person. Let's agree about that second condition anyway, because when Caleb loses his temper, he acts before he thinks.'

'Oh, very well. I promise. Now, in a minute I'll fetch Caleb up from the cellar and he can pack his bag but I'll give you the money first.' He went across to his desk and unlocked one of the drawers, pulling out a roll of money, studying it thoughtfully then adding another. 'You are not to give him any of this and you are to remain in charge of the spending at all times. The second roll is for your own expenses on the journey back to America after you've left him.'

'Very well.'

When his father went to fetch Caleb up from the cellar, Cameron quickly split up the money and hid some in each boot, tucking other little bundles here and there among his clothes. His half-brother wouldn't hurt him, but he'd steal from him or from anyone, friend or stranger, to pay for his gambling.

It was sad to see him so gripped by the desire to throw money away, and the obsession seemed to be getting worse, not better.

6

Lancashire

Maude and Elinor set off from Blackpool after an early breakfast, but it proved to be an even slower journey than they'd expected. They had to change from one small branch railway line to another because there was no direct route across to the part of the northern Pennines where Cousin Walter's farm was situated. Both times they had to wait an hour for the next connection. And such small stations didn't have refreshment rooms.

Maude walked to and fro on the short platform. 'My mother told me Walter's farm was in a small valley that led nowhere and commented on how difficult it was to get there. I can see now what she meant. It was near a place called Ollerthwaite, which no one's ever heard of. The locals called it a town, but it seemed more like a large village to her. The valley was called Ollindale and she found the names confusing.'

'It's hard to get to, isn't it? But I suppose that's a good thing for us, because it means it'll be less likely that Jason will be able to find us.'

'You seem so sure he'll pursue us. Why would he bother?'

'If you'd seen how he looked at me when he was trying to grab me this last time, you'd worry about it too, Maude. I've read about lust and I saw it clearly in his face. He wanted *me*, not just any woman, and it wasn't the first time he'd tried to maul me around as you well know.'

'Some men just want a woman in their beds, and any woman will do.'

Elinor shook her head. 'He seemed quite set on marrying me. I'd never marry him, though, whatever he did, because he's as nasty and twisted as his uncle was, perhaps worse. Oh, thank goodness! This must be our train.'

It was mid-afternoon before they climbed wearily out of the final train, which ran on the local one-track railway, with the passing places only at the various stops, which were just platforms with a small shelter on them.

There were a surprising number of people on it, mostly women carrying full shopping bags and chatting happily to one another after their day out at a bigger market in a different town.

When Elinor and Maude got out of the train they watched the other passengers stride briskly away and looked round for a taxi to take them to Cousin Walter's farm. Only there wasn't any sign of one.

A man in uniform came up to them. 'Can I help you, ladies?'

'We need to find a taxi.'

He shook his head. 'There isn't a full-time taxi, I'm afraid, just a man who carries passengers occasionally.'

'Oh, no! We need to get out to my cousin's farm in Upperfold.'

'Who would that be? There are several farms in that part of the valley.'

'Cross End Farm. Walter Crossley is my cousin. I haven't seen him for ages and he doesn't know I'm coming.'

The man's name brought a smile and a nod. 'Well, you're in luck today because I saw him go into the farm shop a few minutes ago. Um, you say you haven't seen him lately?'

'No.'

'So you don't know about the accident?'

Maude looked at him in dismay. 'What accident? Has he been injured?'

'No, no! It wasn't him. The poor fellow lost his son *and* his grandson a few months ago. They were in an accident with one of them big drays skidding on an icy stretch of road in front of them. The driver wasn't able to stop and the dray was overloaded, top heavy. The dray toppled over and pushed your relatives' little cart over the edge of the cliff. The horses were all killed too.'

'How terrible!'

'Never seen Mr Crossley look as downhearted as he has since then, and who can blame him? I hope you don't mind me mentioning it?'

The two women exchanged worried glances and Maude said. 'Thank you for telling us. I'll try not to say anything that upsets him.'

'Shall I send a lad to find him for you? You can stay here and keep an eye on your luggage. Perhaps your arrival will cheer him up a bit.'

'That would be very kind of you.'

'Why don't you sit on this bench while you wait? You both look exhausted.'

'We are. Thank you so much for your help.'

'It's a poor lookout if we can't help one another.'

The lad he gave the message to stared at them then ran off down the street. He came back shortly afterwards accompanied by a tall, grey-haired man, who looked fit and well, if rather grim-faced. He studied them both then said to Maude, 'You must be a relative of mine.'

'Yes, I'm Angela Crossley's daughter.'

'Ah. You have a look of our family.' He studied Elinor. 'You're not a relative, though.'

Maude intervened. 'Elinor's a very close friend. I've been with her family for near on twenty years. I just about raised her, young as I was then, because her mother was an invalid.'

Mr Crossley surprised Elinor by saying, 'I can see you two are close. It shows in the way you look at one another.'

'There are only ten years between us, so we've decided to call ourselves cousins from now on, because that's how we feel about one another.'

He nodded as if encouraging her to continue.

'Elinor's mother died a few years ago and now her stepfather has died as well. He's left everything to his nephew instead of Elinor, as we were expecting, and well, we had to run away from him. So I came to ask your help, because I think you're my closest relative and, well, we don't have much experience of the world.'

He stared at them, then nodded again. 'What exactly are you ladies running from? Or should I ask who? Doesn't Elinor have any other relatives to turn to?'

They looked at him then glanced at one another in dismay. Was he going to tell them to sort their own lives out?

'None close enough to help her, I'm afraid. And anyway, we want to stay together.'

'Tell me the details,' he urged gently.

Maude explained the situation. 'He's a dreadful person, so I won't work for him, even for Elinor's sake. He turned up as soon as he heard and tried to take advantage of her. She had to lock herself in her bedroom to escape his attack and he said he'd knock the door down if she didn't let him into her bed later.'

That caught Walter's full attention. His face turned a dusky red and anger rumbled in his deep voice. 'They should shoot men who act like that. They're no better than animals if they can't control themselves. What's this chap's name again?'

'Jason Stafford.'

'I'll remember it. He'd better not come after you because if he shows his face round here and tries tricks like that, I'll give him what-for and I won't be short of friends willing to help me do it. What made you think of me?'

'My mother used to talk about you, said you were a kind man. So I'm here to beg your help and advice for us both, Cousin Walter.'

Elinor felt she should say something. 'We're not frightened of hard work, Mr Crossley, and we'll help out with anything we can at your farm till we've found a place to go. Only we're really worried he'll come after us.'

'Nay, I'm not turning you two away. I'd never do that. Blood's thicker than water, always has been, always will be, so you were right to come to me. And I'll take your friend in as well.' His eyes settled on the bags. 'Is that all your luggage?'

'It's all we could grab, we were in such a hurry to get away.'

He shook his head sadly, not needing to put into words how little they'd got, then he bent and picked up the two bags as if they weighed nothing. 'My cart's over there. It'll not be a comfortable ride because the road's quite rough and it's not a big cart, but my mare's a sturdy creature and she'll get us all to Upperfold. My farm's on the other side of the nearby village on the edge of the moors.'

'I can't thank you enough, Mr Crossley.' Elinor couldn't stop her voice wobbling.

'If Maude says you're like a cousin to her, you're as welcome in my house as if you really were one of the family. Come on, now.'

He led the way across the road to a well-maintained cart, the sort used to get around in and carry smaller loads, not one made for heavy loads. It had a brightly painted name on the side: *Cross End Farm*. The mare was standing quietly with a nosebag on and looked well cared for.

'I'll have to put your things in the front seat with you, I'm afraid, because I'd let my stocks of food and animal fodder get a bit low, so I've a bought a lot of things today.' He slung their sacks up then asked, 'Can you get up on the cart on your own?'

'Easily.'

'Good. I hope you won't mind waiting for me. I'll be another quarter of an hour or so because I might as well finish getting my order filled now I've come into town.' He smiled at them and strode off without waiting for an answer.

'Can it really be that easy to get help from a stranger?' Elinor whispered.

'He's not a stranger to me, well, not exactly, and my mother was right: he has a kind smile. You won't mind what work you do on the farm till we sort out our future, will you?'

'Of course not. You didn't need to ask. There's no shame in honest work. I'm used to all sorts of housework, anyway, because you were the only maid who'd stay with my step-father. Apart from the scrubbing woman and the washing, you and I have shared the chores for years.'

She looked up at the blue sky patterned with a few drifts of cloud then gazed round at the quiet little town and let out a long sigh of relief, adding, almost as if she was talking to herself, 'It'll be paradise to live without *him* nagging us, don't you think?'

'That Jason seemed worse than his uncle, more cunning somehow, though both Staffords were bad men.' Maude patted her younger companion's hand. 'We'll be safe in a place like this if we're going to be safe anywhere, love.'

'Yes. I feel that too, though I don't know whether I shall feel completely safe for a long while. Your Cousin Walter has a kind face, though. No one could ever be afraid of him.'

Maude patted her hair, which was scraped tightly back into a bun as usual. 'I can wear my hair in nicer styles now and maybe you'll plump out a bit once you start eating better and worrying less. You're far too thin.'

'I found it hard to swallow food with my stepfather mocking and nagging whenever he bothered to eat a meal at home.'

'We'll be all right from now on. Just you wait and see.' Maude knew her friend was still having trouble trusting anyone, so took hold of her hand, clasping it in both hers and patting it. It'd take time for both of them to feel fully at ease again, she knew, but longer for Elinor, she suspected.

It was nearer to half an hour before Walter came back, accompanied by two lads pushing a handcart containing several large bundles and sacks, paper carrier bags and cardboard boxes of various sizes. He was carrying a large brown paper bag.

'Are you two as hungry as you look?'

'We can manage till we get back.'

'No need.' He held out the bag to Maude, who was sitting on the outside of the driving seat of the cart. 'I bought you a muffin each and got the lady at the bakery to put butter and jam on them. And there's good drinking water from my own well in that bottle in the holder in front of you if you don't mind swigging out of it. I haven't had a drink from it since I filled it, so the bottle's clean.'

'That's so kind. Thank you.' Maude opened the bag and beamed as she handed one of the freshly baked muffins to Elinor.

As they both started to eat, they made happy murmuring noises, which brought a smile to Walter's face.

He took the nosebag from the mare who immediately began to gulp water from the nearby horse trough, then he went to the back of the cart to help the lads finish stowing his purchases and lock up the tailpiece. After slipping coins into their hands, he tipped his hat to a woman walking past, then climbed up on to the driving seat and clicked to the mare to set off.

He didn't try to chat until the muffins had been devoured and gulps taken from the water bottle.

'You two look a lot better now. It'll take us about fifteen minutes to get to Upperfold because we can only go slowly with such a load. I'd have brought my bigger cart if I'd known you two were coming.'

'I hope we aren't causing you too much trouble.'

'On the contrary, I've had too little to do lately.' He shot them a quick glance. 'You know about the accident?'

'Yes. The porter told us.'

'That's all right, then. I shall welcome your company. It can get very quiet on your own.' He swallowed hard and stared ahead, blinking his eyes.

Maude saw the sadness return to his face. What terrible losses he'd had in the past year. But he hadn't hesitated to take her and her friend in, had he? That showed what he was like as a person.

In her opinion kindness made the world a better place and she had no time for people who didn't care about others.

7

As they came to the edge of the town, Maude saw a glint of silver to the right through some trees. It was clearly more than a small pond. 'Is that a lake? We saw some water in the distance from the train but couldn't see enough to make out what exactly it was.'

Walter glanced sideways. 'Aye, it's a lake. The train goes past it on the far side. It's not much of a lake. A few of us started trying to make it bigger in 1885. We dammed the stream and drained a marshy bit of low-lying land nearby. We were intending to finish it in time to celebrate the Queen's Golden Jubilee in 1887. The town council even named it "Jubilee Lake" and threw a party on the shore for the whole village.'

'What a lovely idea!'

'Unfortunately, we never finished the work because it took longer than we'd expected and people got disheartened. Then, when I was thinking of organising a new start on a smaller scale, there was that Russian 'flu epidemic in 1889. It killed a lot of people and the damned 'flu has returned since then in smaller waves.'

'I had that Russian 'flu mildly,' Maude said. 'It left me with a reduced sense of smell for a while. Fortunately Elinor had it even more mildly but one of our neighbours died of it. His turned into pneumonia and there's not much you can do when that sets in if it's a bad bout. Eh, it was a sad time.'

'My horrible stepfather escaped the 'flu completely,' Elinor said bitterly. 'He would! It didn't seem fair.'

There was a pause in the conversation, during which Walter let the pony slow down to a halt as all three of them stared towards the water glinting in the distance and remembered the illness that had swept across the country, killing so many and returning twice in later years, though not as fiercely. How afraid people had been, because they felt so helpless against an invisible enemy.

Walter clicked to his pony to carry on. 'The locals still call it Jubilee Lake, even though it wasn't finished in time for the Queen's Golden Jubilee. My grandson always said he was going to make it into a proper lake one day.'

He gave them a sudden urchin's smile. 'I used to be famous for getting ideas and nudging folk into doing something about them. Maybe he'll get his wish and I'll get it done in his memory in time for Her Majesty's Diamond Jubilee. Who knows?'

Elinor smiled at the water. 'I think a lake looks much prettier than the sea. I was a bit disappointed at the bare sand in Blackpool. The paved promenades were full of strangers and it felt strange not to say good day to them. This water is much nicer with the trees and bushes nearby and the moors looking down on it, sort of framing it from above.'

'I prefer it here too,' Maude said. 'And isn't that a farmhouse just above it on the other side, nestling in the trees?'

'Aye. Holtby Farm, they used to call it, after the family as lived there and rented it from the Crossleys for several generations. The last of them died about twenty years ago and his wife moved away to live with their daughter in Whitehaven. There was no family left to carry things on and no one else wanted to take it over. It's still part of the Crossley lands, but it's only ever been a small farm and the house has been standing empty for years now, like a few other local houses. I keep the buildings weatherproof and use it mainly for storage.'

'And are those ruins I can see in the distance on the left?' Elinor asked.

'Yes. That used to be the manor, the biggest house in the district, Ollerton House they called it. But it burned down a few years ago and there's no one living there now. They still have an agent who comes here to collect the rents, though they do nothing to maintain the smaller buildings properly.'

'What a pity.'

Everything round here seemed a bit rundown, Elinor thought, and yet she found the countryside attractive, especially the great rolling curves of the moors cradling it all like a giant cupped hand. Dry-stone walls criss-crossed the lower slopes and she admired the skill it must have taken to build such solid walls without mortar.

'Why are there fewer people round here now and houses standing empty?'

'Because of the big cotton mills. Spinning used to be done on a much smaller scale and the machinery was turned by water wheels. Quite a few properties were abandoned once steam engines took over running the cotton machinery because they needed more flat land to build them than you can find in the smaller valleys like this one.'

He shrugged. 'They called it progress and it meant riches for some but there was no other obvious way for poorer country folk to earn a living if their watermill closed and all the spinning and weaving got done in other places. When they had to move to the towns to find work in the new mills, some of the villages died for lack of work. The folk left in our valley are barely managing to survive. And even the mills in the towns haven't been doing as well for their owners lately because countries overseas have built their own mills and don't have to pay their workers as much.'

'How sad!'

'Eh, I must be boring you to tears with all this.'

'You're not,' Elinor said. 'Do go on.'

He studied her face as if trying to tell whether she meant that, then inclined his head and continued speaking. 'I own the old watermill in our valley now. It didn't cost much to buy it and it's soundly built. Maybe one day I'll think of something to do with it. My grandson used to say we should turn one of the bigger houses into a place for hikers to stay so that they could have a holiday in the country. I never got round to doing anything about it, though. Eh, our Tim was full of ideas. He made notes about them in the back of his diary and said he'd work his way through them when he was older. I can't even bear to read it now so I put it away somewhere.'

Elinor dared to pat his arm. 'I'm so sorry you lost your family, Mr Crossley.'

He took a deep breath and patted the hand as it lay there. 'You lasses seem to have lost everything, too. I'm not the only one that life's hurt. And you might as well call me Cousin Walter from now on, lass.'

'I'd like that.'

A couple of minutes later he pulled his mare to a halt and pointed further up the gentle slope. 'That's my farm, on the right just past the crossroad. Folk call it "Cross End", whether because of our family's name or because of it being at the crossroads no one knows. My ancestors built it and they built it well. It's stood in that spot for a couple of hundred years and I reckon it'll stand for another couple of hundred.'

He was obviously proud of his home and rightly so. The farmhouse was a substantial building. It was well cared for and looked lived in, unlike the two other farmhouses they'd passed which had curtains drawn across all of their windows and were surrounded by unkempt gardens.

There were various outbuildings showing behind the farm and a few plump chickens were pecking about in a run to one side. And those distant white blobs dotted here and there on the slopes above the farm were surely sheep, and were the smaller blobs lambs gambolling near their mothers? How sweet they looked!

A woman came to the back steps and shook out a cloth, then stopped in the doorway of the house looking surprised to see the two strangers sitting on the cart. 'I wondered where you'd got to, Walter. You're later than usual.'

He waved one hand towards her. 'This is Joan Rossell, my very kind neighbour from that last house we passed on the left before the crossroads. She's been helping me occasionally with the cooking and such, for which I'm deeply grateful.'

'Joan love, these two ladies are Maude Crossley, a young relative of mine, and Elinor Pendleton, who is Maude's cousin on her mother's side.'

The two women still sitting on the cart smiled and exchanged quick glances at this. With just a few words he'd made Elinor sound as if she really did have a right to be here, for which she was deeply grateful.

Joan waved a dirty hand. 'Pleased to meet you, but I won't offer to shake hands at the moment for obvious reasons.'

'They're in need of a roof over their heads for a while, so they'll be able to take over the housekeeping and I won't have to trespass on your goodwill.'

'Pleased to meet you, Mrs Rossell.' Maude and Elinor got stiffly down from the cart.

'They've come all the way from Blackpool today,' he added. 'Done nothing but change trains since early morning. Well, you know how tedious it can be getting to Ollerthwaite.'

'Eh, you poor things! Come on in and I'll get you all something to eat.'

'I bought them some jam muffins at the bakery, so I think we'll be more ready for a cup of tea to start with if you don't mind getting us one, Joan. I'll have to unload. You ladies go inside. I won't be long.'

'We'll help you with the unloading,' Maude said. 'As they say, many hands make light work.'

After they'd done that Walter said he'd put the cart away and let the pony out into the field for a run.

Joan began talking as soon as the other two women joined her in the kitchen. 'You look like a Crossley, Maude. I'm an even more distant relative of Walter's – cousin sixteen times removed, we joke, so there will be a similar relationship to you. The little room's outside the back door if you need it.'

When they came back to join her, Maude said. 'I can't believe how kind everyone we've met has been so far.'

Joan shrugged. 'It's in the Bible, something like: I was a stranger and you welcomed me. I forget the exact words. Most folk round here are pleasant enough but there are always one or two in every village or town, who aren't honest or like to take advantage of strangers if they can. But Walter will keep you safe, I'm sure.'

She whispered unnecessarily as she added, 'I'm glad you've come here, for his sake. That poor man needs something else to think about than the empty seats at his table. Folk haven't known what to do to help him because he isn't one to talk about his feelings. And of course we're all still sad ourselves about losing Frank and Tim, and always will be. Fine men they were, really good-hearted and hard workers, just like him.'

They nodded to show they were paying attention. She clearly enjoyed chatting.

'Eh, what am I going on about that for? That tea will be ready by now.'

In the simple warmth and acceptance of Walter's and Joan's welcomes, Maude saw Elinor start to truly relax for the first time since her stepfather had died. She must have been worrying about her reception here.

Walter joined them for a big farmhouse mug of tea then stood up. 'I'd better get on with my work. Can you find them bedrooms, Joan, and something for us all to eat this evening?'

'Aye. Did you bring the meat?'

'I did. I'd not dare forget it again or you'd give me what for.'

She smiled at his teasing. 'As if I'd dare. But I'll put a nice lamb hotpot together for you and set it to simmer on the stove before I leave.'

Once he'd left, Joan took over the conversation again. 'Me an' my husband have a farm down the hill. It's small compared to this one and I can't really spare the time to help keep things up to scratch here, except Walter started to let things go to rack and ruin in the house after the accident, and I couldn't bear to see it. He's insisted on paying me, though I'd have helped him without, but I must admit the money has been useful.'

She smiled at them. 'Now, let me find hooks for your coats and hats and you'll know where to put them from now on. We usually hang them near the back door as we come in and put our boots under that little bench there.'

She unhooked some coats and sighed. 'These belonged to his son and grandson, and he wouldn't let me remove them, but I think it'll be all right to do it now. I'll put them in the attic for the time being when I show you round up there.'

After they'd hung up their outdoor clothes their weariness must have shown, because she said abruptly, 'I'll just show you round quickly and come back tomorrow morning to go through the house with you properly and tell you how he likes things done.'

She took them upstairs, where there were five bedrooms, two in a newer part of the house, then along to a door at the far end of the landing. 'This leads up to the attic.'

They stood near the top of the stairs looking at a huge attic that stretched across the whole house, but didn't go any further.

Joan carried the coats across to an old sofa and laid them on the back of it. 'They'll no doubt come in useful for someone in need in the future. There are some smaller attic rooms at the front which would have held servants in more affluent times.'

'It's a big house,' Maude said.

'Too big for small families. Let's hope someone in the family fills it up with children one day. She led the way down to the first floor again. Now, let's talk about the practicalities. Flora comes in to do the washing. She's a good worker so you can leave things to her.'

'Perhaps we should sleep in the attics?' Maude suggested.

'Nay, you're family and family sleeps on the first floor. It's children and servants up there.'

She pointed to two doors. 'I'll help you clear out his son's and grandson's bedrooms tomorrow. I don't think Walter has been in them since the accident, wouldn't let me touch them. Just so that you know, Frank was a widower and about forty-four, or was it forty-five? His son Tim had only just turned nineteen, a lovely cheerful lad, but still boyish in his ways. Everyone liked him.'

She paused to sigh and stare into space. 'You never know what life will dish out, do you? Make the most of it while you can, I say. You have to carry on, can't give in.'

She moved to fling two doors open. 'Now, these two smaller bedrooms at the back haven't been used for a while but you two can have them for the time being till we see how everything goes. There are plenty of sheets in the linen cupboard, which is on the landing at the other end from the attic stairs. As you can see, the blankets and quilts are folded up and piled on the beds, waiting for them to be made up. There are plenty of towels in the linen cupboard too.'

She got them some sheets and towels, then checked that there were washing sets in their rooms. 'It must be lovely to have a plumbed-in bathroom. We're very old-fashioned here in the valley.'

She hesitated at the door of the big front bedroom. 'I think Walter's sheets need changing and washing but I don't like to intrude into his bedroom. I'm only a neighbour, after all.'

'You're a very good neighbour by the sound of it,' Elinor said quietly.

Joan shrugged, but couldn't hide her pleasure at the compliment. 'I do my best.'

'We'll make up our own beds,' Maude said. 'But do you think he'd mind if we had a little nap, just an hour or so? It feels to have been a long day already.'

'Can you stay awake for a while longer while I show you how to work the kitchen range? The meat should be cooking nicely now, so you can help me peel the potatoes and carrots. After I've gone, just go and lie down for an hour or so. I'll find you an alarm clock to wake you up. He'll be out in the fields till it starts getting dark, so he won't know whether you're having a nap or not. He often walks around out there. It seems to comfort him.'

'Right.'

Back in the kitchen she chopped the vegetables and tipped them into the big two-handled saucepan. 'Perhaps you can check on the hotpot when you get up, see if it needs a bit more water adding so that it doesn't dry out. He'll have brought home some shop bread to go with it, I should think. I don't have time to bake bread for him.'

'Yes, he has.'

'That's good. You'll be a bit late getting your tea, but it'll give you time for a rest.'

She was like a small, plump whirlwind and by the time she left the vegetables were simmering gently on the top of the kitchen range and the kitchen table was set.

She was still talking as she went out. 'The chests of drawers in the bedrooms are empty. You can leave your travelling bags in the attic.'

As the kitchen door closed behind her, Maude sagged back against the wall. 'Lovely woman but I thought she'd never stop talking. I have to get some sleep and I bet you do too. I can hardly keep my eyes open.'

'I feel the same. I peeped out of the window in my new bedroom and Walter's still out there in one of the upper fields, standing staring into the distance, just as Joan said he would be.'

They lay down on their beds and Elinor closed her eyes and let peace settle round her. She was glad to be alone for the first time in ages, however dearly she loved Maude.

It felt as if life had taken her by the scruff of the neck and dumped her out into the world.

She was hugely grateful to Maude . . . and Walter and . . . She'd close her eyes, just for a minute or two.

There was soon complete silence in both bedrooms.

8

New York

Caleb sulked all the way to New York and refused point-blank to stay hidden in their sleeping compartment. While Cameron was using the amenities on the train he slipped out and when his half-brother found him shortly afterwards he was chatting to a group of men playing cards.

Cameron hesitated for a moment in the doorway of that compartment then left Caleb where he was and since the train wasn't full, he took a seat further along the carriage. From there he could keep an eye on him. At least Caleb couldn't join the game without any money.

'Want to join in?' one of the men asked Caleb idly after a while. 'Your hands are twitching as if you'd like to hold the cards.'

'I would, but I haven't got any money at the moment.'

'You could deal for us if you like.'

Caleb brightened. 'I'd like that. I'm a good dealer and I shall enjoy watching the play. It'll be good to keep myself in practice.'

He acquitted himself so well the group applauded him and one man, better dressed than the others, studied him thoughtfully. When this man dropped out after the next hand, he beckoned Caleb across and began to speak very quietly to him.

Cameron was tempted to go and join them, a bit worried about what was going on, but when his brother shrugged and shook his head in answer to a question from the man, he stayed where he was. He hoped this meant Caleb was refusing to do whatever the fellow had suggested.

By now Cameron was longing to get some sleep, because he'd put in a lot of hard work on the farm earlier before Caleb's problem blew up and his father sent for him. He knew better than to leave his brother unsupervised, however, so forced himself to stay awake.

Unfortunately the conversation and the game both seemed to go on and on. He found games of cards tediously boring at the best of times and must have dozed off because the next thing he knew Caleb was shaking him awake, calling him an old sleepyhead and suggesting they go back to their compartment for an hour or two's rest.

The group of men were still playing cards but there was no sign of the man who'd been speaking to Caleb. 'Finished with those fellows now?'

'Yes. I can't join in and anyway, they're fools. The chap I was talking to took a lot of money off them. *He* isn't a fool and I enjoyed chatting to him.'

'Why did he leave, then, if he was winning?'

'He says it's not good to take all a man's money and anyway, he might have lost what he'd won if he'd gone on. I wish I'd met him before. He earns his living gambling and talks a lot of sense about how to do it and come out on top. I could have learned a lot from spending time with a man like him instead of shovelling cow dung for my father.'

'Well, unless he's coming to England with us, you'll never see him again.'

'I know. Life isn't fair.' He scowled and flung himself on the bunk, closing his eyes.

Cameron wished every evening he'd be spending with his difficult half-brother could pass as easily as this one had and climbed into the top bunk, sighing quickly into sleep.

*

When they got to New York, Cameron still felt tired and had to force himself to concentrate. They went straight to the shipping office and found that their father had already wired and booked them a modest cabin, the last one available apparently.

'See. I'm lucky,' Caleb said immediately. 'I'm a born gambler.'

Cameron didn't contradict him, didn't believe in luck in the same stupid way as his brother seemed to. How Caleb would even begin to cope with helping run a farm in a foreign country, he couldn't imagine. He didn't envy the grandfather.

There were a couple of days to wait before leaving, however, because the ship was unloading at the moment and would have to load its next cargo and take its new passengers on-board before setting off eastwards across the Atlantic again.

The clerk at the shipping office directed them to stay at a small hotel near the harbour, where a room had already been booked for them. From here they'd be summoned to the ship when it was ready for boarding. 'I see that a room has been booked for you gentlemen at the hotel. Please don't go too far away from it in case we have to call you on-board early.'

Once they were in their twin-bedded room at the hotel, his brother looked at him pugnaciously. 'I'm only going to answer to the name Cal from now on. Caleb is such a stupid, old-fashioned name.'

'Cal it is, then.' Their father wouldn't know, so what did it matter?

'Don't you ever think of shortening your name permanently? It's a right old mouthful and you've got three Christian names: Cameron Alan Michael. What was your mother thinking of?'

His father had apparently chosen his name, but it wasn't worth arguing about.

'Actually, my close friends shorten it to Cam, the ones I meet when I go travelling on business I mean. But as you very well know, our father has made it all too plain to all the family and people working for him that he won't put up with any shortening of our names, so I have to respect his wishes when I'm at home.'

Caleb laughed. 'Why he wanted all his children to have so many names and such old-fashioned ones too, I've never understood.'

'I thought it was your mother who chose yours.'

'No, him. Anyway, who cares? I've been Cal in my own head for a long time now and I'm only going to answer to Cal from now on. Are you going to continue travelling and selling things when you come back?'

'Probably,' answered Cameron.

'You ought to have quite a bit of money stacked away by now after all this buying and selling you've been doing. You couldn't lend me a little, could you? I'll pay you interest on it.'

'I've not got all that much saved. I had to buy my house and land. And even if I had money to spare, I'd definitely not lend you any. It takes hard work to earn money, something you don't seem to understand. Any money I make is going to stay tucked away safely in a bank till I can buy more land, thank you very much.'

'You're not dependent on him so I don't know why you always do as he wishes. He won't be able to leave you anything. My mother won't let him. So what would it matter if you shortened your name or even bought a small farm somewhere else than near him?'

'Unlike you, I prefer to tread gently through life and not upset people for no reason. And our father is as near as I get to having a family, and he's put one or two business deals my way. No, I'd rather stay nearby and build up my finances. If I ever do decide to move, I want to make sure I don't spend my life scraping a living on poorer land because that's all I can afford.'

'Oh, you're as much a stick-in-the mud as *him*.'

After breakfast the next day Caleb said, 'I really do need to move about a bit.'

'We can go for a short walk round the harbour this morning if you like. We needn't be away for more than half an hour. I'd enjoy stretching my legs too. The hotel receptionist told me we have to get our main luggage down to reception by three o'clock and it'll be loaded on the ship tonight so we can go out for another quick walk after that. Or else, we can board with the luggage today, if we'd rather, because the ship leaves tomorrow mid-morning.'

Caleb muttered something and let out an angry little growl. 'I'm not setting foot on that ship till tomorrow, and not till the latest possible minute, either. If I had any money of my own, any at all, I'd not be going to England, I can assure you.'

'Well, you don't have any money, so you might as well do it with a good grace. After all, if you tread carefully, you stand to inherit money.'

Caleb's scowl said he was still furious about being forced to go to England.

'Don't vent your temper on me. It's not my fault you're being sent there. Actually, if you want the truth, I agree with you. You're definitely not cut out to be a farmer. But you might at least give it a try.'

His brother shrugged, definitely in a foul mood today.

As the day progressed, Cameron tried to ignore a series of grumbles and snappish remarks, reminding himself that he was earning a piece of land by escorting Caleb to England. His father should be very grateful to him for this and that field would double the size of his land. But it was going to seem a long journey with his brother in such a bad mood.

He had to remind his brother to take his luggage down to the lobby, and then suggested another walk.

As they were going back into the hotel Caleb began complaining about being tired. But when they bumped into the man who'd been successful at cards on the train, his scowls vanished abruptly.

The stranger smiled at them. 'Fancy meeting you two here.'

Caleb brightened up immediately. 'Where else would I be when I'm being carted off to England like a sack of wheat? This is my half-brother, Cameron, by the way. We're staying here till we board the ship tomorrow morning.'

Cameron couldn't help feeling a bit suspicious at this meeting. Was it sheer chance or had it been arranged? No, surely not? What reason could there possibly be for that?

'I'm Daniel Jones, by the way.' The stranger offered his hand and added, 'I always stay here when I'm in New York because it's clean, comfortable and inexpensive. How about we have our evening meal together? My treat. I'd really enjoy some company, and *not* for the purpose of playing cards.'

'Are you catching a ship somewhere as well?' Cameron asked, still feeling suspicious.

'No. Meeting someone arriving by ship later tomorrow, only I got here early thanks to the railway timetables. So we'll share a meal, then?'

Cameron answered. 'Thanks for your invitation but we're thinking of going on board tonight.' They hadn't intended to but he was feeling worried about the way Caleb had perked up when they met Daniel, so maybe it'd be best to play it safe.

His brother's scowl deepened. 'You may be thinking of it. I'm refusing. I can wait till tomorrow to get seasick, if you don't mind.'

Unfortunately, Caleb didn't do well on water and even bobbing up and down in a harbour could make him throw up, as his family had found when he was younger and they'd gone away on holiday. Cameron gave in. 'Very well. We'll stay here overnight and board early tomorrow morning.'

Daniel beamed at them. 'So we can eat together for a meal. I'm in Room Six. Just knock on my door when you're ready. I've stayed here before and they'll serve a meal in your room, ordered in from that café next door. And it's not bad food, either. There's a table in my room that we can squeeze three people round.'

'That'd be great,' Caleb said at once.

Cameron forced a smile because it would have been rude to refuse, and after all, they'd never see this fellow again.

When they went to Room Six after having a wash, Caleb seemed to be rather excited and Cameron began to feel suspicious again.

'Don't even think of escaping,' Cameron warned him. 'I'll be keeping a close eye on you tonight. I'm sorry now that I let you persuade me to stay here overnight.'

Caleb's voice was mocking. 'Yes, Daddy.' Then he added bitterly, 'How can I escape? I don't have any money whatsoever, remember?'

But something still seemed to Cameron to be exciting his brother, only he couldn't work out what. To his relief Daniel made such a pleasant dinner companion that he couldn't help relaxing.

When they went back to their room after a final nightcap provided by their host, Cameron took out his book and sat near a lamp, intending to read a few pages before going to sleep.

He didn't get very far down the page before the words began to blur into one another. He must be tireder than he'd thought. He tried to put the book down but it dropped from his hand and then the room began to waver and sway around him.

When Caleb came to stand over him with a triumphant smile, he managed to force a few words out. 'What . . . have you . . . done? Murdered me?'

'Hell, no. Just put you to sleep. I'll see *you* safely on board the ship tomorrow, but I'm *not* going with you to England and I'm never, ever going to be a farmer.'

Caleb was already searching his pockets and Cameron couldn't move, couldn't think clearly, was utterly helpless to resist as his brother stole his money, hesitated over his pocket watch, then put it back.

What had they drugged him with? Was Caleb telling the truth about taking him to the ship or were they going to kill him?

His brother must be more ruthless than any of the family had realised.

But try as he might, Cameron couldn't do anything about that, because the darkness whirled him away completely.

9

Lancashire

Walter walked up and down the field for a while then sat down on a bench he'd placed by the stream, his favourite place for thinking things over.

What a day of surprises this had been! He was glad to give the two women shelter, of course he was, but their arrival had only emphasised that life goes on. He had to start working out what to do with them because he believed in planning ahead with important matters, and he clearly knew his way around the world better than they did.

People's lives were as important as things got in his opinion, and he not only liked the looks of them both, but was grateful to them. Their arrival had made a difference to him so quickly he was surprised. It was as if they'd nudged him right out of the darkest depths of his sorrow.

Helping the two women was something well worth doing, even if not what he'd planned to do with his life. He wondered suddenly what they wanted to do with their lives, whether they had made any plans before they'd had to run away. He must tread carefully and make sure he was helping them do something they really wanted.

What a terrible person that nephew of Elinor's stepfather must be. He'd better not come here chasing after them.

It felt good to have people living with him and depending on him again. Human beings weren't meant to live alone and he'd felt very alone indeed since the accident.

Now, if he could only hear from his son James and be able to welcome an American grandson into his life, things would get even better. Not the same as before, but with hope for something truly worthwhile in the future – and hope for some sort of family once again to share his life with.

When he went back to the house for his evening meal, the grief was still there and probably always would be, but at least he now had a purpose in life.

There was enough work to keep them all busy, but it was their company he needed most of all, though, he admitted to himself as he reached for the door handle. With them living here, the house wouldn't echo with emptiness each night and he'd stop drinking too much, he definitely would.

They ate their meal together, chatting and sharing information about themselves, but he could see how exhausted they were and after they'd insisted on clearing up, he insisted on them all going to bed.

'There will be plenty of time to talk,' he said. 'Go on. Get your heads down. I can see how tired you are. And I wouldn't mind an early night myself.'

Walter greatly enjoyed eating that first breakfast with the two women the next morning as well. Maude was a fine, sturdy lass and the other one looked a bit less haggard now she had had a good night's sleep.

He still hadn't worked out why she was so thin. She had that starveling look which people got when they didn't have enough to eat, yet Maude didn't have it. He might ask his cousin about it when the two of them were alone.

He didn't waste time on idle chit-chat but told them how he thought they might make a start. 'I can offer you two paid work here looking after the house. I have to pay someone so it may as well be you. You'd also have to care for the chickens, deal with the eggs and keep an eye on the woman who does the washing and the heavy scrubbing. I'll pay you one wage between the two of you—'

Maude interrupted, staring him in the eye indignantly. 'That isn't fair!'

'If you'll let me finish, that's just for starters. I don't know how hard you work and I can't get references. And for your part, you don't know whether you can settle happily here. That's important too.'

Elinor put one hand on her friend's arm. 'We can start that way, Maude, for a month perhaps. Walter's right. We might not like living here or working for him, and he might not like the way we do things. Besides, we don't know how to look after chickens and deal with eggs, so we'll need a few lessons.'

He nodded approval of this sensible attitude. 'Another advantage for you two is that you can stay together if you settle here. And of course once you prove to be good workers, I'll pay full wages to each of you. Oh, and farmers' wives usually keep the money from selling their eggs to people at market. You'd have that as well. The hens are starting to lay better now the weather's getting warmer.' Then he added, 'I hope you'll like living here. I love Ollindale and Ollerthwaite.'

'I've been wondering about the place names,' said Maude. 'I've never heard of Oller before. Does it have a meaning or is it just made-up sounds?'

'Oller is an old name for an alder tree. Ollerthwaite must have originally been a clearing or meadow with alder trees. I read somewhere that it's an old Norse or Viking name, and more often found in the north-west of England.'

'You sound as if you've memorised the details,' Maude said.

'Not intentionally. I just have a sharp memory for details. Sometimes I remember the stupidest things that are no use to man nor beast.'

She gave him a hug that surprised him. 'I like collecting words. It must run in the family.'

He smiled down at her, because tall as she was he was taller still.

'I'm already glad you're here.' He turned to Elinor and added, 'I'm glad you're here too.' She was quietly spoken but not timid, judging by the way she had raised her chin and returned his stare when asking about wages. It came to him suddenly that they were an interesting pair of women as well as potential employees. They'd had the wit to escape from a terrible situation, hadn't they, not given in to it? And to find help.

But they hadn't brought much with them. How would they manage for clothes?

He had a sudden idea. 'I couldn't help realising that you weren't able to bring many clothes with you and I wondered if you'd like to go through my wife and daughter-in-law's clothes, which are stored in the attic and see if there's anything useful?'

'Are you sure?'

'I'd not have offered otherwise. You can have any of them you like, all of them if you wish, but you'll have to alter them because obviously you're taller than they were, Maude especially.'

'And skirts are shorter these days, so that may be a good thing.' Maude chuckled suddenly. 'Elinor is a really good needlewoman, but I'm only fit to do the straight seams under her supervision. Are you sure about giving them to us?'

'Yes. They've been up there for years so will smell of moth balls, but I can't really remember what my wife wore, so you're welcome to take them.'

He took a deep breath and said the other thing that he'd been hesitating about, 'There's something you can do for me, though. Will you please clear out the two bedrooms that belonged to—' He had to pause and swallow hard before he could finish speaking and only managed a husky wobble of sound. 'They belonged to my son and grandson. I didn't feel able to tackle that job and I still don't.'

It was Maude who answered, her voice gentle. 'We'd be happy to do that for you, Cousin Walter.'

He nodded. He liked their low, pleasant voices, the way they didn't shout or argue. They were very easy to listen to. He couldn't have lived comfortably with a strident or shrill speaker.

'Joan is coming here this morning to help us get to know the house so she'll help us with sorting out the rooms as well, I'm sure. '

'She's a very kind woman, salt of the earth.'

'Can we give her anything that we don't want but might be useful to her or to people she knows? I don't like to waste anything.'

'Of course. I don't like waste, either,' Walter said. 'And if there's anything lacking in the kitchen or house, make a note of it and tell me. I haven't been paying the house the attention I should have been. We probably need all sorts of bits and pieces replacing by now.'

If they stayed permanently, he thought, he'd tell them about his quest for an heir. Not yet, though. The pain of having needed to do that was still so raw – and he hadn't heard anything from James, who might never even reply. And then what a fool he'd look if he'd told them an heir would be coming.

He banished that thought and said quietly, 'It sounds as if you two have had a few hard years. Elinor looks rather strained still and no wonder.'

Two nods and gazes from over-bright eyes were his answer but he noticed with approval how they reached out instinctively to clasp hands and comfort each other.

'Since we've all had upsets recently, perhaps we can help one another through to better times, eh?'

He didn't wait for an answer, but took a deep breath and decided he needed some quiet time on his own. He'd taken some big steps in the past couple of days, but he just couldn't face any more heavy emotion for a while. 'If you need me, I'll be in the farm office which is that add-on building sticking out at the side of the barn. I'll feed the chickens for the first day or two, then show you how to do it, Maude. We usually save the scraps of food and peelings for them and cook them up in a mash with some grains, and they love a bit of greenery like the tops of carrots. I give them that sort of thing raw.'

He got up, raised one hand in farewell and left them to it.

They watched out of the window to see where he went then Maude said quietly, 'I think we can stop being so afraid of Jason Stafford coming after us. We can trust Cousin Walter and his friends to help protect us, if necessary.'

'I agree. He's very kind, isn't he?'

'Yes, and his eyes remind me of the way my mother used to look at the world. Calmly, as well as kindly.'

Joan arrived soon afterwards calling out a greeting to Walter as she passed the pen where he was feeding the chickens. She made a mental note to teach the two women how to do that, and how to collect and wash the eggs each day. And then she'd take them to sell their farm produce at the small Friday markets in Upperfold where she sold her own. The big markets were held in Ollerthwaite but that was too far for some people, especially the elderly and women with several children or very young ones.

You could hardly call them proper markets, but there was a place where people set out any produce they had for sale, some on temporary little stalls provided by the council, others on a piece of sacking or in a basket on the pavement. A little extra money could make a big difference to some people.

Maybe Walter could teach the newcomers to drive his pony and cart. It wasn't far to get into the village, but they'd need transport of some sort to carry their eggs and bring home their purchases. Eggs always sold well, especially to people without much land, because they were an economical way to feed families. She'd speak to him about it.

When she went into the house she was pleased to see that the kitchen had been cleared up properly. That boded well for the two newcomers. She couldn't be doing with slovenly ways.

She didn't waste time on chit-chat. 'Right, let's get started. I'll show you how Walter likes the various tasks done – or at least the ways he was used to before and how you do them from then on is up to you. Also, we'll go through the cupboard where the cleaning goods are kept and check whether he's run out of anything or is likely to. I'm not trying to tell you how to breathe properly, and when I'm gone you can work out how you want to do the various tasks, but this will give you a starting point. We all have our own ways, don't we?'

She chuckled. 'He doesn't keep his own cows now, but he's fussy who he buys milk from and he loves porridge with the cream off the top of the milk on it.'

While she'd been talking she'd taken her outdoor things off, pulled a pinafore out of her basket. She slipped the loop over her head and tied the strings firmly round her waist, then stared round to see where to start.

The three of them didn't stop working till she left.

Then the two friends sat down to a cup of tea and a midday meal.

'I think I'm going to like living on a farm,' Elinor said. 'I didn't realise chickens were such friendly, inquisitive little creatures.'

'Neither did I. I'm already hoping we can stay here.'

'I am, too. Joan's a pleasant neighbour to have, isn't she?'

'Yes. I'd never even touched a live chicken before, let alone collected eggs. I didn't realise how warm the newly laid ones were.'

'This is a big fine house, in a much nicer state of repair than our old home. After we've cleared out those two bigger bedrooms Joan says we should move into them.'

Elinor frowned. 'I know they've got nice furniture and a lovely view from the windows, but I like the smaller room I'm in at the moment. It feels cosy and safe.'

'I feel a bit the same. We'll stay in them, then, shall we?'

'Yes. And I can start work on the clothes we've been given because there's enough hotpot left for our tea. It'll save us so much money not having to buy new clothes. I had a quick glance at them when we brought them down from the attic and they're of good quality materials and quite nice colours.'

'I'll do the straight seams.'

They both laughed. It was a standing joke between them that Maude couldn't be bothered with fiddly sewing.

'And even though we can dress how we please now, we won't have big puffy sleeves. They might be fashionable but they're not very practical and they must be hard to iron properly.'

A little later Elinor said, 'What I love most here is the peace and quiet, and the sheer *sanity* of how we're living here already. I'm so grateful to your cousin for taking me in as well as you.'

'I wonder where he is. I'd expected him to come and join us for his midday meal but he drove the cart out earlier and didn't come back for something to eat.' Maude glanced out of the window.

'Talk of the devil. He's just driving up to the farm. Let's push the kettle on to the hotter part of the range. It'll be boiling by the time he's looked after the pony. That man loves his mugs of tea.'

Walter came in, murmuring a greeting. When he saw the teapot being prepared without him even asking for a cup, he smiled and took what they now knew was his usual seat at the head of the table. He didn't say much but asked for a cheese sandwich. 'I didn't get time to eat any dinner.'

He ate it with relish, looked round and nodded as if approving of what he saw.

'My wife used to keep the place nice, like this. Frank's wife was the same, only she died in childbirth, poor thing, so we didn't have her for long. Tell me what you've been doing so far today.'

They explained and mentioned the list they were compiling of things they needed for the house.

'We'll go into Ollerthwaite on market day and buy most of it there. You'll want to have a look round the town. I'll introduce you to the people I'm most closely acquainted with and they'll soon start thinking of you as one of us.'

'Joan said she'd introduce us to some of her acquaintances as well.'

'Good. She knows nearly all the women. Is there another mug of tea in that pot?'

'Yes, of course.'

He sat and watched her prepare it. 'Eh, it feels good to sit here and chat.'

'We haven't made a start yet on clearing out those two bedrooms,' Maude said. 'We like the ones we're in, so we'd as soon stay in them, if that's all right with you. There's a nice view over the moors at the back.'

'Sleep where you want.'

'Also, it's quite important to have a washday soon and Joan's going to send a message to Flora that we need her for an extra day. If you'll sort out any dirty clothes you've got and put them into your linen basket, she can deal with them.'

Elinor joined in. 'Or we can sort them out for you. We'll need to change your sheets, too, if you don't mind. We didn't like to go into your bedroom without your permission, but Joan showed us which clean sheets to use from the laundry cupboard.'

He looked a bit embarrassed. 'I'll tidy my room up a bit in there tonight and sort out the rest of my dirty washing, then you can change the sheets tomorrow. I'd be ashamed for you to see what a mess I've let that room get into. My wife would have thrown a fit, so would my daughter-in-law. They were capable housewives, both of them, a credit to the family – and they were nice lasses.'

After frowning for a moment, he added, 'Don't ever do the heavy washing, just any clothes of your own that you're going to need in a hurry or that are delicate. Flora has an invalid husband and she needs the money she earns from washing. She's good at it too. Besides she has all the necessary equipment at her house. I take the heavy stuff to her and pick it up.'

'That'd be a good arrangement. Thank you.'

'Another thing I did today when I went into town to post a letter was to arrange for the gas to be brought out to the farm. It'll take a few months, apparently. Fortunately for us they've already got it in Ollerthwaite so it won't be a huge job. I shall need to buy us a gas cooker then. I hear they're much better to work on. Is that right?'

'They're a lot easier to use and you can get gas geysers to heat the water, too. We had one in the house we just left because even my stepfather liked a warm bath occasionally. You'd need a hot water geyser in the kitchen and if you can find somewhere to fit in a bathroom, you'll find that a big help too,' Maude said. 'Not that we can't manage as we are, but it's time consuming heating water on the kitchen range.'

'I'll look into putting in a bathroom, then. There's a little room at the side of the house downstairs which is never used, so that might be suitable.'

He waited for this to sink in then asked, 'Did I do the right thing, arranging that?'

This time it was Elinor who answered. 'Definitely. A gas cooker is not only more efficient than a coal range but far easier to use. Most people in the towns have changed to them now. I think the people in Upperfold will be delighted to have gas run in. These modern inventions make life so much easier for women.'

'That's what the man at the gas office told me.'

'And gas lights would give us more light to work or read by in the evenings.' After a moment she added, 'They're changing over to electric lighting for houses in the bigger towns now. That's even easier to use and you don't need to clean them every day like you do oil lamps.'

'They've not brought the electricity out to our valley yet.'

He looked at them both very solemnly. 'Don't be afraid to tell me if I'm going wrong or something's needed or you know a better way to do a job. We should keep up with the times.'

That was when Maude knew for certain she wanted to stay here, she realised later. She had never met such a kind, reasonable man in her entire life as her cousin, never felt as comfortable in a house since Mrs Pendleton married her second husband.

She was never going to work for someone as horrible as the two Stafford men again. But she'd stayed there for Elinor's sake and didn't regret that. She hated to think what might have happened to her dear friend if she hadn't. Their companionship had been a light in the darkness.

10

A few days later Maude found a bicycle in one of the sheds near the hen run. She was gradually exploring the rest of the outbuildings and their contents, partly out of sheer curiosity but also to check whether there was anything useful there. She felt quite sure Walter wouldn't mind. He left quite a lot of the domestic details to them now.

It was a modern safety bicycle and had simply been shoved inside and left lying on the ground. It was dusty, looking as if it hadn't been used for months. There was a big metal basket at the front of the handlebars, the sort used for carrying shopping home or for making deliveries from shops.

She stood it up and examined it, guessing it had belonged to Walter's grandson. That would explain the reason it had simply been thrown to one side and left. The tyres were modern pneumatic ones and needed pumping up again. In fact, the whole thing needed a thorough checking and cleaning before it could be safely ridden on public roads.

She wondered if Walter would let them use it. She'd love to learn to ride it, had read in the newspapers about how much more practical the modern safety bicycles were. Lots of younger people were buying them these days, men and women both, because it made such a difference to their lives. And some of the not so young were buying them too, so it couldn't be all that hard to ride one. It'd be so much easier to cycle into the village for supplies and into Ollerthwaite as well.

You'd be able to get round on one far more quickly than you could on foot.

As they ate their evening meal together, she risked mentioning the bicycle in the shed and felt guilty when a spasm of pain passed over Walter's face.

'That's Timothy's bike,' he snapped before she could ask about using it.

'Oh. Sorry.' She concentrated on her food.

A couple of minutes later he said quietly, 'I'm the one who should apologise, Maude lass. You didn't deserve to be snapped at like that. And if you'd like to use the bicycle, go ahead and do so. My grandson was very proud of it and wouldn't want it to lie there rusting.'

'It, um, needs a bit of attention first. The tyres are flat and I've never learned to ride one. It can't be hard, though, and I'd love to try.'

Elinor risked joining in. 'So would I. My stepfather refused to allow us to have one, you see.' Probably because it'd have given her more independence.

He looked from her to Maude and back. 'So neither of you can ride a bike?'

'No. But I'm sure we could learn.'

'I'll take this one into Upperfold tomorrow in my cart. There's an old chap there who repairs bicycles and sells second-hand ones. Peter can check the tyres and brakes, then once I'm sure it's safe, you two can learn to ride it. When you can do that without falling off, we'll talk about using the roads safely and thinking ahead to avoid other traffic. Horses can't always move out of your way as quickly as pedestrians, for instance. Thank goodness no one round here has a motor car. Well, there's no one rich enough these days, is there?'

His face looked grim as he added, 'People need to learn to use roads safely in these changing times and I can see that it'd be very convenient for you two to have the use of a bicycle if you wanted to nip to the shops in Ollerthwaite for fresh food. And if things go well and you show promise at riding it safely, we can buy another one second-hand and you can ride out together, not only for shopping but to go to the lake. There's still a path along by the water there and you haven't walked down there yet.'

They exchanged delighted smiles.

'Also, and I should have said this before now, we don't need to wait any longer about the money. You two have more than proved yourself good workers so I'll be paying you both a full wage from now onwards. You've made my life much more comfortable and I thank you for that.'

'That's good. Thank you for taking us in, Cousin Walter,' said Maude. It felt more than good; it was a wonderful relief to feel secure.

But she still couldn't persuade Elinor to take up her hobby of painting again. She was shy about showing her work to anyone else and had her drawings and paintings hidden in a drawer.

Maude wondered if her friend still worried about Jason Stafford coming after her, still felt she might have to run away. She didn't intend to run away from anyone again, if she could help it.

They had to wait till the following Monday for the bicycle to be checked properly and cleaned up. It looked so shiny and new when Walter brought it back to the farm, the two women hardly dared touch it.

After the midday meal he leaned back and asked, 'Who's going to try riding the bicycle first, then?'

They both stared at him, then Elinor gestured to Maude because she could never quite forget that it was her friend who belonged to this family not herself.

Maude shook her head. 'No, you go first. I'm rather nervous about it. You've got a much better sense of balance.'

So they went outside and Elinor wobbled up and down in the yard and along the stretch of little used dirt road at their side of the crossroads. She felt more and more secure as she learned how to balance on it, and suddenly stopped worrying.

She'd have loved to ride for longer, but once she felt secure, she stopped near the two watchers and dismounted. 'Your turn now, love.'

Maude wasn't as good at it and fell off twice. But she was going so slowly she didn't hurt herself and she fell on the grass by the side of the road. She simply dusted her clothes down and got straight back on again, her expression so grimly determined, Elinor wished she could give her a hug.

It took Maude longer than her friend to learn to ride steadily, but after a while she managed it.

Walter applauded and said, 'Now let me go over what I consider to be good road rules for riding along safely in busy streets like those in Ollerthwaite.'

They knew why he was telling them that, though the accident to his son and grandson had happened on a country road, not a street in town. But they too had seen articles in the newspapers about traffic accidents, so they listened very carefully and took on board the idea that you had to be ready for problems to pop up.

And then he stood it next to them. 'Yours now.'

As Walter had said, the bicycle gave them freedom to go into the village without troubling him to get out the pony and cart, and the basket at the front held quite a lot of provisions of various sorts.

The first time Elinor went out on her own she felt nervous because there was no one in sight on the dirt road leading down the gentle slope from the farm except her. She felt better when she got into the village and better still in Ollerthwaite, in spite of the increased numbers of carts, horses and other bicycles in the streets, not to mention pedestrians stepping off the pavements without warning as Walter had warned them about.

To their surprise, a couple of weeks later he brought home another bicycle, this one with a few dents and scratches in the paintwork but still in good working order. 'As I said, if things went well, which they have done, you might like to go out cycling together, so I asked Peter to find me another bicycle.'

Without thinking what she was doing, Maude gave him a hug.

He held her close for a minute then blinked hard, gave one of his tight little nods and stepped back.

'I don't think he minded the hug, do you?' she whispered to Elinor when they were alone.

'I think he's starting to welcome it. Let's go and visit the lake now we can do that together.'

'Ooh, yes. We'll do it tomorrow.'

To their annoyance, it rained the following day, heavy showers that made it unsuitable for a bicycle ride. There were still puddles lying here and there in the road the following day, but a brisk wind gradually dried up the moisture, so that by afternoon they were able to go out and practise their skills.

When the following day turned out sunny Maude suggested they ride to the little lake because they'd both been dying to see it more closely. When they checked that Walter didn't mind them going out, he laughed. 'On the contrary, it's about time you two had some time off. I'm not a slave driver.'

He came out to see them off, still giving instructions. 'Don't forget: if you stay on that track it'll lead you straight to the lake. You'd better watch out for potholes, though. It's not much used these days. And there may be rabbits running around.'

'Is there anything he hasn't thought of warning us about?' Maude whispered and they smiled at one another.

The path was just where he'd said and they turned on to it without seeing anyone else out and about.

'It feels strange to be able to go where we want, doesn't it?' Maude said. 'And I love the feel of the wind in my hair as we're riding along.'

'I don't think I've ever felt so free. And look, you can already see the water glinting in the distance. It's not as far away as I'd thought.'

Before they reached the lake, however, they could hear children's voices and they didn't sound happy. Then one yelled, 'No, don't! Ow!' and it sounded like a little girl. She cried out again and begged someone to stop hurting her.

Elinor didn't even ask Maude what they should do but speeded up, hating to hear a child being hurt. What on earth was going on? Who was attacking this little girl?

When they came to a bend in the path close to the water, they saw a big boy ahead of them hit a smaller child across the side of the face and another, even smaller child try to hide behind some bushes, sobbing in fear.

Even as they looked the big boy hit the little girl again and shouted, 'Give it to me!'

'No. It's mine. Ow!'

He couldn't have seen the two women arrive because he knocked her to the ground and drew his foot back to kick her.

Elinor jumped off the bicycle, letting it fall to the ground, and ran across to them, shouting, 'Stop it! Stop that at once!'

He turned to stare at her, nearly as tall as she was when he straightened up, though still with a lanky lad's body.

'Who's going to make me?'

'I am.'

'You and whose army?' he mocked, using the age-old saying.

He clearly didn't think much of her and didn't seem to have noticed Maude getting off her bicycle and bending down to comfort the small child.

But Elinor wouldn't back off whatever this rough lad did, because she'd vowed when she escaped from Jason never to let people force her to do anything she didn't want to again. And she was never going to allow things which were wrong, either, like bullying a child, if she could help it.

As if to prove his point, the boy kicked the little girl in the ribs, making her scream in pain.

Elinor grabbed his arm and he thrust her away so violently she stumbled back a few feet and almost fell.

Horrified at the lad's attack, Maude abandoned the small child, stepped from behind the bushes where the lad had been hiding and yelled, 'What do you think you're doing anyway, hitting a little girl and a woman like that? You're a coward and a bully.'

'That girl has got my money.'

The child had seized the opportunity to roll away from him and stand close to Elinor. 'It's not his, missus. It's our spending money an' he knows it. He tried to get it from us last week as well, but we ran away. He were hiding an' waiting for us this week, though.'

The two women stared at the lad in utter disgust but he tossed his head defiantly.

'I've a right to it!' he insisted.

'It's not his, miss. It's my spending money.'

'Can't your father have a word with him?'

'I haven't got a father now, only a grandfather an' he says he's too old to fight. Mam's working long hours an' she says we have to learn to defend ourselves. I've tried, really I have, but I'm not big enough to stop Jezzer Catlow. He takes other people's money as well as mine an' he can beat all the other lads in the village, so no one's managed to stop him.'

The lad had been studying Maude and looking round beyond them, obviously checking in case there were any other people nearby. When he saw no one else, he said, 'You should both mind your own business, missus.'

'I consider it my business when I see bullying going on.'

'Well, it isn't. Get away from her an' stay away from our village too after this. You're not from round here, an' we don't want no fancy folk riding bicycles into Upperfold an' trying to interfere with how we do things.'

Maude was amazed that a mere lad could be so rude to a strange lady. He was wearing rather worn clothes and he wasn't all that clean but he was going to be a big man one day. She didn't back away but took a step closer to him, which seemed to surprise him. 'We live in Upperfold now and I'm going to make it my business to interfere if I see you or anyone else bullying a small child, let alone stealing from one.'

'It's not stealing; it's paying for my protection against outsiders.'

He let out a sneering laugh and took a couple of quick steps, giving Elinor a hard shove that sent her stumbling backwards again. Then he grabbed the girl's pinafore with one hand and shook her hard. 'Give me that money.'

But as he fumbled in the pinafore pocket, Maude darted forward and clouted him round the ears. 'You let go of her this minute!'

By that time Elinor had got to her feet and since he was occupied with Maude and the child, she gave him a quick, hard shove as well.

He tried to keep hold of the pinafore but the girl managed to yank it out of his hands and run behind Elinor again.

By that time Maude had seen a stick on the ground and grabbed it, hefting it in her hand.

He hesitated at that, glaring at them. 'You won't allus be around, missus. She'll pay me what she owes me next time she goes out, or I'll make her really sorry.'

'I'll be reporting this attack to the police.'

He laughed. 'There isn't a policeman in Upperfold an' there's only an old one in Ollerthwaite. How's he going to see

what I do, let alone stop me? You wait. I'll get that money.'
Then he ran off, laughing loudly.

By that time the girl had her arms round the little boy, who
was still sobbing, shushing him in a motherly way. 'Thank you,
missus,' she said across the top of his head, then kissed him again.

'Why did that horrible lad say you owed him money for
protection?'

'He makes all the smaller kids who get spending money pay
him a halfpenny every week out of it. It's not fair. Some of us
only get a penny.'

'Well, I never heard anything so mean. Do their parents
know? Why has no one stopped him?'

'Some of them have stopped him going near their own kids,
but he's a Catlow an' there's other people who worry that his
family will come after them if they touch him.'

She took the boy's hand. 'We'll have to walk home the long
way round, Jimmy.'

'But I'm tired.'

'I know, but he'll be waiting for us if we go the short way.'

'We can push our bikes and walk home with you in case he's
lying in wait?' Elinor offered.

The girl's expression showed how relieved she was. 'Thank
you, missus. What do they call you, please?'

'I'm Miss Pendleton and this is Miss Vernon, who is a cousin
of Walter Crossley at Cross End Farm. What's your name?'

'Kessie Baxter, an' this is Jimmy. He's only six. I'm nine.'

The two children let themselves into a cottage at the end of
a row of four, calling for their grandfather to come and meet
the ladies.

The old man who came to the door was twisted with rheu-
matism and looked unwell. 'They haven't been naughty, have
they?' he asked anxiously before they could even speak.

'No. They are very nice, polite children, a credit to you.'

That brought a smile to his face.

'Miss Vernon is a cousin of Mr Crossley an' she's come to stay with him,' the little girl explained. 'She stopped Jezzy Catlow from stealing our pennies.'

'Eh, I told him not to do it, but he doesn't listen to anything except a good thump an' I'm not strong enough to do that. He's a right bad 'un, that one is. He'll end up in prison if someone doesn't teach him a lesson or two.'

He gave the little girl a quick hug. 'I thought he'd got a day's work in Ollerthwaite today or I'd not have give you your pennies. An' he seems to grow taller every time I see him. If he gets to be as big as his father, there'll be no stopping him.'

He turned back to the ladies, looking sad. 'Eh, old age is hard to face, missus, when you can't do what's right to help your family.'

'I'm sure you always do your best,' Elinor said. 'No one can do more.'

'We'd better get going again now. Nice meeting you, Mr Baxter. Oh!' Maude stopped and looked round. 'What's the best way back to Cross End Farm?'

Mr Baxter insisted on hobbling along the street with them to point out a ginnel between two more sets of cottages. 'It's a shortcut to the Upperfold road.'

'I never expected that,' Elinor said once they were on their own. 'We'll have to get to know the village better now we're living here permanently, and we'll be able to do that with the bikes.'

'We'd better tell Walter what happened,' Maude said grimly when they got back.

He was furious at what they told him. 'That lad has caused more trouble in Upperfold than any half dozen others. I'll have a word with his father again. Terry's a rogue and a wily fellow, but at least he has the sense not to foul his own nest. And he doesn't usually attack people openly, let alone thump young children.'

He sighed. 'I'll have a word with Cliff Nolan too. He's the police constable based in Ollerthwaite. Only he's getting old and near retirement, and he doesn't like to upset Terry Catlow. In fact I'll go and do it now.'

That evening Jezzy's father clouted him round the ears as soon as he came in for tea.

He ducked out of the way of a second blow. 'What's that for?'

'Getting yourself noticed by Walter Crossley and his family. He came to see me about you.'

'I'll do more than get myself noticed next time. Them women aren't getting the better of me.'

Terry grabbed his son by one arm and shook him good and hard. 'I'm not pleased with you for bringing the Catlow family to the attention of Crossley who was going next to mention your behaviour to the police. If you're going to get money out of people, find a way to do it quietly, or you'll end up in prison and what use is that to the family?'

'I need more money than you give me.'

'You can find yourself a job and keep your nose clean until you learn to be more clever about getting money.'

'Work for some idiot who treats you like a slave? I won't do it.'

'Son, if you're earning money and find a way to get your hands on a bit extra, no one will notice. If you're not earning anything and start spending money, people will get suspicious and come to find out what you've been up to. You don't see me getting myself carted off to prison like that Al Stoner, do you? Stupid, he is. I thought I'd taught you better. What do you need money so badly for anyway?'

'To treat the other lads of my age, so they'll look up to me an' do as I say.'

'You're not old enough for that sort of thing yet, or smart enough.' Terry frowned in thought. 'I'd better send you to stay with your uncle Eric in Manchester for a few months till the fuss has died down. You pay attention to what he says. You can learn a lot from him.'

'I don't like living in cities.'

'An' I don't like my son getting the family into trouble in our own backyard.' He turned to his wife, who hadn't joined in. 'Pack his clothes. I'll take him to Eric tomorrow.'

So when Walter came round again to check that Terry had dealt with his son's misbehaviour, he found that the boy had been sent away.

'Is he here?'

'No. I got him a job for this morning.'

'He's going to get into serious trouble if he goes on like this. And I'll be watching what he does, I promise you.'

'I agree, Mr Crossley. He'll be staying with his uncle Eric in Manchester for a while and learning a bit of sense. I'm taking him there tomorrow.'

'Good idea. You and I don't always agree with one another, but I've never known you bully little children or bash women. That's pitiful behaviour. Your Jezzy is going to make a lot of enemies if he hurts people's kids and women.'

Terry was furious at being put in this position and gave his son another clouting when he got back from digging a neighbour's garden.

He had his own plans for the future, had watched Hatton, the land agent getting money out of people little by little and had intended to follow his example. Hatton got away with a lot and Terry was making plans to act similarly if he ever got the chance. After all, the land agent didn't come here very often these days because the Kenyons didn't look after their land.

Maybe Hatton would be forced to find some other job one day and then Terry would be ready to step into a few of the money-making activities.

★

The morning after Walter's visit to the Catlows, Maude found the fences round the chicken run trampled down and as a consequence three of the hens had been killed by foxes.

Walter surveyed it angrily.

'Who can have done this, do you think?' Maude asked.

'I'd guess it was that Jezzy Catlow getting his own back before he left, but I doubt I'd be able to prove it. I'm glad he's leaving the village for a while. And I will have another word with Cliff Nolan. Unfortunately he's getting past it. What we really need is a younger constable in our valley.'

'That Jezzy Catlow is a real bad 'un, isn't he?' Maude said. 'He saw me in the street and talk about if looks could kill!'

'Yes. Most of that family flout the law whenever they think they can get away with it, but they don't usually *hurt* children and women. We'll have to keep an eye on Jezzy when he returns. In the meantime perhaps those children can spend their pennies in peace.'

11

In their hotel room in New York Caleb stared down at Cameron's motionless body regretfully. It felt wrong to treat him like this when his brother had always been kind to him and he felt a little twinge of guilt. But he had to do something. He wasn't being sent to England.

Daniel came to stand by his side. 'We should kill him and tip his body in the harbour.'

'No. I'm definitely not killing my brother. He's stupidly honest but he's the only one of my family that I care about.'

'Let's at least take his money.'

'I'll do that. He doesn't have much, because my father's a stingy devil, but I'm going to need something to live on so what Cameron has should be mine.'

He saw Daniel look at him angrily but he stared right back at him. He wasn't starting off this new life by acting like a slave. 'I'll more than make it up to you, I promise. I'm a quick learner and I already have some of the skills you want. You did say you'd never seen anyone deal the cards as skilfully. You'll be buying a lot of hours of practice with these.' He flourished his hands.

There was a threatening silence for a moment or two, then Daniel shrugged and stepped back. 'Oh, very well. But don't ever let me down, or it's you who'll be knocked on the head and tossed into the harbour.'

'I won't let you down. I enjoyed watching you on the train and could tell immediately that you were a cut above the rest of them.'

'I enjoyed playing cards with those fools, making sure I haven't lost my old skills, but I don't often do that sort of thing nowadays. I'm into a much bigger game here in New York and I select new employees very carefully.'

Caleb looked at him eagerly. 'I'm looking forward to learning anything I can from you.'

'If you follow my orders to the letter and continue to build up some other skills that I'll pass on to you, you'll not regret it. I reward loyal employees.'

'It sounds like the sort of life I want. I've been going mad with boredom stuck on a damned farm and I'm truly grateful to you for giving me this chance.' He wasn't sure how long he'd stay, because he could never settle anywhere for long, but he wasn't going to say anything but 'yes, sir; no, sir' to start off with.

'At this stage, that's all it is, a chance,' Daniel warned.

'Yes, I realise that.'

'Hurry up and finish packing, then. I'll be waiting for you down in the lobby.'

After Daniel had left, Caleb did another check of Cameron's pockets and found more money than he'd expected, hidden in various places among his clothes as well as in his pockets. Not as stupidly trusting as he'd thought, his brother. He hesitated and put some of the money back, tucking it into the rear pocket of his brother's trousers. Cameron was going to need something when he got to England if only to pay his fares to this cousin Walter's farm.

If he had any sense his brother would take advantage of the opportunity and claim to be him. He'd make a much better heir.

A burly man knocked on the door and poked his head in. 'Mr Jones says to hurry up.'

'Two minutes.'

Once he'd re-packed the few things left out of Cameron's hand luggage, Caleb went to find Daniel, who told him what to do next.

Afterwards, Caleb spoke to the owner of the little hotel. 'My idiot of a brother has passed out. He got drunk because he's prone to seasickness and doesn't like going on the ocean. I've decided to deliver him to the ship tonight and I might as well stay on board with him. I should have insisted he board the ship at the same time as the luggage was taken there, then he wouldn't have got into this state.'

'You'll have to pay me for tonight's lodging before you leave. I shan't be able to let the room again at this hour.'

'Of course.'

Daniel came back into the lobby just then, followed by a couple of men whom he'd hired to carry Cameron on board.

'He must have got very drunk indeed. I hope he hasn't vomited,' the owner of the hotel said as the unconscious man was brought down the stairs. 'The smell lingers, you know.'

'He hasn't done so far. And if we take him straight to the ship, he won't get a chance to be sick here, will he? Or do you want us to wait until he vomits before we leave?'

That brought him a scowl in response and the man signalled to his doorman to keep them there. 'I'll just go and check the room before you go any further.'

Caleb sighed and tried to look as if he was waiting patiently.

The owner came back and nodded to the doorman to say they could go, then called to Daniel, 'Hope to see you back here again soon, Mr Jones.'

When they got to the ship Daniel supervised Cameron being taken into a cabin and told the steward the unconscious passenger's name was Caleb Crossley.

Caleb said. 'I'd better scribble a note to the poor fellow. His companion has been killed in a brawl because of cheating at cards, so he'll be travelling to England alone now.'

He signed it 'A well-wisher'.

Daniel gave him a small bottle. 'Tip a bit more of the drug into Cameron's mouth before we leave him. There's enough here to keep him asleep until after the ship sets sail. We don't want him sending the police chasing after us, do we?'

Caleb saw him smile and suspected this might be a lethal dose, but he managed to spill most of it down the side of his brother's head on to the blanket without his companion noticing as Daniel was now waiting for him in the doorway.

'Let me see that note,' Daniel read it, nodded and handed it back.

'Just a minute.' Caleb pricked his finger to make it bleed on to one corner of the envelope. 'The blood makes a nice artistic touch, don't you think?'

Daniel chuckled.

Caleb gave the note to the steward to pass on when the unconscious man recovered. He knew his brother would recognise his handwriting and guess he wasn't dead but had run away.

He took a final look at the still body, which looked so strange for his always-busy brother. What would Cameron do after he read the note and realised he'd not been brought on board under his own name? He really ought to take advantage of the situation. After all, the English grandfather had never seen either of them so wouldn't know the difference. And Crossley was old, so probably too stupid to work it out.

But then, honest people often were fools. At least Cameron had been given a chance to achieve his big dream of inheriting a farm and this would surely bring home to him how determined Caleb was to avoid farming as well.

'Come on, lad. Time to go,' Daniel called from further along the passage.

Caleb took a quick glance sideways as he and Daniel walked away from the ship, wondering if his suspicions about the extra drug were correct. There was such a smug look on the other man's face that he decided he had been right about that.

'That's done, then,' he said cheerfully. 'The heir will soon be setting sail and will sleep soundly till he's well out on the ocean.'

'You seem very sure that he'll take this chance to claim the inheritance.'

'I'm hopeful. He really loves farming and has no chance of inheriting anything from our father.'

'Well, maybe we can stop talking about him now and concentrate on you. With your manual dexterity better focused, you'll love your new life and you'll end up rich if you do exactly as I say. Though not as rich as I intend to become.'

'I shall look forward to it.'

During the next few days Caleb found that the feeling of sadness about how he'd treated his brother lingered, which was something he'd not expected. He'd actually miss Cameron, who was the only member of his family he did care about.

Do it, he prayed several times in quiet moments spent practising with cards and a variety of small objects. *Seize this chance, Cameron. Don't be a fool.*

Well, he hadn't hesitated to seize his own chance and his life was suddenly full of promise. With a bit of luck he'd never see his father or that damned farm again.

Cameron opened his eyes as someone gave him a shake and said, 'Wake up!' very loudly.

He groaned as light from an oil lamp speared into his eyes. Closing them again quickly, he tried to work out where he was.

'Ah, you're awake at last, are you, sir?' a man asked.

He turned towards the speaker, not recognising him and still keeping his eyes half-closed. 'Where am I?'

'If I only had a dollar for every passenger who said that when he woke, I'd be a rich man. Look, Mr Crossley, I'm the steward who deals with your cabin and you've been asleep so long the chief steward got worried about you and told me to check that you were all right.'

'Cabin?'

'You're on-board a ship, sir. How are you feeling?'

'Oh. Well, apart from a headache, I'm all right, I think.' He rubbed his aching forehead but remembered suddenly what had happened. He was about to blurt out that he hadn't been asleep but drugged when he realised the man had addressed him as 'Mr Crossley' and his innate caution took over.

What the hell was going on? Or rather, what had Caleb done now? Better not say anything till he found out exactly what was happening here. 'Where's the other man – the one I was travelling with?'

The steward sighed, avoiding eye contact as he said, 'I'm sorry to have to be the one to tell you, sir, but your friend got into a fight and was apparently killed just before the ship left. A Mr Melton that was, I gather.'

'*Mr Melton?*' Definitely Caleb up to something. That was Cameron's surname and he felt very much alive. 'Then how did I get here?'

'Another friend brought you to the ship, Mr Crossley. He left a note about what had happened and since you were unconscious I took the liberty of reading it in case it was important. Which it was, I'm afraid. It's how I found out that your friend had been killed.'

Cameron still couldn't make sense of this, but first things first. His mouth felt dry, as if he hadn't had a drink for a million years. 'I'm desperately thirsty. Could I please have a drink of water?'

'Aha! I thought you'd say that. People who've been boozing heavily nearly always do when they wake up, so I brought
a bottle of water with me. Let me help you sit up first, Mr
Crossley. You don't want to spill it down yourself, do you?'

He tried to heave himself into a sitting position but found he
was so weak he needed help. He took a big gulp and couldn't
help letting out a mew of protest as the steward whipped the
bottle away from his lips.

'Best to take it slowly, sir. If you drink too much too quickly,
you'll be sick and we neither of us want that to happen.'

Cameron suddenly realised something else. 'Is it my imagination or are we at sea now?'

'Yes we are, sir. The ship sailed several hours ago, actually.'

It was hard to think what to do except he'd learned to tread
carefully through life so his instinct was still to keep quiet
about the truth. Why did the man keep calling him Mr Crossley?
And who was this person with Cameron's surname who had
supposedly died? Something was very wrong about this whole
situation and it looked as if he was in for an ocean voyage
whether he wanted it or not.

Where the hell was Caleb now?

'You said . . . a Mr Melton had died. Tell me again how you
knew that. I'm not thinking very clearly yet, I'm afraid.'

'The gentleman who brought you here told me, Mr Crossley.
I put his note back in your pocket after I'd read it. Here.' He
pulled it out and handed it to him. 'You read it while I send
word to the captain that you're alive and all right, except for
the usual boozer's headache. Oh, and just to let you know, I'll
be bringing another passenger back with me. He wants better
accommodation than steerage and we have a spare bunk in
this cabin now.'

He stopped to study the man on the bed and add, 'You're
looking rather pale. Do you feel bad? Do you want to see the

ship's doctor? Only, he doesn't usually see people who've come aboard drunk. I mostly deal with them.'

'No. No doctor.'

Cameron eased himself into a more comfortable position on the lower bunk in the tiny cabin, relieved that at least it had a porthole, though it was dark outside at the moment. He studied his surroundings. How long had he been asleep? Surely not for a whole day? But it was definitely night and the steward had said he'd been asleep for long enough to worry them, so a whole day must have gone by. There was a lantern hanging on a hook on the wall close to him. It was barely bright enough to read by.

He opened up the sheet of paper and saw Caleb's handwriting. What was all this talk about the friend he'd been travelling with being dead? Caleb couldn't be dead if he'd written this note and there wasn't another friend.

This was definitely a trick and that thought made him even more determined to say nothing until he'd worked out what exactly was going on. Damn Caleb! Causing trouble as usual.

He read the scrawled note slowly and carefully. It had clearly been written in a hurry.

Dear Mr Crossley,

I'm sorry to tell you that your friend Mr Melton was killed in a bar brawl so you'll be travelling alone.

The gentleman he was drinking with has promised to see him properly buried and as you had passed out, I brought you to the ship.

We were sure you'd still wish to travel as arranged and claim your inheritance in England. After all, you can do nothing to help a dead man, can you?

Your grandfather sounds to have a large farm, and we all wish you well in your new life as his heir.

There was a squiggle at the bottom where a signature should be. It didn't matter what the squiggle was meant to indicate because Cameron could recognise his half-brother's hand-writing.

If Caleb had written this, he definitely wasn't dead. So this must be all part of a trick to get Caleb out of going to England. He'd been more determined not to go to England than anyone in the family had realised. But how had he got the money to do this?

Sending him to become a farmer willy-nilly had been a badly conceived plan anyway, as Cameron had told their father. But once James Crossley had decided on something, that was it. He ruled his farm and his family as he saw fit and heaven help anyone who tried to defy him.

The letter gave no clue as to where Caleb was going or what was he planning to do to earn a living. He snapped his fingers as he suddenly realised it had to be that Daniel fellow who'd arranged this and probably offered Caleb a job, something to do with gambling it'd be.

So Cameron was left to travel to England alone and what the devil was he going to do when he got there? It'd be nearly a week before he arrived, so he'd have time to think about that. And it'd take just as long for him to get back again, even if he could get a berth straight away. By that time Caleb would be long gone.

Their father would be furious and so was Cameron.

Oh hell, what a tangled mess this was!

He groaned and closed his eyes, but could neither sleep nor feel fully awake. What on earth had been in that damned drug?

12

It seemed a long time before the steward returned and by then Cameron had decided to remain 'Mr Crossley' for the rest of the journey. It'd save a lot of complicated explanations, which the captain might not believe anyway.

He read the note yet again. It was obvious what his half-brother had been hinting he should do – remain 'Caleb Crossley' and inherit the farm. What a ridiculous thing to suggest! That would be tantamount to stealing.

Only, who would he be stealing from? This Walter Crossley chap in Lancashire had suffered a terrible tragedy and was clearly desperate for an heir from his own blood line.

The other two legitimate sons had inheritances already promised in America. Cameron couldn't help feeling envious of them, always had done. They'd had such an easy path in life. What's more, he'd heard both of them say that they never wanted to travel, not even to visit the country where their family had originated.

Which left only Cameron available to inherit as a direct descendant. He had as much of Walter Crossley's blood in his veins as the other three did, even if he wasn't born within wedlock.

All he'd have waiting for him if he returned to America would be a smallholding with an extra field added to it as a gift from his father for doing an unpleasant job. And since he'd failed in the job of delivering Caleb, would he even be given that now?

This would leave him in the same position he'd been all his life – bastard born and living only on the fringe of the family. This was why he'd worked so hard at a variety of jobs, so that one day he could buy himself a small farm in a place where he could put down roots. His tired brain kept bringing him back to the reality that there was now no close legitimate grandson to inherit what sounded like a large farm, thanks to Caleb's irresponsibility . . . unless . . . unless he took over his half-brother's name and inheritance, and stayed there.

No, he couldn't do that.

Could he?

After all, what harm would he be doing? He not only had Crossley blood in him but was a good farmer and business-man, with a far better grasp on how to work hard and earn money than Caleb could ever have had. And actually, he con-sidered himself a better businessman than their father, too, and hadn't told him how well he was doing.

Oh, hell, he was getting as bad as his brother, twisting the arguments round to give himself the right to obtain what he wanted so desperately: land and a legitimate place in the world.

He buried his head in his hands. Not only were his thoughts in a terrible tangle, his morals were too, but he'd not be hurt-ing anyone if he took this opportunity.

When he felt in his pocket for a handkerchief, he realised abruptly that his wallet was missing. How could he not have noticed that before? He felt frantically in all his pockets, but it wasn't there, nor were the other small bundles of banknotes.

What he did find were a few crumpled letters and docu-ments identifying him as Caleb but nothing to identify him as Cameron.

He missed it the first time round, a small bundle of notes in his rear trouser pocket, somewhere he never normally put money. Then he remembered something else and bent down to check inside his shoes, groaning in relief as he found that the banknotes he'd put under the insoles of both shoes were still there.

When his brother had robbed him, he must have been in a hurry and had missed finding those, thank goodness. But he must have returned some money to the back pocket, so he hadn't taken everything.

Cameron had a decent amount of money back in America, in a bank account none of his family knew about. The local banker was a close friend of his father's and wouldn't have hesitated to tell him about it if Cameron had opened an account there.

Thank goodness his brother didn't know about that.

Cameron had deliberately chosen a large bank, one that had branches he could access from all over the east coast of America if he ever decided to buy a farm or business elsewhere. He'd made an agreement with the manager to use a special password if he tried to draw money out from elsewhere in the country. Surely he would be able to retrieve this money via a bank in England as well? He'd hate to lose his whole life's savings. He'd worked extremely hard for that money.

He rubbed his forehead, which was still aching, then looked up as footsteps sounded in the corridor leading towards the cabin. It was probably the steward returning, so he didn't try to count the money his brother had left him, simply shoved it into his inside jacket pocket.

He felt cheated and upset by being dumped on board a ship like this, helpless to get back to America for a couple of weeks. The only thing he was certain of was that he never wanted to see that half-brother again as long as he lived.

The footsteps stopped and he saw the steward standing in the doorway, studying him.

'Sorry I took so long, sir. You're looking somewhat better now, I'm glad to say.' He moved forward and slightly sideways, gesturing to the man who had been standing behind him. 'This is Mr Fordham, who will be sharing your cabin from now on.'

The man looked to be a little older than Cameron and must have been just about as tall, because he too towered over the steward. He had rumpled clothes and a tired face. He didn't come any further in, was still looking across the cabin as if trying to work out what Cameron was like.

'I hope you don't mind me sharing with you, Crossley?' he said eventually.

'No, of course not. You'd better take the top bunk, though, since I've already slept on the bottom one.'

'I've no problem with that. Thank you for agreeing to share. It'll be a lot more pleasant here than in a crowded dormitory cabin full of about twenty travellers. A couple of them are already feeling seasick.' He grimaced at the memory.

He spoke like an educated man, which was a point in his favour as far as Cameron was concerned. 'Why did you go into a common sleeping cabin, then?'

'I was late booking a passage so there were no places in cabins left and I didn't want to hang around in New York. I soon regretted that, though.'

The steward interrupted them, speaking in a falsely jovial tone and holding out a bottle. 'I can see you two are going to get on well, so I'll leave you to become acquainted. I'll give you the drinking water now, Mr Crossley. Remember to sip it gradually.'

'Thank you.' He didn't slip the man a coin because he wasn't sure exactly how much money he had left, let alone how much he'd need to sort this mess out once he got to England. To his relief the steward left straight away and didn't seem to expect a gratuity.

The newcomer busied himself taking items from a battered carpetbag and putting them on the small shelf at one inside corner of the top bunk.

'You may as well call me Bryn since we'll be living in close proximity for the next few days.'

Which immediately left Cameron in a dilemma about which name to use. 'Cam,' he said hastily when the other man looked up, showing his surprise at his delay in responding to the friendly offer of first name terms.

'I, um, never know whether to use my nickname or my given name,' he offered as an explanation of his hesitancy.

'I can use either name, whichever suits you best.'

'Then call me Cam. It's based on my initials.' He indicated the side of the carry-on bag which Caleb must have brought on board, thank goodness. Surely by the end of it, he'd have come to a decision about exactly what he should do and could revert to his own name.

He couldn't help adding mentally: *or not.*

'According to the steward, you'd been drinking and were brought on board by your friends, unconscious. And the companion who should have shared this cabin had been killed in a drunken brawl.'

Bryn gave him a disapproving look and said slowly and clearly, 'I'd prefer us to be frank from the start, so I should warn you that I'll be more than a little annoyed if you expect me to put up with drunkenness or pugnacious behaviour in a small space like this. And, I might add, that I am quite capable of defending myself if necessary.'

He heaved himself up on the top bunk and sat upright with his back against the wall.

Cameron suddenly decided to tell Bryn the simple truth. If he didn't, he'd be bound to give himself away while sharing such close quarters for several days. 'I'm not a drunkard. Someone must have spiked my drink because I never, ever drink to excess. In fact, I can't remember ever passing out from drinking in the whole of my life until yesterday. What's more, my wallet is missing and most of my money with it.'

'Ah. I see. Did this happen on board the ship or before-hand?'

'Beforehand. I was apparently unconscious when brought on board and have no memory of that at all. I regained con-sciousness about half an hour or so ago and my head is still not all that clear.'

'Ah, well, I can sympathise, because I was robbed by two men a few days ago. They were armed with particularly nasty-looking knives and at the time I chose to give them my money rather than risk having my throat cut. I'm not sure they'd have left me alive even then except that a group of people came round the corner at that moment and came to my rescue, though the thieves got away. Unfortunately that has left me short of money for travelling once I get to England. And without money for any extras during the voyage.'

'Don't you have any other money at all?'

'I have some in Lancashire, which I was glad about after the robbery. Some close friends are looking after my possessions and money for me, but I shall have to work out how to get to the north.'

'That's hard luck.'

'Where are you heading to eventually?'

And Cameron surprised himself by telling the truth again: 'Lancashire as well.' He'd thought he hadn't yet decided whether to take Caleb's place there, so why had he said that? Oh, hell. He wasn't sure of anything, not really.

'Whereabouts in Lancashire?'

'I don't know. I just have an address. My father took a sud-den desire to send me to visit my grandfather. I've never even been to England before.'

'Well, you're obviously an American from your accent, but it's got a hint of Lancashire in it, too, somehow. Did your fam-ily come from there originally?'

'My father did but my mother was born in America.' Cameron had trouble holding back a yawn and stopped fighting against the tiredness. 'I still feel rather dopey. I have to get some sleep. I hope I'll make more sense in the morning.'

His companion was soon fast asleep, judging by the smooth even breathing, but even though he was exhausted Cameron couldn't stop his thoughts whirling round and round.

The trouble was, he really was contemplating taking his brother's place as heir. And that made him feel uncertain of everything, including his own morals.

By the time the ship docked in Southampton, Cameron had become genuinely friendly with Bryn, who was a decent chap. He was from a town called Rochdale, in the southern part of Lancashire.

'Have you been away for long?' Cameron asked.

'Yes, for a few years, but I expect to find one or two people I still know there, as well as the people I used to work with. I trust them absolutely. I trained as a carpenter and I love working with wood.'

'I'm a farmer but I do a bit of buying and selling as well. Have you got family to go back to as well as friends?'

'Sadly, my parents died while I was overseas and we were a small family. I did hear that my brother had moved away, but we were never close so we haven't kept in touch. Which Lancashire town are you going to?'

'It's called Ollerthwaite and I'm told it's located in a small Pennine valley in the north of the county that's not remarkable for anything – well, that's how my father always describes it.'

'I must admit I haven't heard of the place.'

On the final evening, Bryn confided more personal details. He'd had his life neatly planned till the woman he'd been going to marry had gone to nurse her sick aunt in the south. She'd broken off their engagement soon afterwards and was going to marry someone she'd met there, someone with a lot more money than Bryn and, she said, a much livelier approach to life.

'I never got that close to another woman. To my surprise, I enjoyed travelling and spent the last decade moving round the eastern side of America. It's an amazing country.'

'Did you never think of settling there?' Cameron asked.

'I thought seriously about it a couple of times, but I never met a woman I wanted to spend the rest of my life with.'

'So you're on your way back to England?'

'Yes. I surprised myself by growing deeply homesick a few months ago and strangely enough, what I longed for most of all were the moors. I used to go for long walks across the Pennines and I always seemed to solve my problems up there. I won't be able to solve one of my present problems, though. I don't have any close family left. It leaves you a bit . . . well, uncertain of your place in the world.'

'I feel much the same.' Cameron laid a hand briefly on Bryn's shoulder and they exchanged sad smiles.

By then Cameron had grown used to being addressed by the stewards as 'Mr Crossley' and as 'Cam' by Bryn. But a few days still didn't seem long enough for him to have become certain of what to do with the rest of his life, no, not nearly long enough.

He wondered whether to confide in Bryn about his dilemma and ask his new friend's advice, but in the end he didn't.

Eventually he decided he'd better at least go and visit this Walter Crossley and either continue pretending to be Caleb, or tell his grandfather the truth, depending on what the man was like. He kept coming back to the fact that he was as close a blood relative as Caleb had been, even if bastard born. Surely that counted for something?

If his grandfather simply told him to leave, so be it.

If he didn't, well, who knew what might happen?

He didn't like the thought of inheriting the farm by cheating, though, so he hoped his grandfather was the sort of person he could tell the truth to.

13

Lancashire

Jason Stafford grew furious all over again when days passed and there was no sign of Elinor running out of money and coming back to the only home she'd ever known. He'd pictured her confessing that she'd been wrong to leave, wrong to defy him, and submitting meekly to him in bed.

If she was humble enough, he might still marry her because people near his uncle's former home had hardly spoken to him at the funeral and he doubted they'd make him welcome in the area. But they'd spoken well of Elinor, so he reckoned marrying her would pave the way for him to be accepted. Should he move there and risk it?

How could that stupid bitch have escaped like that? There had been ground trampled below her bedroom window but she could hardly have jumped out and no ladder that long had been found in the garden.

And where could she have gone to? Had she been seeing another man all along and gone running off with him? No, not possible. His uncle hadn't been stupid enough to have missed something like that. Why, she'd hardly ever left the house except to go shopping or to church, had spent most of her spare time with that ugly maid.

They must have gone off together but where?

Thank goodness for Denby, who had discovered where she was likely to be heading. It looked as if his uncle's manservant was going to prove useful in helping sort out Jason's new life.

After some consideration he decided to offer Denby a job and sell the smaller house he'd inherited from his parents and been living in for the past few years. He could use what it brought to pay off those of his uncle's debts that were inescapable, though not those from gambling. He'd check with the lawyer but he was fairly certain you weren't obliged to pay off gambling debts and he'd make it plain to people that he wasn't going to do anything about those.

Moving to another village would allow him to leave the worst of his reputation behind. If he behaved carefully, acting meek and proper for a while, surely people would gradually start speaking to him civilly and consider him to have turned respectable? He'd even go to church to prove he was a reformed character, tedious as that was.

But he needed a wife to add the final layer of respectability and a wife who was an undoubted lady. Elinor Pendleton would have been perfect for that. Not to mention her being just the sort of woman he liked to bed, nice and thin, meek and grateful.

Jason managed to persuade the lawyer handling his uncle's will to hold the creditors back from foreclosing and give him time to sell his house. He had to pay a little money on account to prove that there was some chance of him paying off the various debts, but he regarded that as an entry fee into a new life. Fortunately he didn't share his uncle's love of gambling.

As soon as he could, Jason moved into the house. His next step would be to find out what had happened to Elinor, damn her. He called Denby in to discuss this.

'I could go and check whether she's arrived in this Ollerthwaite place if you like, sir. It's the only lead we have now, though why she's gone there, I can't think. I never heard the place mentioned by my late master, that's for sure, nor did any letters come from that part of the world.'

'How the hell do you know that?'

'I was the one who always brought in the mail. I saw the postmarks.'

'Ah. Right. I see. Good idea to check this Ollerthwaite place, then. She must be there. She hasn't got anywhere else to go, I'm sure. But even if she is there, we can't just seize her and bring her back here by force, can we?'

'She must be short of money by now. She'll probably be working in some menial position and will be relieved to be allowed home. And I'd guess she'll still be with that maid of your uncle's. Hard worker, Maude was, got through twice as much work as most maids. Wouldn't hurt to bring her back as well.'

He looked at his master and waited. What a slow thinker the man was.

'I'll consider it.'

'In the meantime, I could find out how to get to this place and what would be involved in bringing her back? Always supposing she's still there, of course. We'd better not leave it too long to go after her or she might have moved on again.'

'Good idea. Yes, you do that.'

'I'll need some money to pay the expenses, sir. I have an invalid aunt to support, don't forget, and I'm always short of money. She costs me a great deal, but I don't begrudge it. She brought me up when my parents died, after all.'

Denby didn't smile, though it always amused him that both Staffords had believed his tale of an invalid aunt. Had deliberately lost touch with his family years ago, at the same time as he had changed his name. But this story sounded realistic and had always stopped his former employer expecting him to pay his way himself then wait to be reimbursed.

It worked just as well with this new one.

Denby set off a few days later, his ears still ringing with instructions from his fool of an employer on what to do and not do. It felt good to get away, not so good to have to waste so much time travelling to this stupid place. Talk about the back of beyond.

Why was Jason Stafford so obsessed with Elinor Pendleton? How could this possibly be worth it?

When he arrived in Ollerthwaite, he took an instant dislike to the place, which was far worse than he'd expected. There was no small cosy hotel where he could be fussed over – he'd been looking forward to that – nothing but nosey farmers and their even nosier wives staring at him when he asked directions. In fact, he'd not even call it a town; it seemed more like a village to him, and an old-fashioned one at that.

He asked the porter where he could find a room for the night and the man studied his clothing, then told him about a lady who took in occasional travellers, as long as they seemed respectable.

Denby had to walk to her house, though, with a lad to show him the way and carry his bag because the town didn't even have a taxi cab, only a man who occasionally plied for hire but he wasn't well at the moment.

The house was clean, he'd give it that, but it was a poor sort of place and he was disappointed that he'd not be spending his little holiday in more comfort.

He told the lady of the house that he was looking for a Mr Pottle and pretended to be dismayed when told there was no one of that name living in the town that she'd ever heard of, and she had lived here all her life so knew every family.

He escaped to the local pub after tea and consoled himself with a pint of best bitter, sipping it slowly as he settled down to watch the regulars. He also chatted to the barman, who grew noticeably friendlier after being treated to a half pint. But the man said he'd never heard of any Pottles either.

Good choice of name, Denby thought smugly. He'd never met anyone called that, either. It'd have been disastrous if there really were such a family living in the town. He only just managed not to smile openly at his own cleverness.

When he wondered aloud whether his cousin Mary Pottle had married someone local and whether any female newcomers had come here lately, that drew some useful information from two slovenly looking women who'd turned up and were sitting in a little women's area just off his side of the public bar.

'There are two new women come to live here,' one of them said, shooting a suggestive glance at her empty glass.

He took out a couple of coins. 'Do you know what they're called? Are you *sure* they're not Pottles?'

'They're Crossleys, sir, relatives of Walter Crossley, who has a farm out at Upperfold.'

Wasn't that the name the porter had overheard from the fleeing women? He wasn't sure but he thought it was. This was looking promising. 'Where is this Upperfold?'

'Just up the hill from here.'

'What do these women look like?'

'One's a great tall creature, about forty I'd say, and very plain in appearance. The other's younger and tallish as well, with brown hair, rather scrawny, nothing special to look at.'

'Hmm. Not my relatives, then. The Pottles are usually quite short.'

'I'm sorry you've had a wasted trip, sir.'

Denby managed to heave a convincing sigh. 'It's my second wild goose chase. But I'm determined to find my cousins. They're the only relatives I have left.'

'Aw, that's sad.'

Before he left, he felt obliged to buy them a half of shandy each and he thanked the barman profusely, slipping him a shilling. If he had to come back here again, the barman would remember and be helpful. But Denby would take as little money out of expenses as he could and put what was left into the Post Office Savings Bank before he got back.

He felt quite optimistic that it hadn't been a wasted trip. If the description was to be believed, the two women he was really seeking were now living nearby, out at some farm or other.

He'd have liked to catch a glimpse of them to be sure, but with no taxi and this Upperfold village only accessible on foot or by pony cart, he wasn't even going to try.

He heard footsteps running along the street behind him and swung round, ready to defend himself, but it was the barman again.

'I just thought of something else, sir. There's a market here in Ollerthwaite on Thursdays and one of the ladies who've moved into Cross End Farm has started coming to sell eggs at it. So you'll probably be able to see them. People come from all over this area to our market, so you may even find your relatives as well.'

'Thank you so much for telling me. I'll recognise my cousin instantly if she's there.' He fumbled for another coin and handed it over reluctantly.

He'd deposit his luggage at the station early tomorrow and check out the market before he left the town. It meant he'd have to hang around and see if he could catch a glimpse of this woman but it was an opportunity not to be missed. He could take the midday train back to civilisation instead of the morning one. It'd be well worth the boredom if he caught sight of either of them because it'd mean the other would be around. Those two stuck together like a pair of leeches.

Denby packed his things the following morning and left them at the station with the porter. No trouble finding the market in such a small place, even though it was a rather pitiful collection of displays set out on rickety wooden stalls. He walked to and fro, trying to stay in places from which he could see those selling foodstuffs without being seen himself. They all seemed to be at the far end.

He was just thinking there was no one there who looked at all like either of those two bitches when Maude turned up on a bicycle with a big iron tray at the front. She lifted a heavy basket out of it, from which she unloaded eggs and some green stuff that looked like little cabbages.

No missing her. She was, as usual, the tallest woman there. He stepped back till he was partly concealed behind the corner of a building. So they had indeed taken refuge here. He wasn't going any nearer to her, didn't want to risk being seen and sending them running away again.

Jason Stafford had better pay him a bonus for this.

It'd be very interesting to see how his employer dealt with them. He was absolutely set on marrying Elinor Pendleton, which was ridiculous. How did he think he'd persuade her to come back, let alone marry him? He couldn't just drag her through the streets.

He was a stupid man, that one.

Denby would rather jump into the nearest canal than marry either of those two human maypoles. He liked his women to be small and dainty.

When Walter dropped Maude at the market, he said he'd be back in an hour or so.

She smiled and waved at him. 'I may even have sold everything by then.'

She arranged her goods to best advantage on the stall she had started sharing with two other women, humming to herself. As she turned, she caught sight of a man lurking round a corner. Was that—? It looked like Denby. Surely it couldn't be him?

She kept an eye on the man but when he left, he kept his back to the market. He seemed to be heading towards the station, which made her feel it was even more likely that it might be him. She left her produce in the care of one of her friends, saying she had to go to the lav.

She hurried along a nearby gap between two shops, hoping to get a better view without him seeing her. And when she did, she felt literally sick because it *was* him. How could he possibly have found out that they'd come here?

She decided to continue following him, whatever the risks, because she wouldn't feel safe again till she saw him get on a train and leave the town.

A few steps further along he stopped to consult his watch and she ducked back, standing perfectly still, not wanting to attract his attention. Not till he'd started moving again did she move.

On the way there she suddenly lost sight of him and to her horror, when she slowed down to check all the approaches to the station, he suddenly appeared in front of her.

He gave her that superior smile. 'How nice to meet you again, Miss Vernon.'

She wasn't even going to attempt to be polite. 'Well, it's not nice to meet you. What on earth are you doing here?'

'Finding out what's happened to you and that other fool. Mr Stafford is paying me to do that, or I'd not be here, I promise you. For some reason he's still interested in your friend.'

That made her feel even worse. 'How on earth did you find us?'

'You were very careless about hiding where you were going. When I asked at nearby railway stations, I soon found a porter who told me two young women had been asking how to get to Ollerthwaite. You were neither of you born to be conspirators, that's for sure. Might I ask why this place? I could understand you going to Blackpool but this place isn't worth a second glance.'

'Because I have relatives here who have given us a home and will protect us if necessary.'

'A likely tale. Mr Stafford won't let this drop, you know. Where will you run to next?'

'We won't need to run anywhere else. If you ask around about a Mr Crossley, you'll find that he's well known in the area. I doubt your master will find it easy to play nasty tricks on us here, let alone get away with attacking Elinor as he tried to do after the funeral.'

He gave her a scornful look. 'Well, he's still determined to have her, goodness knows why he's still prepared to marry her. She'd be better off with her own home.' And Denby would be paid a nice amount of money for helping get her there.

'Well, she's not prepared to marry him and my cousin won't let anyone hurt us.'

A man walking past proved her point to Denby.

'Are you all right, Miss Vernon?'

'No. This person is annoying me.'

'I'll walk you back to the market then.' He glared at Denby. 'I don't know who you are but you'd better not hurt any of our women.'

He offered her his arm and they walked swiftly round the nearest corner. 'I'm John Brooks, a friend of Walter's, by the way.'

A short distance down the street she stopped. 'I won't feel safe till I see him get on a train and leave.'

'I can understand that. Mean-looking chap, wasn't he? Let's go and watch him go. I know just the place.'

'Do you mind?'

He smiled. 'I'm curious as well now.'

Mr Brooks took her round to the other side of the station and they stood behind a pile of luggage without Denby noticing them.

Fortunately he had quite a penetrating voice and she could hear most of what he was saying as well. First of all he asked the porter if he'd heard of a Mr Crossley, and was told how wonderful and important that man was.

That put a very sour expression on Denby's face.

Then the porter came and announced that the train would be a quarter of an hour late, due to a problem further along the line and the passengers began to grumble to one another.

Mr Brooks looked at her apologetically. 'I'm sorry, but I can't wait any longer. I've arranged to meet someone.'

'I'll be all right now.' Maude decided to wait and see Denby leave, even though Walter might wonder where she'd got to. She wouldn't feel safe while he was in town.

But Denby came across and pulled her behind a pile of luggage, grabbing her arm and giving it a twist that made her yelp in pain. 'Think about what I could do to you one night after dark if you don't give my master what he wants.'

When someone came up to them, Denby let her go. To her relief it was Walter and as Denby tried to walk away, he grabbed the fellow's arm.

'Why was this man hurting you?'

She quickly told him who Denby was and the threats he'd made, even after Mr Brooks had tried to help her. She saw her cousin's expression grow grim.

'We'll see about that.' He twisted the other man's arm behind his back. 'See how you like it, you bully.' He made Denby yelp then said slowly and clearly, 'Stand still and listen. If you ever come back to Ollerthwaite, I'll beat the living daylights out of you and if you bring anyone else with you I've plenty of friends who'll help me deal with them. We don't want people like you in our town, threatening our women and who knows what else. And my niece and her friend are never coming back to where they used to live.'

The porter walked past, staring in amazement but he didn't attempt to intervene except to call, 'Are you all right, Mr Crossley?'

'I shall be when this bully has left our town. He was attacking my niece.'

'What? Shame on him. I'll remember his face.'

Walter turned back to Denby with another of his fierce looks. 'As you can see, people know and trust me here.'

'Let go of me, damn you!'

'Not till the train comes.'

Maude had been watching in amazement, seeing a new side to her cousin.

When the train pulled in, he threw Denby towards it and watched him board it, then waited, with arms folded, till it drew away.

'I don't think he'll be back. Bullies don't like getting a taste of their own medicine.'

Maude walked slowly back to the stall and was relieved to see that her friend had sold the rest of her produce.

As Walter drove them home, he said, 'That bully won't come back.'

'I've never seen you look as angry.'

'I can't abide men who ill-treat women.'

'I'm grateful.'

Walter insisted she keep the money for the eggs and garden stuff and that made her feel good. She and Elinor were now building on their original savings and they hadn't had to sell her former mistress's jewellery.

She didn't think there was much chance of Denby coming back to Ollerthwaite. He only cared about money, not Elinor.

It was Stafford who lusted after Elinor. Would he come after them on his own? She shook her head at the mere idea. He'd bully someone weaker but wasn't likely to face someone like her cousin Walter. And Denby would surely tell him about the encounter.

She was so glad they'd come here, so very glad. And was getting very fond of Walter

As they sat having their evening meal, Walter saw that Elinor was looking worried.

She looked at him as they finished eating. 'I don't trust Denby or Stafford. We'll have to run away again if they come back. I don't want to put you in danger, Walter.'

It was he who answered, saying very firmly, 'No, you shouldn't run anywhere, lass. That'd be the worst thing you could do and only put you in more danger. There's trouble everywhere in this world at some stage. You must stay here, where you've made friends and will make more.'

He hesitated then added in a voice grown suddenly a little husky, 'Apart from anything else, I'm grateful that fate brought you and Maude to live with me. Your company makes a big difference to my life.'

The two women discussed it in whispers after they'd gone up to bed that night, with Maude sitting on Elinor's bed, a shawl over her nightdress.

'You do want to stay here, don't you?' she asked.

'Yes. I really like your Cousin Walter, and he's so kind. I think I panicked when you told me about Denby. I have to learn to be braver.' Elinor took a deep breath. 'I *will* learn to face up to troubles rather than running away.'

'There are two of us here as well as Walter, don't forget. We'll face up to troubles together.'

'I love you like a sister,' Elinor said suddenly. 'I'm so glad we stayed together, and that you brought me here. I love the place already.'

They clasped hands for a moment, smiling mistily at one another.

14

When the steamer arrived in Southampton, Cameron waited impatiently to disembark. He wasn't looking forward to finding his way around in a country that was new to him. Thank goodness he spoke the same language – well, more or less. Some words were different and he and Bryn had laughed sometimes about that.

After thinking carefully about what he'd need to do on arrival, he asked Bryn what his plans were. Perhaps he and his new friend could help one another.

Bryn shrugged. 'Haven't a clue what I'll be doing. I don't have enough money to travel by train, so I suppose I'll go on the tramp and see what sort of work I can pick up as I move north. I've done it before and it can be interesting. I'll get there eventually.'

Cameron was startled. 'You didn't say things were so bad.'

'I decided to enjoy the journey on the ship and save my troubles for after I'd arrived in England. There was nothing I could do about them while we were at sea, was there? I've enjoyed your company, so I hope we don't lose touch after we land. I'll give you an address to which you can send letters, if you like?' He cocked his head, waiting.

'Shouldn't you have stayed in steerage class and saved your money?'

'Just between you and me, the steward let me move in with you for no extra payment on condition I kept an eye on you.'

Cameron couldn't hide his shock at this. 'Did they think I was a danger to the other passengers?'

'They didn't know what to think of someone who was carried on board and dumped on them. If those who brought you hadn't had your ticket and if your luggage hadn't already been brought on board, they'd not have let you on at all.' He gave one of his slightly twisted smiles. 'Bit of luck for me, that, but it could have been a difficult situation for you.'

He slapped his friend on the back. 'I soon realised you weren't a shady character, though, and so I told them.'

Cameron couldn't help smiling. 'You sound very sure of that.'

'Well, you have a very direct gaze, and anyway, someone as tall as you probably doesn't grow up with a need to prove himself by fighting, not to mention being rather visible if he does something people disapprove of. At least, that's what I've found, being nearly as tall as you. Though we do have problems with bunging our heads on low doorways like the ones on this ship.'

They grinned at one another, both having experienced that more than once.

'Didn't your father give you any idea of how to get to his old home from Southampton, Cam?'

'No. I don't think he understands the modern railway networks in England but from what I've heard people say, train services are quite extensive these days and can take you to every corner of the country. All he cares about is the family farm he's created in America, which is a big one. It's well over twenty years since he first arrived there and he rarely says much about his previous life.'

He shrugged. 'Unfortunately I had to leave in a hurry – at his instigation I might add – so I don't have the faintest idea how to get to this Ollerthwaite place, except that it's in Lancashire. I'd been thinking maybe I'd need to go to London first. Isn't that the centre of the railway networks? It's the capital city, after all.'

'You don't need to go there, from what I remember. You can't always get directly to places in Lancashire from London anyway because the main railway line north goes to Yorkshire. I reckon you'd be better going to Swindon first.' He frowned, then added slowly, 'Then I think you'd go to Manchester via Chester. We'll have to check that, though. Things will have changed since I was here, too.'

Cameron sighed. He hadn't even been sure he was going to visit his grandfather till yesterday, because he'd kept vacillating about whether to even look at claiming a possible inheritance. It occurred to him now that he and Bryn might both benefit from travelling together. He could afford to pay his friend's fare if they went at the cheapest rate and he'd welcome the company. Bryn seemed to be almost as alone in the world as he was and would be penniless till he managed to retrieve some of his money.

There was another consideration he admitted to himself. As Bryn had said, the two of them got on so well, it was as if they'd known one another for years, and he didn't want to lose touch, either. He wished he'd had a brother like Bryn, not the three half-brothers who all considered themselves highly superior to him by a mere accident of birth.

'I don't know much about English geography except for what I've looked at in the atlas in the ship's library. And that didn't show the newer rail networks. I'd never planned to come here, just did it to oblige my father.'

'Are you sure you want me to join you?'

'Very sure. Look, if no one's expecting you and you haven't anywhere you need to go in a hurry, why don't you stay with me for a while once we find our way to this Ollerthwaite place? I'll pay your fare and you can stop me making stupid mistakes in a strange country. From what you've said, by doing that you'll end up closer to your own destination as well.'

Bryn gave him a searching look then nodded slowly. 'All right. It's a bargain.'

'And if I decide to stay in the Ollerthwaite district, you may find there's work available round there for a carpenter. Who knows?'

There was a pregnant pause, then he nodded. 'I'd like that if it's where you're going to settle permanently.'

They shook hands on their unspoken bargain then Cameron frowned. 'What are you going to do about tools, though? If you're a carpenter, won't you need some in order to get work?'

'I've looked after my tools more carefully than I've looked after my other possessions while I was travelling. I sent most of them ahead when I booked my passage to England and they should be waiting for me at my old boss's place in Rochdale, but I do have a few old favourites with me in my trunk. I knew Lionel and his son would keep the main set of tools safe till I returned, just as I knew they'd never move away from Rochdale. Once I decide on somewhere to settle, I'll retrieve them all, and I'll either go and visit Lionel or they'll come and visit me, I'm sure.'

'That sounds good, then. We'll travel together.'

'Are you sure you can afford to pay for me, Cam? You said the chap you were travelling with had taken most of your money.'

'I have enough to get us both there in the cheapest seats and a bit to spare. Fortunately, I kept money in my shoes as well as in my wallet and pockets, and they didn't find that. You'll probably save me money by showing me how to do things here, and it'll undoubtedly make for a more pleasant journey. Strange, isn't it, how fate tossed us together?'

'Yes. But good things happen to people by chance as well as bad.'

'I have to confess that I don't know much about my grandfather. My father has never talked about him. He simply ordered me to go to him; it wasn't my choice but it suited me to agree. I have no idea what sort of reception we'll get and whether I'll want to stay there permanently. But if I don't, then I'll come with you to Rochdale and look round there.' He offered his hand and they shook on that.

'It'll be safer with two of us. Look how you got drugged and we both got robbed on the way here.'

'Stupidly careless, wasn't I? I can't even remember what we were drinking. Not booze, cups of tea, I should think. I'm not much of a drinker.'

Cameron hesitated. Even now, he hadn't told Bryn the complete truth about who he was, let alone explained his dilemma about taking over the inheritance offered to Caleb. Maybe he would never tell anyone the full truth. It all depended on what his grandfather and Ollerthwaite were like.

'You were no more stupid than I was to go wandering round on my own in a strange city,' Bryn said. 'America is a fascinating country, but not always safe for lone travellers, especially in the big cities. I've mostly enjoyed my travels, though.'

'You said you wondered about settling there.'

'Yes, I did. A couple of times, when I met a woman I liked. But nothing came of either attachment. A footloose wanderer isn't the best prospect as a husband, especially in the areas of the country where there's still a shortage of women and they can take their pick of the eligible men.'

There was silence for a moment or two and then Bryn suddenly smacked one hand down on the table. 'All right. We're agreed. I'll not only come with you, but if you decide to settle there, I'll look the place over on my own behalf.'

'I'm glad.' More than glad, delighted. To be absolutely on your own in a strange country made Cameron more nervous than he'd expected, as did having no family to guard his back, so to speak. He might not have been accepted as part of his father's legitimate family, but he'd never doubted that they'd help him if he was in trouble.

'Might it be best for you to send a telegram to your grand-father, telling him you're in the country?'

'Yes. But I'll wait until we've found out for sure about trains and I know when we'll be arriving before I do it.'

They travelled to Swindon, found a double room for the night in a cheap hotel near the station and booked their fares for the earliest train that fitted their itinerary, which would leave the next morning.

Only then did Cameron send a telegram to his grandfather, a brief one saying only that he had just arrived in England and would be arriving in Ollerthwaite the following afternoon. He hesitated then signed it 'Caleb' but felt bad about that.

Then they went out to look at the town for an hour or two. It seemed to be made up of railway workshops and dwellings for those who toiled in them. Both men nearly jumped out of their skins when a loud hooter sounded late that afternoon and the streets were suddenly full of crowds of railway workers going home after their day's work.

Both men were tired and as they had an early start the fol-lowing morning, they didn't stay up late.

Once again Bryn fell fast asleep quickly, as he did every night. *Lucky fellow!* Cameron thought. He had another restless night, just couldn't settle to sleep. He had never slept so fitfully before. But then, he'd never been facing such momentous decisions. Whatever he decided to do, there would be huge changes ahead of him, because the only thing he was fairly sure of was that he wasn't going back to his old life as the only halfway accepted relative.

For once he had no way of knowing what to expect, let alone how to prepare for it as he usually liked to do when facing a new situation. His grandfather was a complete stranger on whom he might be about to play a serious trick, something that still didn't sit easily with him.

All he knew was he desperately wanted a proper home and family of his own, but he didn't feel good about getting one this way. Only life and his youngest half-brother seemed to have pushed him into it.

If he did take on the job, however, he'd work hard. That at least he could do in return. He knew he was good at managing a piece of land and had an eye for business opportunities. He would no doubt learn quickly how things were done in Lancashire.

He was longing for some time out of doors in the countryside, tending animals or simply turning over the soil and planting things. He was sick of the sight of the ocean, sick of walking on surfaces that heaved up and down beneath you, sick of living cheek by jowl with other people, even Bryn.

The ship had felt like a prison and in one sense that was what it had been.

15

Over a month had passed since their arrival in Ollerthwaite and the weather had grown gradually warmer with a few lovely sunny days, even in the rainy county of Lancashire. Elinor and Maude smiled to see people come to stand at their doors with faces turned up to the sun, drinking in its warmth as much as the plants and flowers did.

She and Maude were enjoying getting to know people in Upperfold and Ollerthwaite. They were also enjoying learning about the work on Walter's farm and were developing routines so that they could each take a fair share of it each day.

Maude preferred looking after the chickens and doing outdoor jobs, but they both shared the housework and took a pride in keeping their new home clean. Elinor was delighted to find an old cookery book and had mastered a few new dishes. She hadn't realised how much she would enjoy cooking when she didn't have the problem of eking out the skimpy amount of food provided by her stepfather.

One day she'd found an old-fashioned sewing machine in the attic, half-hidden under all sorts of oddments. She'd guessed that this had been put there on the death of Walter's daughter-in-law. After some hesitation, she mentioned it and asked if she could use it.

This time he didn't snap as he had at Maude about the bicycle, thank goodness. 'You take it if you have a use for it, lass. There's no point leaving it to gather dust when you two are in need of new clothes.'

'Thank you so much.'

After that she was able to make much quicker progress remaking and altering clothes for them. She had a flair for it, if she said so herself.

Walter came and went frequently, and his sturdy little pony got plenty of exercise. He said he didn't do as much farming these days because he had various small businesses to tend to. The two women wondered what those could be in this remote and sparsely populated valley.

He didn't share any details of what he was doing and they didn't like to pry, but they wondered if he was helping people as he'd helped Mrs Gleston with offering folk beds for the night. That might partly account for how well thought of he was. People not only showed respect in the way they greeted him but regularly asked his advice.

There were a few people, however, who scowled at him after he'd passed by, though not to his face, and these included the family of the lad who'd tried to bully the other children. They hadn't seen the boy again and Walter had said briefly that he'd gone to stay with a relative in Manchester and he wished he'd stay there, as he was a 'bad 'un' and not likely to come good, a typical Catlow. The family were part of the small minority of people who were not well thought of generally.

From time to time they met the two children Elinor had helped and were always greeted with shy smiles. There didn't seem to be anybody with the time to take an interest in them, because from what Kessie had told them, their mother was working all the hours she could just to put bread on the table and their grandfather was 'poorly' and had to rest a lot.

As they went about their daily tasks, the two women couldn't help noticing how Walter kept a careful watch for the postman who usually turned up early in the morning if he was going to bring anything to the farm. They guessed he was disappointed at not yet receiving a reply from America beyond the initial brief response that James would look into sending his youngest son.

'How do you think the arrival of an American heir might affect us, especially if he's married?' Elinor worried to Maude at one stage. 'I don't think a wife will want two other women hanging around in her house.'

'Who can tell? Walter seems to think the heir is unmarried. I'm sure *he* won't throw us out, whatever the situation, not without helping us find somewhere else to go, anyway. We'll have to see what happens. This youngest son may not like it here and if he isn't prepared to move to England, Walter will be forced to look elsewhere for an heir.'

'He must have other relatives he can leave the property to.'

Maude shrugged. 'It's obvious he wants to leave it to a direct descendant, as would most people, but there's nothing we can do to change matters, so we should stop worrying about the future and concentrate on enjoying the present.'

'You're right. Did you get many eggs today?'

'Even more than yesterday. Will you take them back to the house while I clean out the nesting boxes? There are a couple of broody hens and Joan says she'll show me how to encourage them to hatch out some eggs in a safe place.'

Maude watched her friend carry the basket of eggs across the yard to the kitchen and smiled. The sun highlighted the glints of almost red in Elinor's hair, which was the exact colour of ripe chestnuts. It pleased her to see how much better her friend was looking now that she was eating properly. In fact even she, fond of Elinor as she was, hadn't realised that her friend could be quite as pretty when she no longer looked gaunt and worried.

It must be nice to be good looking. This was something Maude knew no one would ever say of her, however healthily she ate and lived, and however much care she took with her hair, which was her best point she always felt. Well, the Crossley women weren't known for their good looks but for their height, general healthiness and strength. Farmers married women like them because they would make good wives, not because they fell madly in love with them.

Oh, well, there was nothing you could do about the body and face you were born with but at least now she could present herself as well as possible.

She smiled and held up her face to the sunshine, feeling like one of the flowers opening up.

The next evening after they'd finished their meal Walter said, 'When you've cleared away, could you please leave the washing up for a while? I'd like to talk to you about something.'

They removed all the dirty dishes from the table and left them soaking in the washing-up bowl, then sat down again.

He looked at them thoughtfully. 'I've been wondering about the future. I never like to tread blindly forward, as you must have realised by now. Us Crossleys are like that. So in case my letter to America bears fruit, I'd like to discuss something with you both. And we also need to think about your futures as well as that of my potential heir.'

This remark made them exchange apprehensive glances. What was he planning? Surely he hadn't already found them somewhere else to live and work once the heir came to live here? They had settled in nicely at Cross End Farm and both loved living there. Anyway, he'd still need their help in the house, surely? A man coming to live here wouldn't take over the housework.

He took a deep breath and began, sounding less sure of himself than usual. 'I've been thinking about my grandson. As you know I'm hoping he'll come here, marry and settle down. I've also been thinking about you two. What do *you* want to do with the rest of your lives? You're both quite young women still. Well, you seem young to me, especially you, Elinor.'

She stared in surprise at this unexpected focus on herself. 'Why do you ask that?'

'Did you never think of getting married and raising a family? I've seen you both smile as you watch the little ones in the village play, especially you, Elinor, and you seem to get on really well with them. Why, that little lass you rescued beams at the mere sight of you now. I hope you don't mind my asking, but why have you never married?'

She couldn't hold back her sadness and felt comfortable enough with him to tell the truth. 'It never seemed possible, somehow, with my stepfather controlling the money and therefore everything we did. And for a long time my mother needed me. She was rather sickly.'

He looked at her sadly. 'I've seen it more than once, a daughter's life sacrificed to caring for a parent.'

'There was another thing that stopped me marrying. I didn't want to bring children into an unhappy home totally controlled by him. And I knew he'd only allow me to marry someone he approved of. I couldn't stand his friends or acquaintances. They were nearly as nasty as he was. Respectable people didn't deal with him unless they had to so how would I meet anyone decent? So I made myself look as plain and uninteresting as I could and he mostly ignored me.'

'You could have moved away.'

'I thought about it but it's not easy to do that when you have no money and no close relatives to help you, no real friends either because most women of my age were married and raising children. Besides, he'd promised my mother he'd bequeath the house to me in his will, because it came from her family not his. So I wanted to keep an eye on it. If I'd left things to him, the place would have gone to rack and ruin.'

She bent her head, not enjoying remembering how things had been. 'After my mother died, I think he saw me more as a cheap servant than as a family member so he mostly left me alone. His main interests were gambling or boozing with his pal from up the road or with his equally horrible nephew, the one he said in his will that I had to marry.'

She shuddered, as she still did every time she thought of Jason Stafford.

'What if you had a chance to marry someone else now, a decent bloke mind? Would you take it? Wouldn't you like a chance to have a family?'

She stared down at her hands, which were clasped tightly together in her lap, thinking hard. She knew he must have a good reason for asking her such personal questions and by now she'd grown to trust him enough to respond honestly, because she'd seen him be kind to people in small ways several times, in secret or openly. She doubted he'd push her into an unhappy situation, but if he thought she'd be happier married, she wouldn't put it past him to look round for a suitable man and give her a nudge or two.

She answered him with a question of her own, 'I gave up hoping to find someone I'd *want* to marry years ago. No one would call me a young woman any longer and I'd not bring any money or property to a marriage. So how would I find a husband?'

'You still haven't really answered my question.' He didn't hurry her but he waited, clearly determined to get an answer before he said anything else.

As the silence continued, Maude looked at Walter and opened her mouth to speak, but she closed it again when he put one fingertip briefly to his lips as if to tell her to keep quiet and let her friend speak.

'I don't think I'd want to risk getting married, Walter. How do you know someone is going to be kind to you before you're tied to him? And by that time it's too late to do anything about it. I saw how my stepfather changed after he'd married my mother. And her mistake not only ruined both our lives but Maude's too.'

'So you don't even want to get married now?'

'I can't see it happening. And . . . well, I'd be afraid to take the risk, especially with a stranger.'

'Do you have any special dreams about what you'd like to do with your life, then?'

'Doesn't everyone have secret hopes and dreams? What I'd like would be to own a little cottage where Maude and I could live comfortably and know no one would be able to throw us out. I was going to sell the house after my stepfather died and buy a smaller one for us in the country, then live on the interest from the rest of the money. It might sound heartless, but I didn't think my stepfather would make old bones, he lived such a rackety life and looked so unhealthy.'

She shrugged and stopped talking, didn't admit, even to these two, that she'd love to get married and have a child or two before it was too late. It seemed so hopeless, the sort of dream best kept private at her age.

He studied her and said softly, 'No one will ever force you to get married while you're living with me. Never forget that, lass. And I'll always make sure you two have a home that no one will throw you out of. I'm not like your stepfather. I don't gamble my money away.'

'You're very kind. I've never met anyone so kind.'

He flushed slightly at the compliment. 'Well, enough about that. There's something else I want to talk about. If my plan works out and I do get a grandson from America coming to live here, I've warned them it'd be a condition for him to marry a woman of my choice—'

He saw the sudden suspicion and wariness on Elinor's face and added quickly, 'So I'd like you two to help me find a suitable woman for him. You're getting to know people in the village and at that church you attend in Ollerthwaite. Can you keep your eyes open for someone? You'll talk to some people that I don't.'

A sigh of what was clearly relief escaped Elinor.

'Mind you, I'd have to get to know my grandson first before I change my will, see if he's a decent chap, or I'd not let him inherit the farm, let alone bother to find him a wife. That's where you two come in. You can get to know the unmarried women of his age and maybe invite them round to tea. Now, that's enough about that. Any other problems, either of you?'

They both shook their heads and he smiled at them across the table. 'We won't talk about this again until we see if an heir turns up and what he's like.'

Later he said, 'It's grand to have company in the evenings. I'm right glad you came to live with me, I really am.'

He pushed his chair back and stood up. 'I'll just take my last walk of the day round the lower field. I love to say goodnight to my land in the moonlight.'

When he'd gone, Elinor let out a huge sigh of relief. 'Goodness, he did give me a shock. I thought for a few minutes he was going to say that I should marry his nephew.'

'If he had raised that idea, it'd have been a suggestion, not a command.'

Elinor shuddered. 'I'd not dare look the heir in the face if Walter had suggested that. I'd find it hugely embarrassing to live in the same house even.'

'You shouldn't close your mind to getting married, though, love. Men aren't all like Reginald Stafford and his horrible nephew.'

A little later she frowned and said, 'The trouble is, I can't think of any single women of the right age living in the village or even in Ollerthwaite. Can you? They all seem to get married young or not married at all.'

'True. Anyhow, let's sit and read for a while. I do enjoy my half hour with a book or newspaper before we go to bed.'

But though Maude opened her book, she didn't turn many pages because she was still thinking about Elinor. She'd been watching Walter very closely. When he started talking about his nephew, she'd seen him study Elinor in a thoughtful way and had wondered if he'd been going to suggest that she might consider marrying the American. Then he'd noticed how frightened Elinor was at the mere thought of marrying anyone at all, so had changed what he was going to say.

It would be a great pity if Elinor's experiences with the Stafford men had made her so wary of men. She was younger than Maude and there was probably still time for her to have a child or two. It might not be likely, but if it did happen, Maude decided that she would not only welcome it but even encourage it, if necessary.

Thinking about marriage made her consider her own situation and pull a wry face, as she always did No one was likely to offer to marry such a plain Jane as herself, especially one taller than most men. But if a miracle did happen and someone took an interest in her, she would definitely take a good look back at him and even consider accepting an offer A widower might do such a thing, perhaps. People usually got married quite quickly if their spouse died, because they needed help in their daily lives. Someone older and needing that sort of practical help might not care as much what she looked like as they cared about how strong and healthy she was, especially if he had children to finish bringing up.

Maude shook her head at herself. Why was she thinking about finding someone for herself? She was long past hopes of marriage, even in her sweetest dreams, and she should face that squarely.

It amazed her sometimes to think how quickly the years had passed. She didn't feel to be getting old but she was at an age now when women didn't have children easily, and she supposed she would soon be past the age of being able to bear a child at all. In one sense Elinor had been like a child to her, only she hadn't dared show her affection for the younger woman too openly.

Her dreams were more like the stories with happy endings that you found in novels. They were a pleasure to contemplate then afterwards you returned to reality and got on with real life, where happy endings didn't always turn up, even for those who deserved them.

When a young man in a shabby uniform cycled up towards the front door of the farm a few mornings later, Walter hurried out of the barn to see who it was.

'Hoy! If that telegram's for me, I'm over here.'

The lad turned round with a smile. 'It is for you, Mr Crossley.' He held out an envelope.

Walter took it from him, tore it open and read it quickly, then murmured. 'Thank goodness!' and then smiled at the lad. 'There's no answer needed.'

After he'd slipped the lad a threepenny bit, he didn't even watch him ride off but hurried into the house, beaming at the two women and waving the piece of paper with its brief message at them.

'This is from my son in America. My grandson Caleb is on his way to England. James doesn't say exactly when he'll arrive, though.'

The mood at the farm brightened considerably after that.

Another telegram arrived just over a week later and brought an even broader smile to Walter's face. 'This one is from my American grandson. He arrived in England yesterday.'

He swallowed hard and held the telegram out with a hand that shook slightly. 'Look. Read it for yourselves. He says he'll be here this afternoon.'

Elinor read it quickly. 'He doesn't say what time he'll be arriving. And who is the friend he's bringing? I thought he'd never visited England before.'

'As long as he brings himself, he can bring Queen Victoria herself to keep him company. He's the one who matters to me. We've always welcomed friends of the family here. Eh, we often used to have people to stay. I've missed it.'

He closed his eyes and shook his head slightly, with that sad look, so Maude tried to distract him. 'We'll have to check the times of trains.'

'No need. There's only one in the afternoons that connects with those from the south. But he'll be like you were, expecting to find a taxi, so I'll take the pony and cart into Ollerthwaite and meet that train. There won't be many men on it, especially younger ones. Those who work in the outlying farms or workshops further along the line usually come home on the later local train. It's mostly the women who've been shopping elsewhere and those coming from outside the area who catch the one I'll be meeting.'

'Your grandson didn't give you much information, did he?' Maude commented.

'Telegrams are expensive. I'd not waste my money sending a long message either.'

Walter began walking to and fro as if studying the big farm kitchen. 'You always keep this room nice. I'm glad about that. What's for tea? Do we need to buy anything else? He'll want a good hearty meal after several days of ship's food, I should think.'

'We're having beef stew with pickled red cabbage sprinkled on it,' Elinor said. 'I've grown to like your Lancashire way of serving it. And there will be freshly baked bread to go with it, of course, followed by an apple pie – or there will be once I've baked it.'

'That's good. You make delicious fruit pies, lass. And some custard too, eh? Is there a bedroom ready for him?'

Maude took over. 'Yes. We finished clearing out the big spare bedrooms a while ago. They just need dusting and the bed airing. I'll fill some hot water bottles after we've finished our discussion and put them in the beds. What about the friend? Shall I give him the other big bedroom?'

Walter waved one hand dismissively, clearly not very interested in the friend. 'Is it ready?'

'It is.'

'Good, good.' He stood up. 'I think I'll have a quick walk round and check that everything is neat and tidy outside.'

When he'd gone, they looked at one another.

'He's nervous,' Maude said quietly.

'Who wouldn't be? This is a very important meeting for him.'

'Well, we'd better get on with our share of the preparations.'

Elinor stopped her. 'Are you nervous about meeting the heir, love?

'I am a bit. Walter has said it won't make any difference to our staying here, but you can never be quite sure when someone else joins a household what changes will occur. This man's one of the family so I hope he'll be as nice as Walter.'

'And you.'

'What?'

'As nice as you,' she said.

'I'm only a distant Crossley relative; this American will be the closest Walter has in England now. I hope he's a nice chap.'

Elinor went across to check that the three loaves she'd made earlier were fully risen and put them in the oven to bake, then got a few more ingredients out of the pantry. 'Right then, it's time I started on that apple pie. And I think I'll make some scones as well.'

'We'll have to make bread more often or perhaps buy it from the village baker sometimes. Men usually eat more than women.'

Maude got out two hot water bottles, well-used earthenware 'pigs' that Walter said had belonged to his grandparents, then she kept an eye on the kettle. 'There! It's nearly boiling, plenty hot enough to use.'

By the time Walter left to meet the train, they'd got nearly everything ready and Maude said abruptly, 'Let me redo your hair, love. It's coming loose.'

'Only if you'll let me do yours in the style you wear it on Sundays. We'll both want to look our best.'

'All right. It takes longer to do my hair that way, but I'm thinking of fussing with it a bit more every day because it is more flattering, don't you think?'

'Yes, I do. Isn't it nice to be able to dress how we please?'

'Wonderful. And lovely to do what we want.' Maude proved how happy that made her by starting to sing 'After the ball is over'. She grabbed Elinor and waltzed her round the table in time to it.

Laughing, Elinor let her finish the second rendition of the chorus, then tugged her towards the staircase. 'Stop that, you fool. We need to tidy up.'

As they were finishing getting ready, Elinor said, 'You know what? It's just occurred to me that I've never met an American before.'

"They don't have two heads, but they do talk differently. Like the man who gave a talk at the church group that time. You didn't go because you had a cold but I remember him clearly.' She smiled as she added, 'It seemed a strange accent to me. He told us he spoke with a Texas drawl, so who knows what the heir will sound like because he comes from further north, Walter said.'

But even dancing and fiddling around with their hair hadn't made the time pass quickly enough and they were ready too soon. Neither wanted to start a new task which might mess up the kitchen or themselves, and if truth be told, both of them were a bit on edge.

Still, Walter was such a lovely man and so easy to live with. If the American grandson was at all like him, things would surely go well.

You couldn't help feeling insecure, though, Elinor thought, when you were dependent on someone's goodwill for the roof over your head like she was – especially when you weren't a relative and the others all were.

16

Cameron wriggled uncomfortably and grimaced as he sat down in the final train of the day. 'The seats on this train seem even smaller than those on the two others we've travelled on today.'

'Well, at least it's the last stage and the train's not full, so we've got window seats,' Bryn said.

Hardly had he spoken than there was a rush of passengers pushing their way on at the last minute and the carriage filled up with people and bags of shopping. At least everyone gave them a cheerful nod.

As the train set off, chugging slowly along the mostly single-line track, the two men studied the scenery.

'I like the appearance of those great rolling stretches of hills,' Cameron said.

'Is that an American accent?' the woman next to him asked.

'Yes, ma'am.'

'Well, just so you get the right words, young man, we call that sort of hill a moor round here.'

'Thank you, ma'am. Moor it is.' He caught sight of a glint of silver among the trees in the distance. 'Is that a lake? Water always looks so pretty when the sun is shining on it.'

'The lake never got finished, though,' one man said.

'Well, if folk had known Her Majesty was going to live this long, they might have made a bit more effort to finish it later on,' another woman said. 'They reckon she may even live long enough to celebrate her Diamond Jubilee in 1897. Just imagine that! Sixty years on the throne. It's a long time to reign over us, isn't it?'

'They may still finish the lake in time for that then. What it needs is someone to pull us all into action.'

Another man chipped in, sounding to be in a bad mood. 'What's the point of bothering? The queen will never come to a little valley like ours to see it, whether she has her Diamond Jubilee or not, will she?'

'We'd be able to enjoy it, though. Might even put some little rowing boats on it.'

'And like this American chap says, it'll look pretty.'

The bad-tempered man just snorted at that and went back to his carefully folded newspaper.

Cameron joined in again, enjoying listening to their accents as much as they seemed to be enjoying his. 'I read somewhere that the queen always wears black. Is that true?'

When a couple of people nodded, he said, 'She must have loved that husband of hers to mourn for him like that.'

The man opposite winked at them. 'You don't get nine children unless you're rather friendly with one another.'

The sour-faced man muttered, 'Anyone can get children. It's too damned easy, if you ask me.'

'Well, I hope she does make it to sixty years on the throne,' the woman said. 'No one else has managed that, queen or king, not that I've heard tell, any road. Nor I can't remember having anyone but her on the throne in my whole life. One of her other sons died before her, poor chap. Leopold, wasn't he called? And her eldest son's an old man now and he might even die before her too and never become king at this rate. He sounds to be a rackety sort of fellow.'

'She must be getting a bit feeble by now at that age, queen or not.'

A woman squashed in at the other end of the carriage scoffed loudly at that. 'Get away with you! My parents have been wed for nearly fifty years and they're both still working on the farm. Some folk are lucky and live long, healthy lives; others die younger.'

'Easier to live a long time when you're a queen. You'll be looked after and given whatever you need.'

'Fresh air, good food and hard work is what keeps you going, I reckon,' the woman with old parents said firmly, causing him to scowl at her.

The train started slowing down for the next stop just then and three men got off, two of them calling a cheerful goodbye to everyone, the grumpy one pushing to go first.

Soon afterwards the train slowed down again and the rest of the other passengers stood up and began gathering their things together. When the train pulled to a halt, Bryn opened the carriage door for the woman who was nearest to him.

She paused to say, 'Thank you. Next stop is Ollerthwaite. End of the line, that is.'

'Good. I'll be glad to get there and stretch my legs.'

Shortly afterwards a porter slammed the door of their compartment shut and the train jerked into motion again, leaving them alone in the compartment.

'Friendly folk, weren't they?' Cameron said.

'Most of them. One chap was an old misery, though.'

'I hope my grandfather is a friendly sort.'

'Nervous?' Bryn asked.

'Yeah. I didn't expect to be but I am.'

'You'll be all right.'

Cameron wasn't nearly as sure of that, given what he was about to do.

He got out of the compartment first in Ollerthwaite as agreed, leaving Bryn to deal with the luggage from both the compartment and the baggage van with a porter's help while he found them a taxi.

Other passengers bustled past him, mainly women carrying heavy baskets and bags full of shopping, chatting happily. He looked round but there was no sign saying 'Taxis' anywhere on the small station.

An older man standing in front of the small waiting room was staring at him fixedly and when Cameron caught his gaze, he suddenly realised that this had to be his grandfather because he looked just like an older version of James Crossley. He hadn't expected such a close resemblance between them.

The man was almost devouring him with his eyes and he turned his head to flick away a few tears surreptitiously. That reminded Cameron that he'd lost his son and grandson only a few months ago, and he prayed that he wouldn't make any more trouble for his grandfather.

Oh, hell! Was he doing the right thing? But it was too late to stop it now. He took a deep breath and walked across to him. 'Mr Crossley?'

'Aye, but it might be more appropriate to call me Grandad, don't you think?'

'I didn't want to presume till we were sure of each other's identity.'

'Well, I was sure as soon as I saw you, because you look like a Crossley, so we're both sure now and I'd prefer you to call me Grandad, even if you do say it with an American accent. What do they call you?'

'Cam.'

'I thought your name was Caleb.'

He took a deep breath. First lie coming up. 'My friends call me Cam, based on my initials, C. A. M. But my father doesn't believe in nicknames.'

'I'd rather call you Cam as well, if you don't mind. Let alone I'm hoping we'll be on good terms, I never did like the name Caleb. I read in a book about the meaning of names that it meant "Dog" or "Courageous" which seemed a strange mixture of possibilities.'

He stopped and looked at Bryn, now standing a short distance away from them. A porter who had their luggage on a trolley was next to him, looking somewhat impatient. 'Is this your friend?'

'Yes. This is Bryn Fordham, who helped me on the ship. I'd been attacked and left unconscious in New York, you see, but someone put me on board the ship. I was feeling rather shaky. We became good friends and decided to travel together. Bryn, this is my grandad, Walter Crossley.'

He moved to shake hands with Bryn. 'You're another tall one. Six foot three?'

'Yes. And you're not much shorter, I'd guess, Mr Crossley.'

'Six two. Welcome to Ollerthwaite. I have my pony and trap waiting outside the station.'

After the two younger men had loaded all their luggage on the neat little cart, the porter was tipped and took the trolley away, looking happier now.

Bryn studied the seating arrangements and said, 'I'll ride in the back with our possessions, shall I? You can't fit three big fellows like us on that driving seat comfortably.'

'Aye, you're right. There's an old cushion you can sit on and in the middle of the panel behind the driving seat you'll find a rope loop I fixed for passengers to hold on to when it gets bumpy. Not that we'll be going all that fast. My farm is only about a mile away, just beyond the village of Upperfold. It's mostly a dirt road up a gentle hill and I don't overwork my animals, especially this lass. She's one of the most willing mares I've ever had, my Sally is.'

Walter then turned sideways to continue his intense scrutiny of Cameron. 'You look older than I'd expected.'

'Do I?' Oh, hell, he hadn't considered that aspect.

'We Crossleys often start off with baby faces and never really look our age, at one end of life or the other. But you look as if you're several years older than twenty-two.' He frowned and continued to stare at his grandson.

'And you look younger than I'd thought you would. I've always had to work hard, so perhaps my appearance is due to that. Not that I'm complaining.'

'People don't die of hard work as long as they get enough to eat, and our family are usually long-lived, barring accidents.' His face creased into deep sorrow again and it took him a few seconds to pull himself together.

Cameron guessed that his American grandson's arrival had brought back memories of those he'd lost, memories that were biting sharply. 'I'm sorry about my cousin and uncle,' he said quietly.

'Aye. We all are. They were grand chaps, both of 'em. Life can hit you hard at times. Ready?' He clicked to the pony and they set off.

After a while, Bryn tried to find a happier topic of conversation. 'What sort of work do folk round here do to earn a living? They can't all be farmers.'

'There are all sorts of jobs in Ollerthwaite, but Upperfold is a small village, as you'll see shortly, so there isn't as much going there. People do whatever work they can find to bring in money, sometimes two or three part-time jobs. Most of the ones who're not working in farming find jobs in Ollerthwaite these days, but there's a young woman who's started up as a dressmaker in Upperfold, old Peter Horton who mends and sells bicycles and Mrs Tyler, who's a widow and sells groceries out of her front room.'

'Good for her,' Cam said.

'It's not big enough to be called a shop an' she only stocks everyday items, but it puts bread on her own table if we buy some of our groceries there, so most of us do. And of course, it's also very convenient for housewives with small children to care for, having a shop so close is.'

'It's always good for folk to look after one another,' Bryn said.

'Most of us do, but there are one or two bad eggs in the valley, as there are everywhere. In general, our folk are decent enough, though. There's a Methodist chapel or a church in Ollerthwaite, if you like to attend Sunday services. I don't go to church now.'

'We saw a lake in the distance before the train reached the town,' Cameron said, 'and a man told us it was called Jubilee Lake.'

'Aye, but it were never finished, so it's not much of a lake. I own some of the land at this side of it, an' other folk have bits of land around the shore as well. There's a nice walk down to it from my farm and folk from Ollerthwaite go there in the summer. I don't try to keep folk away from my land. They're usually very good about not leaving a mess. The childer like to go paddling in it and the lads skim pebbles across the water.'

'You own land by a lake?' Cameron asked in surprise. 'Who owns the other pieces of land?'

'The Kenyons own the biggest stretch and two or three people own smaller pieces, and the town owns the southern end. If the Kenyons cared about their estate, we'd all have got together and finished the work we started on it. Maybe we'll do the rest of it without them, like we did the first bit, and finish in time to celebrate the Queen's Diamond Jubilee.'

'The lake's gone back to marsh in a couple of places. Still there's enough open water to catch the light nicely, especially when it reflects a full moon.'

'My father owns a small lake. It was useful for providing water for the animals in dry weather, but he used to get angry if kids dug up the edges. As if you can stop kids mucking around in water in hot weather.'

'I like to see children dabbling in the water,' Walter murmured.

Cameron stared up at the sky and made a sweeping gesture above them with one arm. 'I like the way the moors frame the valley land. You can't see much beyond the houses in towns. I prefer to be out in the countryside.' His pitiful pair of small fields were on the edge of a town. He wondered sometimes how Tom was getting on there.

After a couple more minutes, Walter said, 'It'll be a bit different farming here to what you're used to, I should think, Cam lad.'

'I shall look forward to learning about it. I have a bit of land of my own in America, not big enough to be called a farm, though. I bought it myself; it's not part of the family farm which will one day belong to, um—' He nearly said to his legitimate brothers but changed it hastily to 'my oldest brother'. 'I keep one field as a meadow and folk pay to pasture their horses there temporarily. I grow this and that on the rest of the land, mostly vegetables that sell well at nearby markets. I've left a young friend looking after it for the time being.'

'Your father didn't mention that.'

'No, he wouldn't. He only cares about land he owns and controls.'

'According to him, the land on his farm is fertile and produces well. We have to coax ours into giving us a living. I dabble in a few other things as well to bring in money.'

'I had to coax my land a bit too. The best land was claimed many years previously when my father first settled in the area.'

Walter had been listening with interest but now he reined in the pony and gestured. 'We're nearly there. That's the Crossley farmhouse: Four Lane Ends, it's called.'

There was pride in his voice and rightly so, because it was a very pretty house, larger than Cam had expected, and balanced in style, not a mish-mash like some country places where he came from that had had rooms added haphazardly over the decades.

'It's a very attractive house,' he said softly. 'And a lovely setting.'

It sat happily against a dramatic upward sweep of hillside leading up to the top of the moors, and was built of an attractive mixture of buff and grey stones, with a dark slate roof. There were some outbuildings to the right-hand side and clustered around them were a few small trees some of which were in blossom. It looked like a small orchard.

He realised afterwards that he'd fallen in love with it straight away, before he even saw the interior. Somehow, even its windows seemed to be twinkling a welcome to him.

Oh, how he longed to put down roots somewhere. Would he be allowed to stay here? He did hope so.

Maude watched the cart turn into their drive. 'Let's go out to greet them. It feels silly to sit here and wait. We never do that when it's just Walter. We'll go out and help him unload whatever he's brought back.'

'All right.'

The men didn't see them at first because Walter was pointing out something on the slopes above the farm, so the two women had an opportunity to study the newcomers.

'It's obvious which one is the grandson,' Maude said. 'He looks like a younger version of Walter, doesn't he?'

'Yes. And there's a distinct resemblance to you, as well.'

'Blood will tell, but I'd rather be pretty like you.'

'I'm not pretty!'

'You weren't before but you are now. Don't look so disbelieving. You *are* pretty.'

By this time Elinor was a bit pink, but smiling because Maude would never lie to her.

The man who wasn't a Crossley must have heard their voices because he looked across as he got down from the cart and nodded to them. The other two men were still talking.

They went across to him.

'You must be the friend,' Maude said to him. 'Welcome to Upperfold.'

Elinor echoed her welcome then said, 'What tall people you all are! I'm not short but I feel it compared to you four.'

Walter and his grandson came round from the other side of the cart to join them just then. 'This is Cam, as you'll have guessed. This is a distant Crossley cousin, Maude Vernon, and this is her cousin on her mother's side, Elinor Pendleton. They came to live with me recently and are now acting as house-keepers and Maude is also turning into a dab hand with the chickens.'

'Lovely to meet you, Maude and Elinor. I'm Cam to my friends.'

'Why not Caleb?'

'Because Cam is what my initials spell.' He gestured to the white letters painted on his luggage.

Maude said, 'It must get confusing. Thank goodness no one can shorten my name, friend or foe.'

'It does cause confusion sometimes.' He was relieved that they'd accepted his explanation.

'Can we help you take your things inside?'

Bryn was already lifting one of Walter's boxes off the rear of the cart. 'Cam and I will see to the unloading. The trunks are a bit heavy for ladies.'

'How about you lasses make us all a cup of tea while we do that?' Walter suggested. 'I'll show the lads where to put my things, then take them upstairs to see the bedrooms they'll be using.'

When they went inside, Elinor whispered to Maude, 'They look nice, don't they? Cam's quite good looking, isn't he?'

Maude nodded and was secretly glad to hear her say that. She was hoping her friend would get on well with the heir. It'd fit so neatly. 'Well, Walter seems comfortable with the two of them, which can only be a good sign.'

By the time they produced the tea, the men had unloaded the cart and seemed glad to be offered some refreshments.

Cam took a mouthful of tea and smiled. 'Ah, that's good. It's nice to drink real tea again. A lot of Americans don't seem to make it properly, but my father taught the whole family what he called "the right way" to do it. He loves his mug of tea.'

After they'd enjoyed the cups of tea, the two visitors went up to unpack, while the women set the table for the evening meal.

Maude found herself next to Bryn when they sat down for their meal and asked him whether he was a farmer too.

He shook his head. 'No. I'm a carpenter.'

Walter looked across at him. 'Have you done your apprenticeship?'

'Yes, sir. In England a couple of decades ago, but even though I've been travelling, I've kept up with my skills, because I still had to earn my way. And I've picked up a few other skills, like carving.' He waited, head cocked enquiringly, because he guessed there was a reason for asking this and wasn't sure how much detail to go into.

'I have a small barn near the old watermill that's in need of some woodwork replacing. It's the oldest barn in the district and I'd like it done properly, so I'd be happy to pay you to do it if you're looking for work. You'd be in demand for other carpentry work round here, too, because we had a bad storm last winter and we don't have a carpenter in the village at the moment. Most folk have kept their places waterproof but some of them look a right old mess.'

'I'll be happy to take a look at your barn, sir, but if you're putting me up, you don't need to pay me.'

'I prefer to. As the Bible says, the labourer is worthy of his hire.'

'And *her* hire,' Maude put in with a challenging look.

'Aye, you're right there, lass. And you two are shining examples of being worthy of your hire. I respect hard workers, male or female.'

Maude felt happy at his response. After the years of Stafford treating her as if she was invisible and never saying thank you for anything, she was determined never to be ignored again and treated as if she knew nothing.

'I shall enjoy doing some work with wood,' Bryn said. 'I might have to send for the rest of my tools first, though. A friend in Rochdale is looking after them for me.'

'I have plenty of tools. You may find what you need among them and I'd be happy to lend them to you. We'll check the barn in a day or two and then go through my tools to see if the ones you need are there – but not till you've had time to recover from your travels and settle in.'

He looked out of the window. 'It's getting to the warmer weather and I'd recommend a few walks in the fresh air to set your bodies to rights. You're looking very tired now.'

'We could take them for a stroll down to the lake tomorrow afternoon,' Maude said.

'I'd like that,' Bryn said.

Cam concentrated on his meal, making appreciative noises as he ate. When he'd cleared the plate he smiled across at his cousin. 'Who's the cook or do you both do it? That was absolutely delicious. I should warn you that I have a hearty appetite.'

Maude gestured to her friend. 'Cooking is mainly Elinor's job. I've never had much to do with that sort of thing but she's taken to it like a duck to water since we came here.'

'It's easy to cook good meals when you get good fresh ingredients and plenty of them,' Elinor said.

The plates were cleared away and dessert served. The apple pie won everyone's praise and vanished completely once the visitors were persuaded into second helpings.

When the women started to clear the table, the two men immediately got up to help.

'We can manage,' Elinor said.

'Why should you? It'll be much quicker with us all helping you and I bet you started early in the morning if you had to bake the bread as well as do everything else around the house.'

'You're right.'

'I hadn't thought about bread,' Walter said. 'We'll order ours from the village bakery from now on. It's a thankless, never-ending task. But I'd far rather have your apple pies than theirs, if you don't mind, lass. I'm very fond of fruit pies. The bilberries will be ripe in August and they're delicious in pies too, particularly good with a few strawberries added.'

'What are bilberries?' Cameron asked.

'Small near-black berries that grow on low bushes on the edge of the moors.'

'They sound like American blueberries. I'll look forward to tasting them.' Cameron fell silent, realising he'd already started thinking of staying here.

When he caught his grandfather's eye, the old man gave him a friendly nod, and it made him feel accepted in a sense he'd never experienced in his father's house. He didn't want to do anything to disappoint the old man, and he doubted he could keep his secret for a lifetime, but he would prefer to choose his own time to tell him the truth about who he was.

Later, when the visitors couldn't hold back yawns, Walter waved one hand towards the stairs. 'Travelling leaves a person weary, doesn't it? If you two want to have an early night, we won't take offence. We're not late owls ourselves.'

'If you don't mind, I will go to bed,' Cam said.

'Me too.' Bryn pushed his chair back.

The room felt very quiet without them because even when they weren't talking they had been 'there'.

'They seem a nice pair of chaps,' Walter said softly. 'I'm looking forward to showing them round the farm tomorrow. But don't forget to take them for a walk in the afternoon.'

'I'll look forward to it,' Elinor said. 'I love walking by the water.'

'Might be a bit of luck that Bryn is a carpenter. We're lacking one in the valley.' He stood up. 'I'll leave you to finish your reading and get off to my own bed.

Maude put her book down. 'I'm tired too. I think I'll go straight to bed as well.'

As she snuggled down, she thought of how easily Elinor and Cam had chatted. She'd sneaked a few glances at them. She hoped she wasn't imagining this and hoped it would continue. Who knew what might come of it?

It'd suit everyone so well. She musn't push them though. It was early days yet.

Walter was lying awake feeling rather puzzled about this heir of his. He kept trying to work out why. He liked Cam, who was definitely a Crossley, but he couldn't quite figure him out. His grandson seemed far more mature than the twenty-two years he was supposed to be, according to what James had told him in his letters.

What's more, he distinctly remembered James saying a couple of years ago, that Cam – only he'd always called him Caleb – wasn't showing much interest in farming. But this young man's understanding of how to grow things and care for animals was broader than could have been expected at that age and he clearly enjoyed it.

Nothing quite fitted.

He'd have to wait and see how things went. If a person was hiding something, it often came out if you gave them enough time.

Cam seemed like a decent young chap, though, if Walter was any judge. People were not always easy creatures to figure out, but he didn't usually make big mistakes about their basic nature.

Already he didn't want this young man to turn out to be anything but the expected heir.

17

When he got up the next morning Walter found Cam standing outside studying the hillsides near the house.

'Couldn't you sleep, lad?'

'I've never needed a lot of sleep and I'm an early morning person.'

'Me, too. Let's walk round the nearest fields. I like to check that the sheep are all right, even though I don't look after them myself these days. It'll give you a bit of a feel for this sort of land.'

'I've never farmed sheep. They're not common in our part of the world. If I ask any questions that sound stupid, please bear with me. I'm a quick learner.'

'Sheep like these do well on the moors here, because they're hardy. There's shelter in the sheds in the lower fields during the worst of winter. I've never kept a big flock, though, and a neighbour looks after them now.'

Cam listened with obvious interest to explanations, asking intelligent questions, and by hell, the longer Walter spent with him, the more he liked him.

But there was still something that seemed not to fit the type of person he'd been told to expect. He didn't like any sort of mystery about someone who might inherit the family farm.

When they got back to the farmhouse, they saw bread on the table, a toasting fork next to the open fire of the cooking range and bacon to hand on a plate near a frying pan. Bryn was already tucking into a hearty meal while chatting to the two women, who were waiting to cook breakfast for the others.

After everyone had eaten their fill, Walter said, 'Why don't you two lasses take Bryn and Cam for a walk down to the lake? It's such a sunny morning you'll see it at its best. And you'll get a good idea of what our valley is like by walking round some of it.'

Four people stared at him, clearly surprised by this suggestion, then Maude said, 'If you don't need us for a while, Cousin Walter, I'd like that. The lake is one of my favourite places. Sometimes the water glints so brightly you feel as if you could pick up a handful of silver.'

Cam turned to his grandfather. 'You're sure there's nothing we can do to help you?'

'Not till you're properly recovered from travelling.'

'You'll have to leave me out, I'm afraid,' Elinor said. 'I need to bake another batch of bread.'

'Well, as I have a bit of business to sort out in Ollerthwaite, it'd suit me to have the morning free. And I could bring some loaves back, Elinor, and save you the trouble. I'd not like you to miss out on a walk with your friends, especially on such a lovely day as this.'

She stared at him, then at Maude as if asking her friend what to do. 'Well, I would like to go down to the lake. It's my favourite place.'

Maude put an arm round her. 'Mine too. I'd hate to move away from here. I love the valley already.'

They set off soon afterwards, with Maude leading the way at first, and then the group forming and reforming as one conversation led to another and changed the pairings. She was surprised at how well they all got on. It was rare to feel so comfortable with people you'd only just met. But then, Cam was Walter's grandson and therefore some sort of cousin and she'd felt the same instant rapport with him, too.

Once again, they could see the water before they got to it, sparkling in the sunlight, and since the grass was dry, they sat on a grassy mound, looking out over the lake.

'Walter said he'd be out for a couple of hours, so we could go right round the lake,' Maude suggested after a while. 'There's no proper path round the top end, but so many people have walked there that there's a clear way through.'

'Will you two be all right to do that?' Bryn asked. 'The terrain looks a bit hilly and rough.'

Elinor laughed. 'We're not weaklings.'

Which she and Maude both proved.

The following morning after breakfast Walter said, 'You two lads are looking a lot livelier today. Let's go out to the old watermill this afternoon. It's a nice drive along by the river. I like to check up on the place regularly, since no one lives there now. I've chased tramps out of it more than once.'

'Are you keeping an eye on it for the owner?'

'Well, um, actually, I'm the owner. I've bought one or two old buildings round here whose owners were moving away.'

Cameron looked at him in surprise.

'You can pick them up very cheaply indeed when no one is able to live there any longer because there's no work to be had locally in the foreseeable future. I don't like to see buildings fall into disrepair when they might be needed again one day. I own one or two places in our village. I had some money saved. What better use to put it to? And I do get rent money in return from some of them, if not as much as people paid before.'

He didn't tell the two younger men how many properties he now owned scattered up and down Ollindale. He'd tried to keep that a secret from everyone. 'If I've learned one thing in life, it's that circumstances change, and you never know what'll come in useful in the future. I don't like to see our valley going to rack and ruin.'

'You said there were some houses not occupied in the village, even so,' Bryn commented. 'Why is that? These days people can usually travel to work.'

'It started happening all over Lancashire years ago when steam engines took over providing the power in the mills. People gradually shut down the small water-powered mills, especially if they were in narrow valleys with less level land, because those places were harder for the bigger new drays carrying goods to reach. The mill owners wanted places where they could set up to do work like spinning or weaving far more cheaply on a huge scale. In one sense, I'm glad they never built any of the huge, steam-driven cotton mills here, but I wish they'd found other uses for our part of the world so that there would still be work on offer.'

'You've lived through times of great change,' Cameron said.

'Aye. And heard the tales of previous changes from my father and grandfather. Many of the old watermills are in ruins now, unlike ours, or demolished and the stones reused to build homes or barns. I'll find a use for my old mill one day, if only as a dwelling. It'd make a nice home for a big family, actually.'

'You should write down all you've experienced,' Elinor said. 'One day people will want to know about how life has changed. I find your tales very interesting.'

'Nay, I'm no wordsmith.'

'But you are! You paint a vivid picture of times gone by.'

He just stared, not seeming to believe that.

'It's a pity the cart isn't bigger,' Maude said. 'I'd have liked to see the old watermill after hearing you talk about it, Walter.'

He looked at her thoughtfully. 'Would you now?' He shot a questioning glance at Elinor and she nodded.

'We could all fit on the cart if you two lads don't mind jolting around in the back. We're not carrying anything else today except for a few tools in case of repairs being needed. And we'll not be going up any steep hills. I don't see why you lasses should always have to stay at home.'

He watched Elinor's face light up, surprised at how pretty she was looking these days. He noticed Cam studying her, and Maude watching them both.

She was a bit of a dark horse, his cousin Maude was. He reckoned the phrase 'still waters run deep' fitted some quiet people as much as it fitted waterways. But he thought she shared his interest in finding out whether Elinor would make a good wife for Cam. No use pushing the two of them towards it, though. It seemed to him that these two were both a bit wary of marriage.

They set off soon after their midday meal. 'It'll be a bumpy ride, I'm afraid, because the river road is more of a track than a road,' Walter said apologetically as they turned right at the crossroads and started up the gentle slope. 'But it's the prettiest route by far. Not many people use it these days and I can see it needs a bit of repair work. Eh, there's always a list of things needing to be done.'

'I could help you with that, Grandad,' Cameron said without thinking, then hoped it'd be true.

When the horse slowed down to avoid some even deeper ruts, Walter shook his head in dismay. 'This is worse than I'd expected. I usually come out here to fill in the worst of the potholes towards the end of winter, but I wasn't feeling, um, very energetic this year.' He'd let a lot of small things slip this year.

'Bryn and I could put a bit of work in on this track,' Cam said. 'With two of us, we could soon sort out the worst of the potholes.'

'I'll take you up on that and thank you for the offer.' Walter couldn't fault Cam on his attitude to work, that was sure. Or Bryn, who had already done a few small repair jobs on the farmhouse outbuildings without needing to be asked.

The lasses were rosy-cheeked now, clearly enjoying their ride in the fresh air. They'd told him they weren't young any longer and were past being called lasses, but they still seemed young to him because in some ways they'd been untouched by life, shut away almost.

'We have to go past the old mill when we come this way, but you can't see the water wheel properly because of the wall built to stop children playing there and falling in. There's a turn-off beyond it that leads round to an open space at the other side of the mill. Folk used to tether their horses and leave their carts there when they came on business. There's another track leads to it from behind the village but it's not in as bad a condition as this one because there are a few small farms strung along the far end.'

They drove round the mill buildings to the rear space, which was gravelled but had weeds sprouting all over it at the moment. Walter pointed to one side. 'The owners had a vegetable garden there and they built up some good soil, but I haven't had time to touch it so it's badly overgrown now. The fruit trees are still producing, though. You get a nice cooking apple from one of them and I've been letting some of the women from the village come out to pick them, and I've taken baskets of them along to some of the old folk.'

When they'd got down from the cart, he led the way further round the side of the building to where the water wheel that powered the mill was situated.

Elinor exclaimed in surprise at the size of it, because it was taller than any of them. It was set in an artificial, stone-lined channel into which water was diverted from the River Oller.

'When they built the mill, they put it where the river narrows and flows more rapidly,' he said. 'Perfect spot for it.'

'That channel is like a miniature canal, then,' she said.

'We call it a mill race.'

The wheel was turning slowly as if it were tired and as it swooshed in and out of the water, they could see that quite a few slats of wood were missing.

Walter flapped one hand towards it. 'That wheel will need repairing before it can work properly again. I haven't done anything about that because that job is beyond my skills. I don't know whether it's the sort of thing you could deal with, Bryn?'

'I could have a closer look at the wheel, Mr Crossley, but I'd also need to find out how to stop the water flowing through into the channel before I could get to it safely, wouldn't I? And I'd need help. It'll be a two-man job.'

Walter pointed. 'Those are gates lying flat against the wall and you wind them out to cut off the water, but they haven't been opened or shut for years so I don't know if the gates would still work.'

As they walked back to the open space he stopped and pointed to a small wooden building he'd passed without comment before. 'That's the barn that needs repairing properly. It takes the brunt of the wind when there's a storm. They should have built it of stone like the rest, but I suppose it was put on later as an afterthought and they saved money by doing it like that. Ah well, I knew about that when I bought it so I shouldn't complain. We'll look inside the mill now we've seen all the outside, shall we?'

'What state is it in?' Bryn asked.

'The inside of it never seems to need much by way of repairs, and fewer than I'd expected have been needed to the outside, either, apart from that blasted barn. They were built to last in the old days, using good solid stone, unlike some of them terraces of shoddy houses in Ollerthwaite. The bricks are starting to crumble on them after only a couple of decades, while the walls of this mill are intact nearly two hundred years later. Look! There's a date stone set in the wall: 1710.'

They all got down from the cart, with the two younger men helping the women, then Walter led the way into the mill itself, turning left into a large room full of the machinery attached to the shaft from the water wheel. They all stopped instinctively to study the unfamiliar shapes.

'I always feel as if this machinery is sleeping, waiting for someone to wake it up.' Walter rested one hand on the nearest structure as if greeting it.

Maude stood with her head leaning back, looking round the room. 'There don't seem to have been any leaks in here but it could do with a good clean. Look at the dirt on those windows.'

'I'll have it cleaned if and when there's a prospect of someone finding a use for it; otherwise it'd be wasted effort.'

He gestured to some doorways in the walls of the big room. 'The working areas and storage rooms are all at this side of the building and there's an upstairs part that's not used. You can also get to that from the other side, where the family lived. The main entrance to that family area is through that other door in the hall. I'd just like to check that there's no tramp broken in anywhere. I had to board up the kitchen window last time and what with one thing and another I haven't replaced the glass. One intruder had left a broken window to let the weather in. I'd like to give him a good drubbing. Good thing it was summer and I found it before we had any storms.'

To Walter's relief, there were no signs of broken windows or intruders this time.

The others walked round the living area, where there was a huge kitchen table of scrubbed but now dusty wood. The sink was an old-fashioned slopstone made of sandstone with a pump style tap at one corner. The sitting room was next door and still contained a couple of heavy wooden settles. Upstairs there were some bed bases which needed the ropes restringing to hold the mattresses evenly but were otherwise perfectly usable still.

'They didn't take the really heavy stuff and it's just stood here for years,' Walter said. He went to find Bryn, who seemed more interested in the mill's interior and was pacing up and down it.

'I'll show you the inside of that barn now.'

Bryn studied it. 'Your repairs have certainly kept it water-proof, Mr Crossley, but I think I can make it look neater than this and still keep the weather out.'

'Can you give me a price for the repairs?'

'Not yet. I'd need to check more carefully and look at prices of new pieces of wood. Where do you buy your milled wood from?'

'There's a wood merchant in Ollerthwaite, but if it's any-thing fancy he has to order it in. He can't afford to carry a large stock.'

Bryn looked round the shed thoughtfully. 'It might be best if I charged you for my work by the hour and you covered the costs of material. I'm out of touch with prices of wood in Eng-land after so long overseas. And if you want it doing straight away, I'll need to borrow some of your tools till mine can be sent on to me. I'm out of touch with wages here too, so how about you pay me what you consider fair?'

'All right. I'll have a think and ask around, then we'll discuss money again.' Walter pulled out his watch. 'It's about time we went back now.'

He locked up carefully and drove them back along the river track.

As they passed the two small cottages, Cameron pointed to them. 'Those cottages don't look occupied, either.'

'No, they're not at the moment. They used to look pretty when the gardens were in bloom and the windows sparkled at you. One of the families who used to live there went off to work in the Midlands. There's a fellow there who's started to build motor cars. I've read about that sort of thing in the newspaper, how several people are starting to build cars in England. If they go on at this rate, there will be a few motor vehicles in every town and then how will people stay safe?'

He scowled and fell silent for a moment or two, then burst out, 'They should never remove the need for a man to walk ahead of motor vehicles with a red flag even in the country, if you ask me, and they should imprison people who drive at more than the legal limit. Four miles an hour is plenty fast enough.'

'They go faster than that in America,' Cameron said. 'There were quite a few motor vehicles on the roads where I lived. People are getting used to seeing them driving round and learning to listen or watch out for them.'

Walter scowled at that thought.

'I'd have bought a motor car if I could have afforded it. They get you about far more quickly than horses and they don't need feeding and grooming every day, so they're easier to look after.'

'Do you know how to drive?' Maude asked.

'I've had a go. It's not all that hard. My father was thinking of buying one. He liked to keep up with modern inventions.'

'I'd love to ride in one,' Maude said. 'I've only just learned to ride a bicycle and I enjoy doing that. Would I be able to drive a car, do you think?'

Cameron smiled at her eager tone. 'It can be harder to get the car engine started than to actually drive the vehicle around once it's going. You're probably strong enough to turn the starting handle, but smaller women often aren't.'

'I never thought about that side of things.'

'Not as many women seem to want to drive cars anyway, but younger men are often wild to have a go at it.'

'Well, I'm going to try doing all sorts of new things now I'm not working for that horrible man,' Maude said, with a defiant toss of the head.

Walter smiled at her, his anger at the thought of motor vehicle speeds subsiding in his admiration for her spirited approach to life. 'You're a true Crossley, my girl. It's tomboys we breed, not mimsy-pimsy misses.'

'Elinor might not be a Crossley but she's not mimsy-pimsy, either,' Maude declared.

'Neither of you are in any way that I've seen, thank goodness.'

When they got back to the farm, Walter showed the two men where he kept his tools. 'You can borrow any that may be of use to you, Bryn. Have a look through them. I need to go out again.'

He gulped down a quick cup of tea, harnessed Sally to his small cart again and drove off, this time not heading down towards the village but going straight across the road from Upperfold. He hadn't said where he was going but when Maude noticed where he went she wondered yet again what lay on the other side of the crossroads. He'd said there was an old ruined house, but hadn't gone into details.

Cameron came to the front door of the farm. 'I think I'll walk into the village and have a look round. There's still time before tea, isn't there?'

'Why don't you take one of the bicycles?' Maude asked. 'I was going to cycle in to order bread to be delivered every day from now on, which Walter suggested we do. But if you're going perhaps you could save me a journey and call in at the baker's. Order three loaves for tomorrow morning, to be charged to Walter and delivered here, then alternating two and three loaves a day.'

'All right. Happy to help you'.

Cameron was glad to be on his own for a while. He cycled slowly, feeling even more guilty about taking Caleb's place as heir now that he'd got to know his grandfather. It wasn't because he was taking it away from his half-brother, with whom he was still furiously angry, but because he liked and respected his grandfather. At least he hadn't engineered this situation himself.

Walter was clearly delighted to have gained an heir and yet he sometimes frowned slightly as he looked at Cameron, as if he knew something wasn't quite right and couldn't work out what it was. And he'd commented a couple of times that Cameron looked older than he'd expected. Of course he did. He was several years older than Caleb. He hadn't considered that when he decided to come here and take Caleb's place.

Oh hell, what was he going to do about it all?

He went to the baker's first and caught them just about to close, buying some leftover scones and a cake, then making sure they'd continue to deliver loaves to the farm every day.

The woman smiled at him. 'Happy to do that but it'll be an extra penny per loaf each day as you're further out than everyone else.'

'That's fine.'

Cameron wandered out again and strolled round the village centre, which didn't take long. It wasn't a well-planned village but a higgledy-piggledy collection of houses that had gathered there over the centuries. Some were tiny cottages, but one or two double-fronted two-storey houses were bigger than the others. None of the dwellings on the main thoroughfare was nearly as large as Walter's farmhouse, though, and Cameron saw nothing either in or near the village that looked like a manor house or an imposing home.

He realised now that his grandfather was one of the leading lights of the district, if not the most important citizen. There was a mayor in Ollerthwaite but people shrugged when he was mentioned.

When he met an old man sitting on a wooden bench, who seemed eager to get talking to him, he stopped to say good afternoon and introduce himself, garnering information that Joe Silcock was only too ready to volunteer.

He asked Joe if there were any gentry resident in the village, but learned that there wasn't anyone like that now, because the Kenyons' house had burned down a decade ago. The old man spat sideways when he mentioned them, so clearly they hadn't been liked.

'That family still owns the land, well, we think they do because no one else has come and took it over, have they? Nice land it were once when it were looked after proper. And of course they still own cottages in the village, and send that agent of theirs to collect the rent every week or two. He's a nasty chap, that Hatton is.' His expression said that he thought very badly of the family and the agent both.

'Is the burned down house far out of the village?'

'It's up your way, only you turn left instead of right at the crossroads to get to it. It's only a few hundred yards away, but the trees hide what's left of it.'

'What happened to the Kenyons?'

'As far as we know they went to live somewhere in Halifax when their house burned down and they never came back. Nor we don't want 'em back, either.'

'They weren't liked?'

'No. And look how they left it! The ruins are still standing, all black they are, but some other walls have fallen down lately. You'd think they'd have had the rest of them knocked down, wouldn't you, in case children get themselves hurt because lads will go and play there, whether anyone forbids them to or not. No, the damned Kenyons have done nothing to look after the place since they left!'

Cameron made an encouraging noise and Joe took it as a sign to continue.

'Before them it were the Ollertons as lived there – the town were named after them, well, after the Oller part of their name anyway. It's an old-fashioned name for alders, the trees, that is. But the last of the Ollertons lost a lot of money on something called stocks and shares, whatever that may mean, an' they had to sell the estate.'

'It's a form of gambling, but on whether businesses will succeed or not, instead of on cards.'

The old man shook his head disapprovingly. 'Stupid folk, gamblers of any sort, if you ask me.'

'I agree absolutely with you there.'

'Anyway, Dick Rainford used to be the lodgekeeper. He and his wife still live in the old lodge and keep an eye on the place, but they only get paid a pittance for doing it these days.'

'How do they manage, then?'

'Walter Crossley does what he can to help them. He takes them eggs and such. They're getting a bit old now. Dick must be over seventy I reckon because I'm seventy-five, and I'm five year older him but I've got a daughter as looks after me.'

Cameron sneaked a quick glance at his pocket watch and realised he was spending too long chatting. He thanked Joe for the information, slipped him sixpence to buy himself a drink and asked for directions to the lake.

He found it easily, pausing to study it again. Eh, it was lovely. He went past it to one edge to throw stones in and see if he could make them skim across the top of the water, but didn't let himself stay long. Time to go back to the farm.

He found it an easy walk back up the hill and Walter was in the kitchen sipping a cup of tea.

'Go far, did you?'

'Into the village and back by the lake. I got talking to an old man. Joe was telling me about the Kenyons and their house burning down. He didn't think much of them.'

'No one did. Nasty lot they were, thought themselves kings of the earth because they'd made a lot of money and bought the biggest house in the village. Our Lancashire folk are independent-minded, and not given to kow-towing, so the Kenyons didn't get the reaction they were expecting when they moved here, except from those who went to work for them as servants an' had to bow an' scrape, so to speak.'

Cameron was a bit surprised at the scowl that accompanied this description of the Kenyons because Walter didn't usually speak ill of people. He didn't comment on that, however.

'Joe said there's someone still living at the lodge, even though the big house was burned down.'

'Yes, the Rainfords. Nice old couple but they're struggling to feed themselves, they're paid so little. Only they've been there for decades, so even the Kenyons didn't like to throw them out.' Then Walter said he had some accounts to go over, so Cameron went outside and followed the sound of hammering. He found Bryn repairing the side of a small shed and helped him out for half an hour till they were called in to wash their hands and eat their tea.

And all the time he found himself glancing up at the moors. One day he'd go for a walk up there. They felt to be calling to him, wide open spaces where you could stride out for miles.

He really liked the feeling of the countryside in this part of the world: the village, the moors, the stone walls making patterns on the hillside. Most of the houses were built of stone too. He didn't know why he liked that so much more than brick or wood, but he did.

He wanted very much to stay here. But the trouble was he didn't want to base his presence on the lies he'd told.

Only how was he going to tell Walter the truth without being sent packing?

18

The next day Bryn decided to go to the barn at the old mill to take accurate measurements and work out how to make proper repairs to the place. As they were finishing breakfast he asked Walter if he could go round the inside of the mill again, because he'd enjoyed looking at the machinery. 'And is it all right if I take one of the bicycles to get there and back?'

'Of course it is. As long as the ladies don't need it.' He looked at them across the table.

'I'll be working outside here, so I won't need one,' Maude said.

'I'm going to reorganise the pantry today, so I'm not going anywhere,' Elinor said. 'It's making a big difference to my time already not to have to keep baking bread.'

'Well, I've been eating loaves from the village baker's for years,' Walter said. 'They're good and I'm happy to continue buying from them.'

'I think theirs is better than mine, actually.'

He gave her a slight smile. 'Well, let's say they are both delicious and yours got an advantage by being warm from the oven.'

She laughed. 'You're being too kind.'

'I'll show you where the keys are kept, Bryn lad.' He opened the pantry door and pointed out which key to take from a line of them hanging out of sight of visitors on this inner wall. 'Make sure you put it back where you got it from when you return it.'

'I'll do that, sir.' He couldn't help wondering what all the other keys were for, but as Walter didn't volunteer that information he didn't ask.

He whistled cheerfully as he cycled along the path beside the river with a few basic tools clinking about in the metal basket fixed over the front wheel. This wasn't a big river but it was pretty. The water was sparkling clear and sounded cheerful as it made its way over the beds of pebbles. Could water sound cheerful? Well, it did to him today.

The air here in the valley tasted good and he breathed deeply as he rode. This was better than the smoky air of mill towns, that was sure.

He didn't see anyone on his way there and that suited him just fine. He hadn't had much time to himself since he got to New York and he'd loathed the crowded conditions on the ship. Thank goodness he'd been able to share that cabin with Cam.

It didn't seem to take him as long as he'd expected to get to the old mill this time. Well, he could cycle faster than the pony could trot, especially when it was pulling a cart full of people.

He went first to study the stonework holding up the sides of the mill race. The walls didn't look as if they needed any attention; it was the wheel itself that wasn't in good shape. When he studied it closely, it looked as though someone had deliberately damaged some of the struts. Why would anyone do that? There wasn't even anyone living out here. New ones were needed in a few places and he wouldn't be able to move the wheel around to repair these on his own. It was clearly a two-person job.

He took his bicycle inside the mill with him and locked the door behind him. Walter had mentioned break-ins, presumably by men on the tramp seeking shelter for a night or two, or for even longer perhaps. You couldn't be too careful when you were on your own. The mugging he'd suffered in New York had made him a lot more wary about safety.

What did people say? *Fool me once, shame on you; fool me twice, shame on me.* He'd read somewhere that it was a very old saying, centuries old. No wonder it had stayed in use; it was very apt. He definitely wouldn't be taken by surprise again if he could help it.

He pottered around the mill side of the building's interior, checking out the various pieces of apparatus, comparing them in his mind with machinery he had seen in America. Some of this could be adapted to working with wood. But would people need or want the sort of wooden articles he could provide?

If he did set up a business here, it'd be best not to set up in a big way to start off with, but build it up step by careful step. He'd bet Walter Crossley would have contacts in the district and would help him. He'd ask the older man's advice about whether it'd be worthwhile to set up at all, and which products might sell more easily.

Afterwards he went to explore the living quarters in the other part of the mill. He found all sorts of oddments left lying around in the backs of cupboards and drawers. You wouldn't have to buy a lot of household equipment if you were just one person living simply.

All in all, he came away from the old mill feeling thoughtful and fairly optimistic that the place might serve his purpose.

Would he make doing this dependent on Cam settling in the district? Or did he want to stay here whatever Cam did? He'd prefer to have a friend nearby, but he'd come to realise that there was some problem about the inheritance. Cam hadn't shared the details with anyone, so Bryn couldn't be sure what it was and how things would go. All he could be sure of were his own plans and hopes.

What staying would be most dependent on was Walter Crossley being willing to let the old mill to him and not charging too high a rent. Surely he wouldn't? In return Bryn could take over the maintenance of the mill, which would save its owner time, trouble and money. And later on Bryn hoped to be able to create a job or two. Walter would value that possibility greatly, he now knew. That man cared so much about his valley folk.

Bryn decided to raise the matter tonight. He was always like this with a new project: analysing the situation carefully and once he'd come to a decision acting on it quickly.

Well, why delay when something felt right?

As the evening meal came to a close, Bryn took a deep breath and said it. 'Could I have a private word with you if you've finished your meal, Mr Crossley?'

Walter looked slightly surprised but said, 'Yes, of course. We can go into my office and leave the others in peace.' He led the way across the yard and into the cosy little office, gesturing to a seat. 'Is there some problem about the jobs I asked you to do at the mill?'

'It's not about those, sir. It's about an idea I have for setting up a business here in Ollindale.' Bryn noticed how much more alert his companion suddenly became.

'You want to set up a business in our valley?'

'Yes. Well, I think I do. Just a small one. But I'd really appreciate your advice about my idea first.'

'I'm happy to give it. Go on.'

'Well, you know I'm a carpenter, but while I was travelling I also learned to do wood carving. I started as an amateur, fiddling around with small pieces to pass the time. I loved it. In one town there was a carver and when he saw my work he asked if I'd like to train to do the carving properly. I stayed there for three years doing an unofficial apprenticeship with a man who was a master craftsman.' He paused, wondering whether he was telling too much.

Walter smiled. 'Go on.'

'Edgar produced some absolutely beautiful pieces that took my breath away. It turned out I had a talent for it too – at least he said I did. And I'd already sold some of my carvings as I travelled so I know people really do like them enough to pay me.'

He paused and looked at Walter, receiving a nod to continue. 'I intend to do two sorts of carvings as part of a carpentry business: one sort ornamental and the other sort carvings that fit into pieces of wooden furniture, such as the tops of chair backs or mirror frames. Both types sold well over there and should do all right here.'

Again, Walter nodded. 'I agree.'

'Makers of furniture seemed to like small embellishments. I can do gilding too. Mirror frames look particularly good when gilded.'

'And you want to do that sort of thing from the old mill?' Walter frowned. 'Do you need somewhere as big as that?'

'Long-term I hope to need it, if I succeed. I've been planning pieces in my head as I travelled and sketching them. I'm longing to start now. I really liked how it felt out there by the river, so peaceful and beautiful too. I think I could work well there and to have a home there as well would be . . . well, absolutely wonderful.'

'It is a nice, peaceful spot.'

'I'd start by working on my own but later, if my pieces sell here as well as they did in America, I'd hope to employ a couple of people to work for me, one of them at least a proper apprentice.'

'But why not open a workshop in Ollerthwaite or Upperfold? It'd be more convenient for transport.'

'Because I'd like to put the water wheel to use again in a small way driving machinery, once I can afford to buy some more components, that is. We could produce parts for chairs, tables, mirror frames, that sort of thing, so much more easily with water power to do the hard work. I have no ambition whatsoever to become a large-scale manufacturer, just to – well, make a niche for myself and earn a reasonable living.'

He'd probably talked for too long so he forced himself to stop and be patient as Walter sat looking thoughtful and staring into space.

Eventually he focused on Bryn again. 'I think that's an excellent idea. You can have the place rent free for a year, on condition that you do all the maintenance needed and that you supply me at the end of the year with a new carved frame for the mirror on my sitting-room wall, a fancy, gilded one.' He leaned back and waited.

It was a moment before Bryn could respond, because the offer was so generous it took his breath away. 'That's incredibly kind of you, sir.'

'It would suit both of us because you'd be helping with one of my principal aims, finding more jobs for people here. I've seen my valley fade and die as one family after another moved away. I want to put life back into Ollindale. Our main need for that is jobs. You starting up a business here with the potential to employ two people would please me.'

'And you think it might work financially?'

'If your carving is good, yes. I'd have to see a piece or two first, then I can introduce you to a few people who might be interested in buying or taking on consignment the sort of pieces you can produce. These are mostly people in a small way of business in our little town but I know one or two folk in Halifax and Lancaster.'

Bryn swallowed hard, trying to keep calm, though he felt more like shouting for joy. 'That's a wonderful offer and I accept it gratefully, sir. I won't let you down.'

Walter stuck out his hand and they shook on their agreement.

'How quickly can you get started, Bryn?'

'I'll need to send for my tools and a few other bits and pieces that my friends in Rochdale are looking after for me, and I'll have to buy a few household objects before I move out there, like a mattress and bedding, cooking equipment too. But if I can use the furniture and oddments that have been left in the mill, I can manage with very little.'

'I can help out there too. I have a lot of household oddments stored in one of my little cottages, enough to stock a second-hand shop. They were just throwing some things away and I can't abide waste, so I kept it and gave things to people in need. Some of them were bought from people who've fallen on hard times and didn't even have the money to travel to other towns to live with their relatives. Eh, it's heartbreaking to see that happen.'

'You're incredibly generous, sir.'

'I enjoy helping people to get through life, especially folk like you who want to start a business. I don't want to see my valley die for lack of jobs. It was all I had left in my life until Cam came here.'

'He's a good man, sir. Hasn't always been treated decently by his family, though.'

'Yes. I guessed that, more from what he didn't say about them than what he did. Have you told the others about your idea yet?'

'No. Not even Cam. What would have been the use if you hadn't wanted to rent me the old mill?'

'Let's go and tell them now. I'd guess those two lasses will want to help you set up your house, and they'll enjoy rummaging through my stuff to provide you with furnishings. Cam will be happy to have you settle here.'

He sat thinking for a moment, head on one side, then added, 'My grandson seems a bit lost at times. Well, he's in a strange country living with people he hadn't even met before. I think he'll settle down here eventually, though.'

But Bryn caught a flicker of doubt on Walter's face when he spoke about Cam and his future. He wasn't surprised that the astute old man had realised that his grandson was still hiding something from them all.

★

The others were highly enthusiastic about Bryn's new venture and immediately began trying to work out how they could help.

He could see how touched Bryn was by that.

All four of them had needed stability and seemed to be forming a new 'family', even if they weren't blood relatives. He did too, he realised suddenly. He had needed this just as much as they had.

He listened to them swapping ideas but waited for the initial hubbub to die down a bit before joining in. 'If it's all right with you, Bryn, I'll arrange for us to have a chat with a friend of mine in Ollerthwaite as soon as you have a carving of some sort to show him. He's got a lot of contacts in businesses within reach of our valley and I'm sure he'll give us good advice. Then we can go to the bank and open an account so that your friend in Rochdale can arrange to have your money paid into it. You must trust him greatly to have simply left the money in his care.'

'I do. And if anything had happened to me, he could have kept it with my blessing.'

'How soon can you have a carving done?'

'I shall need the right sort of wood before I start, but I can do a small one in a day's careful work. Do you have any pieces of wood that might be suitable?'

'I have a pile of pieces of wood, just oddments. I don't throw that sort of thing away either. Come and look through them. It's still light enough if we go outside straight away.'

Bryn found a few pieces of wood suitable for smaller carvings and took his first piece inside the house to do some initial shaping. He saw Elinor studying the mess even a few cuts made and pretended to be terrified of angering the two women, making them all laugh. But he took care to sweep up the mess afterwards.

As they sipped their nightly mugs of cocoa, Cameron asked, 'Would it be all right if I come into Ollerthwaite with you? I need to visit a bank and see about bringing my money over here from America.'

'If it's money you need, I can let you have some to be going on with,' Walter offered.

'That's very kind of you, Grandad, but I have some savings and they'll not be much use to me in America, will they?'

'Well, it'll suit me to go into town the day after tomorrow. You and I will visit the bank first and arrange for your money to be forwarded, Cam, and we'll send Bryn to have a walk round and study the local shops while we do that. There is one selling furniture quite close to the bank and a wood merchant too.'

He added with a wry grimace. 'You won't want to hang around while Mr Simpkins deals with us. Our bank manager is a pleasant chap but a real fusspot and everything takes far longer than it needs to.'

Bryn nodded. 'It'll be interesting to walk round the town. Thanks.'

If things went well, Cameron thought, he'd need to arrange for the sale of his land in America as well, but he didn't mention that. Not yet because he was starting to think that even if things didn't go well with his grandfather, he might stay in this country anyway, though he wasn't sure where else he could go.

The people round here were so friendly and didn't treat him differently from others. And the moors seemed to call to him in a way he'd never felt before: as if he'd come home.

Before he made an irrevocable decision about his future, he had to discuss the true situation with his grandfather and that wasn't going to be easy. He couldn't wait much longer to do it and was praying that Walter would understand how he'd been pushed into this situation by circumstances and his half-brother. Surely he wouldn't throw him out?

He had not only fallen in love with this part of the world but had grown fond of his grandfather and his cousin Maude, too.

Wanted to be with them because they already felt like a real family.

And then there was Elinor. She could easily become rather special. But nothing could happen between them till he knew where he stood with his grandfather.

He thought she liked him, but she was somewhat reserved, probably as a result of years of ill treatment, so he couldn't be sure she'd welcome the idea of him courting her. He couldn't help hoping, though.

Two days later the three men drove down into Ollerthwaite, leaving the mare and cart at the livery stable. Bryn made sure he had his letter to his former employer in Rochdale with him, ready to post once he'd set up a new bank account.

He needed his tools to be sent on as quickly as possible and his money transferred to his new bank account. He'd sent money from overseas for his friend to look after for him every now and then, and would need access to it now if he was to start up a business.

He took a walk round the town while the other two went to visit the only bank there, looking for the furniture shop and finding it quite quickly. He liked the display in the window, so went inside and examined it more carefully. The owner looked across at him to see if he needed help, but he shook his head.

Not yet.

Walter took Cam into the bank where he was a long-term customer and was greeted by name. He introduced his grandson to the manager then said quietly, 'You'll want to chat privately about this, lad, so I'll leave you two together.'

Once they were seated in his office, Mr Simpkins asked how he could help Cam, who explained about his American bank account and wanting to bring the money across to England now that he was here to stay.

'I've set up the account in another name to keep it private from my father who is a very, um, controlling sort of man. But I have a special password for when I can't get to the bank in person, so it should be all right.'

'Ah. Do you have proof of this other identity?'

'Not exactly, no. I wasn't expecting to stay here in England when I set off.'

'That could be a problem. How much money do you have?'

He named the amount and when the manager looked surprised at how much that was, he added, 'It's my life savings.'

'This is putting me into a very difficult position, I'm afraid, especially as it's a rather large sum of money.'

Walter went out into the main area of the bank and sat down on the nearest seat. It was unusually quiet today and it wasn't until he'd been sitting there for a minute or two that he realised by some quirk of the building's design, he could overhear what was being said in Mr Simpkins' office. Well, he could if he strained and paid attention.

He felt a bit guilty about eavesdropping. Perhaps he should find another seat?

But at that moment a woman came in with a small child and sat down on the only other seat with a weary sigh.

Walter stayed where he was and gave in to the temptation to listen to what was being said.

It seemed strange that Cam would have opened an account under another name. The bank manager was naturally suspicious of this and it sounded as if he were going to refuse to arrange a transfer of the money to someone who could only produce proof of the identity of Caleb Crossley.

Should he take a hand and help sort this out?

19

Suddenly Walter remembered something James had said in one of his early letters and realised its significance now. James had another son, an illegitimate one born in his early years in America. He hadn't mentioned this son again, so Walter had gradually forgotten about his existence.

The information came back to him with the force of lightning today because it made nearly everything about this puzzle fall into place: the surname Melton must be the name of James's former mistress and was therefore Cam's proper surname. The age he appeared to be was more in line with the illegitimate son's age.

Cam's occasional hesitation in giving some piece of information about his life in America was now explained. He'd had to make up stories from time to time. He'd have given himself away eventually. He wasn't glib enough to tell lies easily. Oh, yes, it all matched!

And yet, you couldn't doubt that Cam was a Crossley.

Where was the real youngest son, Caleb Crossley, then? Even his absence fitted in with other information James had shared sparingly before Walter offered to make one son his heir: not just Caleb's age, but the fact that he didn't particularly like farming, hadn't been as easy to raise as his two eldest sons. No wonder he hadn't come to England.

Why had Cam come instead, though? Walter still couldn't believe him the sort to plan a trick like this, one he'd have to keep up for the whole of his life. No, he'd stake his life on the fact that Cam was basically honest. So something must have pushed him into this tangle of identities. What?

The bank manager was trying to refuse to bring the money in from America without giving offence, not making a good job of it. This had to be sorted out quickly.

He'd worry about the whys and wherefores later; he needed to intervene now. He stood up and hurried round to the manager's office. Before the clerk at a nearby desk could stop him, he'd knocked on the door and walked in without waiting for a response.

'I'm sorry for barging in like this, but I could overhear your conversation from the waiting area, and I thought I should join in the discussion.'

Mr Simpkins looked relieved. 'I think that might be a good idea, Mr Crossley.'

'I'll start by saying that I can vouch for my grandson's honesty. There are family complications behind this change of name but he is who he says: Cameron Alan Melton. He's taken the place of his youngest brother at my farm, and thank goodness for that.'

His grandson was gaping at him, obviously shocked rigid by this intervention. He didn't deny what his grandfather had said but looked so miserable Walter reached out to give his hand a quick squeeze. 'I think it will help to avoid future confusion if you change your surname to Crossley officially from now on.'

As they stared at one another, Cam seemed to realise what he meant by that and nodded. 'I'd like to do that and I appreciate your trust in me.'

Walter turned his attention back to the bank manager. 'Cam has been protecting his youngest brother, Mr Simpkins. I think it's time to leave his scapegrace of a brother to fend for himself. You know how older children can sometimes be too protective of the younger ones.'

Mr Simpkins smiled at that. 'My grandchildren certainly are. But if *you* vouch for this man as your grandson, then I believe you. May I ask why this happened in the first place to cause the problem with identity? It would help if I could explain things to the bank managers in London who deal with foreign transactions.'

Walter looked at Cam apologetically. 'I'm afraid I'll have to reveal your secret, lad. Mr Simpkins, this grandson was not born in wedlock and knowing how prejudiced some people can be about that sort of thing, he's been trying to keep the knowledge secret for my sake, as well as trying to hide how his brother forced an exchange of identities on him. There are scapegraces in every family, are there not?'

Mr Simpkins nodded sympathetically.

'Cam is a fine young man, however he was born, and I'm delighted that he's come to help me and be my heir when the time comes. In fact, I shall be glad to stop obfuscating.'

Cam had tears in his eyes at this. He gave Walter a searching look then said huskily, 'Thank you, Grandad.'

'I should have brought it out into the open sooner, lad. None of it's your fault.'

'I was afraid of losing you.'

'You'll not do that.' He turned once again to Mr Simpkins. 'I shall probably have to sign a legal statement to the effect that Cam is my grandson, but has lost his identity documents. I'm happy to do that or whatever else you require.'

'I believe you absolutely. Apart from anything else, I need only look at him to see the family resemblance. That connection has been proved beyond doubt to my mind and so I shall tell them.'

'How about we come back to see you on Monday and complete any other formalities your head office may see fit to ask for then. I think my character and standing in the community will speak for what I've told you and there is no rush to bring the money across, though of course we can't leave it in America long term.'

'That'll be a good way of dealing with it. I'm sure once head office is apprised of the circumstances – in absolute confidence, I assure you – they won't try to block the transaction.'

'As usual, Mr Simpkins, I'm very grateful for your support. It's no wonder I've remained a loyal customer over the years. Now before I go, may I mention that another young friend of mine will be coming in later today to open an account on my recommendation. His name is Bryn Fordham and his money will be coming from a friend in Rochdale. He's going to rent a property of mine and start a small business in our valley.'

Mr Simpkins smiled at him. 'Always glad to welcome a new customer, especially when recommended by a long-time and well-respected client like yourself, Mr Crossley.'

When they got outside, Walter pulled his grandson into an alley next to the bank. 'We need to talk, just you and I, before we find Bryn. About our joint future.'

'Are you quite sure we have one?'

'Oh, yes. I shall be very happy to have you as my heir. I took to you from the start. I think you want to stay, don't you, lad?'

'Very much indeed and not just for the money. I love the farm and there's something about this valley that touches my heart.'

'Good. I didn't have to spend long with you to realise that you were an honest soul, and from the sounds of it, you're a good businessman as well as understanding farming. I'd appreciate it, however, if you would change your surname legally to the one you should have been given from the start. You're a Crossley through and through, lad.'

Cam's voice came out hoarse with emotion. 'I'd be happy to do that.'

'You've never had a proper family life, have you? Just been given a sort of half-life and grudging acceptance as your father's illegitimate son.'

'His wife has made it very difficult for him to deal with me, especially as she dotes on Caleb. But you're right: I've never had the feeling of being truly part of the family. My father has always kept me separate from his *legitimate* children.'

Oh, the pain that rang in that word, Walter thought, and in the whole faltering explanation. Damn James! He'd been selfish as a lad, and seemed to have continued with this sort of behaviour, always looking to gain what he wanted, and not necessarily prepared to do what he owed to others. This Caleb must be like him in that way.

'Leave it to me to write to my son and tell him I've decided you will be my heir, not Caleb. I'll do that once your name change is legal.'

Cameron looked at him in wonderment. 'Are you really so sure of me already?'

'Yes, I am, lad. I can read your face because you're very like the son I lost. As far as I'm concerned you're my closest family now. And I know exactly how it feels to be alone in the world.' He almost whispered as an afterthought, 'By hell I do.'

As Cameron bent his head and tried not to weep, because men weren't supposed to give way to such a weakness, Walter made an inarticulate choking sound and pulled him into another embrace. It was a while before they drew apart.

'Eh, what a place to choose for such a difficult conversation. We're a right old pair of softies, aren't we?' Walter pulled out a handkerchief, wiped his eyes and blew his nose.

Cameron fumbled for his own handkerchief and couldn't find it, so Walter passed his over.

'One day soon, lad, we'll go for a walk on the tops, just you and I, and you can tell me exactly how Caleb tricked you into coming here and posing as him, and exactly what he's like. I feel better talking about important matters in the open air. "I will lift up mine eyes unto the hills" has always applied to me. I couldn't live anywhere else but near the moors.'

'I feel better in the fresh air, too.'

'Come on, then. Let's get on with our other business.' He led the way towards the café where they'd arranged to meet their friend.

Bryn was sitting near the window, scribbling in a little notebook and seeming unaware of their approach.

As they sat down at his table, he looked up and as soon as they'd ordered a pot of tea, he began to tell them what he'd been doing. 'This is a nice little town, isn't it? I got on very well with the owner of the furniture shop. He has good taste in what he offers for sale and will be happy to buy furniture from me.' He chuckled. 'I was even able to adjust a piece of his stock that had got slightly damaged.'

Walter nodded. 'Good, good.'

'I just need to open a bank account and add the details of it to my letter, then I can seal the envelope and post it. Only, could you please lend me some money to start the bank account with Mr Crossley? I have almost none left.'

Walter fumbled in his pocket and pulled out a five-pound note, handing it over to Bryn. 'Now, we're just only a street away from a friend of mine who runs a timber yard. He knows about furniture manufacturing in the area, so might be able to introduce you to some useful people, and not just in Ollerthwaite. He's called Frank Beaton and is usually in his office at this time, so drink up your tea quickly and we'll go and see him. You can go to the bank later.'

The meeting with Walter's friend went well and after studying the small carving of a dog that Bryn had brought with him, he seemed genuinely interested in making use of such skills.

'Bring me some more samples of your work once you've started producing things again, Mr Fordham. And, er, this carving is delightful. You wouldn't care to sell it today, would you? I have a granddaughter who'd adore it and she has a birthday coming up soon.'

'I'm happy to sell it but I don't know what prices are like here, so I'll take your word about its value.'

Frank named a price and Bryn glanced at Walter, who nodded. It felt good to earn money again, however small an amount. The man's interest also showed that his carvings would appeal to people round here.

'I'll have to find a supplier of the right sort of wood for my carvings, Mr Beaton. I wonder if you could recommend someone locally?'

'There's a man who works for me and who will probably be able to help you. He looks after my timber yard, because I have other interests. We may not have the sort of wood that you want in stock, but I'm sure he'll be able to get it for you. He might even take you with him on his next buying trip so that you can check what's being offered by his supplier and show him exactly what you'll want in future. Clarry might even have a few bits and pieces in stock that would do to get started again on carving small items.'

Walter could see the longing on Bryn's face, but knew his young friend didn't have any spare money yet, so intervened. 'Let's all go and see him then, shall we?'

So off they went and to his delight, Bryn found several good chunks of wood.

After this they went on to the bank where Bryn opened an account then added the information about it in his letter to his friend and posted it.

Once they'd collected the cart from the livery stables, they went back to Clarry's yard to pick up the wood.

They were all rather quiet as the pony jogged back home, but it was a peaceful silence not a stressful one, because they'd had a useful day.

Cameron felt hugely relieved that revealing who he was to his grandfather had brought them closer together, not driven them apart.

He caught Walter's eye a couple of times and once his grandfather winked at him and he felt a warmth run through him.

Left on her own in the house, Elinor cleared out the pantry and rearranged its rather meagre contents, by which time Maude had finished her work outside and the two of them could sit down and enjoy their usual mid-morning cup of tea.

'Let's have a look in the attic now and see what we can find for Bryn's new home,' Maude said as they cleared their things away.

'Good idea. Isn't it amazing that he's going to settle permanently near here?'

'Yes, and it's also amazing how willing my cousin Walter is to help people. I've never met anyone as kind in my whole life. Look how he took us two into his own home.'

'You're a relative so that's not surprising. But I had no call on him.'

'He's made you into a relative of us all.'

They had a quick hug at that.

The attic was a dim, shadowy place and rather than go down for an oil lamp, they struggled till they'd managed to pull back the blinds on the two dormer windows.

Elinor shuddered at what was revealed. 'Ugh! There are a lot of cobwebs.'

'Never mind that. I'll bring a broom and deal with them later. Let's find out what that pile of things in the corner is first. It seems newer than the rest, less dusty, anyway.'

They threaded their way through the haphazardly dumped debris from who knew how many lives.

They found some clothes, a battered old teddy bear, some well-worn books and all sorts of oddments.

Then Elinor picked up a large box which had been behind the pile of bags containing clothing and personal items. It contained all sorts of oddments, artists' brushes and some half-used tubes of paint and she fingered them longingly. 'One of your two cousins who died must have been artistic. He had some lovely equipment and looked after it carefully.'

Maude tugged an old blanket off what they'd thought to be just some bits of wood. 'Look, there's even an easel.'

'I wonder if there are any of his paintings or sketches?'

They had a careful look round and Elinor pointed. 'That folder on top of the old wardrobe may contain something. You're taller than me. Can you reach it?'

Maude stretched her arm out and managed to grab it, opening it to show sketches with the name Tim Crossley on the right-hand bottom corner of each. She flipped slowly through the sketches and they both studied them.

'These are lovely! He was very talented,' Elinor said. 'Did he do any paintings, do you think?'

Maude stood up and began poking around in that corner. She tugged at the wardrobe. 'Help me move this. There are some things covered in sacking behind it.'

They managed to edge it forward a little, enough to discover some canvases.

'He was good,' Elinor said.

'What a waste of talent. I'm not going to shove them back. They should be seen.'

'That's not up to us. It might hurt Walter too much to look at them.'

'I'll think about it. I wonder if my cousin would let you use the rest of these paints. Don't tell me you're not missing your painting. And you're talented too.'

'Of course I'm missing painting, but I'd give up my hobby for ever to stay clear of Jason. And I could only do it while my stepfather was away from home, so I didn't do it nearly as much as I wanted to.' Elinor shuddered. 'We both know that Reginald would have taken delight in burning my paintings in front of me if he'd found out about them.'

'Well, he didn't find out. It's a good thing you only did small ones and were able to fit the ones you'd kept into your pillowcase when we escaped. I'll wait for a suitable moment and mention these art materials to my cousin. I'd like to see you paint a really big picture.'

'No, don't! I don't want to impose on him and anyway, if he's shoved them out of sight up here, it's because he can't bear to see them.'

'There's a painting in his office. It's a stormy landscape. I've never looked at who painted it, but I wonder if that was done by his grandson. I've seen him staring at it several times.'

'Maude, don't risk stirring up ghosts for him.'

But her friend had that stubborn expression on her face.

'I'll choose my moment carefully, Elinor, I promise. But you're talented too and deserve to be able to use your skills.'

Elinor knew how stubborn her friend could be, so stopped trying to prevent her from intervening. 'Please take great care when you talk to him, then. I don't want to upset him just for the sake of a hobby.'

Maude gave her an irritated look. 'It's more than a mere hobby, and you know it. It's a passion, and you're still doing sketches on bits of paper. I think you'd be good enough to sell your paintings if you worked at it.'

Elinor only shook her head.

'I think it's one of his joys to make people's dreams come true. He'd help you, I'm sure.'

'Well, we've come up to the attic to find things for Bryn's new home, not stuff for my hobby so let that drop now and let's concentrate on furnishing Bryn's new home, which is much more important.'

Only for the moment, Maude vowed to herself.

★

When the three men returned from Ollerthwaite, they looked full of news and seemed both sad and happy. Maude whispered, 'I don't think this is the time to ask about the paints.'

'No. I agree.' Elinor turned to the men. 'Did you accomplish your tasks?'

'More than. Come and sit down and we'll give you the good news.'

When they were seated round the table, he took charge. 'I already wondered that Cam doesn't fit the description of being James's youngest son. And that isn't who he is.'

Both women exclaimed in shock and gaped at him. 'Who is he, then?' Maude asked.

'He's the oldest son by another mother whom his father didn't marry because she wouldn't bring any money to a marriage.' This was as tactful a way of putting it as he could find. 'And he was tricked into coming here by Caleb, who is no doubt now using his identity.'

By the time he'd finished his tale, Cameron had filled in a few more details about his half-brother and the gambling.

'What a dreadful thing to do!' Elinor exclaimed. 'I'm glad he didn't come here.'

'So am I,' Walter said quietly and firmly.

Both women were clearly thinking through the wider implications and Maude said slowly, 'You're as much a grandson as he is and you fit in well here, both of you have done from the very first day. I'm really happy to have you as a cousin, Cameron.'

'He's a real Crossley, just as are you, lass. He's got the family business acumen too.'

'He's kind as well.' Maude stretched her hand across to him and gave his hand a quick squeeze. 'Welcome to the family, Cameron.'

20

The following morning there were footsteps outside the house even before breakfast and before anyone could go to see who it was, someone hammered on the front door and called out, 'Mr Crossley! Mr Crossley!'

Walter hurried to open the door and an old man nearly fell through it, looking distressed and unwell, his complexion a greyish-white.

'Come in and sit down in the kitchen, Dick. Get your breath back then tell me slowly and clearly what's wrong.'

Their visitor collapsed on to a chair, panting. 'Everything's wrong. I set off . . . as soon as . . . it was light.'

'Have you walked all this way?'

'Had to. It isn't my nephew's day to visit us, an' me an' my Peggy are in desperate trouble.'

Maude had poured out a bare cupful of the lukewarm tea left in the pot and put plenty of sugar in. When she offered it to Dick, he thanked her and gulped a mouthful thirstily, not seeming to notice that it was nearly cold. 'Eh, that's good, just what I need.'

Walter sat down next to him and waited till he'd drunk it all to speak again. 'Now, tell me what's wrong, my friend? Take your time.'

'I've been lying awake half the night worrying and I could only think of coming to you for help, Mr Crossley.'

'You did the right thing. What's the problem? I'll help you if I can.'

'Mr Kenyon's agent came to see us yesterday afternoon. Hatton allus seems to enjoy bringing bad news an' he smiled as he told us that they're throwing us out of our house, Mr Crossley. We've been there nearly forty years an' they're just throwing us out, not even a week's notice, only three days. We have to leave and take away our things by noon on Saturday.'

'Good heavens! Did Hatton say why?'

'He said the family were selling the land and wanted the cottage cleared out so people won't be put off by thinking they'd have to take us on as well.'

'They're selling it! I'm not surprised at that, but they don't need to throw you out to do that. And anyway, it may take years to sell it. They've tried before and failed.'

'Well, we've been told by Hatton to get out. Only me an' Peggy have nowhere else to go.' He mopped his eyes, but more tears welled out.

'I'll find you somewhere else to live.'

'We can't afford to pay rent. The Kenyons are stopping paying us our pension as well as taking our home away. Hatton said the pension was only paid for keeping an eye on the estate an' we won't be doing that from now on. An' my nephew hasn't got room for us, not with all those childer. Eight he's got now an' another on the way.'

He had to fight back sobs before he could continue. 'It'll be the poorhouse for us an' them nasty sods as run it will sell all our possessions except for a few clothes and then separate us once we're trapped in there.'

'I won't let them send you there, my friend.'

Dick gave him a miserable, hopeless look. 'How can you stop them? We can't live on the street, can we?'

Walter laid his hand over Dick's. 'I have a cottage you can move into. And no need to pay me rent.'

He had to repeat that before it sank in but Dick gave another hopeless shake of the head. 'Eh, that's kind of you, Mr Crossley, but we need the pension money to buy food an' we won't have the stuff from the garden to eat in a new place, either.'

Walter spoke slowly and clearly, repeating himself as necessary, because the old man was in such a state he wasn't taking anything in properly. 'I'll make sure you have enough to eat. I promise you, Dick, we'll see that you're all right and that you and Peggy have enough to live on.'

At last it seemed to sink in and Dick sniffed back tears. 'Eh, you're a saint, you are, Mr Crossley, a real saint.'

Walter flushed slightly at this. 'I'm no saint, but I like to help people when I can. Now, let me drive you back so that we can tell your wife you have somewhere to live. Then, if you're up to it, I'll take you both to see the cottage I'm thinking of. It's one of the pair near the old mill.'

'The ones next to the river? I used to play with a lad as lived in one of them cottages when I were young. I allus wished I lived there too. Eh, that'd be grand, that would.' Dick blew his nose again.

'What can we do to help?' Maude asked Walter quietly as they waited for the old man to calm down.

'Feed him, I think.' He raised his voice. 'Have you had anything to eat yet this morning, Dick?'

'Nay, food was the last thing on my mind. I were needing to see you. I knew you'd tell me what was best to do. God bless you, Mr Crossley.'

Walter looked across at Elinor. 'Can you make a ham sandwich for Dick and one to take back for his wife? Then I'll drive him back. Cameron, will you harness Sally for me, then come with us? And Bryn, you'll have seen the cottages I'm talking about, the ones near your mill. If I give you the keys, will you cycle over there and check them, please? If they're both all right inside, which I think they will be, Dick and Peggy can choose which one they want to live in.'

'And once they've done that, Maude and I will clean it for them while they get on with their packing,' Elinor said.

'Thank you, lass. If you an' Maude start getting the cleaning stuff together we'll pick you up on the way to the cottages, then we'll all go and look at them together.'

Dick blew his nose again in a thunderous toot and murmured, 'Eh, to think of it.' He was looking better already and eagerly bit into the sandwich Elinor had given him, chomping away loudly and happily.

'I'll put a few tools together in case we have to dismantle any of their furniture,' Walter said quietly.

He then swept Dick and Cameron off to carry the good news to Peggy and left the two younger women gathering cleaning materials and making more sandwiches as well as putting some basic foods together, including a loaf, a pat of butter, a jar of jam and some tinned fruit. She also put in a quarter pound packet of tea.

'Typical of the Kenyons to do something like that,' Walter muttered to Cameron as they helped Dick clamber up on to the driving seat then set off with him squashed between them.

'And I bet Hatton didn't even try to persuade them to leave the Rainfords in peace.'

Cameron hadn't ever gone far into the area on the other side of the crossroads and was surprised at how different it soon looked from the land round Walter's farm. Everything appeared to have been long neglected and weeds were even flourishing on the track they were driving along, as well as beside it. It was clear that not many people or vehicles ever came here.

When they stopped outside the lodge it was just as obvious that it was in serious need of maintenance work.

Walter stared at the house. 'I bet that roof leaks in rainy weather.'

Dick sighed. 'Aye, it does. But we know where to put buckets, so we manage.'

'Would they not do any repairs?'

'No. An' Hatton said if we pestered him again, he'd have us thrown out.'

Walter breathed deeply but held his anger in check. He'd never had any patience with Hatton, who did very little when he came here except spend the evenings boozing with the worst types in Ollerthwaite. He vowed to himself that the Rainfords would have a cosy cottage to live in for the rest of their days.

As they got down from the cart, an old woman opened the front door of the lodge and stood waiting for them, twisting and turning a corner of her pinafore in her hands.

Walter held back and let Dick go to his wife first.

He put an arm round her shoulders. 'Mr Crossley's finding us a house, Peggy love. We shall be all right.'

She looked at Walter and burst into tears. 'I knew you'd help us if anyone could. We don't need anywhere fancy, Mr Crossley, just a roof over our heads.'

'Let's all go inside and talk about how to arrange the move, Peggy.'

'Come on, love.' Dick guided her back into the house.

When she heard where they were going to live, she began sobbing again out of sheer relief. It was a while before she calmed down and even longer before they could persuade her to eat her sandwich.

'Eat it all,' Walter ordered gently when she managed only half. 'There will be more food provided for you later on.'

'I don't feel hungry, Mr Crossley. Please don't make me. I'll save this one for later.'

As if he'd force her to do anything!

★

They had to just about lift the two old people up on the driving seat of the cart and Cameron sat in the rear, thinking how marvellous it would be to have the power to help people in distress as his grandfather was doing.

When Walter began talking to the Rainfords, he could see that even the sound of his grandfather's voice soothed them still further.

'This is my grandson, Cameron. He's come all the way from America to live with me and help with the farm.'

'Eeh, fancy that.' They each craned round to look into the back of the cart at Cameron, staring as if he'd suddenly grown two heads.

'And his friend, Bryn, who's also come here from America, will be waiting for us at your new house. He's gone ahead to check whether it needs any repairs. He's going to be living at the old mill so you'll have someone close by from now on if you need help.'

'Eh, that'll be a blessing, Mr Crossley, a real blessing.'

They called in at the farm, collecting Elinor and Maude plus the cleaning materials and food, which nearly equalled the amount of food brought from the Rainfords' pantry, then went back to the crossroads and turned right towards the old mill.

As they drove along by the water, Dick gave his wife a tremulous smile and whispered, 'Aren't we lucky to have friends like these?'

She nodded, her hand clasped in his, a slight smile having replaced the misery on her face now. But the smile was tentative still, as if she wasn't quite ready to believe in their good luck.

While they were being helped down outside the two cottages, Bryn came out of the first one to greet them.

'I think both cottages are all right, so you could live in either one, Mr and Mrs Rainford. You've kept them in good repair,

Walter. There's no sign of any leaks. They just need the insides cleaning because they're rather dusty and of course, the gardens need attention.'

The idea that they could choose which house to live in rendered both old people speechless again. For a few minutes they tried to make Walter tell them which he wanted them to take.

He steadfastly refused. 'Your choice, not mine, my friends.'

After walking slowly round them both twice, Peggy was persuaded to say she liked the one nearer to the mill best because although they were similar inside, that one had an apple tree in the garden.

'Eh, we shall think we're in paradise living here,' she added in a choked voice.

Only then did Maude and Elinor get down from the back of the cart and pick up their buckets and cloths.

'We'll make a start cleaning it out for you, while you go back and pack up everything you own,' Elinor said.

'Cameron and I will take you back to do that. I want you out of there today, even if it takes all day and all night to move everything. That bully of an agent is not getting near you again. Is the furniture at the lodge yours or the owners'?'

'Ours. The lodge was empty when we moved in. We bought the furniture years ago when we were first wed, saving up for it one piece at a time.'

'Then we'll make sure we bring every single item across to the cottage. My grandson and I will help pack your things. But first we'll drop you off at home while we go and get my bigger cart and harness my horse instead of Sally. Mac's a big lad and will have no trouble pulling a load of furniture. There's only a slight slope up to the cottages, anyway. I'll also find some boxes and sacks to pack your things in as well.'

'I can wrap our clothes in the sheets.' Peggy's face was looking more alert now.

'I've already got some sacks that'll do for the garden tools.' Dick was looking more alert, as if he was starting to recover from the nasty shock. 'I might even try to transplant some of the plants and take them with me. They'll only die if they're not cared for.'

'Good idea. And we'll bring back some food for our meals from the farm as well. I think it's going to be a long day.'

'I can make us pots of tea,' Peggy offered. 'We have nearly a full packet of tea leaves left.

Walter was pleased to see her looking better. 'That'll be good. We'll rely on you for that.'

As the Rainfords walked into the lodge hand in hand, moving slowly with the stiff gait of old age, he muttered, 'I'd like to punch that John Kenyon in the face. Hit him good and hard, too. He doesn't care who he tramples on to get what he wants. And as for Hatton, I wish I need never see his face in our valley again. He seems to enjoy bullying people and I've heard it whispered that he steals stuff.'

By the end of the day they'd cleared every single item from the lodge and the horse had made three trips to the riverside cottage. The two old people were installed there with food in their pantry and a basket of wood by their fire, looking comfortably at home already.

Maude and Elinor had promised to clean the lodge early the next morning because the thought of leaving it dirty for others to move into had fretted Peggy. They didn't think this would be an onerous task because she was clearly extremely houseproud.

After everyone else had left Peggy took Walter's hand as he stood in the doorway.

'I hope you and Dick will be very happy here,' he said gently.

She squeezed his hand. 'I can't find the words to tell you how grateful we are. Bless you, Mr Crossley. You'll be in my prayers every day for the rest of my life.'

'If we can't help one another, we're not worth much. Sleep well.'

The two old people wept in one another's arms for joy and relief when they went to bed.

But they found it easy to obey his order to sleep well. Indeed, they slept better than they had for years, with the quiet sounds of the river flowing by lulling them to sleep.

The following afternoon, Hatton went to check on the lodge and remind the tenants that they had to leave in two more days. To his surprise he saw that the two women who lived with Crossley were bustling in and out of the lodge.

What were they doing there? Then he watched one of them toss a bucket of dirty water on the garden and realised they must be soft enough to be cleaning the place for the old fools. Good. It'd look better for prospective buyers. And be more pleasant for him to live in, as well.

Where were the Rainfords, though? There was no sign of them helping, or of them bringing out their bits and pieces to take to their new place – if they could find somewhere to live. He sniggered. They'd be a bit short of money from now on, and he'd withheld their last two weeks' payments for himself.

He hoped they'd end up in the poorhouse. Best place to put people who were no longer any use to the world.

He saw one of the women stop to stare at him and realised he'd been sitting in his cart watching them for too long, so drove quickly past to the agent's house. He went to continue watching them from an upstairs window. They'd better not steal anything.

About half an hour later Crossley drove across to the lodge in his cart and picked the women up. And still the Rainfords hadn't appeared, nor had there been any attempt to start removing their possessions. They'd better do that tomorrow because he didn't want to have to clear away their pitiful rubbish and take it to the tip.

When Crossley had driven off with the two women, presumably to go back to the farm, Hatton drove back to the lodge, intending to give the Rainfords a sharp warning that they had to take all their bits and pieces with them.

He was surprised to find the front door locked, which wasn't usual in the daytime, so banged on the knocker. There was no answer, so he banged again. In the end he decided they must be afraid to open the door to him and smiled as he hunted for the key in his rent bag, and unlocked the door.

He went inside to confront them but what he saw made him stop in shock. The front room was completely empty. He found the same thing in the kitchen, the room where they usually spent most of their time. Not only was there no sign of the occupants but there wasn't a single piece of furniture to be seen or anything else either. Even the curtains had gone from the windows.

He marched round, checking every single room then stood in the kitchen trying to work out how they'd managed this. It was only just over a day since he'd given them notice. How could they possibly have found somewhere else to live in such a short time?

There was only one answer: Crossley.

He should have stayed around to keep an eye on them. They'd taken every single item. How dared they?

And when he stared idly out of the kitchen window he stiffened and cursed again, because they'd even dug up the plants from the vegetable garden.

Furious, he locked the door, got back up on the cart and slashed the whip at the pony.

He was going to confront Crossley and demand his employer's furniture back, threaten him and the Rainfords with being arrested for stealing it if necessary.

Who but Crossley could be behind this?

Well, he'd gone too far this time.

Those two women had aided and abetted him. They deserved a good hiding. Women should know their place and not get mixed up in men's affairs. They must have helped to clear the place.

By hell, he'd like to take his belt to them and if he could ever pay them back, he would. See if he didn't!

After Walter had brought everyone back to the farm, he stood outside, enjoying the fresh air and keeping an eye on the lodge, which he could just see from here. He smiled as he watched the Kenyons' agent driving from his estate house towards the lodge, knock on the door, then use his key to get in.

He wished he could see Hatton's face when he found the lodge completely bare of furniture with no clue as to where the occupants had gone.

When Hatton stopped at the crossroads and scowled in the direction of the farm, Walter thought for a moment that he was coming to his house, but after a moment Hatton set off again, turning left and heading back towards the lodge.

Elinor and Maude came to stand behind him.

'Don't even answer the door if that man calls when you're on your own and even if you're both here, don't let him into the house. If he wants to see me, he can do so outside.' He looked at the clock. 'I'll just finish this job then I'm going into town. Is there anything you need there?'

'No, thanks. We've enough food for a day or two.'

Half an hour later Walter went back to the house to change out of his working clothes into something smarter for his trip into town. To his surprise, he heard the sound of a horse and cart again but this time approaching the farm. He glanced out of his bedroom window.

What the hell did Hatton want now?

He went down to join the two women.

'What an ugly man he is,' Elinor said.

'And nasty with it,' Walter said.

'He must have seen the empty house,' Maude said.

'But why would he come here?' Elinor wondered aloud.

'Because there's no one else around, and I suppose he's realised that we must have helped the Rainfords move their possessions.'

Hatton drew into the front of the farm and began to tie his pony to a post.

'I've never heard you sound as if you hated someone,' said Maude.

'Despise might be a better word,' Walter said. 'That man is a liar and a thief. He fines tenants for imaginary faults. And he's even given a few of them a good thumping when they refused to do as he ordered. They didn't dare lay a complaint about it because that police constable in Ollerthwaite is utterly useless. He refused point-blank to pursue the matter when I told him about it.'

Walter continued to scowl at the man now approaching the front door. 'I wonder where he's staying? He took away nearly all the furniture from the agent's house a while ago.' He gave them an urchin's grin. 'I know because I sneaked a peep. You don't see Hatton here in the valley very often these days and he usually leaves the same day.'

'I'm surprised he still has a job.'

'He gets away with a lot because the Kenyons never come here to check what he's up to.'

The door knocker sounded and Walter walked out into the hall, but he waited until Hatton knocked again before flinging the front door open. He stood barring the entrance, arms folded. 'What the hell do you mean by thumping on my door like a madman?'

The agent scowled back at him, making no attempt at any sort of greeting. 'I've got an emergency or I'd not be here, believe me. I'm looking for the Rainfords, who seem to have disappeared. You're the closest house to the crossroads, so you must have seen them leaving. Was it their nephew who took them away? Where did they go?'

'What's that got to do with you now, Hatton? You threw them out, remember?'

'I don't give a damn where they live from now on but they've taken all Mr Kenyon's furniture with them and I'm having it back.'

'It was their own furniture, some of which they'd owned ever since they got married fifty years ago, as half the village can confirm.'

'And some of it was rather fine for a pair of near paupers, so it couldn't have belonged to them.'

'Mrs Ollerton gave them a few pieces of furniture in recognition of their long service to the family. That was over twenty years ago, before she left the property that final time.'

'Have you got written proof of that?'

'I don't need written proof. I was there to farewell her and several other locals were there too. They can bear witness about what she gave to the Rainfords.'

'That'll not stand up in court.'

'It will, you know. Her lawyer was also present and made a note of everything she gave to people.'

Hatton breathed deeply. 'Well, it's not theirs morally.'

Walter's words came out as sharp as ice splinters. 'Any attempt to harm the Rainfords will cause trouble for you in the village – and especially with me.'

'What do I care about those yokels? It's that furniture I want. And why the hell should *you* bother about those old fools? You've even got those females who live with you fussing over them.'

Walter continued to stare at him coldly. 'It's none of your business what we do. I'll say this once only and you'd better take note. The Rainfords are under my protection from now on and I'll make sure my lawyer knows about your threats.'

'You can just mind your own damned—'

'There's nothing else to discuss.' He closed the door in Hatton's face, resisting an urge to punch him. He heard the man kick his door before striding back to the hired pony and trap.

No one else he'd ever met annoyed him as much as this man did, and nearly every time their paths crossed he saw something that disgusted him. It wasn't only Hatton's arrogant ways but the cruel decisions he had made about people's lives over the years that upset Walter.

Well, Hatton might frighten some of the people in the village, but he didn't frighten Walter or have any power over him. And he was quite sure neither Bryn nor Cameron would be frightened, either.

He watched from the parlour window to be sure the fellow had left the farm and driven off down the hill before he went back into the kitchen.

'I've never heard you talk to anyone like that before,' Maude said.

'He's a brute and a bully who turns up in our valley every now and then to check on the Ollerton estate – though what there is to check on, I don't know. The house burned down two decades ago and there's nothing being cultivated in the gardens or fields there these days.'

'Why is he so angry about the furniture? It's mostly well-worn stuff.'

'I'd guess he was intending to stay at the lodge while he got the estate ready for sale. That entrance road is overgrown and will make a bad impression on anyone interested in buying. And he probably planned to sell its furniture for his own benefit at some point in the future once the estate had been sold. I wonder if the Kenyons will manage to sell it this time. They tried a few years ago and failed.'

He paused for a moment, thinking about it. 'I did see a chap going round the place a year or so ago. I thought he was an Ollerton from his looks, but if so he can't have been interested in buying the estate because nothing happened after his visit.'

'Perhaps you should contact the Kenyons about Hatton.'

'Even if I wrote to them, I can't see them caring about the money a few pieces of furniture would bring. And if they do manage to sell the estate, I doubt the Kenyons will keep him on in any other capacity, so he'll have to look for another job away from the valley. I'll make sure he doesn't get anything else inside the valley. The sooner he leaves the better. And good riddance to him.'

Over tea that evening, they told Bryn and Cameron what had happened then Walter said thoughtfully, 'The sooner you can move into the old mill, the better, Bryn. How's the work going?'

'More quickly than I'd expected with Cam's help.'

'Good. Hatton will easily find out where Dick and Peggy are living and I'm concerned he'll try to hurt them, just out of spite. I'll give them a loud handbell and if you hear it rung, please go to their aid – and take something to protect yourself with when you do.'

Bryn looked at him thoughtfully. 'Do you think he'd attack me?'

'He's been known to attack people and leave them badly injured, so I don't want you taking any risks.'

'I'd better get my revolver out then and load it.'

Everyone stared at him in shock.

'Revolver?' Walter asked.

'In some parts of America everyone carried a gun. I learned to do the same to protect myself.'

'Well, I don't think the policeman in Ollerthwaite would look favourably on you walking around carrying a revolver, let alone shooting someone, even in self-defence, so be careful to keep it out of sight.'

Walter was quieter than usual during the rest of the meal and they'd learned to leave him to his thoughts when he got that look on his face.

They'd all been surprised at how quickly this situation had blown up and at how angry the usually calm Walter had become.

They had taken a rapid dislike to Hatton, and Walter must have seen him upsetting people for years to feel like this about him.

21

Bryn was surprised at how many household items Walter was able to provide him with. He promised to pay for them but the older man only laughed and said they weren't worth anything.

'Look at them closely, lad. They're none of them new and some of them are well used. I have a whole cottage full of such items. People who're leaving often throw things away and I can't bear to see waste, so most of them didn't cost me anything. I give them away to those who need them and can't afford to buy new items. If they're of better quality I sell them in a little shop in Ollerthwaite. The ones I'm giving you are worthless, just to tide you over.'

'Then I can only say thank you.'

'You're welcome.'

'On another topic, Mr Crossley, are you still going into town on Monday to see if you can finish sorting out the transfer of Cameron's money?'

'Yes.'

'Can I beg a lift into Ollerthwaite?'

'Of course. I've been wondering how you're going to manage for getting into town from your new home, though. I think you should buy a bicycle.'

'I will do when my money comes through, Walter. I noticed a place in town selling them. When the time comes I'll see if there's anything suitable there.'

'No need to shop so far away. There's a chap in our own village who sells second-hand bicycles from his home. We'll get Peter's help. He needs our support more than someone in the town does. All the younger folk are going mad for bikes these days. I've tried riding one, but don't feel comfortable. I will admit those new safety bicycles are not as dangerous as the earlier styles of bicycle used to be, though. They're much better designed.'

'And they're not only much faster than walking, you can carry small loads in the basket. I'm thinking of building a little trolley to pull behind mine as well. It'll be cheaper to deliver the smaller things I make myself.'

'Get one now, if Peter has one available, Bryn lad. I'll lend you the money for that too.'

'Thank you.'

'How are Dick and Peggy settling in? I'd meant to call on them before now, but something else cropped up.'

'They seem very happy in that cottage. Dick has started work on the garden and the young plants he pulled up and took with him are nearly all alive still. He seems to be greatly enjoying setting it in order, says it's much better soil there. Peggy is arranging and rearranging the house and her orna-ments, and she says if I buy the ingredients she'll bake cakes and scones for me.'

'She used to be a good cook.'

'Do you think she'll accept half of what she bakes as my payment for her trouble?'

'If you coax her a little. Tell her you need her help.'

'I do. I'm no cook. Their nephew came to see them yester-day and he brought them some fresh food.'

'He's a good lad. Keeps an eye on them as best he can.'

'They're going to need groceries from time to time and won't Peggy want to go to the shops? Women usually seem to enjoy that.'

'Yes. I'll be happy to take them into town occasionally in my cart, or you can borrow it and take them with you if you need to bring back heavy items.'

Bryn stared in amazement. 'You'd let me do that?'

'Aye. I'm glad you're nearby to keep an eye on Dick and Peggy, and on my two cottages as well. Saves me a job. I have someone watching for that agent when he comes back to the valley and my friend will let me know if anyone sees him.' He scowled again. 'The sooner someone buys the old place and Hatton stops coming to our valley, the better it'll be for all of us.'

Elinor cycled at a leisurely pace along the river path, enjoying the quiet and the afternoon sun on her face. She was taking some freshly baked scones and currant buns to the Rainfords and Bryn, and using that as an excuse to give herself a pleasant outing on this sunny early summer day. It still felt marvellous to be able to do whatever she wanted when she wanted.

Suddenly a stone hit her on the shoulder and another one whizzed past her face, making her cry out in shock and wobble about. Her bike swerved off the path and down the sloping verge, taking her dangerously close to the water. Another stone followed, but by then she'd regained her balance and moved quickly back onto the track, speeding up so that a third stone and the two that followed it missed her completely.

'Get out of the valley, you bitch!' a hoarse voice called from a group of nearby shrubs. 'You're not wanted here.'

She couldn't see anyone and it was clear that the voice had been deliberately disguised. She continued to pedal as fast as she could, relieved to reach the cottages and hopefully be out of reach of the stone thrower. She didn't stop there because she didn't want to take trouble to the Rainfords and went straight on to the old mill. She felt even more relieved when she got round the back of it and into the area where customers usually stopped.

There was no sign of Bryn but when she hammered on the door and called, 'Bryn! Come quickly! Bryn!' she heard running footsteps and it was flung open.

She glanced over her shoulder, but could see no one. 'Someone just threw stones at me as I rode along by the river coming up to the cottages. It startled me and I swerved off the track, nearly ran into the water.'

'*What?*' He pulled her inside and then brought the bicycle in as well. 'Stay here and bolt the door till I get back. I know a shortcut past the cottages at the rear. It's quicker than the river path. I should think whoever it was will have left by now but I'm going to see if I can find where they were hiding and whether they left any signs.'

Before she could say anything, he'd run off through the bushes that lined many stretches of riverbank, quickly vanishing from sight in the direction she'd come. She did as he'd said and locked the door, then leaned against the wall, shuddering in reaction. She'd come very close to falling into the river.

She couldn't understand why anyone would attack her. That hadn't been a child's voice, nor could a child have thrown such big stones so hard. This wasn't idle mischief. Someone must have wanted to hurt her.

She couldn't imagine even Jason Stafford bothering to spend money to pay for a relatively minor attack. The only other person she might have upset was Hatton. Could it be him? Walter had said he liked to get back at people who'd upset him and he'd been furious at them helping the Rainfords get their furniture away.

It had to be him. She hadn't upset anyone else round here that she knew of.

What good would it do him to hurt her?

Bryn pounded past the cottages, startling Dick, who was working in the garden, and shouting, 'I'll be back in a minute.'

When he got past the cottages on to the river path, he stopped. He couldn't see anyone so whoever it was must have got away quickly. It was clearly no use going much further along, but there was one thing he could do. He searched among the shrubs and bushes near the water and found a small pile of the medium-sized river stones and signs that someone had made a little nest out of sight of the track in a natural hollow.

Clearly the attack had been planned, wasn't just a random impulse. Had it always been aimed at Elinor, or was it to deter anyone coming along to the cottages or mill?

He took great satisfaction in tossing the stones one by one into the centre of the river. It was deep enough there to come up to someone's knees and running quite fast, so no one would go so far out to retrieve them.

The trouble was, whoever had attacked Elinor would easily be able to replenish their store of missiles from the shallows at the edge. Still, it'd slow them down to collect more if they came back. Dick or Peggy would be likely to notice them and could come to the mill the back way to fetch him.

He'd come back tomorrow with a couple of tree branches and hammer them deep into the ground in the hollow, with their tops sticking out. He doubted the attacker would find it comfortable to sit waiting here then. That was the best he could think of for protecting passers-by and customers for his business for the moment.

It had to be Hatton's doing. Word was that he'd gone off on the train again, but he could have paid someone to attack people coming along the path. He was known to booze with the Catlows for a start and they were behind a lot of minor trouble in the district, Walter said.

And he was about to buy a bicycle. He wasn't going to give anyone a chance to damage that. He'd better put a sturdier lock on the barn door, which meant going into the town to buy what he needed. He let out a little growl of anger. That wasn't what he'd planned to spend his time and money doing today.

He walked back towards the mill, stopping on the way to explain what had happened to Dick, who was still working in the garden, and asking him to keep an eye open for anyone behaving suspiciously near the river.

'Is it going to be dangerous for us here?' the old man asked in a hushed voice. 'I could have fought someone off when I were younger. I were a strong young chap then. But I couldn't do it now.'

'Don't worry. I'll take care of that side of things,' Bryn said grimly. 'You can help by keeping your eyes open.'

Dick brightened a little. 'Aye. I can still do that at least.'

'Let me show you the shortcut I found to the back of the mill when I was walking round the grounds exploring, in case you need to come and get me quickly.'

Dick walked with him and nodded when shown the way through the vegetation. 'I shall remember this way, don't worry. And not only will I keep my eyes open for trespassers, so will my Peggy. Now, you get back to Miss Pendleton. She'll be worrying about you and she must have been shook up by the attack. I can walk to my cottage on my own now that I know this way through the copse behind it.'

Bryn hurried back to the mill but had to knock on the door and wait for Elinor to let him in.

He explained what he'd found and when he saw her expression, he asked, 'Do you have some idea who it might be?'

'Well, Hatton was very upset about the Rainfords moving out, especially about them taking all the furniture. He came round and had a shouting match with Walter about it.'

'Is the man mad? What has their furniture to do with him?'

'He's definitely someone to be careful about. Walter says he's hurt quite a few people when they didn't do what he wanted and no one dares complain.'

'That settles it. I'm definitely going to carry my revolver with me when I go out and about.' After another pause, he added, 'I think I'd better get a dog, too, but I'd need a fully grown one rather than a puppy. And perhaps I'll hire a lad to live in and help me with the work and be there to keep watch on the place when I'm out.'

'That's a good idea. Can you afford it, though?'

'I'll be able to as soon as my money comes through. I'll ask Walter if he can help me find someone suitable. He seems to know everyone in the valley. He's amazing, isn't he?

'He's wonderful. But it's not fair that you have to spend your money to protect yourself when you're just setting up in business.'

'I was going to take on an apprentice anyway after a while, but I can change my plans and make use of one from now on. I've known for a while that I wanted to start my own business when I got back to England, so I've been extremely careful with my money over the past few years.'

She shook her head, still shocked by her experience. 'I still can't believe anyone would attack me like that.'

'You weren't hurt, were you?'

'I might have a bruise where the first stone hit, but that's all. You know, for a supposedly peaceful valley, there are some nasty things going on. It puzzles me why.'

'There are unpleasant things happening everywhere, believe me, but honest folk going about their business aren't usually the targets for no reason. Well, whoever it is doing this has chosen the wrong person if they think they're going to frighten me away.'

'I did wonder if it might be Denby again, sent by Stafford.' She shuddered even to say that horrible man's name.

Bryn shook his head. 'He knows you've got a protector in Walter and anyway, he could find a wife much more easily close to home, and a willing one at that.'

'I'm being silly about him, aren't I?'

'You had years of trouble with the older Stafford, so it stands to reason it'll take time for you to get over that. But you've got three men here who won't let anyone hurt you or take you away from the valley, Elinor.' He couldn't resist adding, 'And it'd upset Cameron particularly if someone even tried.'

She looked at him in surprise, could feel herself flushing. 'Do you really think so?'

'Definitely.'

'Oh.'

'How would you feel about Cameron being interested in you?'

She hesitated then decided to tell the truth, flushing slightly as she confessed, 'I like him, feel comfortable chatting. I never thought I'd say that about any man after the Staffords. Only, well, he hasn't shown any signs of that sort of interest.'

'Not yet. He's had to make sure he's truly welcome here with Walter first. Haven't you noticed how he looks at you? I have.'

'I . . . I did wonder a couple of times.' Even speaking about it brought home to her that she did hope Cameron was interested.

She was glad when Bryn let that subject drop and continued to talk about the other thing she'd said.

'I'll keep my eyes open for strangers from now on.'

'We'll all keep our eyes open. My best guess is that any trouble is likely to be Hatton's doing.'

'Yes. He's a horrible man, isn't he? Anyway, I'd better start back now or Maude will wonder where I am. Oops! I nearly forgot.' She lifted two large tins out of the basket attached to the front of her bike. 'I brought you some of my baked goods and I have some for the Rainfords. I know Peggy is a good cook, but she's still settling in. It's a good thing I strapped the tins in carefully, isn't it?' She handed one tin to him. 'I'd be grateful if you'd let me have the tin back.'

'That's kind of you. Actually, if I put these goodies away now, you can take the tin back with you.'

He did that then grabbed his jacket from the hook behind the door. 'Just wait a minute till I check that everything's locked up then I'll walk back with you to make sure you reach the farm safely.'

'That's a long walk. I'm sure I'll be all right.'

'I want to speak to Walter about finding a dog and boy, so I need to see him anyway. I'm going to buy a bike myself as well so that I can go where I want more quickly. Come on. Let's get going. We can drop the rest of your baked goods off at the Rainfords on the way.'

When they got back to the farm, they saw Walter working at the desk near the window inside his office and went straight across to him instead of going to the house.

He saw them arrive and came outside, stretching his stiffness away. He listened carefully as Elinor explained what had happened, and frowned at what the unknown assailant had nearly done to her.

'They could have killed you if you'd landed in the water and hit your head on a stone. Please don't go there on your own till we sort it out. I think it's a good idea for you to hire a lad, Bryn. There will be plenty of room for him to stay in the attic at the mill.'

'Do you know anyone suitable?'

'I know several lads who'd jump at the chance.' Walter frowned. 'Hmm.' Then his face brightened. 'There's one that might be particularly suitable because he already has a dog. Why don't I take you to meet him now? Afterwards we'll call on the man I told you about, who repairs and sells bicycles.'

'That'd be marvellous.'

'I can drive you back to the mill afterwards in my cart. Would you harness Sally, please, while I smarten myself up a bit?'

Elinor stood at the door watching them leave then went to tell Maude exactly what had happened and what she'd like to do to whoever had attacked her. The angrier she got the more her fear receded.

'It isn't making me afraid as much as angry,' she said.

'That makes two of us angry about the attack.' Maude gave her a quick hug.

'I'd grown too meek and mild, trying to stop my stepfather noticing me, hadn't I?'

'We should have left sooner.'

'It's easy to be wise after the event. I'm learning to stand up for myself now. I shan't put up with any more bullying, you can be sure.'

22

New York

In America, Caleb enjoyed his new life greatly at first. Then he forgot something Daniel considered important and received a tirade of abuse, which ended in him being threatened that Daniel would dump him in the next town if he didn't take more care about what he was doing.

With that threat hanging over him, Caleb didn't dare be careless again. For a while all went well, though the mood around him was shifting, and he was beginning to feel rather afraid of the man who had seemed so genial when offering him a job.

Then one day everything got even more frightening. He saw Daniel thump someone who'd annoyed him, and when the man fought back, Daniel pulled out a knife and flung it across the room with amazing speed. The man might have noticed it coming but he hadn't had time to react in his own defence. He didn't get up again. Daniel called for Jan, a huge Dutchman who acted as a sort of bodyguard in New York, to clear some 'rubbish' away.

The body vanished and Caleb didn't let on that he'd seen what happened. But he worried about the incident and couldn't get it out of his mind. No police turned up, but he didn't care about that. It was his own safety he worried about if he upset Daniel again.

The killing had happened so quickly!

It made him wonder whether he should carry a knife or a gun for his own protection. Only Daniel had moved so very quickly. Caleb was not only afraid, he was somewhat intrigued, wondering how the other man had managed to do that.

He'd noticed that Daniel had a leather sheath hanging from the belt of his trousers, and now figured out the slight difference between it and other sheaths.

Having learned to do various swift moves in card playing, he couldn't resist buying a dagger and trying to learn how to take it out quickly if there were any trouble. He only practised this when Daniel and Jan were out of the building, though.

Somehow, what he'd seen took the enjoyment out of the card playing from then onwards. He was finding life very boring in between games because Daniel told him to stay at home and stop wandering about the city. It was a good thing he'd already bought the knife.

Staying at home most of the time wasn't the sort of life he'd expected when he ran away. It wasn't fair. Nothing he did ever seemed to turn out well.

He was also getting more of the little fluttery feelings in his chest than he'd ever had before. His father hadn't believed these were real, but Caleb had spoken to their doctor privately about them once and he'd told him it was happening because one part of his heart got out of step with another part and then it started beating irregularly till it got in step again.

'It doesn't usually kill anyone, but you should keep fit and not let yourself put on weight,' he'd ended. 'Oh, and try to lead a fairly calm life.'

Caleb was relieved that this small problem didn't usually kill anyone and since it didn't get any worse, he'd pushed the worry to the back of his mind. But he'd put on weight, couldn't help it when he was leading such an inactive life. And then the flutterings began to get worse. He learned to stand still when that happened and it usually passed quite quickly but it worried him.

He tried to go for walks more regularly, partly to pass the time and partly for his health and Daniel sent Jan with him. But it was difficult to fit many walks in because Daniel got annoyed if he wasn't available instantly when required to play cards unexpectedly.

This seemed to be happening more often with people from out of town coming to play in 'special' games. Caleb was not only needed to make up the numbers but to fiddle some of the deals so that Daniel won.

In fact, when you took everything into account, his new life, which had sounded so promising, was just as tedious in some ways as his old life.

Not that he'd dare say anything to Daniel. Like everyone else he tried not to upset the man who'd turned out to be the leader of a group of criminals, not a mere card sharp.

When that had sunk in, Caleb even wondered about running away again.

But where else could he go and how could he get away completely?

23

Lancashire

When the two men set off for the village, Bryn said, 'Tell me about these lads you know, Walter.'

'Well, I think one of them would be particularly suitable. He's called Tam and he's very clever. What's more, he already has a big dog. He's hard put to feed it sometimes, because his mother is a widow and he has two younger brothers and a sister. But he always manages somehow or other to get food for it, though not as much as it really needs. If he can't get any food, he'll share his last crust with it, he and that dog are so devoted to one another.'

'He sounds interesting.'

Walter reined in the pony outside a small cottage with a tidy garden at the near side of Upperfold. 'I own this cottage. I have to call in to discuss something with Mrs Barrett but I won't be long.' He passed the reins to Bryn and went to knock on the door. It was opened by a sad-looking, grey-haired woman and he followed her inside.

Bryn sat and enjoyed a few minutes' rest in the sun while the pony found a lush patch of grass by the roadside and began to munch the nearest clump.

When Walter came back, he said briefly, 'Mrs Barrett has been recently widowed, poor woman, so I'm helping her sort things out for her new life. She's going to take in a couple of lodgers so I need to get her an extra bed.'

They carried on across the village to the far end where the houses were shabbier and crammed more closely together. Walter tied Sally loosely to a fence and beckoned to a scrawny lad standing at the nearby corner. 'A penny for you if you keep an eye on my pony and cart for a few minutes.'

The lad brightened. 'Yessir, Mr Crossley. Happy to.'

'This way.' Walter set off down a narrow ginnel between two short rows of shabby houses, knocking on a battered door at the rear end of it.

A woman answered it. She looked tired but brightened a little when she saw who it was. 'Hello, Mr Crossley.'

'Hello, Maureen. This is my young friend Mr Fordham, who's new to our town. Bryn, this is Mrs Hayman. Can we come in? I think I may have found a job for your Tam.'

She stepped back, looking at him expectantly. 'Really? Even if I still can't afford to buy him any better clothes?'

'Even so. Mr Fordham urgently needs a lad to assist him in general duties. Ah, and here is Tam.'

A youth had just come into the room from the far side. 'I could hear what you were saying and thought I'd better let you know I'm here, Mr Crossley. And I'll do any work I can to bring in money for Mam.'

'Good lad.'

A big dog that was rather gaunt followed him in, looking round. It went to wag its tail at Walter as if it already knew him and he ruffled the fur on its head in greeting.

Bryn held his hand out and it sniffed that gently and politely. When Tam said, 'Friend,' more tail wagging followed.

'He likes you, sir,' Tam said earnestly. 'You can trust him to be on your side from now on if there's any trouble.'

Walter smiled. 'There's no trouble, Tam. I'm the bringer of good news. When Mr Fordham said he needed a lad I thought of you. You'd better tell them what's needed, Bryn.'

'I can do that but what I pay will be up to you because I'm not used to English prices and wages yet.' He turned back to Tam and his mother. 'I'm about to start a carpentry business in the old mill beyond Upperfold. I need a lad who'll do anything and everything, and if he proves himself a good worker, I can offer him an apprenticeship in carpentry and wood carving at a later stage.'

Tam's face was suddenly full of eagerness and hope, and he mouthed the word 'Apprenticeship' reverently.

His mother clasped one hand to her chest, staring at Bryn as if she couldn't believe her ears. 'My son could get an apprenticeship?' she asked in an incredulous whisper.

Walter smiled at her. 'There's a very good chance of it because he's a clever lad. I've already recommended him for the general job so he'll get that anyway.'

'Oh, Mr Crossley, I can't thank you enough. And Mr Fordham, I'm sure as can be that my Tam will give you satisfaction. I've been at my wits' end to get him a job but there hasn't been anything except odd jobs to be found round here lately. And now you're offering . . . offering—' She burst into tears mingled with smiles and apologies for being so silly as to cry when it was good news. It was a minute or two before she calmed down.

Bryn left Walter to deal with her while he looked at the lad, who was studying him equally carefully. 'What do you think, Tam? Would you like to try working for me?'

'Yes, sir, please. I'd work very hard but . . . ' He gestured to the dog. 'I'd have to bring Spike with me because he's my best friend and Mam can't afford to feed him. I'll buy his food from my wages. He won't cost you a penny.'

Bryn decided he liked the direct way Tam looked at him and his loyalty to his dog. 'I'm going to need Spike as well as you, so if you'll hire him to me, he can earn his own keep. I'll feed him well, I promise you. We've had a bit of trouble nearby and I need a watchdog.'

He watched this sink in and happy tears well up in Tam's eyes too.

'Sir, I promise you he's a very good watchdog and he always obeys my commands. He'll obey yours too once he gets to know you.'

'Then let's give each other a try-out for a week or two, shall we, eh?'

Walter named the wages and said, 'We'll pay most of that to his mother, if it's all right with you, Bryn?'

'Of course. I'll do whatever you say.'

More fat, happy tears rolled down Mrs Hayman's cheeks even as she tried to smile.

'How about we take Tam and Spike back with us today once we've finished our business in town, Maureen? The old mill would be rather a long way for your son to walk, and a waste of energy when I'm driving back there today.'

'Yes, of course. I'll go and pack his clothes, only . . . well, he hasn't got much, sir, and he's nearly grown out of those he does have. I'll buy him some more clothes as soon as I start getting the wages, I promise you.'

'No need,' Walter said gently. 'We can get him some good second-hand clothes from the pawnshop quite cheaply. In fact, we'll do it now and leave the dog here for the moment. I'll send Tam back to show you his new clothes and pick up the dog after we've finished our shopping, and you can keep any clothes he doesn't need for your next son.'

He clapped the lad on the back. 'I'll bring you back to see your mother in a week or two, Tam, then you can tell her all about your new life.'

'Thank you, Mr Crossley,' she said. 'For everything. You've saved me and my family more than once since I lost my husband.'

'You and he used to play with my son when you were both children. I remember you as a little girl. I'm happy to help you any time and never be afraid to ask. It's not your fault your husband died and you've been left struggling to earn enough to feed your family. How people expect women to manage on half a man's wages, I'll never understand.'

They left the dog with her and went to buy better clothes for Tam and when he admitted how many of the clothes he owned were now too small, Walter told him to give all those back to his mother for the use of his next youngest brother. He then bought a few more clothes and sent the lad off to fetch the dog and meet them at the livery stables.

'I like the looks of him,' Bryn said.

'They're a really nice family. I think he'll suit you. Now, let's call in at the bank, but I don't think your money will have arrived yet.'

It hadn't but the manager assured them that it'd be there before the end of the week, so Bryn had to continue accepting financial help from Walter.

When Tam rejoined them, he had the dog walking beside him with a piece of rope as a makeshift lead. 'Mum says to tell you thank you for the new clothes.'

'She already did that in advance, lad.'

'Well, thank you again.'

After they'd harnessed Sally, they settled Tam, Spike and his bundles on the back of the cart and set off for the mill.

When Bryn looked round, he saw that his new employee was studying everything they passed very carefully as if he didn't often get out of town. And there was always a far better view from up on a cart than on your own two feet.

He had to admit to himself that Tam wasn't a very attractive lad in appearance, even though he looked at the world in an honest, open way. He was tall and very thin, showing the unmistakable signs of a youth who wasn't eating enough to feed his growing body properly. His sharp features were topped by hair of a faded ginger colour, and his cheeks and nose were peppered with freckles. At the moment he had a big, broad smile that lit up his whole face.

The dog was of an indeterminate breed, partly collie and who knew what else? He was past being a puppy but still quite young and like his master, he needed better food to reach his full potential. He too was staring round alertly as they drove along, sniffing the air every now and then.

At they got back to the other side of the village Walter stopped to pick up a mattress and bedding for Tam from his storage cottage, then he bought them all fish and chips. A little shop selling these had opened recently in someone's front room to supply this favourite delicacy to everyone who could afford it. Walter didn't mention that he'd funded the venture but noted with pleasure that there was a smile on the owner's face and two women waiting for their food to be cooked.

'Salt and vinegar everyone?' he asked. 'Except for Spike, of course.'

The humans all nodded and the dog wagged his tail as if he understood.

When he got his order, Walter passed out the small parcels of food, each portion of food set on a square of white greaseproof paper then wrapped in newspaper. 'We'll eat it now while it's hot.'

'This is the one for the dog,' the man serving them said as he handed over the last parcel. 'I put some extra scraps of batter in for him.'

'Thank you.' Walter passed it to Tam. 'You give this to Spike. He doesn't know us well enough yet. He must be taught not to accept food from strangers.'

Tam licked his lips. 'Thank you so much, Mr Crossley. We're both rather hungry.'

When the dog was presented with his own portion, placed carefully on the ground in front of him, he too licked his lips but he still didn't grab the food, instead looking at his young master as if asking whether he was allowed to eat it. Having been given permission, he began to gulp it down rapidly, glancing round from time to time as if half expecting someone to try to take it away from him.

That dog had good manners already, Walter noted with approval.

They stopped at the farm on the way to the mill to introduce the two women to Tam and the dog.

Once again Spike sniffed the strangers' hands carefully and looked at his master, who nodded and murmured 'Friends'. Spike wagged his tail and even swiped a quick lick at Maude's hand.

'He's taken a real fancy to you, Miss Vernon. He doesn't lick everyone. He'll remember you both as friends from now on,' Tam assured them. 'He never forgets once I've introduced him to someone. He's a very clever dog, the cleverest in the whole valley.'

Walter hid a smile at the utter certainty in Tam's voice. 'We'll need to borrow one of your bikes for Bryn for a few days. Is that all right?'

When both women nodded, he turned to say, 'You can cycle into the village tomorrow and visit Peter in the house I showed you, Bryn lad. He should have a bike ready for you by then. Tell him I'll pay him next time I'm in town, then you can pay me back once your money is transferred.'

When they got back to the mill, they unloaded Bryn and his two new employees, then their purchases, the bike and the old mattress.

As he got back on the cart Walter said, 'I'll leave you to settle in now.'

'Thank you.' Bryn said in a low voice, 'For everything. And don't worry. I'll look after the lad.'

'And the dog will guard both of you and your home. It'll soon recognise the mill as its home too. I don't know when I've seen a dog that was more promising. In fact, they're a promising pair and they'll do well by you, mark my words.'

After watching Walter drive away and then waiting while Spike christened the approach to his new home in the usual doggie way, Bryn took them inside and found an old bowl in which to put water for Spike. He showed Tam, who also confessed to being thirsty, where the mugs were kept and how to pump water from the old-fashioned tap.

'Shall we look round the rest of the inside now?'

Tam nodded eagerly.

When told to choose which attic room he wanted, he looked thoughtful for a moment, then asked which way Bryn's bedroom faced. He went round the four smaller bedrooms up there again and voted for one which overlooked the back of the building not the front.

'This way we'll be able to keep an eye on both sides of the house,' he said.

Bryn was pleased with this. 'Good thinking. And if you see anything lying about in the other parts of the attic which you can use in your bedroom to make it more comfortable just take it.'

'Really?'

'Yes, really. There are a few odds and ends left by the last people who lived here.'

'There's a broken chair in that far corner, but I can mend it if you'll lend me your tools and a few nails, I could use it to put my clothes on.'

'We'll mend it together. It can be your first carpentry lesson.'

Tam beamed even more broadly at that.

A yawn stopped Bryn checking any more details. 'I know it's early but I've had a very busy day and I'm tired, so let's get ready for bed now. If you want some bread and jam for supper help yourself to a couple of slices but don't forget to put the loaf back in the bread bin, and put everything else away in the cupboard. I do like a tidy house.'

'I can have something else to eat?' He sounded amazed.

Tam licked his lips involuntarily and Bryn remembered how hungry he'd always felt at that age.

'Is it all right if I share my bread with Spike? He's hungry again too.'

'Give him a slice of his own. We'll get him some horsemeat and bones next time we're in town. You'll know when he's hungry better than I will, so feeding him will be up to you.'

A happy sigh greeted this.

'Oh, and don't forget to take some matches up with you to relight your candle if you wake in the night. There are some unopened boxes of them on that shelf. I need to buy us some good oil lamps and I will do as soon as my money comes through to the bank. We'll manage with candles until then.'

Tam looked at him, big-eyed and solemn. 'I'd just like to say thank you for giving me this chance, Mr Fordham, and giving us all that lovely food. I won't let you down. And Spike won't, either.'

'Call me Bryn. If we're going to be living and working together, I don't think we should stand on ceremony.'

'But you're my employer! Mam says I have to show you respect.'

'I've lived too long in America to stand on ceremony. Take Spike outside after you've eaten then lock the door carefully when you come back in and get off to bed, the pair of you.'

Bryn watched the boy and dog eat some more food and clear up after themselves, the dog making sure every single crumb was cleared from the floor. After they'd gone up to bed, he did a final check of the ground-floor doors and windows then followed their example.

As he went into his new bedroom, he was overtaken by another huge yawn. He couldn't wait to get into bed and let himself fall asleep.

When he woke the next morning he got dressed quickly and hurried downstairs, intending to check that there had been no disturbances during the night. He found Tam already up and standing on the doorstep watching his dog check and christen the far edge of the big open area.

There was a fire lit in the kitchen range and the kettle was simmering on the top.

'Did you sleep well, Tam? I went out like a log. I don't think there were any prowlers around.'

'Me an' Spike slept really well, too. He'd have woke me an' let me know if anyone had come near the house.'

'Good.'

Bryn was feeling re-energised by his long, peaceful sleep, ready to start putting his new life together, not to mention training his new employee. But first he needed to go into the village and see if he could get himself a bike, not to mention food for his new dependants.

He left Tam to sweep the floors in the workshop and mop the one in the kitchen while Spike took a nap in a sunny spot just outside the back door, then he rode into Upperfold on Walter's bike, hoping to come back on one of his own.

This place felt so good he found himself whistling as he rode along by the river. Even the sun was smiling on him today.

24

Halifax, Yorkshire

Meanwhile, in Halifax, a tall, well-dressed gentleman who looked to be in his late thirties had just arrived at his solicitor's office.

After exchanging polite greetings, the first thing he said was, 'Don't forget that I don't want the Kenyons, or indeed anyone in Ollindale, to know who is buying the property. Don't even speak my surname aloud in your own office. If you have to call me something, you can call me Mr Smith.'

Mr Filmore inclined his head. 'You made that very clear last time we spoke, sir.'

'Make sure it always stays clear in your mind and discourage your employees if they're too inquisitive. *You* must make the offer, arrange the contract on behalf of my company according to my instructions and then sign it for me.'

'You seem very sure they'll agree to sell at that price, sir. It's rather a low offer, you know.'

'I've been keeping an eye on John Kenyon for a few years and when I discovered recently that he was deep in debt, I moved to Halifax to keep a closer eye on the situation because I'm interested in buying the Ollerton estate. Since then he has lost even more money in gambling. His wife is absolutely furious and he's desperate to pay off those debts before he gets declared bankrupt and the rest of his money and property taken by the authorities.'

The lawyer shook his head and made a disapproving sound at the mere thought of this carelessness with money.

The man continued, 'According to what I found out, the Kenyons have never been back to Ollindale since the big house burned down two decades ago, nor have any of them shown any signs of wishing to rebuild it. In fact, they put the property up for sale several years ago, but didn't receive any offers to buy it because they were asking too much money.'

'Not many people would want to live in that part of the world even if there were a big house there that was still habitable,' said the lawyer. 'Why did the family buy it in the first place?'

'It was his late parents who bought it because they wanted to live in a big house but didn't have a large enough fortune for a grand one in a more popular area. After their deaths it passed to him, but he already lived in a house belonging to his wife's family. All he's done with the one in Ollindale is appoint an agent to collect the rents. His wife has never even seen the estate. I'm told she comes from a moderately wealthy family, and why she married a man like him puzzles me greatly.'

The gentleman gave a wry smile, as he went on. 'I, on the other hand, will be very happy to build a comfortable home and live there for the rest of my life because I do love the north country. I've visited the estate secretly and I shall be able to stay in the agent's house for a year or two while a new house is being built – well, I will once the roof is made fully waterproof and the interior cleaned out properly.'

He paused, waiting for the lawyer to speak but all he got was another frown, so he said gently, 'Give this offer a try, please, Mr Filmore. What have we got to lose? I think you'll find that I've chosen my moment and my price rather well. I gather from one of my informants that Mrs Kenyon is increasingly ruling the roost now that her husband is so deeply in debt that he can't pay any of their household bills and her family has had to step in.'

'You're sure of this?'

'Very sure.'

'Very well. I'll make the offer. I presume you would raise it a little if he wished to bargain?'

'No. I'm not paying a penny more for it, and he's lucky to get that because he hasn't looked after the place.'

'Excuse me asking but it still puzzles me why you are so determined to live there, Mr—um, Smith?'

'I've had a busy few years and I want a quiet life from now on. I also have a fancy to build a large modern house to my own specifications and am looking forward to doing that. I may even see if I can find myself a wife. It's not too late for me to start a family.'

'Ah. I see.'

'Go ahead with the offer, Mr Filmore. Please get in touch with me immediately it's accepted and we'll push the sale through a few days after that.'

'You seem very sure it will be accepted.'

'I am.'

'A few days would be difficult, sir. Things don't usually move that fast when buying and selling houses.'

'I was told you are one of the most capable lawyers in Halifax, but if you can't make this sale happen quickly, perhaps I need to look for a lawyer who is able to facilitate this matter. What do you think?'

There was a pregnant silence, then Mr Filmore gave in. 'Very well. If they accept the offer, I'll send a message to you immediately and then I'll set to work to push things through rapidly, whatever it takes. I have a very efficient lady typewriter working in my office and she will produce the actual contract documents rapidly. These machine-written documents are so much better than the old handwritten ones that we used to use. And the carbon copies are far clearer when made by typing than writing by hand, too.'

'I'd appreciate your efforts to speed things up and will continue to value your services once the sale is completed. I shall not be giving up all my businesses by any means and shall need legal help in the north.'

The lawyer nodded and smiled after his client had left. He would do it, whatever it took.

He sent his clerk to the Kenyons that very afternoon, asking them to visit him at his office because he had a client interested in buying their property in Ollindale.

When he got back, his clerk described their residence as 'modest' and that made Filmore wonder whether their situation was more difficult financially than he'd thought.

Perhaps 'Mr Smith' had been right. He didn't allow himself to think of that man by anything other than this assumed name in case he inadvertently used the latter.

When the Kenyons were shown into Mr Filmore's office the following day, he studied them with interest. Mr Kenyon proved to be a gentleman who had grown plump in his middle years, with a face that might have once been handsome but now bore testament to a dissipated lifestyle.

Mrs Kenyon was extremely thin, with greying hair worn in a severe style. She was wearing expensive dark garments which were neither flattering nor fashionable, and frowning as if she knew no other expression. She offered the lawyer the briefest of nods when he greeted them and asked them to sit down on the hard chairs at the other side of his desk.

A tense atmosphere seemed to follow them into the room even before Mr Filmore told them the details of the offer. It grew noticeably worse when he fell silent and waited for their response.

John Kenyon stared at him in patent shock. 'That's a ridiculously low amount. I can't possibly sell the estate so cheaply. There's a lot of land involved, you know.'

Mr Filmore stared back at him, adopting the bland expression he used in court so that his face didn't betray his feelings. 'It's not very fertile land, though, is it? And it has no residence on it.'

'The land has its, um, uses. Grazing for sheep and rent from several houses in and near the village. And a new house could easily be built there. The views across the valley are very pretty. Perhaps your client could raise his price a little, say by a couple of thousand pounds?'

'That isn't possible. The rent roll doesn't bring in enough to justify a higher price and there are no sheep or other stock there at present. In fact, my client has told me specifically that he will not raise his price by a single penny because there are always other houses available for purchase.'

Kenyon's mouth opened and shut. He didn't seem able to form a word of protest, however, and shot a nervous glance at his wife.

Filmore waited a few moments to add, 'And if I may remind you of one rather important thing, sir, my client and his partners are offering to pay cash within two days of signing the contract. That would surely be a considerable benefit to you – given your situation.'

The last phrase clearly struck home and Kenyon gulped audibly, while his wife's frown deepened.

When Kenyon did manage to speak, his voice wobbled slightly. 'Not possible for him to raise his price, you say? What do you mean by that?'

'They won't pay any more than the offer I've made. He and those involved with him in this sort of business always do it that way: fixing a price in advance and sticking to it. I have never known them raise the price they offer, not in all the years I've been representing them.'

Which was a lie because this was the first time he had acted on behalf of Mr 'Smith', and his client had stated from the beginning that there were no other people except himself involved.

'I'll . . . need to think about it.'

'You have until noon tomorrow to accept their offer or else they will move on to the next property on their list and buy that instead. He and his partners have made a lot of money over the years by this method of doing business and they're not going to change it now, believe me. You must decide quickly whether to take their offer or leave it.'

The lady sitting bolt upright beside her husband had been silent so far, her lips clamped closely together, the expression on her face suggesting any affection between them had completely vanished and been replaced by hatred. Now, she stretched out her arm and twitched her husband's sleeve to get his attention, because he was still staring at the lawyer.

'Do it, John.'

He turned to her, looking even more shocked than before. 'Amelia, no!'

'When you lost that much money you also lost the ability to bargain about prices and it's my guess these people know that only too well. What's more, if my family is to get you out of debt, we must have the final say in the selling of your assets. So do as I say and accept that offer. It'll reduce considerably what my family has to pay to keep you from bankruptcy.'

As he opened his mouth to continue protesting, she said sharply, 'If you think about it, we shall also save paying some of the interest which would accrue each month should we pay off the debt quickly. Why you borrowed money at such a high rate of interest, I shall never, ever understand.'

Filmore watched with interest the way Kenyon's shoulders sagged. His client had been right. The wife did have the final say in matters financial now and there was something about her that said she was utterly determined to do this her way.

He'd guess that she would find a way to prevent her husband gambling again, as well.

He waited, watching Kenyon bite his lip and then say jerkily, 'As my wife has pointed out, we'll save money elsewhere by accepting the offer now, so we'll sell to your client as long as he really can pay quickly.'

'Good. I can personally guarantee the rapid payment.'

'I'd like to know the name of the purchaser.'

'Smith and Company.'

'I meant the name of the man behind the company, the one leading the group. I doubt he's really called Smith.'

'My client and his colleagues prefer to stay in the background. I have full authority to act on their behalf in this sale, as I have done in their other ventures, which obviously includes signing contracts to buy or sell on their behalf.'

'This man has other companies?'

'Oh yes, sir. Several.' Filmore didn't know how true this was, because his client had been very sparing with information about himself, only admitting his real name on condition it went no further. However, saying this stopped the vendor protesting further, as he'd hoped it would.

This time Mrs Kenyon gave her husband a sharp poke with a bony forefinger. 'His name isn't important, John. Let it drop.'

As he closed his mouth and sagged against the back of his chair, she favoured the lawyer one of those bitterly sharp looks. 'You're sure the payment will be made within two days of the contract being signed, Mr Filmore?'

'Oh yes. I can guarantee that because the money is already waiting in the bank. Once both parties have signed the contract itself, I shall see the manager and arrange to transfer the payment to your account immediately.'

'Very well. Make sure that is a written requirement in the final contract. I have a separate bank account, which is used for my family trust. I've written down the details. All contracts are to be in both our names. Is that clear?'

At the lawyer's nod, she pulled a piece of folded paper from her handbag, which was a much larger one than was currently used by ladies of her class, and pushed it across the desk to him. 'The purchase money is to be paid into this account, *not* into my husband's former account, which has been closed.'

Kenyon scowled down at the floor but made no attempt to correct this statement.

Mr Filmore pulled out the provisional agreement to buy and sell that he'd already prepared and inserted both their names in the relevant place then pushed it across the desk.

Kenyon signed this without a word, not even bothering to read it.

His wife picked it up, took out a pair of spectacles and read it carefully before signing.

A time was then set for them to come back to the office the following day to sign the contract itself.

Filmore didn't let himself smile until they'd left his rooms.

When he heard the outer door close, he couldn't resist watching out of the window as they walked down the street. Mrs Kenyon's arm was linked in her husband's and even from this distance he could see that she was grasping his arm rather tightly.

They didn't seem to be conversing at all. Well, what else was there to say?

Kenyon was looking utterly miserable, both in his expression and in the way he moved his body. At one stage he threw a quick sideways look at his wife which said he hated her.

She didn't glance in his direction once while Filmore was watching, simply held herself erect, kept that tight hold on her husband's arm and walked briskly along. There was something implacable about her, but if she was having to deal with a gambler who had lost most of their money, she'd have to be a

very determined and capable woman to sort their finances out
and prevent him from losing the rest of their money.

When they'd vanished round a corner, Filmore went back
to sit at his desk and rang the handbell to summon his senior
clerk.

He looked astonished at what the lawyer told him to do. 'I'm
afraid it can't be done so quickly, sir.'

'It has to be done rapidly for the gentleman we are now
representing, and since he will be a very valuable customer in
future if he gets what he wants from us this time, we must find
a way to do it. I'm quite prepared to stay up all night working
on the contract if necessary. And we can pay you and Miss
Becker double wages for any extra time needed, which I'm
sure you will both appreciate.'

'Very well, sir. Um, do we know this client's full name? For
the contract, that is.'

'I know it. For the contract we need only know the name of
his company and that is the sole information about himself
that he wishes to be given on the contract or indeed to anyone
at all.'

'Very unusual, sir.'

'Yes, but I can assure you he is acting legally, if in an unusual
manner, so we must do as he wishes.'

When the clerk left his office, Filmore sat quietly for a
moment or two, wondering what his client intended to do with
this estate, which was in the middle of some valley that few
people had heard of. Did he merely wish to build a house on
it, or was there some other reason for buying it?

Then he shrugged and walked along to the post office himself to send a telegram across the city to Mr Smith, something
normally left to junior staff. The secrecy required by his client
made even this minor task too important to leave to anyone
except himself, but he didn't mind because he saw a great deal
of benefit in having this man as a permanent client.

Filmore's father had been content to work slowly and quietly, earning a comfortable living as a lawyer and not striving
for more. Ezra Filmore was rather more ambitious about his
own finances.

In addition, when his client had talked of rebuilding the
big house he had started to wonder whether this transaction
might provide a turning point for the valley where the estate
in question lay. A large building project was bound to provide
jobs and bring money to the valley's one and only town.

His mother had been born in Ollerthwaite and had lived
there until her marriage. Her best friend had been the wife of
a farmer called Crossley. Filmore had always enjoyed his visits
to her family there as a child and youth. Sadly, both his mother
and Crossley's wife were dead now, as was his father, but his
happy memories were still vivid.

He wondered from one or two remarks Smith had let fall in
the early stages of their negotiations whether some personal
connection with the valley was the reason Smith had chosen
him to act in this matter.

He wished he could tell his mother about this development.
He still missed her greatly. She'd have been very interested in
the possibilities. His father would just have nodded and said,
'Yes, yes. Very interesting. You must do what you please about
this, Ezra.'

Walter Crossley was an admirable person, who had been
a major influence for the better on the valley for many years,
something Filmore was happy to facilitate. He might wish to
make money, but he intended to do that in an ethical way.

But sadly he couldn't betray a confidence and tell either Mr
Crossley or Mr Smith about one another.

His father had always said there were wheels within wheels
in this world, and he had been right. A very shrewd man, his
father, about how people interacted, even if not deeply interested in making money for himself.

It would be extremely interesting to see how all this turned out.

The following afternoon the Kenyons came to the office to sign the contract and Filmore couldn't help suspecting that John Kenyon had drunk himself to sleep last night, he looked so heavy-eyed.

He read the contract in a cursory manner and shrugged. 'Looks all right to me.'

Mrs Kenyon twitched it out of her husband's hand, making an angry little growling sound. She read it through from cover to cover while he fidgeted beside her.

She then asked Mr Filmore for two small changes in wording, changes which put all dealing with the money entirely into her family's hands.

After that had been done and initialled, she then agreed that they should both sign the contract. She pushed her husband's hand out of the way when he reached for the pen. She signed it first, her signature black and in a perfectly formed copperplate script. John Kenyon signed beneath her, but his was a mere scrawl.

She cast one scornful glance at that then ignored her husband and turned to Mr Filmore. 'We shall stay in Halifax until the money is paid into my family's account, after which we shall be moving permanently to a small estate my family owns in the north of Yorkshire.'

From the startled look on her husband's face, this was news to him. He opened his mouth as if to protest, caught her scornful glare and shut his mouth again.

She turned back to Mr Filmore, pulled out a folded sheet of paper from her handbag and handed it to him. 'I doubt this will be necessary, but in case you need to contact us after this transaction is completed, this will be our address after our move and for the foreseeable future thereafter.'

'Thank you. Um, I was thinking. Shouldn't we let your agent in Ollindale know what's going on, give him notice and so on?'

She stared at him for a moment then shook her head. 'He's our former agent now and has not been a loyal employee. He has been filching money from the rents, my father discovered when he took over my husband's accounts, so we owe him nothing. Let him find out about the sale when the other people in that benighted valley do.'

'How do you intend to inform people? Do you wish me to put an announcement in the local newspaper?'

'It's not up to me now. The company which has purchased the property can inform people – or not. Their choice.'

He was horrified at how she was behaving, glanced at John Kenyon to see if he had anything to say about this, but the man just looked away and kept silent.

It was a relief when the Kenyons took their leave. Filmore let out his breath in a relieved whoosh once they'd left his room. The atmosphere had been most unpleasant.

He'd not like to cross that woman. But he felt that anyone who was stupid enough to gamble away most of their fortune deserved whatever adverse outcomes such behaviour led to.

He'd not agree to work for unpleasant people like them again if he could ever help it. Perhaps the two of them deserved one another. And clearly their former agent deserved no sympathy either.

Once the Kenyons were home, Amelia said, 'Come into the sitting room. You can spend the rest of the day here, John.'

'I think I'll go out and stretch my legs for a while.'

'No. And if you try to get out by the rear way, the gardener has instructions to bring you back by force if necessary. He's a strong man. The front door will be guarded by another equally strong man provided by my family. Both of them are more than capable of preventing you from leaving.'

'I say, old thing. I can't sit around indoors all day.'

'You will probably be staying indoors for two entire days, actually, three if necessary. Once the money for the estate is paid, we'll leave immediately for North Yorkshire. My family's strong man will be travelling with us to make sure you don't . . . get lost en route.'

She gave him one of her vicious looks and added, 'You and I will be staying there until further notice, so you'll be able to get plenty of exercise riding a horse provided by my family, since yours have all had to be sold.'

As he opened his mouth to protest, she glared at him. 'I do not intend to let you lose the rest of our money, not for any consideration, John. Our son is already facing a much-reduced inheritance and the need to earn a living. And be warned, if you try to move away from our new home, I shall have you brought back by force if necessary and then I shall send for my family's long-time doctor who lives nearby. My father has already told him that your behaviour is becoming erratic, so I shall put you permanently in his hands as having lost your wits.'

He could only gape at her in shock, which turned slowly into terror.

'Remember, too, that it will be useless for you to go against my father in anything from now on. He is determined to keep you from gambling and save the rest of what I regard as *my* money for our son to inherit.'

Her husband sagged visibly, looking suddenly shrunken and older.

She gestured to a side table. 'There are sporting magazines and daily newspapers available for you to read. You can remember how to read, I trust? I recommend reading as a future hobby. It costs far less than gambling. The maid will fetch you any refreshments you need but has been instructed not to bring you any alcohol.'

She moved to the door and stopped again. 'I nearly forgot to mention that we shall no longer be sharing a bedroom or spending much time together. Now, I'm going to rest in *my* bedroom because I can't bear to look at you for one minute longer. You are a *pitiful* excuse for a man.'

For the first time her voice cracked and she showed signs of breaking down. But as he knew from past experience, she was at her most dangerous at such times because she hated to show any weakness.

Would her family doctor really do as she asked and certify him as insane?

Probably. She had never before failed to carry out a threat. He shivered at the thought of being locked away in an asylum for the rest of his life, wasn't prepared to risk that.

At least in Yorkshire he would be free to ride, hunt and shoot.

As for Hatton, he must surely have heard about the sale of the property by now. Kenyon didn't intend to deal with him again or anything to do with Ollindale.

All he could do was bide his time. Surely he'd find some way to escape from her eventually? Or she might die before him. That would be a very happy release.

Only, she'd never had a day's illness since their marriage, even when carrying their first and only child.

How was he going to bear a life like that now facing him, though? Surely he'd find a way out?

The money was paid to the Kenyons the next day and Filmore washed his hands of them mentally.

When Mrs Kenyon contacted him to ask if he'd deal with a small transaction for her, because it concerned matters in Halifax not their new location, he wrote to say that he was very busy and could no longer take on any other clients. They should find a new lawyer closer to their new home from then onwards.

He grimaced even to think of them, but ended the letter by wishing them well. That was a lie. He was very glad he had been representing Mr Smith, not them, because they were neither of them decent people from what he'd seen. He didn't believe people should cause unhappiness in the world, or that being rich was an excuse for doing what you wanted, regardless of how it affected others.

He didn't consider it his duty to tell the agent that he no longer had a job. Mr Smith hadn't mentioned doing anything about the agent and anyway, he'd gone down to London now to complete some important business there.

Hatton would find out soon enough that he was no longer employed by the Kenyons and that they no longer even owned the property. Word of a big sale like that usually got round quite quickly.

25

Lancashire

Hatton hadn't heard from his employer for a few days and was fed up of hanging around, not knowing what to do with himself. He'd sold all the furniture from the agent's house weeks ago as soon as he found that the estate was going to be put up for sale. He rarely stayed there and Mr Kenyon never did, so who would notice?

He hadn't expected it to be sold quickly, if at all, because the parents of this Kenyon had tried to get rid of it for years. A couple of times, people had come to look at it, turning up when Hatton was away and not even staying overnight in the village. But they hadn't attempted to buy it.

He wished now that he hadn't sold all the contents of the agent's house yet. He'd intended to use the lodge if it was necessary to stay overnight to deal with a potential buyer, but those doddering old fools, the Rainfords, had taken all the furniture away with them.

He might have gone after them and taken some of it back by force if Crossley hadn't been involved. He'd come off badly any time he'd gone against that man and now found it safest to avoid him completely.

He didn't know whether to hope there would be a quick sale or not, because a sale might put his job at risk, unless he could persuade a new owner to take him on as agent. Surely the person would need his services? After all, who knew the tenants and properties better than him?

Faced with an empty lodge and agent's house, he had no alternative but to find temporary accommodation. He tried Mrs Gleston's, but she wouldn't let him have a room, even though he knew she had no one staying there. He was tempted to come back after dark and break some of her windows, but unfortunately she was another person under Crossley's protection, damn the interfering sod.

In the end, the only person offering to house him on his occasional overnight stays was Terry Catlow, a man he'd drunk with occasionally at the local pub, and who had done small jobs for him every now and then. Terry had been particularly good at frightening people into paying one of Hatton's 'fines' then they'd shared the extra money.

When he received a message from Mrs Kenyon to say he was to stay in Ollerthwaite and wait there for further instructions, it surprised him, but you didn't go against that woman on the rare occasions she poked her nose in. But though Catlow and his wife said he'd be welcome to stay for as long as he needed because they wanted the money he was paying, he was finding it rather unpleasant there.

The house was crowded and he was sharing a bedroom with his host, though not a bed, thank goodness. He'd rather have slept under a bush than do that.

Catlow didn't seem concerned that he was now sleeping on a filthy straw mattress on the floor as long as Hatton paid him two and sixpence a night. His host had no trouble sleeping soundly, but snored in fits and starts and Hatton found it hard to ignore that, because when each session started there was a lot of grunting and snuffling before settling into a steady rhythm.

Mrs Catlow was sharing her daughters' bed and refused point-blank to provide any food for their visitor, saying she had nothing to spare and she hated cooking anyway. Terry apologised and said Hatton had better eat elsewhere or bring his own food. Bread and jam was filling and easy to make, and he could get fish and chips in the early evenings. That was how Catlow mostly fed himself.

Hatton put up with the situation because it would only be for a few days, and waited to hear from the Kenyons. When several more days passed without a word, however, he began to get worried and risked sending Mr Kenyon a letter.

There was no response.

He began to worry that someone had offered to buy the estate. No one had been to look at it recently, or he'd have known, but still, something must be going on.

He considered going back to Halifax and trying to catch Mr Kenyon on his own. Only, his last instructions from Mrs Kenyon had been very specific. He was to stay in Ollerthwaite and wait for her further instructions. The only thing he was certain of at the moment was that on the rare occasions when she gave orders like that, you either obeyed them or you suffered.

At the moment, he was bored and uncomfortable, but he wasn't suffering and he still had a job. Well, Mr Kenyon had assured him more than once that there would always be a job for him.

There was another worry fluttering at the back of his mind. What would that new job be if there were no rents to collect, no properties to check on and no tenants to manage?

Hatton had been doing that job for the past ten years because he knew how to suck up to a vain fool like Kenyon. He had never found a way to suck up to Mrs Kenyon.

Why was no one telling him what was happening? Something must be going on.

Why were there not even rumours about it?

That was the most puzzling thing of all.

Walter was also puzzled by the situation at the property next door to his farm. If it were for sale, why hadn't there been any strangers coming and going? And why had Hatton stayed on in Ollerthwaite? The agent only came for a day or at most two usually, and not often. It was years since he'd stayed this long.

Well, Walter had enough on his plate without having to keep a watch for strangers coming to visit the estate, so he paid someone who lived on a smallholding to one side of the Upperfold Road a small sum per week to keep his eyes open. But his watcher said the only person he ever saw going there now that the Rainfords had moved away was Hatton, and the agent didn't do anything, just wandered round, looking miserable.

Then another man from Ollerthwaite who owed Walter a favour told him that the estate had been sold but would he please not say who'd revealed that. They both spent a few minutes wondering who had bought it and how anyone could have done that without the prospect of a sale becoming generally known?

'You didn't hear anything from the lawyer in Ollerthwaite, then?' Walter asked his friend, almost thinking aloud.

'No. The person who told me said the news came from someone he knew in Halifax who had overheard a conversation and thought he'd be interested.'

Walter had wondered occasionally what would happen to the place when it sold, so he was concerned about what was going on. The estate was close to his farm and neighbours could have a lot of influence on your life, for good or bad. At the moment the land was full of weeds and the small houses and outbuildings on it badly needed repairs. Not to mention the blackened ruin. It ought to be dealt with and it was a miracle the rest of it hadn't fallen down. It must have been very well built in the first place.

Since there was nothing he could do but wait and see, he turned his attention to his immediate family. Well, he thought of them as family now. He'd never forget the loved ones he'd lost, but you could either sink or swim in this life and he'd always managed to swim away from problems, as his grandfather had phrased it.

It pleased him that Elinor and Cameron looked to be getting along well, but they were both holding back from taking the necessary next steps to form a close relationship. Were they not interested in marriage and children, or was something preventing them from getting closer to one another?

Then he overheard a conversation between Maude and Elinor one morning and it gave him hope about the future.

The two of them were clearing up after breakfast and working out what to make for tea.

Walter had been in the boot room next to the back door, about to kick off his muddy shoes and go back into the kitchen to get another drink of tea. He froze just outside the inner door when he heard Cameron's name and stayed there, unashamedly eavesdropping.

'Have you done as Walter asked and looked round for a woman who might make a suitable wife for Cam?' Maude asked out of the blue.

Elinor didn't respond immediately then said, 'No. I haven't looked at all. I didn't feel comfortable talking about him in that way to anyone. Have you tried?'

'No. There's never seemed to be a good time to do it and anyway, it's so personal I've been a bit hesitant to broach the subject. As you say, it made me feel uncomfortable.'

'Exactly.'

'And I wondered . . . aren't you even a little bit interested in him yourself?' Maude asked suddenly. 'When you two chat, you seem to get on really well and you share several interests.'

There was dead silence, then Elinor said, 'If I wanted a husband I'd certainly think about him, because he's such a nice person and as kind as his grandfather. But as you know, I don't want to get married, not ever.'

'You can't let how Reginald Stafford behaved towards your mother stop you getting on with a normal life of your own, Elinor love. I thought that feeling would fade once we got away from him. Most men aren't like him, you know.'

'Well, I learned the hard way that marriage is too risky because men can change once they've tied the knot.'

'It doesn't have to be like that.'

'There are no guarantees.'

'There are no guarantees about anything in life, love. Don't expect the impossible. You should think seriously about finding a husband, even if it's not Cameron.'

'I daren't.'

'You're not usually a coward.'

'Is that what I am?'

'I'm afraid so.'

'Oh.'

Another dead silence followed and it was broken by Maude saying quietly, 'Well, let's think about something different. Since it's going to be a lovely day, how about we go for a bike ride down to the lake?'

'Cameron has taken one of the bikes. But you could go on your own.'

'I'm not leaving you here alone, Elinor. Let's walk there and back instead. It's not all that far.'

'I always feel guilty if I take too much time off looking after the house.'

'Don't be silly. My cousin isn't a slave driver. Anyway, we'll only be away for an hour or two and Walter said he had to go into town shortly so he definitely won't need us here.'

'Oh, all right, then. I would like to go out for a walk. Come on. It won't take us long to finish clearing up the kitchen. But if you try to talk about marriage when we're out, I'll turn round and come back.'

'You don't need to talk about it, just think about it. Will you promise me to do that?'

'Yes.' Elinor immediately began putting the crockery away, making a clattering noise that prevented further conversation.

There was another long silence and the sound of cupboard doors opening and closing, so Walter judged it time to go about his business because he didn't want to be caught eavesdropping. But from what he'd overheard, he guessed Maude thought Cam might be a good prospect for marriage, so she might help him nudge her friend in his direction.

He smiled. He didn't think his grandson would take much nudging from the way he looked at Elinor sometimes when he thought no one was watching him.

A short time later Walter watched from the window of his office as the two women left. They looked rosy and healthy these days, striding out across the yard and disappearing down the path to the lake. That pleased him greatly.

A short time later he saw Cameron returning on one of the bikes from a visit to one of their tenants. He smiled to see the tall young man riding across the yard towards him. He was a good lad.

It was about time he gave his grandson more information about his various businesses, Walter decided and greeted him with, 'It's about time I brought you up to scratch with what I'm doing. We can have a little chat about one thing before I go out if you've time.'

'Happy to do that.'

The two friends were glad it was such a warm day and they didn't wear their outer coats. Maude snatched the beret Elinor had been about to put on from her and tossed it on one of the chairs.

'Let's not bother with hats either. It's rather old-fashioned to wear a hat every time you poke your nose out of the door. As if that proves you're respectable! Anyway, we won't be meeting many people near the lake at this time of day. Come on.'

As they walked, Elinor turned her face up to the sun and let out a happy sigh. 'How about we go all the way to where the lake path ends since we won't have any shopping to bring back?'

'Good idea.' Maude looked down at her new skirt and gave it a little stroke. 'It's easier to stride out with these shorter skirts you've altered for me from the clothes in the attics, isn't it?'

'Much easier. My stepfather would have had a fit at us showing so much of our lower legs when we go out, though.' She peered down at her friend's ankles, then her own. 'We've both got nice slender ankles still, haven't we?'

'Yes, we have. I don't ever want to wear floor-length skirts again. I'm glad the fashions have changed.'

'Aren't we lucky that your cousin kindly gave these clothes to us? We couldn't have afforded to buy a whole new wardrobe.'

'Yes. And I'm double lucky that you're good at sewing because I'm useless at doing anything except mending and sewing straight seams. I'd rather be working in the garden any day.'

A short time later she asked, 'When are you going to ask my cousin about the paints and pencils, Elinor love? They're just lying around there up in the attic. That's such a waste.'

'I'm not going to ask him yet. I've still got plenty of sewing to do and he has enough on his mind without being reminded of Tim's painting. I think he's still worrying about what's going to happen to the big house. Haven't you noticed how he stops talking to listen when anyone in the village mentions it?'

'Why does everyone suddenly think it's going to be sold?'

'Who can tell? Rumours sometimes seem to float around in the air we breathe for no obvious reason. Never mind that now – let's enjoy our outing.'

By the time they got down to the lake, they were both warm from the exercise. As usual they sat down on the raised hummock of land to stare at the water, arms clasped around their raised knees.

'The lake would look much better if it had been finished off,' Elinor said suddenly. 'I found an old newspaper that had been used for wrapping up some pieces of fancy crockery in the attic and it talked about Jubilee Lake in glowing terms. It even showed a plan and sketch of how it would look when finished. Apparently Walter was the one pushing for it to be done. What a pity it was abandoned.'

Silence fell again, then Maude gestured to the lake with a sweep of her hand. 'The water looks so beautiful on sunny days. Don't you just love the way it gleams like polished silver sometimes, especially when the sun is at a certain angle?'

Elinor pointed to one side. 'Yes, but it'd be even more beautiful without that dark, marshy bit that runs along the edge over there after the cleared part stops. I don't think bullrushes are at all attractive, and they're such a dull colour.'

'I agree. And the ground is not just boggy but uneven there, so you can't even walk across it without risking a sprained ankle. You'd think they'd at least make a proper path all the way round the edge so that people could take longer walks. After all, they went to the trouble of building a weir at the lower end to hold back the water and make the lake bigger. And they did the path more than halfway round the lake.'

'Walter said they stopped because of the Russian 'flu. But that's been over for a while now, surely?'

'We hope it's over. Perhaps my cousin couldn't be bothered about the lake after he lost his son and grandson.'

They were both silent again. They tried to tread carefully around Walter's grief, but you couldn't put your life on hold for ever, whatever happened, as they were both finding.

'I wonder where the detailed plans he had drawn up have got to,' Elinor said thoughtfully.

'I'll ask him about it one day soon. He can only say he doesn't want to talk about it after all. From a couple of remarks he's let drop, it was his grandson, Tim, who was the enthusiast about it.'

'Maybe we could help him finish it off as a sort of memorial to his son and grandson.'

Maude frowned. 'Hmm. I'll think about it. I'll have to choose my time to ask him very carefully. I wonder what Cam thinks about it.'

'Who knows? Anyway, we'd better think about starting back now. I need to put the meat on the stove to stew gently for tea.'

As she stood up Elinor began to brush some grass seeds off her skirt. Suddenly the ground at that side gave way beneath her and she flailed wildly as she lost her balance. She tumbled sideways and let out a yelp as she fell awkwardly, twisting her right foot beneath her.

When she didn't try to get up, Maude hurried round to hold out her hand so that she could pull her up but Elinor let out a yelp of pain when she tried to stand.

'What's the matter?'

'I've ricked my ankle. Ooh, that hurt.'

'You haven't broken it, surely?'

Elinor moved it slightly and stopped, shaking her head. 'No, but I must have twisted it badly because it hurts to move it.' She proved that by waggling her foot slightly and letting out another gasp. 'I can't bear to move it, let alone think of standing on it. How am I going to get back to the farm?'

'I'll have to run back and ask Walter's help and— Oh, no! He won't be back yet. And he's got the cart so how are we going to bring you back, even if one of the others is there?'

'Go and see if Cameron is around. He said he'd be back for midday.'

'I don't like to leave you on your own.'

'Well, we can't both sit here for ever, can we, so you'll have to go for help,' Elinor said sharply.

'What if someone comes along?'

'I don't suppose there's a murderer running loose in Ollindale. I'll be fine.'

'All right. I'll be as quick as I can.'

Maude set off running up the slope and to her relief when she got near the top she saw Cameron fiddling with his bike in the farmyard. She yelled out at the top of her voice and he stood up.

'Is something wrong?'

'Elinor's had a fall down near the lake and twisted her ankle and she can't bear to walk on it. Walter isn't around and he's taken the cart so I don't know what to do. We can't leave her sitting there. How about we take the wheelbarrow?'

'That'd be a rather uncomfortable ride.' He frowned and looked down at the bike. 'I might be able to give her a dink on this.'

'What does that mean?'

'Letting a second person ride on a bike with you. I wonder if she could manage to sit on the bicycle and hold me by the waist so that I could take her home? It'd surely be more comfortable than a wheelbarrow.'

'As long as she doesn't fall off.'

'I'll make sure she doesn't.'

Maude was about to say it still didn't sound very safe, then she suddenly realised it might be a rather useful way to get them together – quite literally. After all, they'd be cuddled up to one another on the bike.

'I'll ride down and see. We don't want to leave her sitting on her own there. You wait at the farm in case Walter comes home.'

Maude watched him go, crossing her fingers for the pair of them and smiling slightly, in spite of her worries about her friend.

26

Cameron set off without waiting for an answer from Maude, cycling recklessly down the uneven path at full pelt, worrying about Elinor.

She was sitting awkwardly on the ground near the mound and a muddle of earth and grass, looking pale and uncomfortable.

He swung his leg off the bicycle and left it resting on the ground, not even looking back to check it was safe as he knelt beside her. 'How are you?'

'I feel better for seeing you.'

'Is your ankle still hurting?'

'Yes. It throbs when I try to move it.'

'You don't look comfortable. Here, lean against me.'

But somehow when she let out an involuntary yelp as she tried to edge across to him, she ended up in his arms instead.

He moved carefully but didn't let go of her, didn't want to do anything but hold her tight. 'Sit still for a moment and we'll discuss what to do.'

She gave in to temptation and rested her head against his chest. 'I don't know how I'm going to stand up, let alone get back to the farm.'

'I can lift you into a standing position.'

'I'll be much too heavy.'

'No, you won't. I'm used to carrying heavier loads than you around and—' Their faces were so close he couldn't resist kissing her on the cheek and made no attempt to lift her up from the sitting position.

She didn't protest, just stared at him as if bemused, so he kissed her soft cheek again, then kissed her on the lips.

And still she didn't try to pull away.

As the kiss ended he drew back a little but she didn't move away, not even an inch.

'I didn't mean to do that yet, Elinor.'

'Yet?'

'I've been wanting to kiss you for a good while. And when you were so delightfully close just now, well, I gave in to temptation.'

She couldn't be less than honest with him. 'I didn't know it could feel so good. A kiss, I mean. It's not something I've experienced very often, only an occasional kiss stolen after church when I was much younger.'

'Were the young men who lived near you blind? You should have been snapped up and married years ago.'

'When my stepfather moved into the house, he was too watchful and I didn't get any more chances even to talk to young men on my own. I think he just saw me as a cheap servant.'

'That was selfish of him. Surely he and your mother weren't that short of money?'

'He preferred to spend it on himself. And then my mother became an invalid so I had to look after her.'

He couldn't help kissing her again and she kissed him back, she really did. 'How did that kiss measure up?'

'It was far nicer. The others were a long time ago but I can still remember that they weren't nearly as good.'

She gave him one of her shy smiles. He loved to make her smile. She sometimes looked faintly surprised to be doing it.

He kept one arm round her. 'I'd intended to wait until we were both well settled in with Walter then begin courting you, if you were willing. I've been only too conscious that I didn't start out as the one he wanted as his heir, you see.'

'Anyone can see that he's very happy with you. He smiles much more often nowadays and he looks at you fondly. I think your poor grandfather must have been dreadfully lonely living here on his own.'

'Yes. But we're changing that. At the moment, since you haven't protested about my last kiss, I'm more interested in finding out whether your lips really are that soft.'

This time when they drew apart he stroked her hair back then whispered, 'To be continued another time. We need to work out how to get you back to the farm now or Maude will be worried.'

She needed to make sure what he meant, whether he had any doubts whatsoever about courting her and the words escaped her before she could stop them. 'You're sure about kissing me?'

'Of course I am. It was wonderful. Did you not enjoy it? I won't force myself on you.'

'I don't regret it at all but—' She broke off, seemed to be struggling for words.

'But what?' he prompted.

'I just don't want to rush headlong into anything.'

'Neither do I. But I would like us to make a start – at courting, I mean – and see how we go? In fact, I'd like that very much indeed and I think Walter will approve. He's hinted once or twice that he wants me to marry. What about Maude?'

'She's already said I should encourage you.'

'Can I ask why you're hesitating, then?'

'I've seen people make mistakes about who they marry.'

'You're talking about your mother?'

'Yes.'

'Well, my mother didn't even get the chance to marry the first time she fell in love. My father wanted her in bed, but he was determined to marry a woman from a wealthy family. And when he found one, he abandoned us, except to provide us with a small house and give us enough money to live on if we were careful.' His tone suddenly took on a bitter edge. 'I used to hear her crying at night.'

'I'm sorry,' she said softly.

'Do you mind that my mother wasn't married to my father?'

'Not at all.'

He moved away from her. 'What a time to talk about this as we're just starting to get to know one another! Maude will be worried sick if we don't get you back soon. Look, if I lift you up, can you stand on the good foot and hold on to that tree. I'll bring the bike across to you and see if I can sit you sideways on the back carrier rack. Leave that to me.'

He was as strong as he'd said and managed to settle her on the back of the bike without too much trouble. *Thank goodness for the tree*, she thought.

When he was sitting in front of her on the bike, he said, 'Here we go!' and set off carefully.

After a couple of wobbles, he said, 'It's harder to stay balanced if I go slowly. Hold tight. I'm going to speed up.'

When he went faster there were fewer wobbles, but bumping around hurt her foot, so she had to concentrate on not letting him know that. He must have guessed because he said, 'Hang in there. Let's get it over with as quickly as we can.'

At the farm, he stopped and put his feet down, then turned enough to pull her off the back of the bike into his arms, nudging it out of the way with one foot afterwards. He staggered a little but managed to stay upright.

Once again they were close to one another. She thought he was going to kiss her but Maude came running out of the house towards them.

'Damn!' he murmured in a low voice, then said more loudly, 'Will you make sure the doors are fully open, Maude, and that the sofa in the kitchen is clear of clutter? I'm going to carry her inside.'

He settled Elinor on the sofa then started giving instructions as if he'd dealt with this sort of situation before.

'Could you get a bucket of cold water and one of hot, please, Maude? If we alternate putting that ankle in cold and hot water for a few minutes each, it should help to reduce the swelling. Good thing the tap water is always cold.'

By the time Walter came home she was sitting with her foot up and the throbbing had started to settle down a little and was more of a dull ache now.

'I'd take you to see a doctor,' Walter said, 'but ours is in Ollerthwaite and jolting about in my cart would probably make the ankle worse again. Anyway, I think you're right and it is only a sprain.'

'I agree. I'll be fine if I can just rest it for a while.'

'You'd better take command of the sofa for more than a while. Rest for a few days is what the ankle will need.'

She sighed. 'I can get on with some sewing, I suppose.'

He remembered what he'd overheard. 'You don't have to work every minute of the day, you know, lass.'

'I like to keep busy.'

A little later, when she and Elinor were alone for a few moments in the kitchen, Maude gave her a sly smile and said in a low voice, 'Something happened between you and Cam when he was helping you, didn't it?'

She could feel her face growing hot and giving her away. 'How can you tell?'

'You're looking at him differently.'

'Oh.'

'And he's looking at you with even more interest than before.'

'Oh.'

Maude chuckled. 'I won't say a word, love, except I forbid you to push him away. He's not like the Staffords.' She didn't add that it wouldn't be necessary for her to say anything. The two of them would give themselves away every time one stole a glance at the other from now on because something really had changed between them. And she was delighted about it.

She only wished she could meet someone who made her feel like that.

She should stop longing for something that was highly improbable at her age. They weren't living in a fairy story or an age of miracles, after all.

But if Elinor ever had children she'd be a sort of auntie to them. That'd be something, at least.

27

In America, Caleb Crossley sighed and stared out of the window of the flat provided by Daniel. He hadn't been outside for three days and was fed up to the back teeth of looking out at sunny days like a prisoner locked behind bars. It was rather hot today so he pulled off his jacket and slung it on the back of a chair.

A few minutes later the door banged open so violently he knew who it would be before he turned round. What could have upset Daniel now?

The other man stood glaring at him. 'What the hell did you think you were doing last night? You were barely civil to my guests and that Canadian guy was getting very fed up of you staring into space instead of playing your cards promptly. I had to let him win more than I'd planned to cover up for you. We could have taken them for far more money if you'd paid attention and not given them so much time to think. And it's not the first time you've acted carelessly.'

He stared at the younger man, eyes narrowed, shaking his head then saying slowly, 'In fact, you haven't lived up to your promise as a card player because of lack of concentration. I expected far more of you, so I've found another guy to replace you, one who will pay attention. I'm sorry but—'

Caleb had seen Daniel show off many times before, boasting how rapid a move he could make with his knife, so out of

curiosity he'd practised doing it like that himself when he had
nothing better to do. Boredom had given him little else to do
because he didn't like reading books and newspapers. He'd
practised the same move till he thought he was even faster
than Daniel, just for his own satisfaction.

If he hadn't, he'd have been taken by surprise, but all that
practice had paid off. Daniel had only just pulled his knife out
when Caleb used his own weapon to slash the other man's
throat, turning his own head away at the same time. He felt
Daniel's knife slice into his arm, but then the grip on it slack-
ened and it fell to the ground.

Thank goodness he'd taken off his jacket!

It felt as if the world stood still. Daniel froze where he stood
as blood poured from his throat. He made a faint gurgling
sound then slowly crumpled into an untidy heap on the floor.

He didn't move again.

Caleb froze too, utterly horrified at what had just happened.
There was no mistaking the look of death. He'd killed Daniel!
Killed a man.

Only, if he hadn't done it, he'd be the one lying there dead.

He looked down at himself, suddenly aware that blood was
dripping from his upper arm where Daniel's knife had cut
through his shirt sleeve into the tender flesh.

Then he forgot that as he realised how quickly he had to get
away if he was to stay alive. He was not only in danger from
Daniel's fellow criminals but from the police.

He jerked suddenly into action, rushing into the stuffy little
bedroom to grab the suitcase he hadn't bothered to unpack
properly. Stuffing the few things from his drawers back into it
any old how, he forced it shut on the jumble of garments.

He was about to put on his jacket when he noticed blood
still trickling from his sleeve so stuffed the handkerchief from
his breast pocket into the wound before slipping the arm into
his jacket.

'Hurry!' he muttered. 'Get going, you fool.'

As he passed Daniel's body he shuddered, but after taking a couple more steps he spun round and went back to it. He'd need money to get away and Daniel always carried plenty.

He found several rolls of banknotes in the dead man's pockets and stuffed them into his own, then went to peer out of the door of the flat. He was relieved to see that there was no one waiting for the elevator but hesitated about his next step.

They were on the sixth floor. If he waited, who knew how long it'd take the elevator to stop here? And it might go on up then not down. Even if it went straight down, he'd probably find some of Daniel's men waiting in the foyer, men he knew wouldn't let him leave without their boss's say-so, because they'd stopped him going out before.

He snatched the key out of the flat's main door, shut it quietly and locked it, then darted along to the fire door at the far end of the landing.

He opened it slightly, stopping again to listen. He couldn't hear any sound of footsteps or voices in the stairwell, so went out into it and ran down the concrete stairs, leaping down some of them two at a time, moving as fast as he could, desperation driving him on.

The suitcase was awkward and slowed him down, but he'd need his clothes. He nearly fell at one stage, but grabbed the handrail and righted himself in time, slowing down slightly after that, but only slightly.

His heart didn't stop thumping erratically in his chest the whole time.

The outer fire doors on the ground floor were closed but he managed to depress the emergency bar and open one of them. Again he peered out before he moved, but luck was with him once more and there was no one around. He ran quickly along the side alley, instinctively turning towards the rear. After that, he took a route that kept him out of sight of people using the main street on which the block of apartments was situated.

He glanced round as he ran, praying that no one would look out of a window and see him. Only there was nothing he could do to avoid that.

He had to clamber over a wall at one stage, something that would normally have been beyond his strength but sheer terror drove him up and he scrabbled over it with nothing worse than a grazed hand on his injured arm.

He had to slow down when the alley stopped at another street in order not to draw attention to himself and felt on edge the whole time he was walking briskly along. He fixed a smile on his face. At least he hoped it looked like a smile. It didn't feel like one.

He didn't have to think about where to go. There was only one way to get out of this alive. He had to get a berth on a ship and go to his grandfather in England.

And he could never, ever come back to America.

If there was a ship ready to leave he might stand a chance. If there wasn't one leaving for a day or two he could be in serious trouble because Daniel's friends and associates would come looking for him. They'd not want anyone to get away with killing one of their own.

28

Lancashire

Hatton drank more than usual one evening because he was fed up to the teeth of hanging around waiting.

It was nearly noon before he woke up the next day and it took him a few minutes to force himself out of bed.

When he came back from using the lav at the far end of the backyard, he went into the kitchen to get a glass of water.

Terry was sitting at the table with a sneering smile on his face. 'About time you got up.'

'Eh?'

'There's a bit of news going round that might interest you.'

Hatton stilled. There was something in Catlow's tone that said he wasn't going to like the news, whatever it was. 'So? Tell me.'

'Ollerton House has been sold. Last week it happened but the news only came out late yesterday round here. When I went out this morning to get a newspaper, everyone I met was talking about it. I'm surprised no one told you last night at the pub.'

'Well, they didn't.' Hatton rubbed his forehead, but the ache only settled inside it more firmly. 'You sure about that?'

'I'd stake my life on it.'

'I'd better go into Halifax to see Mr Kenyon, then.'

'I'd have thought he'd have sent for you before this to tell you.'

'Why do you say it in that tone? What else do you know?'

'I don't know anything else but I'll be watching what happens with great interest. After all, it's my valley too and you're my only lodger.'

When Terry was in this mood you couldn't get anything definite out of him because he liked to play with people, tormenting them like a cat with a mouse. Hatton pulled out his watch and flicked open the top. 'If I hurry I'll just catch the late morning train.'

Terry smiled again and watched him get ready, not volunteering any further information and certainly not offering any help.

Hatton hesitated by the door. 'All right if I come back here?'

'As long as you can keep paying your way.'

Something in his tone made Hatton pack everything he owned and take it with him 'in case'. He wasn't certain whether he'd be coming back here or not. Surely Mr Kenyon wouldn't abandon him now, not after all his years of service, not to mention the constant flattery?

No, Mr Kenyon wouldn't treat him like that but Mrs Kenyon might. He'd have to find a way to avoid her.

It was mid-afternoon before Hatton arrived at the street where the Kenyons lived in Halifax. He went round to the back entrance because Mrs Kenyon didn't like him using the front door and anyway, he didn't want to run into her.

But the back gate was locked and when he piled up a couple of bricks that were lying nearby and stood on them to peer over it, he found he could see straight into the kitchen. There was not only no one working in it, there was no equipment to be seen either, just a bare sink and table.

They must have moved. Where to?

Oh, hell. What would happen to his job now?

He went to the next gate, which was unlocked thank goodness, and knocked on the kitchen door. He could see people working there.

'I was looking for Mr Kenyon.'

'Who is it?' a voice yelled from across the big room.

The lass who'd opened the door looked at him as if asking the same thing.

'I work for Mr Kenyon at his country estate. He doesn't seem to be at home next door.'

The woman chopping onions stared across the kitchen at him. 'You do look a bit familiar, but if you were still employed by them, surely they'd have told you they were going away?'

'I've worked for him for over ten years,' he told her indignantly. 'But I've heard nothing for several days.'

Her expression softened. 'Well, I don't suppose it'll do any harm to tell you, because what's happened is all over the town. Mrs Snobby Nose's husband lost all their money gambling and they've had to sell up and move to North Yorkshire to a house her family owns. Talk about coming down in the world.'

'*What?*' Hatton felt as if the room was wobbling round him and next thing he knew someone was helping him to sit on a chair and steadying him, then he was being offered a cup of tea.

'Eh, if Meggie hadn't of caught you, mister whatever your name is, you'd have fallen on the floor.' The cook looked at him with a little more sympathy than before and her voice softened. 'They didn't tell you they'd sold their country house, did they?'

'No. Not a word.'

'They had ought to of at least told you,' she admitted grudgingly. 'But some folk are like that, don't care about others. I'm glad my missus has a kinder nature.'

'You're sure the Kenyons have moved to Yorkshire?'

'Oh, yes. There's a notice in one of the front windows about where to send any bills. They've not only gone to live there, they're never coming back from what I've heard and the house next door is for sale.'

'I heard Mrs Kenyon shouting at the servants and telling them to hurry up with the packing,' the maid volunteered. 'Really sharp, she was.'

Hatton could imagine that only too clearly. He covered his face with his hands, not knowing what to do or where to go next, wanting only to shut the world out for a moment or two.

'You can't stay here,' the cook said. 'We've got work to do. Look, I'll give you a cup of tea to buck you up a bit, but after you've drunk it you'll have to leave.'

'Thank you. That'd be kind of you.'

When he stood outside in the street again, looking at the front of the Kenyons' house, he saw the piece of card in the window saying where to send bills and it was in Scotland. No use going there after them. He cursed the family in a low voice, using the worst insults he could think up and vowing to get his own back on them one day if he ever got near them again.

More important at the moment was what the hell he should do now?

Thank goodness he'd got some money put away in the bank. But they'd left owing him a whole month's pay, damn them.

If Crossley and them two women who'd come to live with him hadn't helped the Rainfords take away that furniture, he'd have had a nice chunk more to add to his savings, so damn that lot as well.

One thing he'd have to do was go back to the valley to get the more valuable things he'd hidden in the ruins of the big house.

He'd have to work out a way to do that without being noticed by Catlow or Crossley. At least the things he had risked taking over the years would be worth quite a bit when he sold them. He definitely wasn't leaving them behind.

He'd still need a new job, though. The money he'd saved and those things were to look after him in his old age and he was only fifty-five so had a few years to go yet before he could stop work and sell them all.

When he did stop work, he intended to live in comfort. He'd been planning how to do that for years. He was going to have a home beside the sea, not let anyone stuff him in the sodding poorhouse.

Hatton decided to find a place in Halifax to stay for the night. He might as well give himself a little holiday. It'd only cost a few shillings and he needed time to think.

There was a nice little pub nearby and though he had one or two pints, he took care not to get drunk because he'd need all his wits about him tomorrow to get his other things back again without anyone realising what he was doing.

He got up late, ate a very nice breakfast and paid his bill because he could see no way of sneaking out.

On the way to the station he bought a few items he'd need so that he could get the things he'd hidden away. He'd buy some food too so that he could hide out for a day or two.

He was back to Ollindale by the late afternoon train and had to trudge out to the Catlows' house lugging his suitcase and the old Gladstone bag he'd bought to put the other stuff in.

He was glad when Terry opened the door, not his wife.

'Do I still have a room?'

'You can have a bed, same as before. Got enough to pay for it?'

'Enough for a few nights, anyway, after which I need to be on my way again. I've heard of another job that might suit me.'

'Oh, where's that?'

'I'm not telling anyone till after I've got it.' He hesitated, then added, 'In the meantime I can afford to buy you a half pint if you feel like an hour at the pub tonight.' He needed to find out whether anything important had happened in Ollerthwaite while he was away.

Terry brightened visibly.

At the pub Hatton bought two half pints. He'd have liked to pour a pint down, then drink a second pint more slowly, but had to keep up the fiction that he was short of money as well as making sure Terry was on his side so that he'd have somewhere to sleep at least.

The following morning he said he might as well go up to the property and see if there were any other pickings to be had.

He set off openly then ducked into a back alley and watched. Sure enough Terry came creeping along the street, clearly hoping to follow him.

That settled it. He waited till the other man had turned the corner then went back for his bags, after which he took a different route up to the estate. Good thing he knew all the roads and tracks there as well as he knew the back of his hand.

When he got to the agent's house, he sighed for how comfortable it had once been, then went up to sit in the attic, grinning as he watched Terry try and fail to open the front door, then prowl round looking for him in other places. He could see that Terry hadn't brought anything with him to jemmy the lock on the front door and wouldn't dare to break it down so that it showed, so Hatton could wait him out.

Eventually the other man went away towards Ollerthwaite but Hatton didn't come out till he'd seen Terry go right down the road and vanish into the distance.

Only then did he make his way to the ruins and move the stones he'd set in place to cover the coal hatch that led into the back cellar. The big fire had caused the roof of the wine cellar at the front to fall in but the back cellar had survived more or less intact, and he'd dug out a way to get in that he could roll stones across.

He'd stashed a few things here over the years. Small things that he'd picked up when people were stupid enough to leave them lying round. Quite valuable, some of them were. Enough to boost his savings nicely if he could get them out of town without anyone else seeing what he was doing.

He decided in the end to take a train into Manchester once he'd got them. He had a cousin who'd look after the things for him and could be trusted not to try to steal from him because he'd promise her a share and she knew he always kept his promises to her. Besides, she'd have no idea how to sell stolen goods and wouldn't even dare try.

She was all right, though, Flo was, and he'd make sure she had enough money to keep her happy.

Good thing he'd thought to buy some food. It was going to be a long, cold night. He'd have to put another layer of clothes on.

29

Bryn smiled as he finished carving a pattern into the last of the six tops for a set of chair backs. Doing such crosspieces was a small job, easy for him, but he'd accept anything and everything till he'd established himself as a skilled tradesman.

Tam had been watching him so closely he'd had to tell him to stay back a bit a couple of times. But he'd been glad to see that the lad was fascinated by it and only needed telling once what a tool was needed for.

He was starting already to pass him the correct chisel some of the time without Bryn having to say which one. That was good going with a set of thirty to choose from and the differences very slight from one to another.

He smiled at his array of tools. He was glad to have them back. These chisels particularly. They were the best ones he'd ever worked with and felt like old friends.

As he ran a hand over the carvings one by one, Tam asked, 'Why are you doing that again? Isn't it smooth enough now?'

'I have to make absolutely certain that the new pieces are completely smooth so that they're safe for the manufacturer to polish. Feel these chair backs and tell me if you can find anything at all rough that shouldn't be.'

Tam ran his hands over the tops one by one, frowning and concentrating so hard, that Bryn thought in amusement his new assistant wouldn't have noticed if there had been an earthquake.

'They're a lot smoother than last time. But . . . ' He hesitated. 'Is there a tiny rough bit at this corner?'

Bryn felt it and nodded in approval. 'Yes, there is. Well done for finding it. You can't be too careful with the finish.'

He smoothed the corner out and they both felt it again and nodded.

'Right then. We can deliver them to Mr Hartell tomorrow when we go into town. And I'll see if he has any bits of wood that are no use to him but which I can use for side pieces in the smaller boxes I make.'

As he swept the floor afterwards, Tam sniffed the air and smiled happily. 'I love the smell of wood.'

'So do I. Now, if you've finished that, let's wrap up the chair tops and go back to working on that box.'

'There's more work goes into making things out of wood than I thought there would be.'

'Yes. And I won't send anything out of my workshop that isn't done properly. I'd rather burn it on the fire. Now, how about you make us a cup of tea and if you're hungry get yourself a piece of bread and dripping.'

Just then there was the sound of a horse trotting along the inland track and stopping outside the rear of the old mill, so he went to stand by the window and check who it was. Until they'd found out who was causing mischief like the attack on Elinor, he was being very watchful of who came here.

This was no one he knew but there was nothing furtive about the man and his behaviour. He got out of his cart and came straight towards the door.

Bryn could see something on the back of his little cart. It looked like a large piece of furniture but he couldn't see exactly what it was, because it was covered in an old blanket with ropes tied round to hold it in place. He went out to greet his visitor.

The man looked at him, not suspiciously but in a way that said he was checking him out. 'We heard someone had set up here to make furniture. Do you do repairs as well?'

'Yes. I do anything at the moment because I'm just starting up.'

'That's good to hear. I'm John Greeburn.' He held out his hand.

'Bryn Fordham.'

They shook hands.

'And this is my apprentice, Tam.'

Greeburn held out his hand to the boy as well.

Tam looked surprised at this courtesy but shook it.

'How can I help you, Mr Greeburn?'

'My wife says she's fed up of this chest of drawers wobbling about even when we put wedges under the back legs. It's an old piece and been knocked about a bit. The back legs are worn and uneven at the bottom, but it's got plenty of wear in it yet. She wants it making steady and she thinks one foot will need replacing where our puppy chewed the side of it. Oh, and there's a corner of the moulding at the top that got knocked off when it belonged to her father, who wasn't always sober.'

'Let's have a look at it.'

They checked it out together, then Bryn named a price, quite a low one because he had his reputation to make, but which would still give him a profit on what he'd need to spend on materials.

The man stuck out his hand to shake on the bargain. 'Yes. That sounds very fair. But I'll pay a bit more if you find anything else wrong. How long to do the job?'

'A week or so. I'll have to charge you more if you want it delivering because I'll lose working time if I have to do that as well.'

'No need. I live just down the road from here. There's a sign up at my gate with my name on it. But how about I come back in ten days to see it before I take delivery. That'll give you plenty of time to finish?'

He knew he would be judged before he got paid. He also knew Greeburn wouldn't find any shoddy work. 'Fine by me.

You must live at that smallholding with the two cottages on the right just before you reach Upperfold?'

'Yes. We own those two small fields. Ours is the cottage nearest here and my son and his family live in the one next to us.'

'Then we're neighbours.'

'We sell our vegetables if you're interested.'

'I am. Nothing like fresh vegetables.'

'I put things out near the gate and write the prices on a blackboard. People leave the money in a jar. And my wife sells things at the Friday morning market as well.'

'I'll remember that.'

The man studied Tam then said. 'I'll help you carry it in, Mr Fletcher. Your lad looks as if the wind could blow him away. Maureen's son, isn't he?'

'Yes.'

'He needs feeding up.'

'I'm doing that.' He grinned. 'And the lad doesn't mind at all.'

'They're allus hungry at that age.'

When the man had left, Tam came to stand in front of Bryn. 'You called me your apprentice. Did you mean it?'

'Yes. You're a good worker, you learn quickly and I think you're going to develop a good feel for handling wood. I'll get the papers for your apprenticeship drawn up next time I'm in Ollerthwaite.' Then he had to explain exactly how apprenticeships worked.

'You'll be tied to me for three years. At the end of that time you'll get your final papers saying you're fully trained – well, you will if you work hard and learn your trade. You must look after those papers very carefully. They're proof that you're a properly trained craftsman. I've still got mine.'

'I'll be very careful, Bryn. Thank you. Mam will be ever so pleased.'

'I'm pleased to have found someone suitable so quickly.'

All in all, it was a very satisfying day. In fact, life in Upperfold was going well. He'd even got his money and his tools through from his friend in Rochdale now.

There was only one thing missing in his life now, and that was a family of his own. He still hadn't given up hope, but first he'd have to find a wife and as he'd discovered over the years, that wasn't as easy as it sounded, not if you wanted a companion as well as a helpmeet, as he did.

Cam had found someone now, and Elinor was a lovely lass.

Pity he wasn't drawn to Maude. He liked her, but not in that special way.

He was going to keep his eyes open from now on and try to find someone who suited him. He didn't mind a widow, as long as she was young enough to bear children. In fact, it'd be good to have someone who'd proved able to provide them. He'd like at least one son and daughter, preferably more.

He shook his head, amused at himself for daydreaming. But he was so ready to settle down. He thought he'd hidden how eager he was from everyone except Walter. That wise old man missed very little.

30

New York

Caleb went straight to the office of the shipping company and had to hold back a whimper of sheer relief when he found that he was in luck; there was a ship almost ready to leave and he was just in time to book a passage, though only in steerage.

He'd been lucky with the cards lately, too, but hadn't earned as much as he could have done because he'd had to obey Daniel's orders as to when to let his opponents win and never to strip them of all their money.

Worst of all, he'd had to hand over most of whatever money he did win to Daniel, keeping only ten per cent. Well, he'd never have to do that again at least.

If he ever went back to playing, he'd certainly not do it on board the ship, or go back to America.

But what would he do with himself at his grandfather's in England? Muck out cows and kow-tow to an old man? Bile rose in his mouth and he spat it out on the ground. He'd not do that for ever. If the old man didn't die in a timely manner, he'd have to be helped into the next life.

By the time he got through the formalities and was able to board the ship, Caleb was exhausted and all he wanted to do was lie down and sleep. There was no one else in the big cabin. The other men had dumped their luggage to claim possession of bunks and gone back on deck. He'd seen them crowding at the rails to get a last glimpse of New York.

There was only one bunk unclaimed so he had no choice about where to sleep, but it suited him to stay in a dark corner. He put his two bags on the bunk and went back on deck, not wanting to stand out as different if anyone came looking for him. When he joined the other travellers, he took care to stand at the back of the crowd and keep his hat pulled well down, and stared down towards the deck as much as possible to keep his face hidden.

He was relieved when the ship sailed and the other steerage passengers started trickling back down to their quarters. He didn't waste time joining them.

He kept himself to himself for the voyage, pretending he'd just lost his wife to a childbirth gone wrong, because he didn't want to chat to anyone. It wasn't difficult to play the bereaved husband and act as if grieving his loss because all he wanted to do was huddle into himself. He was still coming to terms with the fact that he'd killed a man.

He was grieving all right, but about losing his chance of a future doing what he loved, which was playing cards and gambling. There was nothing to equal the thrill of that.

He didn't like the idea that he was a murderer, though, didn't like that at all. He tried to console himself with the thought that it had been done in self-defence: kill or be killed. He hadn't started the fight, had he? But as the days passed, his biggest worry about what he'd had to do was that he'd be caught and executed.

The other men in the big, crowded cabin left him alone, thank goodness, but the voyage seemed to go on for a very long time. Yet he was dreading arriving, because then he'd have to find his way to his grandfather's farm and come up with a story to satisfy the old man.

The best time of all was when everyone went to sleep and the big cabin was more or less quiet. He let himself drift into the dimness mentally and tried to work out exactly what to say to Walter Crossley. He could usually think up tales and explanations easily, but his mind seemed cloudy and dull since *it* had happened, and he was more tired than usual. And his damned arm was slow to recover from the knife wound.

He wondered if he'd find Cameron installed at the farm as the heir. Well, if he did, he'd unmask his half-brother as a usurper and surely his grandfather would go back to his first choice of heir. After all, Cameron was bastard born, not even a Crossley by name.

There was no escaping the fact that he'd have to pretend he wanted to settle down and work on a damned farm at first. He'd have to do that for a while to consolidate his place with his grandfather, but not for ever. Oh, no. It'd drive him mad.

Once his grandfather died, he'd inherit the farm and sell it. If his brother was still hanging around, he might have to cause an accident to get rid of him as well as dealing with the old man.

The thought of doing either of those things shocked him at first, but after he'd told himself a few times that you did what you had to simply to survive, it didn't seem quite as bad. After all, his grandfather was old, had had a fair chance at life.

He couldn't persuade himself that Cameron deserved an untimely end, though. He regretted that possibility of having to kill him.

But he had to think of himself first, because no one else would look after him. Especially now.

One day there was an announcement that the ship would arrive in Southampton the following afternoon and they were told who would be disembarking first and it wasn't the men in steerage.

When Caleb eventually got off the ship and found his way through customs, the evening was far advanced and it was no use trying to find his way in the darkness.

He did find a station and bought a ticket to this Ollerthwaite place just before the ticket office closed. He asked about getting there and was shocked at how far he still had to go and of course, there were no trains leaving till the next day. No overnight trains at all, it seemed.

Not only would he have to put up with living on a farm, but he'd be in the middle of nowhere from the sounds of it. This was going to be even worse than he'd expected.

He found a cheap lodging house and endured an uncomfortable night on a lumpy bed in a room containing four bunks. In the morning he had to run to catch the train, which made his heart flutter like a captive bird.

He sat looking out of the window at a landscape that looked more grey than green. What a chilly, rainy country England was.

He punched the side of his suitcase as anger overcame him, then winced as pain struck in his upper arm. That knife wound was taking a long time to heal. It must have been deeper than he'd realised.

He had to get on and off trains all day, till finally he caught the last one and had to endure a shabby old compartment full of nattering people.

He ignored them and stared glumly out of the window.

He no longer wanted to get there, wanted only to lie down and sleep.

31

Lancashire

Elinor's ankle took a few days to get better but eventually it was just about back to normal, though Maude urged her to rest it as much as she could and Walter backed her up on that.

She didn't notice at first that Maude was making excuses to leave her and Cameron alone when she had to rest, because she found it so easy to chat to him she often didn't realise how long they'd been talking for until Walter or Maude joined them again.

Then the quietly happy days of getting to know one another ended abruptly when a man from the village came up the hill in his pony and trap, bringing a visitor.

Walter was in his office so he didn't see who had come to the front door and it was left to Maude to answer it.

She stared at the tall young man, recognising at once that he was a Crossley, but not knowing how he fitted in.

'Is my grandfather here?' he asked.

She stilled, frowning. *Grandfather?* That seemed even stranger. 'I'll fetch him.'

'Can I come in while you're doing that? I've come a long way to see him and I'm exhausted.'

She thought this cheeky and, in fact, didn't like the patronising expression on his face when he spoke to her or the way he looked round as if he owned the place as he moved into the hall.

In the kitchen Cameron was wondering why she was taking so long to answer the door. He put down his mug of tea and called, 'Is something wrong, Maude?'

'I'm not sure. Can you come here a minute?'

He hurried out into the hall, stopping dead when he saw Caleb leaning against the doorpost.

'Oh, hell!' He looked beyond him and saw a man pulling two pieces of luggage from the back of the cart and carrying them towards the front door.

Caleb looked at him. 'Can you give him ten shillings, please? I've only got American money left.'

He fumbled in his pocket and handed over a few coins. 'Thank you for your help.'

As the man walked away, he turned back to his half-brother who asked mockingly, 'Am I expected to stay here on the doorstep all day?'

'You'd better come in.' Cam turned to Maude. 'Could you fetch Walter, please? Tell him it's urgent.'

'Who is this?'

'I'll tell you when Walter and Elinor are here.' His eyes pleaded with her not to argue, so she went through the kitchen, whispering to Elinor on the way that there was trouble.

'What sort of trouble?'

'I don't like the looks of the man who just arrived and Cam looks really upset.'

As she went out of the back door Elinor heard Cam take their visitor into the sitting room, not the kitchen where they usually sat and wondered why.

Cameron left the luggage sitting in the hall and gestured to a chair.

'Not a very warm welcome,' Caleb said mockingly, but he couldn't help sighing in relief as he sank down on the chair.

'You don't deserve a warm welcome,' Cam said.

'What do you know about anything? I'm exhausted. Travel's exhausting.'

'So is being in trouble. And you must have another problem now or you'd not have come here at all.'

Caleb shrugged. 'Well, we'll see what my grandfather thinks. After all, he did ask me to come here and offered to make me his heir. I've decided to take him up on that now I've had time to think about it.'

Elinor continued to eavesdrop from the kitchen doorway and gasped at this. It wasn't at all like Cam to speak so brusquely to anyone. She hadn't seen the visitor yet but she didn't like the mocking tone of his voice. Why had he come unannounced and uninvited into their peaceful world?

And why had Cam shown the visitor into the little-used front room instead of the kitchen?

Maude had said she didn't like the looks of him and she was usually a very tolerant person, like the other Crossleys.

Was Cam right and was his half-brother in trouble and using this as a refuge?

Walter was writing in one of his big ledgers. He finished a careful set of additions on a scrap of rough paper before looking up to see who'd disturbed him. The others usually left him in peace when he said he was going to do his accounts, knew it was fiddly work with money coming from different sources.

'A man's just arrived and Cam says he needs you urgently.'

'Can you ask him to give me another ten minutes or so? Offer the visitor a cup of tea.'

'From the look on Cam's face, I don't think you'd better delay, Walter. I didn't like the look of this man, either, and I don't usually feel like that so quickly. I like to give people a chance to show what they're like. Especially when there's a Crossley involved, but this one – he just isn't nice.'

That caught his attention and he put his pen down. 'You're sure this person is a Crossley?'

'Certain. He has the look. You can't mistake it. And he's very tall, though not as tall as Cam, I'd guess. And also . . . he says you're his grandfather.'

Walter stilled for a moment as he considered what this might mean, then stood up. 'We'd better go and see what's going on, then, hadn't we?'

'Yes.'

'Lead the way.'

He followed Maude into the house and when she would have stood back to let him pass, he gestured to her to continue to lead the way, surprised when he realised Cam had taken their visitor into the front room.

Elinor was standing in the hall near the door, also looking worried and clearly listening to what they were saying. She stepped back towards them and whispered, 'This man says you invited him here and asked him to be your heir.'

'You're sure of that?'

'Certain. He has a very loud voice.'

'What did Cam say to that?'

'He didn't say anything. I think he's waiting for you before he does anything.'

Walter stood for another moment or two then took a deep breath and moved past her into the front sitting room. He stopped a couple of paces inside and stared across at the young man, struggling to get out of an armchair. Yes, he was a Crossley, but his expression was . . . well, sly and mocking were the words that came to mind.

'No need to get up. You don't look well.'

Caleb fell back. 'I won't if you don't mind. I injured my arm on the ship and I've found the travel utterly exhausting. The railway system here isn't much good.' He looked at the old man and waited.

'You didn't come here when I invited you. Why now?'

He looked faintly surprised. 'You know who I am?'

'Yes. It's written on your face.'

'Then you must have known Cam wasn't me when you took him in?'

'I guessed almost from the start. Cam is older than you and he knows a lot about farming. Your father warned me that you didn't.'

'Oh, did he? Well, now I'm prepared to learn. I've had enough of a frenetic way of living. I, um, thought I'd enjoy it but I didn't. Sowing your wild oats, don't they call it?'

'That usually refers to dealings with women. There's none of that with you, is there? It's gambling that's your passion.'

A scowl, quickly abandoned for a false smile was the only response.

'Well, we can talk about what you've been doing with yourself later. You look to me as if you need a good, hearty meal and an early night. We'll save any serious discussions about your future until tomorrow morning.'

Elinor gave him a disappointed look and scowled at the newcomer. She hadn't liked how he talked to Cam or Walter, and something about the newcomer continued to grate on her. She went across to thread her arm in Cam's and he looked sideways at her, trying to hide his surprise at her doing that so openly but not pulling away.

'Who's your lady friend?' Caleb asked suddenly, again in that mocking tone, 'I can see that the other woman is a Crossley, but this one isn't. First time I've seen you in a female's clutches, actually, Cam. I thought you were a born bachelor.'

'Elinor is my friend,' Maude said. 'She's part of the family and she lives here.'

'She looks to be far more friendly with Cam than you are, which is going to be disappointing if she's counting on him being the heir.'

'Mind how you talk about her,' Cam snapped.

The timer sounded in the kitchen and Elinor said quietly, 'I need to see to the oven.'

The caring look Cam gave her made it unnecessary to say how much she meant to him.

She smiled up at him and unthreaded her arm from his. 'I need to get the apple pie out of the oven.'

'Ooh, she's definitely got her hooks into you,' Caleb mocked. 'Baking you pies now.'

Cameron gave his brother a scornful look. Caleb definitely hadn't improved since he ran away. 'I certainly hope so. And I've got my hooks, as you so charmingly call it, into her, too.'

Walter had been watching and was wondering why this young man was acting in such an antagonistic manner. Was he drunk? Or jealous of Cam, who was taller and better looking? Or was the younger brother ill? He certainly didn't look well, and was that a feverish flush on his cheeks?

Well, everything could wait until their visitor had had a proper night's sleep, and Walter had had time to work out how best to deal with the situation. He turned to Maude. 'Could you please get a bedroom ready for Caleb?'

'Yes. Of course.' She followed Elinor out of the room.

Walter turned to the two younger men. 'We'll leave any discussions until tomorrow.'

'In the meantime perhaps you can show me round the farm, Grandfather?' Caleb asked.

'You're too tired for that now and anyway, it's going to rain soon. I think you should go and unpack once Maude has your room ready. Then it'll be time for our evening meal. Just come downstairs when you're ready. We'll be in the kitchen.'

He moved to the door and held it open. 'There's only one set of stairs. Cam will show you the way. Take your time and when you come down, go through that door, which leads to the rear of the house.' He looked at Cam. 'I need to finish my accounts while the figures are still clear in my head. I'll have done them before the meal is ready. I'll see you then.'

Cam led the way upstairs, not saying anything because he could sense that Walter didn't want any arguments or heated discussions – though Caleb seemed to want to provoke them.

He was surprised at how slowly his brother followed him up and how haggard he looked in the bright light thrown by one of the new oil lamps they were using in the bedrooms now.

Maude came out on to the landing as Caleb at last reached the top of the stairs. 'This is your room. The bed's ready.'

All she got in response was, 'Mmm.' No word of thanks. Caleb paused in the doorway, staring round. 'Not bad. He can't be short of money then.'

Maude gasped at this and saw the anger on Cam's face. 'Could you bring up a big jug of water for the washstand, Cam, please?' she asked hastily.

He nodded and went down to pump the water, tipping some hot water from the kettle in to take the chill off it. There was always a kettle sitting on the stove.

As he picked up the jug he looked across at Elinor and shook his head, but didn't let his anger loose or try to discuss their unexpected visitor in case Caleb overheard.

Upstairs, Maude said in a toneless voice, 'You'll need to have a wash – and perhaps change into some clean clothes. There's time before the meal.'

'Not easy to stay clean in steerage, I'm afraid. You'll have to wash some clothes for me tomorrow.'

Again the visitor had spoken in a jeering voice, treating her like a servant. She didn't try to say anything else, or tell him she'd do no such thing, just left him to it, glad to get away from him.

Down in the kitchen she looked at Elinor. 'What a horrible person this Caleb is! How can he possibly be a grandson of Walter's?'

'I don't know. Nor do I know how I'll keep from giving him a good telling off if he insults Cam again.'

'Well, at least he's pushed you two right out into the open about how you feel.'

That at least made Elinor smile. 'I suppose so. It was pretty obvious before, I think.'

'You suit one another.'

'I hope so.'

When Cam took the jug of water into the bedroom he found Caleb sitting slumped on the bed. He really did look exhausted. But that didn't excuse his rudeness.

'Will that female still care about you when you're not the heir?' his brother asked suddenly.

'None of your business.'

'I'm making it my business from now on. I was a fool to hand my inheritance over to you. I intend to take it back. And if you know what's good for you, you'll step away from it voluntarily.'

'That's up to Cousin Walter, not you.'

'Does he know you're a bastard?'

'Yes.'

'Does your fancy woman?'

'Yes.'

'You have been busy cosying up to people, haven't you?'

'I'll leave you to wash and change your clothes,' Cam said.

'I suppose I'll have to go down and chat to him. I'd much rather lie down and go to sleep.'

The meal was ready on time but still Caleb hadn't come down to join them.

Cam looked across the kitchen at Walter. 'Shall I go up and tell him it's ready?'

'No. I'll do it.'

When Walter went up he found Caleb lying down, still in his dirty clothes and fast asleep. He went closer and frowned.

His grandson didn't look at all well. Was it the travelling that had exhausted him, as he claimed, or had he injured himself on his travels?

He went back down. 'He's asleep. And if he isn't better in the morning, I'm sending for the doctor. I'm wondering if he's ill. He looks feverish.'

'He's always caught things easily,' Cam said. 'And taken longer to recover than others. His mother has always coddled him because of that and our father has tried to toughen him up and claimed there's nothing wrong with him.'

'Well, I'm a light sleeper. I'll hear him if he gets up during the night. Let's have our meal now.'

Walter pulled out a chair for Maude and sat down beside her. Cam helped Elinor serve the food, then they joined the other two in eating it.

No one said much during the meal.

Afterwards, the two women cleared up, Cam fiddled with a book but didn't seem to be turning any pages, and Walter sat reading a newspaper. But he too did more staring into space than reading.

When Walter got up in the morning, he knocked on the door of the room where Caleb had been sleeping.

His grandson swung round as the door opened, moving to the mantelpiece, hand outstretched. Something seemed to be hidden under a wallet and when he saw it was his grandfather who'd come in, he moved to stand in front of whatever it was.

'How are you this morning?'

'A bit better, thank you.'

'Good. You must be hungry.'

'Um, yes of course I am.'

'If you're ready, we'll go downstairs.'

Whatever was hidden glinted like a knife blade. Why would Caleb need a knife?

In the kitchen they found Elinor and Maude, as usual getting breakfast for everyone.

'Good morning, ladies,' Walter said cheerfully. 'It's going to be another rainy day, I'm afraid.'

No one said anything for a moment, then Elinor made an attempt to fill the awkward silence. 'I hope you slept well, Mr Crossley.' She gestured to the kitchen range. 'Would you like a big breakfast seeing you missed last night's meal?'

'Not really. Just a boiled egg and a piece of toast.'

They all stared at him, because he seemed to think the two women were servants, and even if they had been, Walter would have preferred to hear a please or thank you.'

He was about to make a comment on this when Caleb moved towards the table, staggered slightly and bumped into a chair, sending it flying across the room. He let out a yelp of what sounded like pain as his upper body made contact with the edge of the chair back.'

'Are you all right?' Walter asked. 'What have you hurt?'

Caleb stepped hastily backwards. 'It's just a cut. I had a little accident on the ship and it's not quite healed yet. It'll be all right in another couple of days.'

'Let Maude dress it for you. She's a dab hand with injuries, people or animals.'

'*No!* It's all right.'

But his voice had been so sharp, it made Walter give him another of those thoughtful looks. Then he looked at the chair, annoyed that it was a delicate one that had belonged to his mother and the awkwardness of Caleb's fall had sent it crashing into the side of the fireplace. He picked it up without saying a word and set it by the kitchen door. He'd see if Bryn could repair it.

Caleb didn't notice that he'd broken a chair. He was too busy asking Elinor if they had any coffee, then scowling when she said they didn't and giving her orders about how exactly he liked his cups of tea.

Did he treat all women like that or only servants? Well, even if she was one, she deserved treating politely.

Cam had just come in and frowned at the way their visitor had spoken to her, but once again he caught Walter's glance and obeyed the slight shake of the head that said to leave it be.

'Sit down at that side of the table, Caleb, and take that bigger chair. That can be your place from now on.'

When he gestured to it, Caleb slid into his place, shooting a triumphant look at his brother and not even seeming to notice that he'd broken the other chair.

Elinor and Maude exchanged quick worried glances but like Cam they had soon picked up the message that Walter didn't want them to take issue with anything.

'If he weren't Walter's grandson, I'd be giving him a sharp response next time he orders me around,' Maude fumed.

'There's something wrong with him,' Elinor murmured after Walter had taken Caleb outside to show him round the outbuildings.

'What do you mean?'

'The way he's behaving. It's almost as if he's drunk – or sick.'

'There's something very amiss with his manners, that's for sure.' Maude looked at her friend. 'Surely Walter isn't going to make that man his heir? If he does, I'm not staying here, cousin or not.'

'Neither am I. But I find it hard to believe Walter would do that to Cam. I think he's waiting and watching to see exactly what Caleb is like.'

'Sometimes people care about blood relationships above anything else. And Cam's mother wasn't married to his father.'

'Walter's not likely to care about that.'

'Well, that man is so rude and horrible he doesn't even seem like a Crossley, blood relationship or not.'

32

Hatton spent an uncomfortable night in the cellar of the ruined house. At one stage he decided to go outside and go back into the agent's house, because he not only found the cellar stuffy, he also felt uneasy there, as if someone were watching him.

Which was impossible. It was just the wind making things knock against one another – wasn't it?

However, when he got up and began to gather his things together, intending to sleep in one of the two empty houses, it began raining so hard he stayed where he was. He could hear water trickling into the cellar now through the narrow gap where the edge of the coal chute didn't quite fit. When the rain didn't abate and the sound of water got louder, he lit a candle to see if he could close it properly. But it looked as if rain had been coming in at that spot for years, so he left it alone and blew out the candle. He didn't want to make it worse.

After what seemed a long night, a thin thread of light filtered through the same gap and he realised that morning had come at last. Thank goodness!

When he moved the stones to provide a path for the rainwater to drain away, he moved the coal hatch and looked up at the morning sky. It wasn't raining now but he bet it'd pour down later because the sky was full of heavy clouds.

He ate the last couple of scones and checked the rest of his food, setting it out and trying to estimate how long it would last him, then put it back in the small bag of cotton material.

But his hands were so cold he fumbled and he dropped the big bag before he could put the food away in it. To his horror, it knocked against the smaller bag and sent it down into a gap between some heavy stones.

He tried to move the stones to get at it but couldn't budge it and cursed loudly.

There was nothing he could do now but leave that day.

When he walked slowly across to the coal chute, he trod on a paving stone that wobbled under his feet. Strange. None of the others were loose.

He bent down and studied it, then found a piece of wood and levered one side of the stone up. Two small leather bags were lying there. He let out a crow of triumph when he saw what was inside the first one, and another even louder shout when he opened the second bag.

Someone had hidden these under the flagstone so their contents must have some value. They'd obviously been lying there for many years, from the looks of them.

When he studied the big stone again, wondering why it had suddenly started moving, he realised it was directly below the leak. Rain from the winter storms must have sent enough water into the cellar to gradually wash away some of the soil underneath that particular bit of paving.

These pieces didn't look much but they had to be worth something if someone had bothered to hide them. Was it real silver they were made from? They were so tarnished he thought at first they were cheap imitations, things he could sell at the markets for a shilling or two each.

Then he tried polishing a little brooch and it came up beautifully, gleaming at him in the light from the coal chute.

Who had put them here? Perhaps they'd been stolen by someone else years ago, a maid perhaps who'd filched pieces from her mistress and who'd never managed to retrieve them.

Who knew? Who cared? Not him. All he cared about was that they were worth something and he'd take them with him when he eventually retired. They'd add nicely to his savings.

He gathered all the things he'd hidden down here, intending to take them away. Then he changed his mind. He didn't trust banks, didn't completely trust anyone except himself. He'd seen his grandparents shut away into the poorhouse when they grew too feeble to look after themselves, to die there in meek misery. His parents had gone to an early grave, worn out after working hard all their lives trying desperately to avoid the same fate.

No way was he going to end up like any of them. So he put only half the coins into his suitcase and slipped some of the jewellery into his inner pocket, leaving the rest of the valuables under the stone, which he settled in place more solidly.

He'd come back for them in a year or two. No one knew better than him how to sneak around the grounds of Ollerton House. No one would find them down here in the meantime.

When he was ready to leave, he scanned the area carefully before moving up through the cellar hatch and then, when he was sure no one else was nearby, he covered it up carefully and went out of the ruins into the overgrown shrubbery.

He made his way cautiously towards the road, ducking down when he saw Walter Crossley drive away from the farm with one of the women sitting beside him.

The younger man who resembled Crossley came out of the farm shortly afterwards on a bicycle, but he turned up the hill, heading off along the river road towards the old mill.

That had left only one person at the farm, the taller of the two women. Then she too came out on a bicycle and turned down the hill towards Upperfold with a big basket containing what looked like eggs and some green stuff. Of course! It was market day.

He scowled as he watched her move down the hill. The whole world had gone mad over bicycles in the last few years. He hated the stupid things. They made him puff and pant, and it hurt his knees to turn the pedals.

Seeing all that food she was carrying reminded him that he was ravenously hungry.

Her departure meant there was no one left at the farm, so if he hurried across to it now, he'd be able to steal some food and possibly a few other things as well to add to his savings.

After that he could leave the farm the back way and make his way up the hill. There was an old shepherd's path that led over this part of the tops and down into the far end of the town, going along the far side of the lake. Not many people used it these days because it was a long way round and a bit overgrown – or it had been last time he looked.

But you could still use go this way and reach the town without being seen, he was sure. And best of all, it'd bring him out near the station without it being likely he'd meet anyone.

He wished he didn't have his suitcases to carry. They slowed him right down. But he'd need some decent clothes when he got away.

He hurried across to the farm, feeling a lot more cheerful. No one else seemed to be out and about, thank goodness.

When he reached the farm, he found the front door locked, so crept round to the back and found that door open to anyone who cared to turn the handle and walk in. Laughing softly, he did just that.

Inside the farm Caleb was dozing in an armchair, grateful that they'd all gone out and left him in peace. He wasn't feeling at all well but give him a few days of rest and he was sure to recover. By that time he'd have watched the old man enough to work out how best to treat him in order to worm his way into the role of heir again.

His half-brother wasn't getting the farm. If he had to stay in the middle of nowhere, Caleb was going to make sure he benefited from the time he spent there. And if that meant shovelling cow dung or whatever else his grandfather did with his time, then so be it. How many years would it need? Three or four?

Or maybe Walter would do him a favour and drop off the perch of his own accord. He could then deal with Cameron and—

Suddenly he stiffened. Someone had come to the back door, not only to it but in through it. But everyone was out and there'd been no sound of any of them returning. What's more this person hadn't called a greeting. Damnation! It had to be an intruder. The door couldn't have been locked, then. Which just showed the old man was getting senile.

He got out of the chair and went to peep through the gap in the hall door, which wasn't properly closed at the kitchen end, and found himself clutching the wall as the room wavered round him.

When he regained his balance – he really did need to rest and recover – it looked to him as if it was some old tramp foraging for food. Maybe the fellow would just grab something and go away. If so, he was welcome to it.

Only the man not only grabbed some bread and cheese, but poured himself a cup of cold tea and stood drinking it and staring out of the window, damn his cheek.

Caleb felt for the special sheath in his belt, setting it just so. The throwing knife was there if he had to defend himself, but he'd rather the tramp just went away. He waited, keeping still and silent.

In Ollerthwaite, Walter took Elinor to the butcher's, where they bought a leg of lamb and some sausages, then to the baker's where they bought three extra loaves, plus a fruit loaf and a lardy cake. Having a visitor at the end of the week had caught them a bit short of some foodstuffs and he wasn't having her slaving over that worthless fellow.

He already knew that he didn't want Caleb to stay at the farm for long but if he was ill, well, you couldn't just chuck him out, could you?

On the way back they waved to Maude, who was standing at the market stall chatting to one of her acquaintances as she sold their spare eggs and some of the greens she'd been growing.

Cam had gone to the old mill to drop off the broken chair for Bryn to repair. Walter reckoned he and Elinor would get back to the farm first. The two younger men were good friends and would likely have a good chat over a cup of tea.

Seeing how lush the grass was in front of the farm, Walter stopped the cart there and tethered Sally to a gatepost to let her have a munch.

'You and I can go in through the front door. I have a key,' he said to Elinor. 'Here, let me carry one of those baskets.'

As Hatton lifted his mug to gulp down the last of the tea, he heard something outside and stilled. Had Walter Crossley come back early? Oh hell, he hoped not! He didn't want to be caught here by any of the occupants. But he'd been so ravenously hungry he hadn't been able to resist grabbing something to eat and drink.

He'd better get out of here as quickly as he could. But he needed to grab some food to take with him in case he got delayed again.

They hadn't come round the back or into the house the front way either, so he still had a couple of minutes. He shoved a few bits and pieces of cake and bread into a tea towel and stuffed it into the top of one of his bags.

In the hall, Caleb was growing tired of keeping still and hiding from the intruder. And he was getting cramp in the injured arm, whose painful throbbing had kept him awake for half the night. He moved it inadvertently and hit it on a sharp corner of a small table. Dizziness struck him again and he stumbled to one side, crying out in sudden agony at a sharp pain in his chest.

When he heard movement somewhere, he thought the intruder had heard him bump into the wall and was coming for him. Good thing he had a way of protecting himself. He moved his hand towards the sheath ready to pull out the throwing knife, just as someone peeped through the back door of the hall, a burly, unshaven fellow.

At the same time as that was going on, Walter had unlocked the front door and was about to open it when he heard someone moving inside the house. He assumed it was Caleb but when he heard a cry of pain and the thud of someone banging into something, he was worried that his grandson had got worse and fallen over.

He left the bag where it was and thrust the front door wide open in time to see Caleb draw a knife from inside his belt with astonishing speed. He sent it flying down the hallway into another man's chest with a throw that said he was an expert at using it.

Walter realised the other man was Hatton and watched in horror as the agent clutched his chest and staggered sideways. He had been holding a kitchen knife but it dropped from his hand as he collapsed slowly to the floor, blood pouring out where the knife protruded from his chest.

For a moment Caleb looked triumphant, then his face twisted into anguish and he too clutched his chest. He sank to the floor and lay there, moaning faintly.

Walter moved forward towards him ready to prevent the land agent attacking his grandson again. But Hatton was lying utterly still. Surely he couldn't be dead?

Since the agent was in no state to attack anyone else, Walter turned to his grandson, only to find himself rooted to the spot.

He'd seen the look before, seen it all too often when people died of heart problems. Caleb hadn't been hit by a knife, but by an enemy just as deadly: a problem within his own body.

He knelt on the floor beside his grandson, muttering, 'Keep an eye on the other fellow,' to Elinor.

'I think he's dead,' she whispered.

'Stay vigilant!'

He saw her grab a walking stick from the hall stand and stand watching Hatton.

When he turned his attention back to Caleb, his grandson was staring up at him. 'I . . . can't breathe . . . this time.' His words were punctuated by gasps.

'This time?'

'This happened . . . in America . . . '

He closed his eyes and murmured. 'My luck . . . has run out. Cameron will . . . get your farm . . . after all.'

He had been going to give it to the older grandson anyway, but Walter didn't bother to point that out, didn't do anything but hold his grandson's hand and watch helplessly as he struggled for breath.

There was the sound of a bicycle outside and then an exclamation as Cameron burst into the hall and saw his brother lying there. 'What the hell happened?'

'I don't know what started this, but Caleb had just killed Hatton and then . . . his heart gave out. He said he'd had trouble with it before.'

'He's complained about his heart fluttering for years.'

There was dead silence as they both stared down at Caleb.

He stared at them, tried to say something else then gasped and stopped breathing so abruptly the utter silence that followed was shocking.

'He's never been happy, not in all the years I've known him,' Cameron said in a half-whisper. 'But I never thought he'd die so young.'

As Walter reached out to close his grandson's eyes for the final time, Cameron stood up and moved across to put an arm round Elinor. 'Are you all right?'

'Yes. Is he—?'

'Caleb's dead. What about this one?'

'He died first.' She stared at Hatton, shaking her head. 'I've never seen such a violent death, so much blood.' She shuddered and buried her face in Cameron's shoulder and he hugged her close to him, wishing she hadn't seen these horrors.

Walter came to check on the other man, stared for a few seconds then turned to the couple standing there.

'Can you manage on your own for a while, lass? I need Cameron to go into Ollerthwaite and report this to the policeman.'

She took a deep breath and nodded but Cameron pulled her back and pressed a quick kiss on the nearest cheek. 'I'll be back as soon as I can, love.'

She nodded and watched him turn to listen to Walter's instructions. Two good men, these. She mustn't let them down.

'Our police constable will have a fit,' Walter said grimly. 'He's more than ready for retirement and is pretty useless but we need him to represent the authority of the law and deal with Hatton's death.' He paused for a moment then added, 'Ask for the doctor to come too while you're in town, Cameron. His surgery is just along the street from the police station.'

'He can't help now.'

'But he can say how your brother died.'

'Shall I cover them up?' Elinor asked.

'No. I think we should leave them as we found them. We need to do everything properly.'

He shook his head and gulped, but suddenly he was weeping, one hand pressed to his face, great sobs escaping his control. 'So much death. When will it ever end?'

He wasn't only talking about today's deaths, she realised, but about those of his son and grandson – and at his age, who knew how many other people he'd cared about had died suddenly.

The two of them guided Walter into the kitchen away from the dreadful sights in the hall.

'I'll look after him.' She sat down beside Walter, holding one of the old man's hands with her other arm round his shoulders. 'Go and fetch Constable Tully and the doctor, Cam love.'

She could only hug Walter as his tears still flowed.

It seemed a very long time before the people from the town arrived.

Cameron went into town for help, stopping in Upperfold on the way to let Maude know what had happened. She left the rest of her produce and set off home straight away.

It took a while to find the police constable and doctor, and tell them that they were needed at the farm, then Cameron set off back.

The doctor and police constable were both horror-struck at the scene in the hall, then it was the doctor who pulled himself together and examined Caleb. After that he guided the constable through the formalities with grim determination to do things properly.

It took a while but there could be no doubt what had happened. It was spelled out in blood and bodies.

Walter managed to answer their questions in fits and starts.

After verifying the two men's deaths, the doctor told the constable to stay there and said he'd send help from Upperfold.

As Cameron helped him harness the pony and cart again, the doctor whispered, 'Your grandfather is suffering from shock and he's held in too much of his grief about his son's and grandson's deaths earlier this year. Keep an eye on him and don't try to stop him weeping out his pain. Those two

ladies are towers of strength. Most females would have gone
to pieces.'

'They're wonderful women.'

'I'm going to send the local midwife to help out at the farm
as well. She can always be relied on in any crisis. And I'll
send the undertaker to fetch the bodies out of there as quickly
as he can. He's a good chap, too, used to dealing with folk
who're upset.'

He studied Cameron. 'Will you be all right?'

'Yes. How soon can we have the funeral? I think it'll be best
over and done with.'

'Can't do anything until the police sergeant in charge of
this area has been informed, and the magistrate has given permission to bury them. There's no doubt that what happened
wasn't the fault of any of the family. Any idea why Hatton was
here?'

'Not the faintest.'

'Right, then.'

He went back in to find Maude clearing up the mess and
Elinor still with her arm round Walter's shoulders.

Cameron looked across at her briefly, and she managed to
smile reassuringly if briefly then turned back to Walter.

The following day Cameron walked outside and found Elinor
walking to and fro in the yard. Here was his chance. He moved
forward. 'Are you all right?'

'I'm fine, thanks. I'm just taking in some fresh air and hoping today will be more peaceful.'

'May I walk up and down with you?'

'I always enjoy your company.'

'And I enjoy yours.' He took her hand and stopped her
moving. 'Elinor, I can't hold back any longer. I love you and
well, I want to make you my wife. Will you? Do you care for
me at all?'

She reached up to touch his cheek, saying with a smile, 'Of course I do, you fool. I thought you'd never ask me.'

He pulled her closer and kissed her, then rained kisses on her cheeks and forehead, before dancing her round the farm-yard.

Walter came out as he was doing that and smiled to see them.

When they came to a halt next to him, he asked, 'Does this mean what I hope?'

Cameron beamed at him, 'That she's agreed to marry me? Yes. You may be the first to congratulate us.'

'Oh, I do. And it's wonderful to see such joy after a difficult time.' He moved forward to give Elinor a hug, 'Now you'll truly be a member of the family, though you've felt like one since soon after your arrival.'

She found she was holding a hand of each man so pulled them into a whirl of joy 'I've never been as happy in my whole life.'

'Nor I,' Cameron said.

He turned to his grandfather but Walter had gone back inside the house, so he kissed Elinor again, then just held her close.

It was just over a week before the dead men could be laid to rest.

Cameron sent out word that his grandfather wanted only a quiet, private funeral for his grandson and there were only the five of them there, Bryn coming to give them unspoken support, as he had for the past few days.

Hatton's family were contacted by the authorities but they weren't close to him and no one stepped forward to bury him, so he was put into a pauper's grave. His bags of clothes were offered to Walter by the constable to distribute to the poor as needed.

He pushed them aside with a grimace of distaste, tempted to throw them away, then sighed and pulled the bags back. 'I can't bear to throw good things away, but put them in the attic in the house where I store my bits and pieces, Cameron lad. We'll leave them there for a year or two till people have forgotten the incident.'

His grandson did as he asked, only giving the bags a cursory look inside.

And then at last all the official fuss was over and they could start to build new lives.

33

After two more weeks had passed, Walter claimed to have recovered enough to resume his work on the farm. There was something still missing in the way he behaved, though, at least it seemed so to those who loved him so dearly. It was hard to put your finger on it exactly, but perhaps there was a reduction in his old energy and enthusiasm, and a willingness to leave decisions to others.

The people of the valley also noticed that he was still 'a bit lost' and did what they could to cheer him up, sending him little gifts and messages when they had something to share. They came together as a community in a way they hadn't done for years in their attempts to help him.

One day when the two of them were out for a walk together, a chance comment by Elinor reminded Walter of a small piece of unfinished business at Jubilee Lake.

She'd always longed to be able to walk right round it and that day she stopped to say without thinking, 'I do wish I could walk all round the lake. Are people ever going to finish the work they started? They should at least finish this path, surely?'

He stopped to look at it briefly, then shrugged and walked on. But when he came to the actual ending of the path, where they usually turned back to avoid the boggy patch, he stopped again and stood frowning at it.

Had she caught his attention? She stopped beside him but said nothing.

He turned round on the spot, staring at her and then back at the lake. 'We could do that, couldn't we? A proper path might bring hikers to our valley or people on cycling holidays. That'd give our people more work, in the summer at least.'

He turned round and they began to walk back again. He seemed lost in thought and after a while, she linked her arm with his and risked asking, 'Tell me how it'd look if we finished it. Would the path just go straight along or would it take a few little detours to add interest?'

He grew quite animated describing the way the path could curve round the lake, further from the water in some parts, closer to it in others.

The others listened to him talk about the lake and behind his back they smiled at one another. Something was happening again and the old Walter seemed to be emerging from his sadness.

That evening they'd invited Bryn and Tam round to join them for tea to celebrate Bryn's birthday. After they'd eaten, the idea of working on the lake was mentioned as she told them where they'd been that morning.

'It could be a pretty little lake,' Bryn said.

'It was our Tim who was eager to do a lake, even when he was a young lad,' Walter said. 'He made the idea come to life for everyone. I can put things into words, but I can't draw them like he could. I think people need to *see* what it'll look like to get truly interested.'

A little later he mentioned it again. 'Eh, you were right, Bryn lad. That lake could be pretty. I do wish our Tim were still here. He made a rough sketch or two and they *showed* what could be done. Only I don't know where his sketches have got to. I don't remember where I put their possessions after my lads died, just that I couldn't bear to look at any of their things.'

Maude frowned and raised one forefinger to get his attention, waggling it to and fro as she said slowly, 'I saw some sketches up in the attic. I thought they were just, you know, sketches made for pleasure. Would they be the ones showing Tim's ideas for the lake to people, do you think?'

Walter beamed at her. 'They might be. Do you remember where they were?'

'Yes. I can go up and fetch them now, if you like.'

He stood up. 'I'll come with you to hold the lamp.'

While he was lighting it she seized the moment she'd been waiting for to help her friend. 'I saw some sketching materials up there too. I was going to ask you about those, Walter. Elinor's really good at drawing as well, only she lost her art things when we ran away. And she didn't have much drawing stuff anyway, because we were hard put to find the money for extras like that in those days.'

When they went downstairs, he paused in the doorway and looked across the room. 'I hear you can draw, lass?'

Elinor shrugged and Maude stepped in again. 'She's really good, but we had to hide her drawings and she had to keep them small to hide them and stop her stepfather finding them. He'd have torn them up if he had and mocked her unbearably.'

Walter turned to Elinor, 'Eh, I shan't mock you, lass. We'll fetch the art materials down as well as the sketches. You'll never need to hide your talents here.'

His voice wobbled a bit as he added, 'And I know my Tim. He'd have been glad to see the paints and other stuff go to someone who could use them, he really would.'

A few minutes later, Maude called down, 'Can you come up and help us carry some things, please?'

When they came down they were carrying several lumpy bags and boxes and Cameron and Bryn followed them, carefully manoeuvring a large easel round the bend at the foot of the stairs.

They set it up in the kitchen. 'It's a bit dusty but it's a really good one,' Bryn said as he checked it. 'I can go over it and make sure it'll stand more solidly, as well as cleaning it up. Won't take me long.'

'Can I help you?' Tam asked at once. 'I've never seen one of those before.'

Bryn ruffled his hair. 'Of course you can. It won't take *us* long.'

Elinor had put the boxes she was carrying down on the table and began to open them. They contained both oil paints and watercolours, some partly used, some unopened, plus all sorts of other bits of equipment. Even the pencils were special artists' ones of different hardness and softness.

'Take them and use them with my love, lass,' Walter said.

So she turned round and gave him a cracking big hug. 'You're so kind to us.'

'I'm lucky to have you all.'

'I know you say you're no good at drawing,' she coaxed, 'but could you sketch it out, however roughly and talk me through what he wanted to do?'

'I suppose I could. If you promise not to laugh at my stick figures.'

She made the sign for crossing her heart.

'I love the idea of starting work on Jubilee Lake again,' Maude said. 'I know we need a path all the way round the lake, but what else were you planning? I could make a list and help with anything that doesn't need you to draw.' She chuckled. 'I'm like you, Walter, not skilful at drawing.'

He sat down on his armchair, smiling in a more relaxed way than they'd seen for ages, and she perched on a chair nearby, resting a piece of paper on the nearest side of the table, ready to start writing.

'Well, we need places for older folk to sit on and rest as they walk round, and a sandpit for the small children to play in.'

'And the benches could be named in memory of the people who'd been involved,' Bryn suggested. 'I saw that done in a park in America once.'

'Name the benches,' Walter said softly. 'What a lovely idea.' He tapped the piece of paper. 'Leave that on the table and anyone who gets an idea can write it down.'

Cameron gave Elinor a questioning look and she nodded, so he clapped his hands. 'While we're all together there's something else we want to decide.'

Everyone turned round towards him.

'You know that Elinor and I want to get married. Well, we don't want to wait to do it.'

'Not a fancy wedding,' she said. 'Just one with the people we care about most.'

'And if you'll have us, we'd like to start our married life here,' Cameron said to his grandfather.

'I can't think of anything I'd like better.' Walter's face was absolutely shining with gentle happiness now.

He got his old mischievous look on his face suddenly. 'And after that, we'll have to find a husband for our Maude and a wife for our Bryn.'

The two people mentioned went a little pink and Walter chuckled.

'You don't mind me treating you as a member of the family and calling you "our Bryn" do you, lad?'

'I'm delighted. But I'll find my own wife, if you don't mind.'

'See that you do or I'll find someone for you.' He turned to Maude. 'And for you as well, lass.'

'I'm a bit old now, I think. I'll just be everyone's auntie instead.'

He took her hand. 'No, you're not too old. And I mean it. If you don't find someone to marry, I really will seek someone for you.' He pulled the end of the plain, dark ribbon holding her hair back and cast it aside.

'Let alone this is the sort of ribbon old women wear, you should start by showing off your hair in one of those chignon things I've seen some women wearing. It's really bonny, that hair of yours is and you should make the most of it.' He ruffled it up some more.

Everyone laughed at her as she went an even darker pink, but she knew they were just teasing out of fondness. And surely Walter wouldn't go looking for a husband for her?

That night Walter lay awake in bed, so thankful for his new family he'd been given by fate that he couldn't get to sleep for a while.

Tonight brightness seemed to have shone into his soul again and into their family.

With a bit of luck Cameron and Elinor would create another generation of Crossleys. Eh, he did enjoy having little children around the house. You could never have enough of them to love.

The happiness of that evening seemed to linger in the very air for a long time.

When he woke up after the best night's sleep for ages, the first thought that came into his mind was that two of the people he loved needed spouses.

He'd been teasing them about looking for spouses, but why not? He wouldn't force anyone into marriage with someone they didn't love, but he could try, couldn't he?

He contemplated the idea of doing that in reality for a few moments then thumped his hand down on the bedspread. If they didn't do something about it, *he* would find spouses for Maude and Bryn. By hell, he would!

He had a few good, busy years left in him yet.

Just let them try to escape getting wed. He'd snabble them one way or another.

He laughed aloud at the thought of doing that as he got ready for the new day and sang loudly and cheerfully as he got the kitchen range burning.

And when Maude came down, he pulled the dark ribbon out of her hair the minute he saw it and waltzed her round the room.

Just wait till he got going. She wouldn't know what had hit her. New clothes, new people to meet – a whole bright new life.

Hidden in the hallway, Elinor and Cam glimpsed the merriment through the kitchen door and laughed at Walter's enthusiasm.

'I'm looking forward to seeing Maude married,' she said.

Cam drew her close, his smile mirroring her own. 'When he gets that look on his face, you can't doubt that he'll do what he sets out to. But in the meantime, we have to prepare for our wedding, my love. I'm looking forward to that even more.'

So they started the day with a kiss and stole a few more as the day passed.

If you loved *Silver Wishes*, read on for an exclusive sneak peek of the next gripping novel in the Jubilee Lake series, *Golden Dreams* . . .

I

Autumn, 1895

When Stanley Thursten died suddenly of a seizure, his wife felt nothing but relief. Her parents had forced her to marry him five years ago because they said she'd been left on the shelf at twenty-five. The marriage had brought her no joy. On the contrary. Thank goodness he'd spent as little time at home with her as he could, preferring the company of his friends and his parents to hers.

Their dislike had been mutual. She'd found out that he'd only married her because it was a condition of an inheritance from his grandmother that he should wed by the age of thirty, otherwise the money would be donated to charity.

Now that he was dead, she only hoped there would be some of that money left for her, otherwise she'd have endured his company for nothing. Even the house they lived in belonged to his parents and they'd had to pay rent on it.

The doctor cleared his throat to gain her attention and said quietly, 'I can write out a death certificate for you, Mrs Thursten, because I saw your husband at my surgery only a few days ago. I'd been warning him for months that he needed to moderate his lifestyle if he wanted to make old bones, but he only shrugged. Did he change anything at all? Drink less, perhaps?'

'No. He drank at least a bottle of wine every night.' She watched him shake his head in disgust and write the certificate. After he'd handed it to her, she escorted him to the door.

He said gently, 'You should change your life now. You need to get out more, make friends.'

She dredged up a faint smile and nodded. She intended to change things, she did indeed. And she'd start with her name. Why not? She'd never liked being 'Mary Janet'.

As she closed the door, she stared down at the death certificate and wondered yet again where Stanley had kept their marriage certificate. They were both such important documents for her now that she wanted to look after them herself, wanted to control her own life in every way from now on.

She knew his parents didn't have it because they'd suggested more than once to him that they look after all the family papers and mentioned that one specifically. Only he'd refused point blank to hand it over. That had been one of the few things where he hadn't done as they'd wished.

Where could she hide this death certificate? She wasn't handing it over to his parents.

In the end she put it between the pages of a magazine and put that in the middle of a pile of similar magazines that she'd been given to read by an elderly neighbour to whom she spoke occasionally when she was working in the garden. She doubted the Thurstens would even glance at them.

She went upstairs, took most of the money out of Stanley's wallet, then put the wallet back in his jacket pocket. After some thought, she hid the money under the loose sultanas in their neatly labelled tin in the pantry, together with most of her housekeeping money.

Only then did she inform his parents of his demise by sending a passing lad with a note about what had happened.

As she'd expected, they came at once, grim-faced and tearless, and immediately started telling her what to do with her life from then on. She didn't argue but she was determined to get away from them.

Lemuel Thursten took over the arrangements for the

funeral, which was to be conducted from their house. She didn't care enough about that to argue because it meant the bills would also be sent to them. Anyway, they must know that she didn't have the money to pay for it.

As usual, Eunice Thursten said little beyond, 'Yes, dear,' or 'No, dear,' to whatever her husband ordered her to do or told her to think.

After the poorly attended funeral was over and the few guests had consumed the meagre refreshments and left, she was called into the Thurstens' sitting room.

Lemuel gestured to a chair and remained standing near the fireplace. 'I'm afraid I have some bad news for you.'

She looked across at him and waited. What now?

'As you know, Stanley was not good with money.'

She didn't say anything. He'd been hopeless at managing money, but could spend it faster than anyone she'd ever met.

'By a few months ago he had spent every penny of the inheritance that marriage to you brought him. Since then, I've had to give him money to pay your household bills and he hasn't been paying us the rent he should have done. I don't intend to continue paying for you to live in that house on your own.'

She was so shocked by this she couldn't say a word. She'd hoped and indeed expected that there would be something left for her to live on because the money had come from her family.

'We intend to sell that house, which has too many sad memories for us now.' He took a letter from the mantelpiece and handed it to her. 'This is a formal notice to you to move out by the end of the week. We can offer you a home here with us. In fact, you shouldn't wait to join us.'

She didn't protest, just waited for him to finish.

'You only need stay in that house until you've sorted out your own clothes and small possessions ready for your move.

We'll deal with the furniture and Stanley's possessions after you've left. The furniture you inherited from your godmother will pay our son's other debts.'

She'd rather run away to Timbuctoo than spend one night under their roof and she didn't intend to hand over her furniture. But she knew better than to say that, and only inclined her head.

'We shall need to make sure you are not with child as well,' Mrs Thursten said.

'I'm not.'

'You can't possibly know that yet.'

'I can. I'm absolutely certain.'

'Well, we need to be certain too – so you will move here with us as soon as you can, and I shall myself check that you are not with child. You can make yourself useful around the house to pay for your keep. We would have arranged for that to happen tomorrow but unfortunately your lawyer insists on seeing you alone before he completes the formalities, so that will take a few days.'

'I can't think about seeing Mr Baker yet. I'm too upset. I'll visit him in a couple of days.' She dabbed at her eyes, hoping she had hidden her anger and looked as if she were weeping. 'I'll walk home now, if you don't mind. It'll clear my head.'

'Oh, very well. A few extra days won't matter.'

They had never complained about her doing a lot of walking as it saved housekeeping money being spent on bus fares. But they had set someone to follow her from time to time when she was first married, saying when she challenged them that it was to check that she wasn't associating with undesirable people or taking anyone back with her into their house.

Given Stanley's threats about what he'd do to her if she invited anyone except her parents and his into their home, she'd never been able to make friends.

Her parents hadn't known how strange the Thurstens were and didn't care when she told them. They were only concerned with her being safe in a respectable marriage, as if she were a package to be handed over. They'd threatened to throw her out on the street if she didn't marry him. And they'd have done it too, which was why she'd given in. She'd thought marriage to him couldn't be worse than living with them. It wasn't but it was just as bad.

She breathed deeply as she walked along the street. That house always felt so stuffy. She didn't go straight home, however. Instead she went to see her own family's long-time lawyer since he had asked to see her. She was hoping Mr Baker would find a way to help her escape. She had only met him a couple of times but he'd seemed pleasant enough.

Before she went into his rooms, she walked past and made a detour into a nearby newsagent's shop, buying some sweets and checking the people outside through the shop window to make sure she hadn't been followed.

It had been two years since her last visit to Mr Baker. He'd sent her a message then asking her to see him without informing her husband, so she'd sneaked into his rooms while out shopping.

He'd told her she had a small inheritance from her godmother but it had conditions attached to it. The main one was that he must continue to manage the money and keep it out of her husband's hands. 'Your godmother was very concerned about your husband's drinking so wanted you to have something for yourself. There are also a few pieces of antique furniture for you to receive openly so that they don't suspect there's money as well.'

She felt sure he would keep her money safe so she agreed to leave it with him. She didn't need the quarterly payments until she found some way to escape from her husband and had let the Thurstens think the furniture was all she'd received.

They'd been pleased with it and she'd been afraid they'd

take it for themselves, but Stanley had also taken a fancy to it and they'd let him keep it.

Her parents had died a few months later, both contracting pneumonia after a bout of severe influenza. There had been a lot of such deaths at the time. People had called it the Russian 'flu.

The Thurstens were furious when they found that she'd inherited nothing from her parents, who had left everything to charity due to concerns about Stanley's handling, or as they called it more accurately, wasting of money.

At the moment she had little money of her own except the small amount she'd saved from the housekeeping and what she'd taken from Stanley's wallet.

After checking one last time that she wasn't being followed she turned off the street into Mr Baker's rooms. When she gave her name the clerk showed her into his office immediately.

'My condolences on your husband's death, Mrs Thursten.'

She wasn't going to pretend. 'It wasn't a happy marriage. He might have been a stranger for all I cared.'

She ignored his look of surprise and explained her dilemma, showing him the official letter asking her to move out of the house within a week. 'Can they really throw me out of my home so quickly? It doesn't give me much time to make other arrangements.'

Mr Baker sighed, fiddled with his pen, then looked across at her. 'I'm afraid they can, because it was a weekly tenancy. The letter you've received is an unusually harsh way to treat a daughter-in-law, however. You say they've offered you a home with them. Shall you take it?'

'No. Definitely not. I'd as soon live with a pair of hungry tigers. They'd make my life an utter misery.'

'I must admit that when they spoke to me they showed no sign of affection for you, and indeed, seemed to blame you for their son's death.'

'How could I have stopped him drinking? Or getting into those occasional fights? He'd been like that all his adult life. Everyone knew what he was like. He didn't even listen to the doctor's warnings about his health. Anyway, never mind him. I'm here because you wanted to see me before completing the final formalities.'

'That was an excuse to talk to you about your godmother's will.'

'Surely I can access that money now?'

'Not until you're safely away from them.'

'Oh dear. But I can get it soon afterwards, can't I? I shall need it to live on once I'm away from them. The problem is, I'm not sure where to go.'

'I can help you there. You'd be much safer moving away from Bolton, and doing it secretly.'

She looked at him in surprise. 'Secretly?'

'Yes. I've found out they intend to take action to gain control of you and your affairs by claiming that you are slow-witted and would not be able to look after yourself.'

A shiver ran through her. 'That's ridiculous.'

'I agree.'

'Are you sure? How did you find that out?'

'I happen to know their former lawyer rather well and he said he is no longer acting for them because they had no possible foundation for such an accusation and he refused to be involved in something unlawful and grossly unkind. Unfortunately, he suspects they are still intent on taking control of you with the help of a less scrupulous lawyer, so he let me know.'

She stared at him in shock. 'I've never got on with them and they only arranged the marriage because of the money I'd bring and their hope that I'd provide them with a grand-child.'

'Yes. My friend said that he feels they're still hoping for a grandchild.'

'But I've told them I'm not expecting.'

He cleared his throat, flushed slightly and said, 'I fear they are plotting something to ensure that you do provide them with a baby.'

Horror filled her as the implications of this sank in, especially after the way Mr Thursten had stared at her today. Were there no limits to their nastiness? 'I need to get away from them quickly, then.'

'I think so too.'

'Can you let me have some of my godmother's money?'

'Yes, but only the money you didn't use from the quarterly payments. I'm not allowed to pass final control of the capital to you until you're safely established away from them.'

'Oh. Well, my savings should be more than enough to live off for a year or even longer if I'm careful. Will it be all right if I revert to my maiden name now?'

'It's probably an excellent idea to change your name. But don't use your maiden name, as they know that. You see,' he hesitated before saying, 'I'm rather concerned about your personal safety if you run away.'

'You think they'd try to hurt me?'

'Yes. And my friend does too, which is why he broke his clients' confidentiality to suggest I warn you. You could perhaps use your godmother's maiden name. They won't know that but you and I will.'

'And call myself by my middle name.' She tried them out. 'Janet Hesketh. Yes, that sounds nicer.'

He shook his head. 'It'd be better to make a complete change of name. Don't use either of your Christian names. They're too obvious. What's your favourite woman's name?'

'Lillian,' she said immediately. It had been the name of one of her favourite heroines in a library book she'd borrowed three times to read over the years because it had such a lovely ending.

'That name isn't connected with anything you said or did during your married life?'

'No. Stanley was usually drunk by eight o'clock in the evening so we didn't sit and chat.' Sometimes those evenings had seemed to go on for ever.

'Then how about calling yourself Lillian Hesketh?'

She mouthed the name, liking the sound of it. 'I would be able to live on my godmother's money if I'm careful, but how can I get away without them finding out what I'm doing? And where can I go? I must confess that I'm afraid of them, Mr Baker, and I'm sure they'd keep watch on me every minute if I ever moved into their house. Even Stanley was afraid of them.'

He stared into the distance for a moment or two then looked across at her. 'I have a nephew who has just set up a legal practice in the north of Lancashire, Greville Turnby he's called, my sister's son. He's moved to a rather small town called Ollerthwaite because his wife's family have a farm near there and she was desperately homesick, hated life in a town. May I take the liberty of writing to him and explaining your situation?'

She nodded without hesitation.

CONTACT ANNA

Anna is always delighted to hear from readers and can be contacted via the Internet.

Anna has her own web page, with details of her books, some behind-the-scenes information that is available nowhere else and the first chapters of her books to try out, as well as a picture gallery.

Anna can be contacted by email at
anna@annajacobs.com

You can also find Anna on Facebook at
www.facebook.com/AnnaJacobsBooks

If you'd like to receive an email newsletter about Anna and her books every month or two, you are cordially invited to join her announcements list. Just email her and ask to be added to the list, or follow the link from her web page.

www.annajacobs.com